THE PREMONITION

She bent to pick one of the bluebells that grew so lushly and when she straightened up, Lord Silverbridge was on the path before her astride a splendid gray horse.

It was a moment before she realized that this was a different man. He was dressed in Regency costume and his golden hair was cut in the Regency style. But the resemblance to Lord Silverbridge was astonishing.

She stared at the horseman in stunned surprise. He looked back at her, but Tracy had the distinct feeling that he didn't see her. Then he turned his horse and galloped away. For about twenty seconds, Tracy could hear the footfalls of the horse on the bridle path. Then there was silence.

Tracy stood there, her hands gripped together tightly, her heart hammering so hard she thought it would burst.

Who was that?

But no matter how often she asked herself that question, she could not come up with a reply.

"Joan Wolf is absolutely wonderful. I've loved her work for years."   **—Iris Johansen**

Please turn this page for more praise for Joan Wolf and turn to the back of this book for a preview of her upcoming novel, *High Meadow*.

Silverbridge

By Joan Wolf

The Deception
The Guardian
The Arrangement
The Gamble
The Pretenders
Golden Girl
Someday Soon
Royal Bride

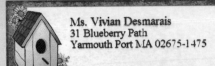

JOAN WOLF

Silverbridge

WARNER BOOKS

An AOL Time Warner Company

WARNER BOOKS EDITION

Cover design by Diane Luger
Cover illustration by Alexa Garbarino
Hand lettering by David Gatti

Warner Books, Inc.
1271 Avenue of the Americas
New York, NY 10020

Visit our Web site at
www.twbookmark.com

 An AOL Time Warner Company

Printed in the United States of America

First Paperback Printing: May 2002

10 9 8 7 6 5 4 3 2 1

For my own Ebony,
who insisted on sitting on my lap,
and doing everything else she possibly could
to disrupt the writing of this book.

"I long to talk with some old lover's ghost . . ."
John Donne, "The Extasy"

Silverbridge

1

"So how did the first reading go, babe?" asked Mel Barker, actress Tracy Collins's agent. The telephone connection from Los Angeles to London was clear as a bell.

"Fine, I guess," Tracy replied. "The frost melted a little when I produced an authentic English accent. And Dave Michaels, the director, was very pleasant."

"He damn well better be," Mel replied emphatically. "You saved his movie when you signed on."

"I have to confess that I'm a little nervous." Tracy leaned back into the cushions of a sofa—one of three in the living room of the luxurious suite the movie company had engaged for her. "I mean, I'm working with Jon Melbourne. He has a voice like God and he does Shakespeare, Mel. All I've ever done is romantic comedy."

"It's a little late to get cold feet," Mel pointed out. "Remember, you were the one who wanted to do this movie; I was against it. The part is too small. Melbourne is the star, you have exactly one-quarter the number of lines that he has."

"Please don't say *I told you so*," Tracy replied with an edge to her voice. "I'm not saying that I'm sorry I took it. I'm saying I'm a little nervous about the challenge. It's not an easy book to make into a film."

The novel Tracy was talking about, *Jealousy*, had won the Booker Prize in Britain for Best Novel of the year and had gone on to become a best-seller in America as well. It was essentially a literary novel about an aristocratic household in the days of Regency England. The film rights had been bought by an American producer, who had persuaded an American film company to invest in making the movie.

But there had been problems over the casting. The studio executives had been reluctantly brought to agree that England's greatest Shakespearean actor would be a good thing for the movie, but they had dug in their heels about the female lead. They wanted a blockbuster name to ensure that American moviegoers would buy tickets, but the part was simply too small to interest most actresses of that stature. The studio had been ecstatic when Tracy had agreed to do it.

The rest of Hollywood had been astounded. The films that had made her a megastar were lighthearted romantic comedies, not serious psychological dramas. The general opinion of her peers was that Tracy had bitten off more than she could chew and was in grave danger of damaging her star status.

"I'm not saying *I told you so*," Mel said soothingly. "You'll be great, babe. You always are."

"And don't condescend to me." Tracy put her sneak-ered feet up on the pale wood coffee table in front of the sofa.

"I wouldn't dream of it," Mel assured her, then hastily changed the subject. "How did the rest of the actors seem? Any crazies?"

"I must say, they all seemed remarkably normal," Tracy said. "But I'm sure that will change as I get to know them better. I just hope no one is a serious drug-gie. My last film was horrendous."

Mel sighed. "I know."

Tracy glared at a nearby vase filled with huge pink roses. "I will *never* work with Matthew Howard again. I don't care how talented and charming he may be."

"I know, I know. I don't blame you. One of these days he's going to go too far and wind up in jail."

"He needs to be in a treatment program, not jail," Tracy said.

Once again Mel found it prudent to change the sub-ject. "How is Melbourne, anyway? Is he taller than you, or are you going to have to stand in a ditch when you work with him?"

"He's about five-ten, two inches taller than I am. If I wear flat shoes, we should be okay."

"Well, don't let him intimidate you. He may be the 'new Olivier' and all that, but your movies take in huge sums of money."

Tracy sat up straighter. "I am not easily intimidated, Mel."

"I know. I know. But you definitely have a thing about Melbourne's acting. Just remember, a movie isn't worth a nickel if no one goes to see it. They'll go to see this movie because of you, not because of Melbourne."

At that point the door of the suite opened and Gail Ramirez, Tracy's personal secretary, entered, carrying a vase of magnificent lilies. Tracy said into the phone, "Gail has just come in, Mel, and she needs to talk to me."

"All right. I'm glad things have gone good so far, babe. Call me if you have any problems."

"I will," Tracy said, and rang off.

Gail lifted the lilies a little higher. "These are from the studio. Where do you want me to put them?"

The room was already filled with floral arrangements. Tracy waved her hand, and said, "Wherever."

"These roses are looking a little droopy." Gail put down the vase of lilies and picked up the arrangement of red roses that reposed on a table in front of a huge gilt-framed mirror. "Maybe I'll toss these and replace them with the lilies."

"Fine," Tracy said absently.

As she was switching the vases, Gail remembered something. "Oh, your mother called earlier. She wants you to call her back."

Tracy sat up and put her feet on the floor. "Kate must have had the baby!" She picked up the phone again and within minutes was listening to her mother rave about the eight-pound girl her sister had delivered several hours earlier.

"Kate and Alan must be thrilled," Tracy said. Once again she stretched her long legs out on the coffee table. "Finally a girl!"

"They're delighted," her mother said. "And so is your

father. In fact, I think he's even more pleased that it's a girl than Alan and Kate are."

"And what about you?" Tracy asked. "Are you pleased to have a granddaughter?"

There was a little silence. Then, "I don't know. Daughters can be a terrible worry—much more so than sons."

Tracy rolled her eyes at Gail. "If that was meant for me, Mom, there's no reason for you to worry. I'm doing perfectly fine."

"I wish you weren't so far away. You won't even be here for the christening."

"Alan's brother won't make it to the christening either," Tracy pointed out. "These things happen, Mom."

"Robert is a naval officer, and he's out at sea. He's working."

"Well so am I," Tracy replied as mildly as she could.

"It's not the same."

Tracy counted to ten, then put her feet on the floor once again and sat up straight. "Do you have Kate's number in the hospital? I'd like to call her."

"She'll be sleeping. It would be best not to disturb her. You can call her at home tomorrow," Mrs. Walters said. "I think it's just terrible, the way they throw young mothers out of the hospital these days. When I had you girls, I was in for five days."

"Are you going to stay at Kate's, Mom?"

"Yes. For a few days, until Kate feels strong enough to cope on her own."

"That's great," Tracy said sincerely.

She and her mother talked for a few more minutes,

then Tracy hung up. "I gather your sister had a daughter," her secretary said.

"Yes," Tracy replied with a pleased smile. "I'm so happy for her. She wanted a girl so badly." She got up from the sofa and stretched her arms over her head.

"My mother always said that every woman should have a daughter," Gail said.

"My mother would agree, as long as the daughter was like Kate," Tracy replied dryly, letting her arms drop to her sides.

Gail regarded her in silence for a moment. "Your mother adores you, you know that. She just worries about you."

Tracy's mother was a very proper Connecticut matron who had never reconciled herself to the fact that her youngest daughter was a famous movie star. She was certain that it was an unhealthy lifestyle, one in which Tracy was exposed to all sorts of disreputable people: people who used foul language; people who committed adultery; people who used drugs. She would have added even more debauchery to the list, but that was about as far as Mrs. Walters's imagination went.

"She thinks my biological clock is ticking away, and she wants me to get married, settle down, and have kids," Tracy said bitterly. "That's the sort of woman's life she understands."

"It doesn't sound like a bad life to me," Gail said.

After a moment, Tracy grinned. "It doesn't sound bad to me, either. But the guy has to be right."

"Now, *there* is the problem," Gail replied. "I have never met a woman as fussy as you. The last guy you dumped was because you didn't like his laugh! Good grief, Tracy."

"He had a laugh like a goat. No one could put up with that."

Gail's only reply was to roll her eyes. Then, as Tracy started toward the bedroom, she said, "You do remember that you have a news conference in an hour?"

"I remember," Tracy replied grimly. She was famous in Hollywood for being an extremely cooperative actress on the set; she was equally famous for her dislike of the press.

"There's no need to look as if you're going to have a tooth pulled," Gail said.

"I really think I would rather have a tooth pulled than meet with the press," Tracy replied. "And the *British* press!" She shuddered. "They're even bigger scandalmongers over here than they are at home."

Gail took a few steps over the thick carpet in Tracy's direction. "Tracy, please try to answer their questions with more than two or three words. You hurt your image by being so terse."

"The hell with my image," Tracy snapped. "I'll be polite, and I'll answer their damn questions, but don't expect me to volunteer any extra information. I learned long ago the dangers of being friendly to the press."

"You can't still be upset about that ridiculous story in the *Reporter*?"

Tracy folded her arms across her chest. "That miserable rag put on its front page the 'hot' news that I was pregnant with Ben Affleck's child. I don't even know Ben Affleck! All I said was that I admired his acting. It took me a whole year to calm my mother down. You know that, Gail!"

Gail sighed.

"I still think I should have sued," Tracy fumed.

"No, you shouldn't have," Gail replied. "You were perfectly right to listen to Mel. No one believed that stupid story, and suing would have only given it credence."

"Well then, you, of all people, should stop telling me to chat up the press. You know what it can lead to."

Gail sighed again. "Yes, I guess I do."

"I'm starving," Tracy said.

Gail looked at her. "I'll get room service to send some food up. Will salad do?"

"Salad will be fine. Be sure to order one for yourself." Tracy wrinkled her nose. "And tell them ASAP. I don't think I can bear to face Britain's press corps on an empty stomach."

Six weeks later, Tracy stood in front of a large, three-sided mirror while a seamstress pinned the back of her dress. The rest of the large room was filled with racks of costumes, an ironing board, and a shoe rack stacked with shoes of all sizes and different-height heels. The seamstress had had a heavy hand with her perfume that morning and the sickly-sweet scent of honeysuckle hung in the air.

"There," the seamstress said, stepping away from Tracy. She turned to look at the man who was standing behind the two of them. "What do you think, Mr. Abbott?"

"I think it's perfect," the costume designer replied in

his flawless Oxbridge accent. Sidney Abbott was a tall, thin man with a mop of exquisitely brushed blond hair. "What about you, Miss Collins?"

Looking back at Tracy from the mirror was an English lady who could have stepped from the pages of a Jane Austen novel. Her ball dress of white French gauze was high-waisted and fell to her ankles over a blue silk slip. The hem of the gown was embroidered with flowers, and her shoes of soft white leather resembled modern ballet slippers. The only thing out of place in the picture was her hair, which she was wearing in her everyday, shoulder-length style.

"It's perfectly lovely," she said sincerely.

"This is the dress Julia will be wearing on the night she first meets Martin," Sidney said. "We'll be staging the scene at the country house Dave rented down in Wiltshire. Dave tells me it has a room that will do the job perfectly."

"Stunning." The word was spoken by a rich, flexible, well-known voice, and in the mirror Tracy saw Jonathan Melbourne move into view. He was a burly man with curly brown hair and light hazel eyes. She turned to face him, and he smiled. "Seeing you, I can perfectly understand how Martin manages to whip himself into such a jealous frenzy."

Tracy had had long practice in deflecting compliments gracefully. "It is a lovely dress," she agreed, and looked at the costume designer. "All of the clothes are wonderful, Sidney. The only question I have is, how on earth did the women of those days manage to stay warm? I mean, there wasn't any central heating, and these dresses are flimsy, to say the very least."

"Oh, we English are tougher than you Americans," Sidney Abbott replied in a voice that held just a pinch of superiority. "Even today we don't coddle ourselves with central heat the way you do."

"Perhaps not, but I notice that you all wear sweaters and long pants." Tracy looked pointedly at the men's warm clothing. "I don't see anyone prancing around with bare arms and gauzy skirts."

Jon said gravely. "I occasionally wear a gauzy skirt, but only in the privacy of my own home."

Tracy laughed.

Sidney turned to Jon. "Have you come for your fitting?"

"Yes, but I'll wait until you have finished with Tracy."

"Tracy's done," Sidney assured him. "We'll be ready for you as soon as she has changed."

"Fine."

Tracy went into the next room, which was filled with more costumes hanging from portable racks, and the young girl waiting for her helped her change out of the elegant dress and into jeans, sneakers, a cream-colored cotton turtleneck, and a Fair Isle sweater. She fixed her floating mass of auburn hair in her usual way, by shaking it, and returned to the other room.

As she joined them, the two men were talking about the location change the company was making that weekend to Silverbridge, the country house where they would shoot the rest of the film.

"Liza is ecstatic," Sidney was saying sarcastically as Tracy came in. "She wants to add a lord to her list of bedfellows."

Liza Moran was the actress playing the older woman who hates Julia and does her best to poison Martin's mind against her. It had become apparent to Tracy over the past weeks that Liza was, to use the technical psychiatric term, a nymphomaniac.

"I doubt that Lord Silverbridge will be in residence while such working-class types as we are hanging about dirtying up his estate," Jon returned dryly.

Sidney was insulted by being designated a "working-class type" and replied in a chilly voice. "I beg to differ with you, but Lord Silverbridge will indeed be in residence. I understand that he trains at his own stable, which is on the property. In fact, Dave told me that His Lordship made a special request that movie personnel should keep away from the stable area so his horses aren't disturbed."

Tracy made an attempt to defuse the obvious tension that had arisen between the two men by saying humorously, "I hope to goodness it's not going to be like the killing schedule he has held us to these last six weeks."

"I'm afraid it will be," Sidney replied. "It cost a fortune to rent Silverbridge, and it's essential to finish shooting there on schedule. Dave told me that he shudders at the very thought of the amount of money Lord Silverbridge will hold him up for if we have to extend our time."

"Silverbridge is probably praying for a delay," Jon said cynically.

"Why would he want a delay?" Tracy asked. "I should think he would want to get us out of his way as quickly as possible."

"These old houses cost a ton of money to maintain,"

Sidney explained. "Every country house owner in England wants to have a movie shot at his home. It helps to pay for the upkeep."

"Oh," Tracy replied.

"Lord Silverbridge is one of Britain's own celebrities," Sidney went on, still addressing himself solely to Tracy. "One sees him photographed all the time at horse shows, dances, nightclubs, with the royal party at Ascot—that sort of thing." From the tone of his voice it was clear that Sidney would adore to be a part of Lord Silverbridge's world.

"I've never heard of him," Tracy said.

"He's a celebrity because he's an earl," Jon explained, also speaking solely to Tracy. "Even at the beginning of the twenty-first century, the British still worship the aristocracy." The tone of his voice made it clear that he did not consider himself part of this monumental delusion.

Sidney did not look at Jon as he informed Tracy, "Not surprisingly, the fact that the Earl of Silverbridge is an unmarried, good-looking young gentleman, who happens to own some of the loveliest property in the country, contributes to his celebrity. But"—he shot a triumphant glance at Jon—"he also won the bronze medal for Britain in the dressage competition at the last Olympics."

"Did he really?" Tracy said with genuine interest. "I know that the American dressage team did not do as well as we had hoped, but I just assumed that the Germans had won all the medals."

Sidney's straight back became a little straighter, and he stood a little taller. "No. Britain won the bronze."

Jon said, "Not all of Silverbridge's press has been as positive as Sidney makes it out to be. Last year a model he was seeing committed suicide when he dumped her."

Sidney made a noise that sounded like *harrumph*. "It was a terrible tragedy, my dear Tracy, and I'm certain Lord Silverbridge deeply regretted the young woman's hasty action."

Jon said conversationally, "Actually he was cool as a cucumber about it."

"If you will excuse me, I must speak to someone for a moment," Sidney said courteously to Tracy. Then, in a very different voice, he said to Jon, "Your costume is in that room."

As he watched Sidney walk off, Jon said, "I shouldn't let him bother me, but he does."

"He seems harmless," she replied.

Jon shook his head, as if to clear it, then said, "Do you realize that we are going to have a day off? We leave for Wiltshire on Sunday, but Dave has left us Saturday free."

"He must have made a mistake. I thought he was ethically opposed to days off."

Jon laughed. "I was wondering if there was anything in London that I could show you, anything you haven't already seen."

Tracy hid her surprise. Jon had been friendly over the past six weeks, but he had never attempted to ask her out.

Not that there's been time to do anything but film, she thought.

She hesitated, then said slowly, "I would love to see

the Tower of London. I've been here at least a dozen times, but I've never managed to tour the Tower."

He smiled. "One of my favorite places. Let's go to the Tower then."

Tracy had not lost any of her initial awe of this English actor; in fact, her respect had increased the more she worked with him. She did not want him to have an unpleasant experience in her company. So she said half-humorously, "I must warn you that if you are seen in my company, the American gutter press will assume that I'm carrying your baby. It will then plaster this news all over the scandal sheets so that every person in America who buys groceries will be sure to see it."

"Surely we can manage to elude the press for one day," he protested.

"There is one reporter who seems to have made me his mission in life. If I were an ordinary person, I could have him arrested for stalking, but my lawyer tells me that I am a public figure, and the press has a right to do its job."

"Good heavens," he said.

"This miserable excuse for a human being is parked outside my hotel just waiting to pounce. I don't want you to be the other pouncee."

"There must be a back way out of your hotel," he said.

Her lips curved in acknowledgment of a hit. "There are several exits, in fact. I prefer the kitchen one myself. As far as I know, that miserable bloodhound, Counes, hasn't found it yet."

"Great. Then shall we say that I'll meet you at ten

o'clock Saturday morning outside the kitchen of your hotel?"

Tracy felt a spurt of excitement. "Okay."

"Uh-oh, Sidney returns," Jon said. "I had better get into my costume before he throws a tantrum."

She laughed, and waved, and turned away.

2

Tracy had a very enjoyable time on Saturday with Jon. They managed to avoid the loathsome Counes and were relatively undisturbed by the tourists at the Tower. They capped the day with an excellent dinner at one of London's best restaurants and ended it with a visit to a nightclub.

Tracy did not find a single flaw in Jon that was egregious enough to complain to Gail about.

On Sunday afternoon, the movie company left for Wiltshire. Tracy was feeling sleepy from a late night and dozed for most of the trip. It was almost six by the time the car pulled up to the front of a half-timbered building that was styled like a large cottage. The front yard was brilliant with massed pink tulips, and, as Tracy ascended the stone steps, a carved panel next to the front door proclaimed THE WILTSHIRE ARMS.

The manager himself escorted her to her suite, which was decorated with what looked like genuine antiques.

"It's lovely," Tracy said politely. "What a charming hotel."

The manager, who had a round, babyish face and horn-rimmed glasses, beamed like a delighted two-year-old. "It's not large, so we can offer personal service to all our guests. Please call me, Miss Collins, if you need anything at all."

Tracy said that she would, and he left as two young men in uniform came in with her luggage. As they took the bags into the bedroom, she went to look at the cards on the magnificent floral arrangements that dotted the sitting room. The flowers were from her producer, Jim Ventura; her director, Dave Michaels; the hotel management; and Jon. She was reading the card attached to the last floral arrangement when the phone rang.

Gail answered, then put her hand over the receiver, and said, "It's Jon Melbourne. Do you want to speak to him?"

"Yes, of course." Tracy went to take the phone from her secretary. "Hi, Jon. How are you?"

"Comfortable. This is a nice hotel."

"It seems to be."

"I understand that its dining room serves the best food in the area. Would you care to join me for dinner tonight? Once we get started filming, we'll be eating off the catering truck I'm afraid."

Tracy smiled. "From the looks of the shooting schedule, I'm sure we will. I'd like to have dinner with you. In an hour?"

"An hour it is. See you in the restaurant."

"Great." Tracy hung up and turned to her secretary. "Jon just invited me to have dinner with him."

Gail's large brown eyes shone. "Now this is promising. He must have passed the first test."

"Don't be ridiculous," Tracy replied edgily. "I don't have 'tests.'"

"Oh yeah? Then how come all the men you know seem to flunk them?"

Tracy's shoulders slumped fractionally and, all of a sudden, she looked very weary. "I don't know, Gail." She hooked a lock of hair behind her ear. "I just don't know."

Gail said something under her breath in Spanish, then came to put an arm around her employer. "Don't mind me, I'm only teasing. My problem is I don't know when to stop. Have fun with Jon. I'd have dinner with him just to listen to him read me the phone book."

Tracy smiled. "I know. That voice! Anyway, you're on your own for dinner. I suggest you order all the best stuff from room service. The movie company is paying, remember."

Tracy was very popular with the moneymen in Hollywood because her modest requests for perks added very little to a movie's budget. Instead of asking the studio to pay for a limo, a cook, a private camper for location shots, and personal makeup, hair, and clothes persons, she only required that the studio pay the hotel, food, and travel bills for her secretary. She was perfectly content to use regular studio personnel for the rest of her needs.

"Filet mignon, I think," Gail said.

Tracy nodded. "Perfect." She glanced at her watch. "We had better get a dress unpacked for me to wear to dinner."

They both knew the "we" was a courtesy, and Gail would unpack the suitcases. She said, "Why don't you take a shower while I'm getting the clothes out?"

"Terrific idea. Thanks."

Tracy went into the bathroom while Gail hung a garment bag on a hook in the closet and began to take dresses out of it. "How about the blue Escada?" she called through the door to Tracy.

"Fine," Tracy called back over the sound of rushing water.

Gently, Gail took a deep cobalt blue dress out of the garment bag and laid it on the bed. Then she went to another suitcase to see if she could find the matching shoes.

Jonathan Melbourne sat in the dining room of the Wiltshire Arms sipping a Glenlivet and waiting for Tracy. He had socialized and worked with many beautiful women in his life, but there was something about Tracy that was particularly striking. She looked so . . . so . . . healthy, he thought, picturing her in his mind. She was slim, not skinny, with a beautiful slender waist, and her flawless skin had a natural glow. Her shoulder-length auburn hair was threaded with a gold that looked amazingly natural, though Jon was quite sure it couldn't be.

When she came in the door, every eye in the dining room turned her way.

"I hope you haven't been waiting long," she said, as the waiter seated her.

"I haven't been here long at all."

She looked around the small, elegant room. "This is charming."

"It's not as opulent as L'Aigrette," he said, referring to the restaurant in London he had taken her to. "But it's more comfortable."

She smiled, showing the perfectly even white teeth that Jon associated with all Americans.

A waiter came to ask what Tracy wanted to drink and, as she gave her order, Jon took another sip of his scotch and watched her. Her hair glowed under the light from the chandelier, and, in profile, the tilt of her nose looked delightfully insouciant. She turned away from the waiter to look back at him, and Jon said, "That dress is lovely. It matches your eyes."

A faintly ironic expression came over the eyes in question. "Why else do you think I bought it?" She picked up the handwritten parchment menu and frowned. "This writing is so elegant that I can't read a word of it."

"Their veal is supposed to be outstanding," he said.

The cobalt eyes looked at him reproachfully. "Do you know what they do to those poor little baby calves?"

"Please don't tell me," he replied hastily.

"If you knew, you would never eat veal."

"I'll order something else," he promised. He remembered that she had eaten fish the night before, and asked curiously. "Are you a vegetarian?"

She gave him a rueful look. "No. I tried to be once, but the dreadful truth is that I don't like vegetables very much. It's difficult to be a vegetarian when you don't eat vegetables, so I went back to eating meat."

"But not veal."

She smiled. "But not veal."

The waiter appeared, and once again Tracy ordered fish. After the waiter had collected their menus and left, she said, "I've been wanting to tell you how wonderful your films of *Hamlet* and *Henry IV* are. I think it's marvelous that people who didn't get to see the theater productions should have an opportunity to see your performance."

He was pleased. "Thank you."

"You're welcome," she replied, and took a sip of her white burgundy.

He buttered a roll. "You appear to be fond of Shakespeare. Have you ever acted in one of his plays?"

"Oh no." She shook her head emphatically, causing her gorgeous hair to float around her shoulders. "I was an English major in college, and so I've read most of his plays, but I never acted in one. I really became an actress by chance, you see. I didn't go to drama school or anything like that."

He was about to ask how she did become an actress when a stir at the door drew their attention. The maître d' and other members of the staff were fawning over two men who had just come in. As the newcomers were ceremoniously escorted to the best table in the room, Tracy said to Jon, "Are they royalty or something?"

He laughed. "Not precisely. The man with the mustache is Robin Mauley, the biggest real estate developer in the country. He's rather like your Donald Trump, I suppose. The other man is Ambrose Percy, the hotel man."

Tracy raised her eyebrows. Ambrose Percy, the scion

of one of Britain's most noble families, built only five-star hotels.

"They must be cooking up a deal," Jon went on. "I know that Mauley is interested in building a world-class golf course here in England, and Percy must be thinking of putting a hotel nearby."

Tracy said, with an edge to her voice, "It sounds like America—golf courses everywhere. Personally, I think they're a blight on the landscape. A few years ago some developer bulldozed a beautiful stretch of woodlands near my parents' home in Connecticut and put in a golf course. Now there's nowhere to ride your horse, or let your dog run, and the deer are reduced to eating from everyone's gardens. What we do have are batches of people dressed in Calvin Klein, scooting around in carts and whaling away at a little white ball."

Jon, who played golf, was amused. "What you just said would be regarded as blasphemy by most of the people I know."

She took a sip of wine. "I really don't mind people playing golf, it's the cutting down of the natural wood-lands that I abhor."

He decided to drop the subject of golf. "You said that you became an actress by chance. If you weren't going to be an actress, what were you going to be?"

She looked a little wary. "I was going to be a high school English teacher."

He thought that she would have been a completely disruptive influence in an environment of adolescent males, but prudently did not share his thought with her. Instead he asked, "And what caused you to change your mind and go into acting instead?"

A subtle change came over her face, and she looked down at her china plate and was quiet.

He said, "You don't have to tell me if you don't want to. I know what a nuisance it is to always answer the same questions."

She looked up. "It isn't a big deal. I took a semester off from college between my junior and senior year and an agent I knew got me a job on a film that was shooting in New York. The director liked me and put me in his next picture, and my career sort of snowballed from there. I never went back to school to finish my degree."

Her voice was calm, but there was suddenly such an air of sadness about her that Jon felt an urge to gather her into a comforting embrace. He said with an attempt at lightness, "So you were never a struggling young actress, pounding the pavements looking for a job?"

She shook her head. "No. I was lucky."

The look in her eyes did not agree with her words.

"Mademoiselle, monsieur." It was the waiter with their food. Once the plates had been placed in front of them, it was only natural to change the subject.

"What do you think about Julia?" he asked, referring to Tracy's part in the movie. "Her husband certainly thinks she is unfaithful, but the book leaves the question open."

She smiled faintly, although her eyes still held that sad look. "I don't think I'm going to tell you what I think. If you're going to play Martin, you need to be in a state of doubt."

He grinned. "That is very astute of you."

She smiled back. "Thank you."

He immediately tried to think of a way to make her smile like that again.

*J*on was called for Monday morning, but Tracy was not needed until the afternoon, which afforded her a chance to sleep in. At precisely eleven-thirty she and Gail came out of the Wiltshire Arms and got into the car with their driver, Tracy in the front as usual and Gail in the back. Tracy always sat in the front of cars because she had a tendency to get carsick.

The two-lane road from the hotel took them through a perfect stretch of English countryside, and today Tracy was awake enough to enjoy it. The new leaves were a clean fresh green, and dense patches of bluebells turned the grassy meadows an even deeper blue than the sky above. Brown cows grazed peacefully in their fields, and ducks floated on a stream underneath a small stone bridge.

"What a difference from what it must have looked like last year, when they had that awful foot-and-mouth disease over here," Gail said.

"That was horrible," Tracy agreed, and opened the window so she could smell the freshness of the spring air. They passed a pasture where ewes were nibbling the sweet new grass while their lambs frolicked around them. A flock of birds passed overhead and settled in the woods at the far end of the pasture.

"Oh, aren't the lambs darling!" Gail exclaimed. She had grown up in the New York City streets of Spanish Harlem, and the sight of animals always delighted her.

Ten minutes later a high iron fence appeared on their

right. "This must be it," Charlie said, and slowed the car.

The gate was open, and a small, discreet sign beside it proclaimed the word: SILVERBRIDGE. Charlie turned in.

The long driveway was bordered by beautiful tall lime trees and eventually opened onto a vista of vast green lawns, budding shrubbery, and flower beds with a brilliant display of erect red and yellow tulips. The centerpiece of this scene was an elegant, Palladian-style mansion, its many tall windows glittering in the afternoon sun.

Tracy stared at the mansion like one who is stunned. *I know this house.* The thought was instant, confident, absolute. Her heart began to pound.

Don't be ridiculous, she scolded herself, trying to account for the odd sensation of *déjà vu. I must have seen a picture of it somewhere. I've never been here before.*

Dimly from the backseat she heard Gail's voice. "What a beautiful house. It's so perfectly proportioned."

"Yes," Tracy managed to reply.

The car pulled up, and for the first time she noticed the movie's trucks and campers parked on the driveway along the edge of the wide front lawn. They looked ugly and incongruous in the golden eighteenth-century setting.

Gail opened her door, jumped out, lapdog in hand, and said cheerfully, "Well here we are. Do you want to go directly to makeup or do you want to check out your dressing room first?"

It was a sensible, ordinary question. Tracy, whose eyes were glued to the house, didn't respond.

"Tracy?" Gail asked. She opened the front car door

and looked worriedly at her employer. "Are you all right?"

Slowly Tracy swung her legs out of the car and stood up. The smell of cut grass wafted to her nostrils. The golden stone of the house was mellow in the sunshine. She stared at it and said nothing.

"You look awfully pale," Gail said worriedly. "Perhaps you had better get back into the car and sit down."

"No," Tracy said. "I'm all right."

"You don't look all right. Do you have a headache coming on?"

Tracy moved her head, as if testing it, then said with some surprise, "I feel dizzy."

"Sit." Gail pressed her back toward the car.

Tracy sat sideways on the front seat, her feet on the ground.

"Put your head down between your knees," Gail said.

Tracy put her head down and closed her eyes. Slowly, as she sat there, the dizziness subsided. She lifted her head and forced a smile. "I'm okay now. I don't know what hit me there for a minute, but I'm okay."

"Are you sure?"

Tracy did not look toward the house. "Yes." She stood up, and this time her legs felt steadier. "I'd better go straight to makeup. I don't want to be late on the set."

Gail walked beside her as she made her way along the drive to the camper that housed the makeup department. Jon was just coming out as she reached the door. "You look pale," he said. "Are you all right?"

He had grown his sideburns for the role, and his hair was brushed into the casual curls of Regency fashion.

His open-neck shirt and tweed jacket looked almost comically out of place.

Tracy said, "I'm okay. Not to worry." She turned to look at the house. "When do we begin to film the inside scenes?" To her own ears, her voice sounded faintly breathless.

Jon did not seem to notice anything amiss. "The schedule calls for us to shoot in the garden while the weather holds. We won't move inside for at least a week. Unless, of course, it rains." He cocked an eyebrow. "You must excuse me while I go and get into my very confining costume."

Tracy gave a genuine laugh. "I think the Regency must be one of the few periods when men's clothes were actually more uncomfortable than women's."

Jon moved off, and Tracy stepped up into the camper, where the studio makeup artist was waiting to do her face for the camera.

3

The garden where her first scene was to be filmed was at the back of the house and, as Tracy walked through the scattered afternoon sun, the skirts of her muslin dress swinging around her ankles, she experienced once more a strange feeling of *déjà vu*. The magnificent beech trees on the sweeping front lawn spread their silvery arms to the sky, each feathery branch misted with green, and she could not escape the feeling that she had seen those trees before.

She stopped for a moment to look up at the house, and her eye was caught by movement in one of the upstairs windows. A woman was standing there, framed in the casement, and she appeared to be wearing one of the film's Regency costumes. Then the sun reflected off the window, Tracy blinked, and the figure was gone.

I must be hallucinating. I hope to God I'm not getting a headache.

But her head wasn't hurting, and there was no pressure in her neck, so she took a long, deep breath and strode purposefully forward to join Dave and Jon. They were standing on a broad graveled terrace, which led down to a sloping lawn planted with more beautiful beeches. Jon, in his blue morning coat, fawn-colored pantaloons, and boots, looked perfectly at home in the setting, whereas Dave's khaki pants and casual sweater looked distinctly out of place.

Tracy went up the two broad steps that led to the terrace and, as she joined the men, she turned to regard the vista that stretched before her. The focal point of the lawn was a large circular basin bordered by a low stone curb. Stone urns on pedestals filled with clematis surrounded the pool and were reflected in its still water. Beyond the pool a gravel path led down the gently sloping lawn to a set of wide stone steps, beyond which were the massive yew hedges that enclosed the garden.

Tracy shaded her eyes with her hand and gazed at the sight before her. She didn't say anything, just exhaled long and slow.

"It's perfect, isn't it?" Dave said. "That's why we chose Silverbridge. It was expensive, but both the grounds and the house are natural settings for us. We'll save money by not having to travel to several places, or build sets."

"It looks like a painting by Watteau," Jon said.

A little silence fell as the three of them regarded the loveliness before them. Then Dave said briskly, "All right, we'd better head on down to the garden. Ivan has everything set up, so I hope we can shoot without much delay."

The three of them stepped off the terrace and began to walk along the graveled path that led to the pool and thence to the yew-enclosed garden. "We've chosen a perfect spot," Dave said, as they went down the stone steps and through an arched opening in the great yew hedge. Inside was a wide grassy pathway that followed the hedge. Tracy looked first left then right, and saw that all along its perimeter the hedge had niches cut in it, which contained either statues or stone benches.

"This way," Dave said, and started along an azalea-bordered path that led toward the center of the garden. Tracy looked up and down a series of smaller paths as they went by, and at the end of each there was a fountain jet shooting water into the air.

The movie company had set up in the center of the garden, which featured a wide, shallow pool, in the midst of which was a fountain of lead cherubs with a jet sending a magnificent spray of water high into the air. The cameras, the audio equipment, the electrical wires hooked up to a truck, and a crowd of people dressed in jeans indicated that this was where they were going to shoot.

Ivan Hunt, the cinematographer, called, "All right, Tracy and Jon. If you'll take your places and walk through the scene, I'll check the lighting."

Like the professionals that they were, the two leads moved to make the first run-through of the scene.

Tracy was actually back at the Wiltshire Arms in time for dinner. Food was not on her mind, however, as she and Gail stepped out of the elevator and headed toward her door.

Gail let her go in first. "Get undressed, Tracy, and

into bed," she said. "Do you want anything to eat or drink? A cup of tea, perhaps?"

"No," Tracy replied in what she always thought of as her "headache voice." "I just want to take some Imitrex and get into bed."

"Do that then," Gail replied. "I'll turn off the ringer on the phone in your bedroom and man the living room phone for the rest of the evening."

"Thank you," Tracy said, and went straight to her bathroom, where she washed down a pill with water. She then changed into silk pajamas and got into bed.

The headache was pounding in time with her heartbeat, and she curled up in a fetal position, as if trying to escape the pain.

What on earth happened to me today? She did not doubt that her headache was connected to the strange sense of *déjà vu* she had experienced at Silverbridge. She had never had such a feeling before. The shock of recognition when first she beheld the house was something entirely new to her; it was also a little frightening.

I must have seen a picture of it somewhere before, she told herself again. *That's why it looks so familiar.*

It took a full two hours for the Imitrex to work and for the sledgehammer pounding in her head to begin to subside. By ten o'clock she was asleep.

She awoke once during the night to go to the bathroom, and the dregs of the headache were still there. She took a couple of Excedrin and went back to bed.

When she awoke the following morning, it seemed to be gone. She sat up and tested it by moving her head. The headache was indeed gone, she decided, but the all-too-familiar hungover feeling she had the day after a migraine was firmly in place. Her mouth tasted like medicine, her stomach was uneasy, and she felt as if she hadn't slept in twenty-four hours.

"Water," she said out loud, and went into the bathroom to fill a glass. She drank it thirstily, then brushed her teeth and washed her face. She came back into the bedroom and was moving to pull the drapes back from the windows when her attention was caught by the collection of silver-framed photographs that traveled with her wherever she went. Gail had set them on the round Regency-style table that was set to one side of the fireplace. Slowly Tracy approached the table and looked at the familiar faces that had been caught by the camera.

There was a picture of her parents taken at their thirtieth wedding anniversary celebration. Her mother wore a long, smoke gray dress, her father wore a tux, and somehow they managed to look both dignified and exceedingly happy. There was a picture of her sister and brother-in-law with their two little sons, and a picture of Tracy holding their eldest, Matthew, in his long white christening gown.

She looked for a while at each of these pictures before picking up the last one, a twelve-by-fourteen formal portrait of a bride and groom. She carried the picture with her to one of the Queen-Anne-style chairs in front of the fireplace, sat down, and regarded it gravely.

We were so young, she thought, looking at her own radiant twenty-year-old face, so bright with happiness, so confident in the continuation of that happiness, so completely unaware that within three months the man who stood so proudly by her side would be dead.

"Scotty," she said out loud. "I still miss you."

He'll remain this way forever, she thought: twenty-one years of age, just married to the girl he had known since third grade, poised on the brink of what everyone said would be a fabulous career in professional basketball.

And then with the crash of metal on the highway and the screaming of ambulances in the night, it had been over. Scott Collins, recently married number-two pick in the NBA draft, was dead. A tractor trailer truck had gone out of control and smashed into his new sports car, and not even the seat belt he had been wearing, not the deploying airbag, had been able to save him from the explosion of fire that had engulfed his car.

Seven years had passed since that dreadful night, and instead of being a wife, a mother and a teacher, as Tracy had planned, she was an actress. A movie star.

It had all happened so quickly. She had not been able to face going back to the University of Connecticut, where she would have been a senior and where Scotty had played college ball. There were too many memories. Then Scotty's agent had suggested she might like a small part in a movie shooting in New York, and she had thought something so alien would be a good distraction. She would spend a few months doing something totally different, then she would go back and finish her degree.

What am I doing here?

Scotty's light gray eyes smiled at her from the picture she held in her lap. He had been dead for seven years, and she no longer mourned for him, but there had never been anyone to fill his place.

"I like Jon Melbourne," she told her dead husband. "He has a great voice."

You've always been a sucker for an English accent. She could almost hear the amusement in Scotty's voice as she imagined his reply.

She smiled. "I have been." She lifted the picture to her lips and kissed the young man's face. "But I'll bet he has a lousy jump shot."

A flash of pain shot through her head, from the left side of her neck to her left eye, and Tracy stiffened. *Oh God. It can't be coming back. Please don't let it come back. I have to work this afternoon.*

She closed her eyes and began to do yoga breathing. *In and out. In and out. Just concentrate on the breath. In and out. You're going to be fine. Relax. In and out.*

After ten minutes she cautiously opened her eyes once more. The pain in her head was gone. *I think it's going to be all right.* She stood up carefully, as if she were balancing a water jug on her head, and went to return Scotty's picture to the Regency table.

4

The shoot was scheduled to go for as long as the light stayed good, but Tracy was finished by five-thirty. Dave called her name as she was walking off, and she changed direction and went to join him by the fountain. "I'd like you to meet Lady Margaret Oliver," he said. "She's Lord Silverbridge's sister and is a great fan of yours."

"How do you do, Lady Margaret. What a nuisance this must be, having all these people tramping around your lovely garden."

Lady Margaret's hair was so blond it was almost white, and her elegant, straight nose was dusted with freckles. She wore jeans, a red sweater, lace-up suede boots, and looked about sixteen. The most noticeable thing about her, however, was that she was painfully thin.

"Not at all," she replied to Tracy's remark. "I think it's great fun."

Dave said, "Tracy, if you are going to get something to eat at the catering truck, will you take Lady Margaret with you and introduce her around?"

The look on his face said clearly that he knew he was asking a lot, but that he badly needed to ditch this young sister of the owner. Tracy opened her mouth to say that she wasn't going to dinner, but then she saw the hopeful look in Lady Margaret's eyes. There was something vulnerable about the girl, and Tracy, who had once wanted to be a high school teacher, changed her mind.

"Of course." She turned to Lady Margaret, and said kindly, "Are you hungry? Would you like to have dinner with some of the cast and crew?"

The girl replied shyly, "I'm not hungry, but I'd like to meet them."

Thank you, Dave mouthed to her, as she prepared to remove Lady Margaret from the area of the shoot. Tracy shot him a look that said clearly *You owe me one*, before she shepherded Lady Margaret away.

"Have you been watching for long?" Tracy asked, as they made their way through the yew-enclosed garden.

"I've been watching the whole time," the girl replied enthusiastically. "It's so super having a movie made here at Silverbridge."

"I hope you still feel that way in a few weeks, Lady Margaret. It can get to be awfully old, having strangers in your home all the time."

"Please call me Meg." The girl's sky-blue eyes regarded Tracy worshipfully. "And it may sound idiotic, but I don't feel as if you are a stranger at all. I've seen all your pictures, Miss Collins, most of them more than once."

"Thank you," Tracy replied. Normally a comment about knowing her through her movies would annoy her, but there was something about this girl that called forth her protective instincts. So she said, "As such a devoted fan, you have earned the right to call me Tracy."

Greg, the assistant director, was hurrying along the path in their direction clutching his clipboard. He gave Tracy a grin as he went by, and she flapped a friendly hand in his direction. Then she turned to Meg. "How does the rest of your family feel about this invasion?"

"My brother Tony thinks it's super too. I'm sure we'll see him sometime during the course of the shooting." Meg shot Tracy an impish look. "You might even want to put him in the picture. Tony's gorgeous."

"If he looks at all like you, then he must be."

Meg became flustered. "Oh, I'm nothing compared to Tony."

This unsure girl was nothing at all like Tracy's image of an aristocrat, and she replied gently, "I think you are extremely pretty."

Meg shot her a doubtful glance. "I'm not, really."

Tracy, who rarely touched people who were not family, found herself patting Meg on the shoulder. She barely refrained from wincing at the sharpness of the bone under her fingers. "I'm afraid you're just going to have to accept my word for it, Meg. I have seen and worked with some of the most beautiful women in the world, and, in my judgment, you are a very pretty girl."

"Well . . ." Meg said. "Thank you."

"You're quite welcome."

They went up the stone steps together, and the lawn, the fountain, the terrace, and the house stretched out before them, golden in the hazy late-afternoon sun. "What does your brother, Lord Silverbridge I mean, think about having the movie here?" Tracy asked.

Meg said offhandedly, "Oh, Harry was happy to have the money. And he was very pleased with what the film company did with the gardens."

Two small birds arose from among the shrubs that bordered the walk to their left, and Tracy watched them fly off over the lawn. "What did the film company do to the gardens?"

"Cleaned them up. The yews needed cutting, the paths needed a lot of work, and half of the fountain jets didn't work. You also planted all of those marvelous tulips in the front of the house."

Tracy looked around the lovely property. "I guess the upkeep on a place like this is enormous."

"It's ridiculous," Meg replied. "It's a listed house, of course, which means that it's under the jurisdiction of English Heritage. So all repairs have to be done with their approval, which sends the cost rocketing."

"Why is that?" Tracy asked.

Meg shrugged her blade-thin shoulders. "Because Harry can't substitute less expensive, modern materials in the publicly visible portions of the house. For example, we need a new roof, but Harry can't use modern tiles. Instead he has to replace the old slate roof as well as the layer of lead and boards underneath. And the gutters have to be iron, not plastic. The whole job will cost poor Harry five times more than it would cost to reroof with modern materials."

Tracy looked at the expanse of the present roof. "Whew. That doesn't seem fair."

"Between the rules for upkeep and the death taxes, Harry says the government is out to destroy the whole upper class," Meg said darkly.

Tracy considered this statement, added it to the information she had received from Jon about Lord Silverbridge's callous treatment of the model he had broken up with, and came to the conclusion that the owner of Silverbridge was not a very nice man.

When they arrived at the camper that served as Tracy's dressing room, she invited Meg in to wait for her while she changed out of her costume. Inside, the camper was furnished with a dressing table and mirror, a green corduroy sofa where Tracy could take a nap, and two chairs. It was a utilitarian room, nothing like the luxurious surroundings that Tracy was accustomed to, but then she did not usually work on films with such a tight budget.

When they came in, Gail was sitting on the sofa, tapping away on her laptop. Tracy introduced the two young women, then sat at her dressing table to take off her makeup.

She listened to the two girls talking behind her and compared their backgrounds. Gail had been born in Puerto Rico and brought to New York when she was two. Her parents had struggled to put her through Catholic schools, and after high school she had taken a secretarial course at Katharine Gibbs. She had been working at NBC when Tracy met her and offered her a job. She was smart, funny, extremely competent, and intensely loyal. Tracy considered her a friend.

Meg had been brought up in the palatial surroundings

of Silverbridge, yet it was Gail, the kid from Spanish Harlem, who had self-confidence.

"What a great job you have," Meg was saying. "How does one go about getting a job like yours?"

"I did a secretarial course after high school, Lady Margaret," Gail replied with cool politeness.

"A secretarial course? But that sounds like such a bore."

"It is necessary to acquire certain skills in order to find a job like this, Lady Margaret." Gail's voice sounded even cooler than before.

Tracy actually felt a pang of pity for Meg and swung around on her chair. "Have you finished high school, Meg?"

Meg began to pick at her sweater. "We don't call it high school here. And I still have a year to go. I'll probably go back in the autumn."

"So you're not going to school now?" Gail asked.

Meg stood up. "Enough about bloody school! Are you sure you want me to go with you to dinner, Tracy? If you don't, I'll understand perfectly." Spots of color stained her too-prominent cheekbones, and she was twisting her hands together.

Tracy said, "Of course I want you to come. All I have to do is get into my jeans and we can go."

There was a screen at the end of the camper, and Tracy went behind it to change. Gail hung the Regency-style dress carefully on a portable rack, and then the three young women headed for the caterer's truck, where the second sitting of dinner was being served.

The sun was still out, but there was a distinct chill in the air, and Tracy was glad of her wool sweater. She collected her filled plate from one of the caterer's assistants and walked to one of the two dining buses parked nearby.

Twenty or so people were gathered around the table inside, and a loud chorus of greetings went up as Tracy came in. Elsie Anway, who was playing Tracy's maid in the film, called Tracy's name and gestured to the two empty seats next to her. Gail took a single seat between two electricians, and Tracy led Meg to the chairs next to Elsie. Before she sat down, she announced, "Listen up, everybody. This is Lady Margaret Oliver. Her brother owns this place. She's having dinner with us, so behave yourselves."

Laughter came from all around.

Meg's cheeks were flushed with color and her eyes were bright as she took her seat between Tracy and Elsie. She had consented to accept a bowl of soup from the caterers and placed it carefully on the table.

"This is quite some place your brother has here," Elsie said amiably.

"Thank you," Meg replied. "It's so super getting a chance to watch you film."

Liza Moran, who was seated a little way down the table, said, "Is Lord Silverbridge interested in filming, Lady Margaret?"

"I don't think so," Meg replied cautiously.

"You ought to get him to come along to the set one of these days," Liza said. "I think he would find it enjoyable."

"Harry is very busy." It was the first time Tracy had heard that note of aristocratic reserve from Meg.

Conversation flowed easily around the table, and

Meg listened with obvious fascination and did not eat her soup. Tracy suspected that the girl was anorexic, which perhaps accounted for her being out of school.

Elsie also noticed Meg's lack of appetite and said in a motherly way, "Don't you care for the soup, Lady Margaret? I'm sure the caterers have something you would enjoy."

"The food is fine," Meg replied with a trace of annoyance. "Don't worry about me, I never eat much."

Tracy was finishing her coffee when a horse van came into sight through the windows of the bus. It veered off the main drive shortly after it emerged from the trees, and she asked Meg, "Is that the way to the stables?"

"Yes." Meg had been listening to the banter between two of the audio men, but she turned her attention to Tracy. "That's probably Gwen Mauley's horse. She's sending him for training with Harry."

"Mauley," Tracy repeated thoughtfully. "I've heard that name before."

"Gwen's father is Robin Mauley, the big real estate pooh-bah."

"Oh, yes. I saw him at the hotel the other evening."

"Gwen rides dressage, and she has been training with Harry for six months." Meg's eyes sparked, and she added disapprovingly, "Personally, I think she's more interested in Harry's title than she is in his teaching."

The electricians sitting around Gail got to their feet, prepared to go back to work. Tracy caught her secretary's eye and motioned very faintly with her head.

Elsie said, "There's cake for dessert."

"None for me, thanks," Tracy said. Gail was moving

toward the bus door, and Tracy stood up. "I want to go home and put my feet up. I'm tired."

Meg gave her a hopeful look. "Will I see you tomorrow, Tracy?"

Tracy considered her expression, than said, "Come and watch me film."

"I'll do that," Meg replied, and for a moment her flashing smile made her seem as pretty as she would be if she were not so painfully thin.

Meg remained at the table until everyone had finished, watching her soup congeal in front of her and listening to the crew joke around. When she finally returned to the house, she found her eldest brother in the kitchen, microwaving the dinner Mrs. Wilson, the daily woman from the village, had left for him. His two Springer spaniels were eating out of large china bowls and didn't even look up when she came in.

"You should have eaten off the catering truck, Harry," she said as she went to the refrigerator and took out a bottle of diet soda. Two large windows, which were set above eye level, let the dying light into the room. "I did. They have buses fitted up as dining rooms. It was super."

Henry Oliver, fifteenth Earl of Silverbridge, poured himself a beer and sat down at a large scrubbed oak table. "What did you eat?" he asked casually.

"I had some soup."

He frowned.

The microwave beeped. "I'll get it," Meg said, and lifted the plate out, peeled off the plastic wrap that covered it, and put it in front of her brother. He began to eat hungrily.

Meg leaned against the old but immaculately clean sink. "I met Tracy Collins. She's super nice. And she's even more beautiful than she looks in her films."

Lord Silverbridge took another bite of chipped beef. "Would you like some of this, Meggie? It's quite decent."

She opened a cabinet and took out a glass. "No thanks, I ate with the movie people."

Behind her back, her brother closed his eyes.

Meg measured out a half a glass of soda and turned to face him. "Was that Gwen Mauley's horse I saw coming in an hour or so ago?"

"It was." He took a swallow of beer and produced a grin. "And he's even more beautiful than he looks in his films."

Meg giggled, then took a tiny sip of soda. "It's good to see you smile."

He shrugged wearily. "There hasn't been much reason to smile so far this year, Meggie."

"I know. But landing this film was a good thing, wasn't it?"

"It will put on a new roof, at least." He finished the chipped beef and took another swallow of beer.

Meg brought her soda to the table and sat across from her brother. "This house is such an albatross. If you sold off some of the land, Harry, it would make life so much easier. Mr. Mauley's offer is tremendously generous. You're not likely to get a better one."

"We have been through this before, Meg, and I am not selling off my land to some developer," he replied evenly. "The Olivers have been at Silverbridge for four centuries. This land is in my charge, and I will do everything humanly possible to keep it."

Meg looked at his set face and prudently did not reply.

One of the spaniels had already finished dinner and gone to lie on the old corduroy sofa that stood under one of the high windows. Now the second one finished and ambled over to the sofa to join her brother.

Harry got up and carried his plate and beer glass to the sink, where he left them for the housekeeper to deal with in the morning. "I'm going upstairs."

"I'll go with you." Meg followed him, leaving her virtually untouched soda on the table.

The kitchen they had been using was the original and was located in the rustic, or half basement, of the house. The apartment where they lived was upstairs, and brother and sister had to climb two flights of the narrow back stairs that had once been used by servants, to access it.

Their father, the fourteenth earl, had had the apartment built in the west wing when it became prohibitively expensive to live in the original rooms. A sitting room, called the morning room, a drawing room and six bedrooms had been closed off from the rest of the house, and central heating had been installed.

Brother and sister made themselves comfortable in the morning room, which was at the top of the stairs. Three chintz-covered sofas, a number of comfortable-looking chairs, a television set placed incongruously in an eighteenth-century cabinet, two white wood fireplaces, an oil portrait of two teenage boys, and a collection of watercolors depicting the Silverbridge gardens were the room's main furnishings. The rug that covered the center of the polished wood floor matched the orange in the chintz fabric that covered the three sofas. The drapes on the tall windows were of simple yellow silk.

"So is this horse of Gwen's any good?" Meg said from her usual place upon one of the sofas.

A small black cat had leaped into Harry's lap the moment he sat down in his usual wing chair. She purred loudly as he stroked her. "He's extremely talented."

"As talented as Pendleton?" Pendleton was the horse Harry had ridden at the Olympics in Sydney.

"I haven't ridden him yet, so I can't say, but his natural gaits are wonderful."

"He's a Thoroughbred, right?"

He nodded.

"And Gwen wants to ride him?"

They looked at each other. Both knew that Gwen did fine with a big warmblood who took a lot of pushing and pulling, but she did not deal as well with a more sensitive, hot-blooded horse.

Harry said, "I'm charging her double my usual fee. And there's rot in the east wing."

"Uh," Meg said. "And you like Thoroughbreds."

He grinned. "True." He glanced at his watch. "Time for the news. Then I'm going to let the dogs out and go to bed."

"I'll get the telly," Meg said. "I wouldn't want you to disturb Ebony."

A louder purr came from the silky pile of black fur on Harry's lap.

5

During the following three days, Meg followed Tracy around the set like a chick that has imprinted. "I never get a chance to talk to you," Jon complained, as he and Tracy stood together waiting for a light to be set. "We work from sunup to sundown, and any free time you have is monopolized by that girl."

"She does seem to have adopted me," Tracy agreed. She had draped a blue wool sweater over her shoulders to keep warm while she waited and was sipping a cup of tea.

He looked around the set. "Where is she now? She's always here."

"I don't know where she is."

"Why isn't she in school? She looks young enough."

"I think she has an eating disorder," Tracy returned gravely. "Haven't you noticed? She's nothing but skin and bones."

"That's how all the young girls look these days."

"This is different. I've watched her, and she doesn't eat." A slight frown creased Tracy's brow. "She should be in some sort of treatment."

"Well, I fail to see why you should feel obliged to baby-sit her," Jon said.

"She just seems so fragile somehow. I don't want to reject her and perhaps make her problem worse."

At this point Greg, the assistant director, came up to them and said. "We're ready to go."

A costume assistant came running up to take Tracy's sweater and teacup, and Tracy went to take her place.

They shot the scene five times and broke for lunch. Jon was needed for the afternoon, but Tracy's next scene wasn't until the following day. Her intention was to go back to the Wiltshire Arms, but when she came out of her camper dressed in brown wool slacks and an oatmeal-colored sweater set, she found Meg waiting for her.

All Tracy wanted was to have a peaceful lunch by herself. So she said pleasantly but firmly, "I'm going back to the hotel, Meg. They don't need me this afternoon."

Meg smiled timidly. "I know. I was just wondering if you'd care to come with me to see the stables. You said you used to ride, and my brother has some wonderful horses."

Tracy paused. She had honored Lord Silverbridge's request that movie personnel stay away from the stables, but she had definitely been disappointed not to see the horses. She had kept a horse at home for years before she went to college, and she still rode whenever she got the chance.

If Meg invites me, then it will be all right, she thought, and replied, "I'd like that very much."

Five minutes later, she and Meg were following a footpath that led from the side garden, which was filled with a gorgeous profusion of roses, into the lovely plantation of lime trees that served to screen the stables from the house. Stopping as the stable area first came into view, Tracy took in the splendid sight of stone stable, grassy paddocks, outdoor riding ring, and an unidentifiable building built of the same stone as the stable. Horses were grazing in the paddocks, the May sun shining on the healthy dapples of their glossy coats. A single horse and rider were working in the outdoor ring.

A picture came into her mind of her and Scotty loading Portia into the trailer, she dressed in her show coat, breeches, and boots. It was the summer of Scotty's senior year and her junior year in high school. She did not yet have her license and he had driven the truck to most of the horse shows she competed in. They had fought companionably the whole time they were in the truck over what kind of music to put on the radio.

Meg took her hand and gave it a tug, like a very young child. "Come along. Harry is schooling Dylan, Gwen Mauley's horse. Let's go and watch."

Tracy came back to the present and accompanied Meg across an expanse of grass to the outdoor ring, which was enclosed by a five-foot, wooden-rail fence. Inside, a horse was cantering rhythmically on a twenty-meter circle. Meg led Tracy to the wooden bench on the outside perimeter of the fence, where two spaniels were snoozing in the sunshine. They stood up as the young women approached, and one of them went up to Meg, tail wagging.

"Say hello to Marshal and Millie," Meg said as she stroked a canine head. "It's okay. You can pet them. They're very friendly."

Tracy said, "Hi there, puppies. Aren't you pretty?" She squatted to pet them with the assurance of one who knows dogs, and the tails wagged faster. "Are they Springer spaniels?" she asked Meg.

"Yes. Brother and sister. They belong to Harry. They follow him everywhere."

Tracy lifted her head and for the first time looked at the horseman in the ring.

He was not wearing a hat, and his tawny hair shone like a bronze helmet in the brilliant spring sun. He sat deeply into the horse, directly over the animal's center of balance, so that they almost looked like one creature, not two. His eyes were focused between the horse's ears, his gloved hands held the reins in a soft, sure grip, and his booted legs hung long and reassuring against the horse's sides. He was utterly intent on what he was doing and never glanced their way.

Tracy looked at him and everything inside of her went still. Time seemed to stop.

She had no idea how long it was before Meg's voice came floating to her ears. "Harry is in love with this horse."

With a supreme effort of will, she made herself look from the man to the horse. It was a tall, bay Thoroughbred gelding, with long elegant legs and small delicate ears. Those ears were tilted back as he cantered, and his whole expression proclaimed that he was as concentrated on his rider as his rider was on him.

"He's beautiful," Tracy said a little breathlessly.

The man in the ring said, "Come along, boy. Just a little more." The rider didn't appear to do anything but, as Tracy watched, the horse's canter became rounder, fuller, bigger. The rider smiled as he followed the horse's motion, gave the horse's neck a pat, and said, "You see? I told you you could do it."

For the next fifteen minutes, Tracy sat in silence, watching the man work with the animal as delicately and respectfully as a gifted nursery school teacher would work with a four-year-old. When the lesson was finally over, and the rider leaned forward to enthusiastically pat and praise his pupil, the expression on the equine face was so full of pride that Tracy had to smile.

The rider dismounted and reached in his pocket for a sugar cube. A man wearing jeans and paddock boots came out of the nearby stable and stepped into the ring. The dogs got up and trotted toward their master.

"That's Ned Martin," Meg said. "He's in charge of the stables after Harry." She got to her feet. "Come along and I'll introduce you."

Once again Tracy felt that strange stillness as she followed Meg across the sand ring. *What is this?* she thought with a mixture of impatience, bewilderment and trepidation. *Why do I have this crazy feeling that I am walking toward my fate?*

She heard Ned Martin say, "I'll see to him, Harry," as he led the horse away in the direction of the barn. Then Meg and Tracy had reached their destination.

"Hi Harry," Meg said. "I want you to meet Tracy

Collins. We've been watching your session with Dylan."

He turned to them, and, for the first time, Tracy saw the color of his eyes. They were not blue but brown, wide-set, and intelligent. And at the moment, they looked distinctly annoyed.

Tracy's stomach dropped the way it did on the first steep hill of a roller coaster.

"Meggie, I thought we agreed that the movie people would stay away from the stables." His voice was clipped, upper-class. Tracy felt a shiver go up her backbone.

Meg said earnestly, "But Tracy knows horses, Harry. She used to own her own horse, actually."

The earl turned his good-looking face from his sister to the unwelcome visitor she had brought. For the briefest of moments his dark eyes looked directly into hers, and she thought she saw a look of startled recognition in their depths. Then a veil came down.

"How do you do, Miss Collins," he said. "I don't mean to be rude, but I'm sure you understand my feelings in this matter. Horses are easily spooked, and I have some valuable animals stabled here."

Abruptly the stillness inside Tracy was displaced by a surge of temper. She was not accustomed to being greeted in such a fashion. "You may not mean to be rude, but you most certainly are," she retorted.

He looked surprised at this comeback, and Tracy thought defiantly, *Your aristocratic title doesn't mean beans to me, chum.*

Meg said earnestly, "Tracy won't spook the horses, Harry. Really, she won't."

He dismissed Tracy from his attention and turned to his sister. "How did your appointment go, Meggie?"

She shrugged. "Okay, I guess. Beth wants you to call her."

He rubbed his forehead as if he had a headache.

"Please, Harry, can't I show Tracy around?"

He glanced at Tracy, and said, "Oh, I suppose so."

Tracy had been a movie star for seven years and a megastar for three of those years. She was outraged and had opened her lips to say something scathing when Meg's voice intervened. "Did you know that Harry won a bronze medal at the Olympics in Sydney, Tracy?"

Tracy matched Lord Silverbridge's indifferent manner. "No, I did not have the pleasure of knowing that." She gave him a condescending look. "Good for you, Lord Silverbridge."

She was pleased to see that Lord Silverbridge did not appear to appreciate this compliment one bit. Tracy went on, "I would enjoy seeing your Olympic horse. Are you going to ride him today?" She made it sound as if he should give a performance just for her.

The earl scowled at her. He was wearing a well-worn gray sweater, breeches, and high black boots. His thick, silky hair had fallen over his forehead, and he tossed it back with a gesture that looked as if it was habitual. He was quite tall, several inches over six feet. He replied in a staccato tone, "No, Pendleton is turned out in one of the paddocks. He is seventeen years old, and I retired him from competition after the Olympics."

"How lovely." From her manner she might have been the queen talking to a commoner. "So now all he has to do is eat grass all day."

Lord Silverbridge turned to face her, and for some reason Tracy once again felt a shiver run down her spine. He said calmly, "I said he was retired from competition, not from all work. He will be an invaluable schoolmaster for me to use with my students. He has never been brilliant, but he is absolutely correct. Anyone who rides him learns more than they could from a thousand books."

Tracy would adore to ride such a horse, but she would die before she asked this man for anything. She turned her shoulder slightly, and spoke to Meg, "Can we go look at the barn first?"

Lord Silverbridge said, "It is not a barn, Miss Collins, it is a stable. Barns are for cows."

Tracy turned back to confront him. Their gazes met, and a fleeting, puzzled look flickered in his eyes. Then once more the shutters came down.

For some reason, Tracy's heart was racing. She managed to say evenly, "In Connecticut, where I come from, barns are also for horses, my lord."

From behind them there was the sound of car wheels on gravel, and Meg turned to look. "Oh dear. Harry, I'm afraid it's Mr. Mauley."

Tracy turned in the direction of Meg's gaze and saw the burly man she had previously seen at the Wiltshire Arms getting out of a gleaming black Jaguar.

"Shit," Harry said. "If this continues, I'm going to sue him for harassment."

They stood in silence as the burly real estate mogul came to the gate of the riding ring. When it became clear to him that Harry wasn't going to move, he reluctantly stepped into the arena dirt.

"Good afternoon, my lord." He stopped in front of them. "Lady Margaret." He looked at Tracy and smiled, showing oddly small teeth for so large a man. "It needs no introduction for me to know who you are, Miss Collins."

"I'm afraid I can't return the compliment," Tracy replied.

He held out his hand. "Robin Mauley."

Tracy looked at his hand for a moment before she finally put her own hand into his.

Harry said in a cold voice, "What are you doing here, Mauley?"

"I am here to up my offer substantially, my lord," Mauley said genially. "I don't think you'll want to say no to this."

"Screw your offer, Mauley," Harry returned without heat. "You can offer me the moon, but I am not selling any of my land. That is final. Go look elsewhere for a place to put your golf course." And he strode away, the black-and-white spaniels trotting at his heels.

Robin Mauley set his jaw as he watched Harry's retreating figure, then he turned to Meg. "Ambrose Percy has agreed to build a five-star hotel adjacent to the golf course, Lady Margaret. We are determined to build *the* premier golf resort in Britain, and we are prepared to pay well for the property upon which to do it. I know that your brother has little income outside what he gets from agriculture and tenant rents. He would be able to invest this money, and your family finances would be secure."

"You're wasting your time talking to me, Mr. Mauley," Meg said. Her facial bones were almost visible through her skin in the sunlight. "Harry is the one who owns Silverbridge, and I have to tell you that once he makes up his mind about something, a bomb won't move him."

"Once he hears this offer, he'll change his mind," Mauley said confidently. "Will you tell him about the hotel, Lady Margaret? Will you tell him we are prepared to double my original offer?"

Meg blinked. "*Double* it?"

"That is what I said."

Meg's sky-blue eyes were wide. "I shall certainly tell him, Mr. Mauley."

"Thank you. That is all I ask." He smiled, once more showing those baby-sized teeth. "Lady Margaret. Miss Collins. I wish you good day."

"Good day," Tracy returned and stood in silence next to Meg as the real estate mogul got into his expensive car and drove away.

Then Meg said, "Harry will be crazy if he rejects this offer."

Rather to her surprise, Tracy discovered that her sympathy lay with Harry. "Certainly one can understand that he wouldn't want to give up all this." She gestured toward her surroundings.

"Oh, he would keep the house, the stables, and enough of the grounds to make an appropriate setting," Meg assured her. "It's the eight thousand acres of woods and farmland that Mauley wants to buy."

"Eight thousand acres is a lot of land," Tracy said slowly.

"I know. There aren't many pieces of property that large left in nice areas like this. That's why Mauley keeps hounding Harry. He's never going to find property as good as this for his golf course."

They had been walking toward the stable while they were speaking, and as they reached it, Tracy asked, "What kind of farming is done on the property?"

A young man wearing low-slung jeans and work boots came out of the stable carrying a bucket of water. He stared at Tracy the whole while he was dumping the water on the grass that encircled the cobblestoned stable yard.

Meg said, "We have quite a lot of beef cattle, and we also grow wheat and barley and hay. My brother Tony says that in today's world there's no way you can keep a big house going on agricultural rents and profits alone. But Harry is a farmer at heart—he went to the Royal Agricultural College—and he won't give up."

Very slowly, the young man retreated to the stable, his eyes on Tracy the whole way.

"I can sympathize with him," she said. "I have a particular dislike of golf courses myself."

"But why?" Meg asked in astonishment. "It will be very pretty. Mauley is planning a championship course, with expensive villas close by, and now there will be a Percy hotel as well. Everything will be beautifully landscaped."

The young man came back out of the stable carrying another bucket of water as Tracy answered, "I'm just not a big fan of golf, I guess."

"Tony said he would teach me to play," Meg said. "But the best part of the whole deal would be that Harry wouldn't have to worry about money anymore."

Tracy was looking at the stable building before her

and didn't reply. The large sliding wood door stood wide open, revealing a wood-paneled interior with a wide aisle and high ceiling. From her position she could see a series of Dutch doors along the outside of the building. Only one equine head was hanging out, however.

"How many horses live here?" Tracy asked, dropping the subject of the golf course.

"Ten at the moment," Meg said. "Five of the horses belong to Harry and five of them are here for training."

Slowly Tracy walked into the stable and looked down the aisle. All of the inside stall doors were polished to a rich chestnut gleam and most sported a brass plate with a horse's name engraved on it. The stalls were big and bedded deeply with straw. The boy with the water buckets was mucking out one of them.

Meg said, "Most of the horses are out at pasture now, but Moses is inside today. He's my old pony. Would you like to come and meet him?"

"I'd love to."

"Let's go around to the outside, then. We can see him better."

Tracy followed Meg back out of the stable and around the side of the building, where the stalls all had a second door. The roan pony was resting his chin on the bottom part of his Dutch door, and when he saw them coming, he nickered.

"This is Moses," Meg said, as they stopped in front of the stall. "He taught me to ride. Isn't he adorable?"

"He's darling," Tracy said sincerely as she regarded the fat roan pony who was so obviously looking for treats. "Hi there, cutie."

As the pony nuzzled her hand, looking for a carrot, Tracy looked at the paned glass window, which was set above the Dutch door for more light, and then at the stone trim that edged the door and window and made an arch above them both.

I suppose I can see why Lord Silverbridge didn't like having this elegant building called a barn, she thought with a flicker of reluctant amusement.

Meg was holding the pony's face and looking at his right eye. "It's still a little runny, but it definitely looks better. Harry put some goop into it yesterday and this morning. It seems to be helping."

"My mare had a terrible eye infection once," Tracy said. "I ended up trailering her to Cornell, and if I had waited one more day she would have lost her vision. You have to be careful with eyes. They can blow up all of a sudden."

"That's what Harry said." Meg bestowed one last pat on the pony's neck.

"What is that other building that looks like the stable?" Tracy asked.

"Oh, that's the indoor riding school," Meg replied. "It's quite famous, actually. My ancestor, the tenth earl, had it built after he returned from fighting against Napoleon. Unlike Europe, there were hardly any indoor schools in England at the time. The English, you know, like to ride outdoors—galloping after hounds and all that. But my ancestor had learned the classical way of riding in Portugal, and that's why he built the school. Would you like to see it?"

"Very much," Tracy replied, and they turned their

steps in the direction of the elegant stone building that so surprisingly housed a riding arena.

An hour later Tracy walked back to the house alone as Meg elected to stay and help Ned bring horses in for the farrier. Halfway through the lime plantation she passed the path that Meg had told her led to the woodlands that belonged to Silverbridge. "There are bridle paths all throughout the woods," Meg had said. "I ride there occasionally. Perhaps you'd like to come with me one day?"

"I would love to," Tracy had answered.

She glanced at her watch, thought that a walk through the woods would be very pleasant, and turned in that direction. Once she was under the canopy of trees, she knew that she had made the right decision. Bluebells carpeted the ground on either side of the bridle path with their intense color, yellow cowslips and paler primroses grew around the trunks of the trees, and patches of cuckoo flowers gathered along a little stream that followed the bridle path. Overhead, a flock of small brown birds flew from tree to tree, calling to each other.

How horrible to cut all this down for a golf course, Tracy thought. She bent to pick one of the bluebells that grew so lushly and when she straightened up, Lord Silverbridge was on the path before her, astride a splendid gray horse.

It was a moment before she realized that this was a different man. He was dressed in Regency costume and his golden hair was cut in the Regency style. But the resemblance to Lord Silverbridge was astonishing.

She stared at the horseman in stunned surprise. He looked back at her, but Tracy had the distinct feeling that he didn't see her. Then he turned his horse and galloped away. For about twenty seconds, Tracy could hear the footfalls of the horse on the bridle path. Then there was silence.

Tracy stood there, her hands gripped together tightly, her heart hammering so hard she thought it would burst.

Who was that?

But no matter how often she asked herself that question, she could not come up with a reply.

6

At two o'clock Friday morning, Tracy was awakened by banging on her door. She got out of bed, thrust her feet into slippers, and ran into the sitting room. From outside the door came the sound of voices yelling, "Fire! Fire!" She pushed open the door and the hotel manager was standing outside, a towel pressed to his face. The hallway was filled with smoke. "Miss Collins!" he said. "Thank God. I'll show you to the stairs."

"I know where they are," Tracy replied, coughing and waving her hand in front of her face as if she could push away the smoke. "You had better continue waking people up."

She ran down the corridor in her slippers, her eyes half-closed, trying not to breathe in the smoky air. She reached the stairs at the same time as Jon, who was coming from the opposite direction. The enclosed stairwell was still relatively free from smoke and they both ran down the stairs, Tracy right behind Jon. Tracy asked, "What happened, do you know?"

"No," he flung over his shoulder, "but considering the amount of smoke, it must be serious."

They reached the ground floor, and Jon said, "Step back," as he cautiously opened the stairwell door and peered out. "It's smoky, but I don't see any flames. Let's go."

They ran the twenty feet to a side exit and were safely out into the chill of the night.

Fire engines were pulling up in front of the hotel, their sirens blasting, as Tracy and Jon moved to join the huddle of pajama-clad people gathered together on the front lawn. "Gail?" Tracy called, anxiously scanning the group. "Are you here?"

A small figure wrapped in a fleecy red robe and carrying a computer case and her purse separated from the crowd. "Tracy! Thank God."

Tracy gave a shaky laugh. "Am I glad to see you." The two women shared a convulsive embrace.

Most of the people on the lawn had been sleeping in the single rooms on the first floor and consequently had been evacuated first. As Tracy and Jon turned to look at the house, several more pajama-clad guests came around the side of the building. Among them was Dave Michaels, who was pushing his glasses up on his nose and blinking furiously as he hurried across the lawn.

"Thank God!" he said as he spotted Tracy and Jon. He came up to join them, looking very thin and bony in his T-shirt and flannel pajama pants, and hugged both of his stars in extavagant relief that his movie was safe.

"What happened?" he asked after he had collected himself. "Does anybody know?"

"I think the fire started in the kitchen," Gail volunteered.

"That's what I heard," another voice said.

"Look!" said someone else, and the group on the lawn turned fascinated and horrified eyes toward the flames that had suddenly leaped out two of the first-floor windows.

"I think that's my room," Gail said hollowly.

Tracy reached out an arm and once more hugged her secretary. "You're safe, and that's all that matters."

A few more escapees came trailing across the lawn, and Tracy was relieved to see that the rest of the movie crew had made it out.

By this time, the fire personnel had trained hoses on the building. The manager was talking to the fire chief and when the manager came to join the gathering of his restless guests, the first thing he did was announce, "Everyone is out."

A sigh of relief swept through the crowd.

Then a woman's voice demanded shrilly, "It's two in the morning. Where are we supposed to go for the rest of the night?"

"There's a shelter in Warminster," the manager said. "The Warminster Rescue is opening it up for us and providing tea and coffee. We'll soon have you warm and comfortable."

"Comfortable?" The voice sounded even shriller than before. "In a shelter? Surely you can't be serious?"

Tracy was not thrilled about the idea of a shelter either, and asked the manager if there were any area hotel rooms open.

"I'm afraid everything is booked for the weekend, Miss Collins," the man replied apologetically. "There's a big point-to-point tomorrow." He was referring to an event for jump riders that consisted of a cross-country race from one point to another.

A man said furiously, "All my clothes are in my hotel room. I have a meeting in the morning. What am I supposed to wear?"

The shrill woman began to cry.

Jon said calmly, "None of us has any clothes. I think going to Warminster is an excellent idea. It's a large town, and we will be able to replace at least some of our wardrobes there." He turned to the Wiltshire Arms, which now had fire blazing out of its upper windows as well. The sky was filled with black smoke, and the smell was acrid in the air. He said somberly, "I don't think we're going to be able to salvage anything from here."

"It doesn't look that way," Dave agreed. He turned to the hotel manager. "Can you take Miss Collins, Mr. Melbourne, and the rest of the movie crew in the hotel van? Our own drivers and cars aren't on the premises, and I don't want to keep Miss Collins standing about here in the cold."

The manager assured him that he could do that and, as he went to get the van, Tracy looked once again at the burning building. It was frightening to think that fire could take such a hold in so short a time.

"I don't have my car keys," a man said agitatedly. "They're back in the room."

"I'm sure you can go with someone else," Jon said, and another man responded, "He can come with us."

Tracy smiled at Jon. Most of the actors she knew wouldn't have evinced the slightest interest in a small, bald, pajama-clad man who had forgotten his car keys.

There was a flash of light, one that was all too familiar to Tracy, and over Jon's shoulder she saw the photographer. Suddenly she was swept by fury.

"You little shit!" she yelled. "If you take one more picture of me, I'm going to have you arrested!"

"Temper, temper, Miss Collins," replied Jason Counes, the photographer who had been stalking Tracy for six months. "Freedom of the press, you know."

Tracy was so angry that she started for the man, intending to smash his camera. Jon grabbed her after she had taken three steps.

"Calm down, Tracy," he said in a soothing voice. "Look, the van is here, and we're going."

Tracy was shaking. The abrupt awakening and fear from the fire had stripped away the wall she usually erected between herself and her hatred of the smarmy photographer who would not leave her alone.

Jon kept his arm around her and began to lead her in the direction of the van. After throwing one last glare in the direction of Jason Counes, she went.

By the time the refugees got to Warminster it was after three in the morning. The promised shelter consisted of cots and blankets in the basement of a school. Two women were brewing coffee in the kitchen. A silver-haired woman in a fur coat over her nightgown began to cry.

"Oh please," Gail said unsympathetically. "You might have been burned to death, lady. A night in a shelter should look good to you."

The woman replied angrily, "I'll have you know that I am not accustomed to sleeping in a basement, young woman." She sniffed. "It smells like mildew in here."

The shrill woman agreed.

"Frank," said someone else, "do something!"

"What the hell do you want me to do?" her husband replied. "It's three in the morning, for God's sake."

Tracy's emotions were still turbulent from her encounter with her nemesis, and she said acidly, "Guess what, people? I am not accustomed to sleeping in shelters either. But this is what we've got, and we might as well stop whining and make the best of it until the morning."

The silver-haired woman's equally silver-haired husband unexpectedly said, "Miss Collins is right, Eunice. Buck up, will you?"

"I am not going to lie down on one of those disgusting cots," Eunice announced. "God knows who may have slept there before. For all I know, the mattresses have bugs."

This was a sentiment with which Tracy heartily agreed. "Then we'll all sit around the table for the rest of the night and drink coffee," she proclaimed.

It was a plan of action that appealed to most of the other guests, and the majority of them wrapped themselves in the cot blankets and sat around the large Formica table drinking the coffee and tea brewed by the shelter volunteers and trying to figure out what to do in the morning.

Everyone agreed that clothing was the most important thing, and Tracy proposed that they have a local department store send over underwear, sneakers, slacks, and shirts. "At least then we can go out to shop for whatever else we may need," she said.

"I don't have my credit card with me," a man said unhappily.

"I'll take care of the clothes," Tracy said. "It will be easier."

Everyone was happy with this arrangement, and Gail made a list of everyone's sizes. As daylight dawned, the Americans (Gail and Tracy) were the only ones to take advantage of the single tepid shower and, promptly at nine-thirty, Gail called the local department store. The manager was delighted to be able to accommodate Tracy Collins, and by ten o'clock Tracy had shed her silk pajamas and was wearing a turtleneck, jeans, and sneakers.

While most of the other newly clad guests headed for the stores to buy more appropriate clothing, the movie people got into company cars to drive to Silverbridge for the day's filming.

As soon as they arrived on location, Dave put Greg in charge of finding new lodgings for the dispossessed cast and crew. The assistant director spent a very discouraging hour on the phone to various hotels, which were all booked for the next two days. He then drove to check out personally the few bed-and-breakfasts that had reported openings. At two o'clock he returned to Silverbridge.

He found the director watching the camera operators practice moving the camera to keep up with the actors. Everyone else was standing around. Greg went up to Dave, and said, "Can I talk to you for a minute?"

"Sure." Dave moved to stand beside the chair that had been set up for him, a chair that was presently occupied by Meg. Each day she had made herself progressively more comfortable on the set and, because she never intruded but only watched, Dave had reached the point where he scarcely noticed her.

"There are no rooms to be had in any of the area hotels," Greg said grimly. "Because of the big point-to-point this weekend, everything that is decent is booked."

Dave groaned and began to polish his glasses with a handkerchief. "There has to be something available! Did you tell the hotel managers that you wanted a room for Tracy Collins?"

"Yes, I did. But apparently a flock of aristocracy is arriving for the race, and no one was willing to bump them."

Dave polished harder. "There must be something that's open!"

"I've found a B&B in Littleton that has three rooms and two B&Bs in Marlton that have two rooms each. But the rooms are tiny and don't have private bathrooms. I really don't think we can ask Tracy to sleep in them. Jon either, for that matter."

"Shit," Dave said. "What are we going to do?"

Greg pulled at his ponytail and looked unhappy.

Meg said, "I have an idea."

The two men looked at her.

"I couldn't help but overhear." Excitement bubbled in her voice. "We have extra bedrooms. Perhaps Tracy and Jon could stay with us."

The two men looked at each other.

"There's nothing available in the area," Greg said. "We would have to go over an hour away to find anything remotely suitable."

Dave finished polishing his glasses and returned them to his face. He frowned as he looked at Meg. "Do you think your brother would agree to such an arrangement?"

Meg said promptly, "If you're willing to pay him what you were paying the Wiltshire Arms, I rather think he might."

There was a pause as Dave continued to frown, and Greg pulled once more at his ponytail. Then Dave said, "All right, Lady Margaret. Would you be kind enough to ask him and let me know what he says?"

Meg removed her fragile frame from Dave's chair. "I'll go and find him now."

"Great. Thanks," Dave said. Then, as Meg moved out of earshot, he rolled his eyes. "Lord Silverbridge is going to end up being half the bloody cost of this picture."

Greg said nervously, "Don't you think I should look at the setup before we make a deal, Dave? The bathroom arrangements in these old places are sometimes fairly primitive. And Tracy . . ."

Dave groaned. "All right, I suppose you'd better take a look at the bathrooms. But I don't know how we're going to tell His Lordship and Lady Margaret that you don't find their home suitable to house a movie star."

"We shall just have to hope that it is," Greg said. "Because there really isn't much other choice."

Meg went first to the stables, but Harry wasn't there. Next she tried his office, which was a wood-paneled room next to the kitchen. He had left the door partly open, and Meg stopped for a moment in the doorway to look at her brother.

Harry, wearing a brown wool sweater, was seated at a modern desk, his back to her, his eyes on his computer screen. The afternoon light slanting in from the high window over the computer lit his tawny hair and, as she watched, he muttered something under his breath, then slammed his open hand on the desk. The spaniels, which were lying on either side of his chair, raised their heads at the sound.

"Not good news?" Meg asked as she came into the room.

He swiveled around in his chair, causing Marshal to get up and look at him expectantly. When Harry didn't get up, the spaniel lay back down again. Harry took off his horn-rim glasses and rubbed his eyes. "Meg. What are you doing here? I thought you were watching the movie shoot."

"I came to see you." She went to sit in the old leather chair next to the desk. "Did you know that the Wiltshire Arms burned down last night?"

His brown eyes widened. "No, I hadn't heard."

She hooked her rain-straight hair behind her ears. "Well it did, and it has left all of the movie people who were staying there homeless. Greg—he's the assistant director—tried to book them into other hotels today, but the point-to-point over in Castleton is tomorrow, and everything is taken."

Harry leaned back in his chair. "I was planning to go myself," he said mildly. "One of my students is riding in it."

"Who?" Meg asked, momentarily distracted from her mission.

"Matt Alder."

Meg nodded. Matthew Alder, Baron Carsford, was a jump rider, but over the winter he had taken a series of dressage lessons with Harry.

Meg moved the conversation back on track. "Anyway, because of the point-to-point, the only lodgings available are in some bed-and-breakfasts in Littleton and Marlton. Greg says that the rooms are tiny and not appropriate for Tracy. Or for Jon."

Harry crossed his arms behind his head. "God forbid an American movie star should be forced to stay in an English B&B."

"Well you certainly wouldn't like it."

He shrugged.

"Anyway, I suggested that they stay here," Meg said. "We have three empty bedrooms at the moment."

Harry's arms dropped and he glared. "You can't possibly be serious."

"Why not?" Meg asked. "The film company would pay you the same amount of money they were paying the Wiltshire Arms."

A little silence fell. Then he said abruptly, "It's impossible, Meg. I have managed to work around the mess the movie people are making of my grounds, but I don't want them living in the house with me."

"It would just be Tracy and Jon. They're super, honestly, Harry. And they spend most of their time on the set or in their dressing rooms. You'd probably hardly see them."

He said stiffly, "I would like to think that I am not yet reduced to the status of a hotel keeper."

"You'd be a very well paid hotel keeper," Meg shot back. "The Wiltshire Arms charges a fortune, and both Tracy and Jon had suites."

"I can't offer them a suite," he said. "I can't even offer them a private bathroom. Did you explain that to whomever you were talking to? Perhaps your movie star friends won't think Silverbridge is suitable."

"Anyone would rather stay at Silverbridge than in a B&B," Meg said with certainty.

Harry pushed his hair off his forehead. "Jesus, Meggie, what's going to happen if the gutter press gets hold of the fact that Tracy Collins is staying in my house? I really can't go through another Dana Matthews thing."

"You are also training Gwen Mauley's horse," Meg pointed out. "Darling Gwen is going to be hanging around here as well."

"I know." He sounded grim.

"Harry, even the *Examiner* won't have the nerve to say that you're having an affair with two women at the same time and in the same place."

His jaw set. "In my experience, there is very little that the *Examiner* doesn't have the nerve to say."

Meg chewed on a strand of her hair and looked at him.

He sighed. "Oh, all right. If the film company wants to pay me the Wiltshire Arms rate, they can stay here."

Meg jumped up. "Great. You'll like Tracy, Harry. She's not like Dana Matthews at all."

He grunted, put on his glasses, and turned back to the computer. As she was going out the door he turned his head to call, "Tell them I want the money up front."

"All right." She squinted at the columns of figures that had appeared on the computer screen behind him. "What are you working on?"

"Bills," he said dryly, and turned back to the machine.

7

The excitement over the fire had pushed Tracy's vision of the horse rider to the back of her mind, but once she returned to Silverbridge for filming, it came back vividly.

I must be letting the atmosphere of this place get to me, she thought, as she stood on her mark waiting for Dave to direct the cameras to roll. Clouds had come in during the course of the afternoon, and the changing light in the garden had forced them to shoot a scene near the end of the film, when Julia had begun to fear her obsessively jealous husband. Tracy's mind, however, was not on the movie.

I spend my days surrounded by people dressed in Regency clothes. Then I meet Lord Silverbridge, who, however rude and obnoxious he may be, is certainly a striking man. So I have this hallucination where I see a man who looks like Lord Silverbridge riding a horse and wearing Regency clothes. It's weird, but explainable.

The vision of the man on horseback rose again before her mind's eye and her heart began to thud. As if from a distance, she heard Dave call, "Check her."

A studio makeup woman appeared at Tracy's side, dusted a tiny bit of powder on her nose, and went away. Dave called, "Action."

Tracy made a great effort to close her mind to all outside thoughts, and began to walk along the path in the direction of the house. The camera, which was mounted on a dolly, moved beside her. Tracy, as Julia, looked toward the terrace, where she was supposed to see her husband awaiting her. In fact, Jon was not on the terrace. They would shoot the meeting between Julia and her husband later. Consequently, when Tracy focused her eyes on the terrace, she expected to find it empty.

It wasn't. A young woman with auburn hair was there, accompanied by a little boy. The woman wore a plain Regency morning dress of sprigged muslin, and the little boy was dressed in what looked like a gray jumpsuit with a short jacket over it. Even under the cloudy sky, his hair looked bright.

Tracy stopped short, staring in disbelief at the tableau on the terrace. Her hand went to her throat in an instinctive gesture of protection. Then she shut her eyes, trying to get a grip on herself. When she opened her eyes again, the terrace was empty.

"Cut! Dave called. "Were you able to get that, Michael? I know she wasn't supposed to stop."

"We got it," the cameraman called back.

"Then print it," Dave said.

He came up to where Tracy was standing. She had broken out in a clammy sweat, and small tremors were causing her body to quiver. Dave appeared to notice nothing of this, however. "That was brilliant, Tracy. Just brilliant." Behind his thick glasses his eyes were glittering. "Do you think you could do it once more, just in case the first take doesn't come out?"

"No," Tracy said in a thready voice. "Not now, Dave. I can't do it now."

For the first time he noticed her pallor and her trembling. He put an arm around her shoulders, and said gently, "All right. I'm sure the first take will be okay. Come and sit down, and I'll have someone bring you a glass of water."

Tracy nodded and allowed him to lead her to the chair that had her name on it. Gratefully, she sat down and rested her forehead on her lap.

"You're not going to faint, are you?" Dave asked in alarm.

Tracy shook her head. "Where is that water?"

"Here." Someone put a plastic bottle in her hand, and she drank thirstily. The water was tepid, like most liquids in England, but she drank it gratefully. Finally, she was able to offer Dave an attempt at a smile.

"I'm so sorry. I don't know what came over me."

"That's all right," Dave replied. "You didn't sleep at all last night. Perhaps I should have given you the day off."

"No, No, I was fine. Really."

"Well you're finished for today," Dave said. He was still looking worried. "I think you ought to go home and take a map."

Meg said from someplace behind Tracy's chair, "I'll take her, Dave."

"Take me where?" Tracy asked a little forlornly. "My hotel burned down."

As Meg appeared at his side, Dave explained, "We've made arrangements for you and Jon to stay here at Silverbridge."

Tracy jerked, as if a bolt of electricity had just shot through her. "What?"

Dave said soothingly, "All the hotels were booked for the weekend. If you don't want to remain at Silverbridge after Sunday, I'm sure we can make other arrangements. But for now, I think you'll be more comfortable here than you would be at a bed-and-breakfast."

"We have a nice big bedroom for you, Tracy," Meg said. "It even has a painting by Claude."

For some reason, Tracy felt panicked by the thought of staying at Silverbridge. "I don't want to disrupt your family any more than they have been already," she protested to Meg.

"Don't worry about that," Dave said. "We're paying Lord Silverbridge hotel fees for you and Jon."

Tracy racked her brain for a valid excuse not to stay at Silverbridge for the weekend and could come up with nothing.

"Do you feel well enough to walk?" Dave said solicitously.

Tracy slowly breathed in and out. Then she did it again. "Yes," she said.

Despite her assurance, Dave put a hand under her elbow and supported her as she stood up. To her relief, the world remained clear and steady. She smiled at her concerned director. "I'm fine, really I am. Go back to work and don't worry about me."

"You look better," he said. "A little color has come back into your face." He turned to Meg. "Lady Margaret, if you would accompany Tracy to the house, I would be grateful."

"Not to worry," Meg said. "Come along, Tracy. I've already had Mrs. Wilson make up your bed. You can crawl right in if that's what you want."

Tracy made one last plea. "This has to be an imposition, Dave. Really, I wouldn't mind a B&B for a few days."

"That photographer will have much easier access to you at a B&B than he will if you stay here," Dave said.

Tracy thought of Silverbridge's huge extent of private property that Jason Counes could not trespass upon and gave in. "This is very kind of you, Meg."

Meg smiled. "It will be fun having you."

Tracy looked apprehensively toward the terrace. It was empty.

"Go with Lady Margaret," Dave said firmly. "We're finished with you for the day, you aren't on call tomorrow, and we're taking Sunday off. By the time you report for work on Monday morning, I expect to see roses back in those cheeks."

Tracy didn't even attempt a smile as she turned toward Meg and a house she did not want to enter.

A side entrance took them into a wood-paneled vestibule with a green marble floor. The staircase that led upstairs from the vestibule was steep and narrow.

"Our apartment is on the second floor," Meg said.

"My father thought that the rest of the house was just too big for modern living."

Tracy nodded.

"We have an elevator if you're not up to the stairs," Meg said. "My brother had it installed for Mummy when she broke her hip."

"I'm sure I can manage the stairs," Tracy said.

"This way, then." Meg led the way upward.

The first flight of stairs ended in a landing that opened to the left onto a delightful sitting room furnished in chintz and rosewood and bowls of fresh flowers. "How pretty," Tracy said, peering in through the arched doorway.

"This is the morning room." Meg walked into the room and gestured for Tracy to follow her. "This room and the kitchen are where we basically live. You are welcome to make yourself at home here."

Tracy looked around the room, which ran from the front to the back of the house, with tall windows on three sides. In front of the south wall windows there was a rosewood table with six chairs set around it and a magnificent vase of fresh flowers in its center. Six more matching chairs were set along the walls for use when the table was expanded. Meg said, "If we have a dinner party, we usually eat in here."

A small black cat, who had been curled up on one of the chinz sofas, stood up and stretched, arching her back. She then fixed a pair of unnerving green eyes on Tracy and uttered a short, angry-sounding yowl.

"That's Ebony, Harry's cat," Meg said. "She doesn't like strangers."

"Most cats don't," Tracy murmured, her eyes on the

outraged Ebony. "I once had a cat that would hide under the bed every time someone new came into the house."

"Ebony is a little more confrontational than that. She'll glare at you and yowl and prowl around you, but if you ignore her she won't actually scratch you or anything."

"How nice," Tracy said ironically. Then, curiously, "How on earth does she deal with the dogs?"

Meg straightened a copy of *Horse and Hound* that had been carelessly tossed on the coffee table. "They have different territories. The dogs stay downstairs, in the kitchen and Harry's office, and Ebony stays up here." She smiled. "Come along, and I'll show you to your bedroom."

They exited the morning room and went down the wide, picture-lined corridor that lay to the right of the landing. Three large oak doors punctuated either side of the corridor. One of the doors was open; the others were closed.

"These are the bedrooms," Meg said. "The room on the far end of the passage is the original drawing room, which lies at the top of the main staircase. We had the morning room made by knocking down the walls of the two end bedrooms."

"Is the drawing room part of the apartment?"

"Yes, but it's used for entertaining, and we haven't done a lot of that since Mummy died."

They went past the open bedroom door, and Meg said, "That's Harry's room. He always leaves the door open so that Ebony can come in and out."

Tracy stopped herself from looking in. "Your brother seems to have very devoted animals," she said lightly.

"He found Ebony when she was a starving kitten that somebody dumped. People still have such weird ideas about black cats. Anyway, he brought her home, and she worships him." Meg stopped at the end door on the opposite side of the passageway from Harry's room. "This will be your room," she said, and opened the door.

This bedroom, like the other rooms on the floor, had a twelve-foot ceiling, two long, many-paned windows, and a white wood fireplace. The landscape by Claude that Meg had promised hung over the mantel. The bed was a four-poster without a canopy, and the rug was an Axminster. A great bowl of pink roses reposed on the table that stood in front of the fireplace.

"It's lovely," Tracy said honestly.

Meg opened a door that led into a white-tiled, old-fashioned bathroom. It was quite large and, except for the usual conveniences and a scale, exhibited a lot of empty white tile floor. Meg said, "I'm afraid that you'll have to share a bathroom with me. The only rooms with private baths are the two closest to the sitting room, and Harry has one of those and the other one had a leak in the ceiling and has to be redone. The two other rooms on each side share a bathroom. There are locks on the bathroom doors, however, and when you're using it, just lock my side and I won't be able to come in on you." She gestured toward the sink. "Mrs. Wilson has put out a new toothbrush and toothpaste for you, and I will be happy to lend you what you need in the way of clothing."

Tracy privately thought that there was no way she would ever fit into Meg's clothes, which had to be size 00. Out loud she said, "I appreciate the toothbrush,

Meg, but Gail called our London hotel this morning and asked the concierge to send everything we had left behind down to Wiltshire. I expect some clothes to arrive before evening."

After Meg had finally gone, Tracy went over to the window and stood looking out across the front lawn. She was still deeply perturbed by her earlier hallucination. *It must be an hallucination,* she thought. *What else could it possibly be?*

She turned back into the room, and it was then that she realized for the first time that her family photographs had been left behind at the Wiltshire Arms and were probably ashes.

My wedding picture! she thought in panic. The other photos were all blown-up snapshots and could be duplicated, but her wedding picture had been done by a studio, and the only other copy belonged to her mother.

I have to call Gail. She looked around for her purse and realized that it, too, had been left at the hotel. She didn't have her cell phone, and there was no phone in her bedroom.

There has to be a phone around here somewhere, she thought and hurried out into the corridor and back to the morning room. There was a phone there, and she dialed her secretary's cell phone number. Gail answered on the third ring.

"Gail!" Tracy sounded almost as panicked as she felt. "I left my wedding picture back at the hotel. Can you call my mother and see if the photography studio still has the negative?"

"Of course," Gail replied. "In fact, if you have the name of the studio, I'll call them myself."

Tracy shut her eyes and thought. "Wilson Photography," she said finally. "It's in Westport, Connecticut."

"Okay, I'll call. But I'm sure they'll have the negative, Tracy. In fact, they probably have the picture hanging in their showroom."

Tracy slowly hung up. Her irrational fear that if she lost the picture she would be losing Scotty again was slightly abated by Gail's rational words.

She was exhausted, but the adrenaline was still flowing too strongly to make sleep possible. When she saw the closed door at the far end of the corridor, she decided that she would take a look at the drawing room before she went to bed. She walked past Harry's room, Meg's room, and her own room, softly turned the knob on the drawing room door, and opened it.

The drawing room was much larger and grander than the morning room. Hanging over the marble fireplace was a magnificent painting of a mother and child, which Tracy later learned was a Gainsborough portrait of a previous Lady Silverbridge holding the hand of her young son. Green velvet sofas and green-and-rose-striped chairs were grouped around the fireplace, and a large grand piano stood in one pale green corner. Tracy's eyes moved slowly across the stunning room, with its magnificent moldings and chandelier, in the direction of the tall window, which looked out over the back lawn and the fountain.

A man and a woman were standing a few steps away from the window. They were very close to each other, but not touching. The man, who looked like Harry, wore the blue morning coat and pale yellow pantaloons that Tracy had come to recognize as standard for a Regency gentleman. The girl, for she could not have been over twenty, wore a simple muslin dress, and her auburn hair was pulled back into a chignon. Tracy had a clear view of her profile and, except for the darker hair and straighter nose, it was like looking in a mirror.

The strangest feeling settled over Tracy as she beheld this couple. No longer was she startled, or frightened, or upset. It was as though a great stillness had encompassed her, almost like the stillness she had felt when she first met Harry. She stood, motionless and silent, and watched.

The man lifted a hand and gently traced a finger along the girl's cheekbone. He left his finger where it was as he said, "God, Isabel. What am I to do?"

His voice was the voice of a living man. The couple looked completely solid as they stood there in front of the window.

"You can't do anything, Charles," the girl replied. Her accent was English. "*We* can't do anything. You are married, and I am your third cousin. And that is all we can ever be to each other."

"I know that you are right." His voice sounded harsh. "At least my head knows that you are right. It's my heart that tells me otherwise."

The girl did not reply. She just looked at him. Very slightly, her mouth quivered.

He jerked his hand away from her face and turned to stare out the window, the tension in his broad shoulders visible. "Christ, this is a pretty sight. Here I am, trying to seduce my children's governess. I have always despised men who took advantage of their dependents."

"You haven't taken advantage of me," the girl

replied. "Something happened between us. It wasn't something either of us wanted. It just"—she lifted a hand in a helpless gesture—"happened."

He turned back. "I know. But I can't go on like this, Isabel. I can't see you day after day, and want you, and know you are living under the same roof as I . . ."

She crossed her arms over her breast in a protective gesture. "What am I to do, Charles?" There was a desperate note in her voice. "Caroline took me on because there was nowhere else for me to go after Papa died. I'm too young to get a job as governess with any other family."

The sun suddenly peeked out from beneath the clouds, lighting the man's hair to gold. Tracy felt a pain somewhere in the region of her heart. He reached out and gathered the girl into his arms. "I have no intention of putting you out, sweetheart. Forget my ravings. We shall do just fine."

The girl rested her cheek against his shoulder in a small gesture of confidence and trust. She did not see, as Tracy did, the look of grim despair carved into the flesh of the man's face.

Yeeooow! Tracy jumped at the high-pitched screech and looked down to see Ebony standing behind her in the doorway. The little cat's hair was standing on end, making her look twice as big as she really was, her tail was fat and standing straight up, and her glittering green eyes were fastened on the space in front of the window. Once again she let out that bloodcurdling sound.

Tracy looked back to the window, but no one was there. Her heart, which had accelerated at Ebony's yowl, continued to race as she stared at the empty space where just a minute before two people had stood. Then she looked back down at Ebony, who was still staring at the window and still in a state of full alarm.

I'm not crazy, she thought. *There was something there. Ebony knows it.* She looked once more around the empty room and began to tremble. *In the name of God,* she thought, afraid as she had not been before, *what is going on here?*

8

$\mathcal{T}$racy slept for five hours and when she awoke the light outside her window was dimming. The first thing she thought was, *I'm starving. I hope I haven't missed all the food.*

She went to the window to see if the catering truck was still there. It was, but the caterers were packing up to leave.

Damn. Tracy had crawled into bed in her clothes, and she looked with disgust at her wrinkled turtleneck and jeans. She turned from the window to see if her clothes from London had arrived.

Someone had placed a large leather suitcase and a smaller matching tote bag along the wall next to the door. A green garment bag was draped over a chair. Tracy heaved a sigh of relief and went to pull out some warm clothes. She had been delightfully toasty under the down comforter, but the air in the bedroom was decidedly colder than she was accustomed to.

She wanted to take a shower before she dressed, and went into the plain, functional bathroom she was to share with Meg. The old white tub was long and narrow and, to Tracy's relief, a striped shower curtain indicated the presence of a shower.

The bathroom was freezing. Tracy started the shower and stripped off her clothes, praying that the water would be hot. It was. She climbed through the shower curtain, borrowed Meg's soap and shampoo, and was out again in five minutes. She had no wish to linger and find that she had run out of hot water before she had washed the suds out of her hair.

Shivering even more than before, she hurried into her underwear and a pair of wool slacks and a lavender cashmere sweater set, the kind of clothes she would wear to a gathering of friends in Connecticut. She couldn't find a hair dryer in the bathroom, which, except for a few shelves holding towels, was utterly devoid of storage space, so she dried her hair as best she could with a towel. Then she set off for the morning room, hoping to find Jon.

The person she encountered was Lord Silverbridge. He was sitting in a large, comfortable-looking wing chair with Ebony on his lap and a folded newspaper propped up on the chair's arm so it was out of the little cat's way. He looked up as Tracy came in.

"Good evening," he said. "Meggie said that you were sleeping. I hope you got a good rest."

His words were courteous, but his tone was indifferent. He was wearing a pair of horn-rimmed glasses that, outrageously, made him look even more handsome than usual.

He could have been the twin of the man she had seen in the drawing room.

"Yes, thank you, my lord," she replied expressionlessly.

"You must forgive my not getting up, but Ebony dislikes being disturbed."

Tracy narrowed her eyes. *You arrogant bastard, you're the one who dislikes being disturbed.* "Where are Meg and Jon?" she asked.

"They still appear to be shooting down in the garden. I haven't seen either of them since I got in."

Tracy looked at the paper he was holding. "Is that an evening edition?"

"It is indeed," he replied. "And there is a picture of you prominently displayed."

Tracy cursed.

"You look quite fetching in your pajamas," Lord Silverbridge went on. He turned the paper around and held it out to her. "Here, would you like to see?"

She took the paper from him silently and regarded the picture that Jason Counes had taken at the fire. He had caught her smiling at Jon.

"Damn," she said. "Now the gossip will start that I'm having an affair with Jon."

"Are you?" he asked blandly. Then, as she glared at him, he held up his hand. "I'm sorry. I know all too well how the press can distort things."

There was a bitter note in his voice, and Tracy remembered Jon's story about Silverbridge's relationship with a model. Then her stomach gurgled, and she said, "I missed dinner, and the catering truck is leaving. Is there anyway I could get some food? Are there any area restaurants that deliver?"

"No." He took off his glasses and rested them on top of a table. Very gently he shooed the little cat off his lap. She leaped to the floor with a protesting squawk, gave Tracy an indignant glare, and began to clean her paws.

"I'll take you down to the kitchen," he said. "I'm sure there will be something you can eat."

He was wearing brown twill pants, a tattersall shirt open at the neck, and a pair of polished brown moccasins. As he joined her, Tracy could see that he was taller and slimmer than his phantom counterpart, but their faces were almost identical.

"The kitchen is in the basement," he said. "It was much easier to use the original than it was to install a new one upstairs."

"That is understandable," Tracy said, mimicking his carefully polite tone.

She followed him down the staircase that led to the green marble hallway, where he opened a door revealing yet more stairs. He switched on a light, and they went down another flight, ending up in a very large but surprisingly cozy kitchen. When Harry entered, his two spaniels arose from the sofa under the window and came to meet him, tails wagging eagerly. As he greeted the dogs, Tracy looked around. Besides the sofa and table and chairs, there was a large oak sideboard displaying an assortment of china, soup tureens, and a big bowl of fruit. The stove looked modern, as did the refrigerator. The countertops were the same color oak as the table. The wood floor was darker.

The spaniels pattered out into the back hall.

"I usually come down before I go to bed and take them out," Harry said. "I'll just let them out now, if you don't mind."

He disappeared into the back hall, and, a moment later, Tracy heard the sound of a door opening and closing. He returned almost immediately without the dogs and went directly to the refrigerator, murmuring, "I'm sure there must be something here."

When he withdrew his hand from the refrigerator it was holding a plate covered with plastic wrap. He said expressionlessly, "Mrs. Wilson left some stewed chicken for Meg, but she must have eaten with the movie people." He looked at Tracy. "I can warm it in the microwave if you like."

"I don't want to eat Meg's dinner," she said. "Some cheese and crackers would be fine."

He was looking at the plate in his hand. "Meg isn't going to eat this. It will only get thrown away. You might as well have it."

"How can I possibly refuse such a gracious offer?" Tracy said.

He shot her a look but didn't reply. Instead he popped the plate into a large microwave oven that sat on top of one of the counters and expertly pushed some buttons.

"Would you care for something to drink?" he said with exaggerated courtesy. "We have some fizzy water that Meg likes. Or I can offer you a glass of wine."

"Fizzy water will be fine," Tracy said. She went to sit at the oak table, putting him in the position of serving her.

He didn't seem at all discomposed by this maneuver. He opened the bottle top, poured the water into a glass, and brought it to her. The microwave beeped, and he went to remove the plate, which he brought to her as well. "Hold on," he said, and went to get a knife, fork, and spoon from the sideboard drawer.

As Tracy lifted the fork she saw that the kitchen flatware used at Silverbridge was heavy, solid silver with a coronet engraved on the handles. The dinner plate, on the other hand, was the kind of modern stoneware that one could put in the microwave.

"Oh," he said. "I forgot." He went back to the sideboard and returned with a heavy white damask napkin, which he spread ostentatiously on her lap. "There. I believe I've done everything expected of a good innkeeper."

Tracy was annoyed. Somehow he had got the best of her. She ignored him and began to eat.

He hesitated, as if he wasn't sure what to do, then he took the seat across from her. Tracy glanced up from her food and found him looking at her. His open collar revealed a strong, slim neck and an elegant but firm jawline. She quickly looked down at her plate, speared a piece of potato, and said offhandedly, "Do you have any ghosts here at Silverbridge, my lord?"

"Are you one of those ghost-busting Americans who go around collecting haunted houses, Miss Collins?" There was amusement in his voice.

"No, I am not." It was difficult to make an American voice sound as chilly as an English voice, but Tracy managed it. "I am merely trying to make conversation with a very rude man. However, if you prefer to be silent, that is perfectly all right with me."

She shot him a scorching blue look and ate the piece of potato on the end of her fork.

For a moment she didn't think he was going to reply. Then he rubbed his hand across his eyes, and said stiffly, "I beg your pardon. I have been rude. I have a great many things on my mind, but it isn't fair to take my bad temper out on you. Please forgive me."

The words were okay, but the tone was wrong. Tracy picked up her glass, looked at him, and for a brief second their eyes met and held. An electric current flashed from her toes to the ends of her still-damp hair. She mumbled, "Of course," and quickly returned her gaze to her food.

She heard him shift in his chair. "We don't have any ghosts that I know of. They are supposed to lurk in places where they met a violent death, isn't that so? Most of the violent deaths in my family were met on the battlefield, not here at Silverbridge. For such an old house, we are remarkable spirit-free."

Tracy moved a piece of celery to the side of her plate. She kept her voice casual as she asked, "Do you know which ancestor of yours lived here during Regency times?"

"That would be Charles Oliver, the tenth earl," he replied.

Charles.

Tracy returned her fork to her plate with an unsteady hand. She felt as if the wind had been knocked out of her.

"Are you all right?" he asked. "You've gone quite white."

She waited a moment until she was certain she had

control of her voice. "I'm fine." She wanted a drink of water but was afraid her hand was trembling too much to pick up the glass. "You must be very familiar with your ancestors. You certainly came up with that name in a hurry."

He leaned his shoulders against the back of his chair. She noticed that his eyebrows were the color of his hair, but his lashes were as dark a brown as his eyes. He said, "I've always felt a kinship to Charles. He fought in the Peninsula during the war against Napoleon, and he managed to learn the elements of classical riding while he was in Portugal. It was he who built the indoor riding ring here at Silverbridge. Actually, I have a portrait of him hanging in my office."

Tracy reached for her glass and realized it was empty. She asked if there was any more water.

"Certainly." He went to the refrigerator, opened another bottle, and returned to pour it into her glass. She drank half of it.

"Is that chicken too salty for you?" he asked.

"Not at all. It's delicious. I'm just very thirsty. It must be because my sleeping schedule is all out of whack." She put her glass down and stabbed another piece of chicken with her fork.

For a long while the hum of the refrigerator motor was the only sound in the room. It was Harry who made the next attempt at conversation. "So you ride yourself, Miss Collins?"

The refrigerator motor switched off as Tracy answered. "I had a wonderful Thoroughbred mare I used to show when I was in high school. When I went away to college I retired her to a big farm in Virginia, and I've done very little riding since." He actually appeared to be interested in what she was saying, so she continued. "I rode hunt seat, of course. That's what equitation is in America. But I have always loved to watch dressage. It comes the closest to the Greek myth of the centaur of any of the riding disciplines, I think."

For the first time in their brief acquaintance, he regarded her with approval.

A single sharp bark came from outside the kitchen door. "Excuse me," he said as he got up to go and let the dogs back in. They trotted into the room, their nails making scraping sounds on the bare wood floor. Marshal went to take a drink from his water dish while Millie jumped on the sofa and made herself comfortable.

Harry returned to the kitchen table. Tracy had finished the food on her plate, but he didn't appear to notice as he sat back down. She wanted to keep him talking to her, so she resumed the conversation about horses. "Whom did you study with?"

He replied gravely. "I was fortunate enough to spend a year with Nuno Oliviero in Portugal."

"Oh wow," Tracy said, genuinely impressed. "I've only seen pictures of him on horseback, but even in a still picture you can see that he was something."

"So you have heard of him?"

"Yes, I have heard of him," she replied. "I have also heard of Podhajsky. And I once saw Reiner Klimke ride Ahlerich to music at the National Horse Show in New York." Her tone softened. "I actually cried, it was so beautiful."

He folded his arms on the table. "Klimke is my hero. He competed internationally, yet he always remained faithful to the ideals of classical horsemanship. He was able to marry the competition to the art, and that is something I have been trying to do."

His brown eyes sparkled in the light of the overhead lamp. The slight line that had drawn his brows together when first they came into the kitchen had vanished. He looked enthusiastic, and devastatingly attractive.

Tracy felt her back stiffen as she resisted his too-potent appeal. When she spoke her voice was crisp. "By all accounts, you have been successful in doing that. You took a third at the Olympics, which is fabulous, considering the competition from the Germans and the Dutch."

He nodded politely and noticed for the first time that she had finished eating. "Would you like something else? I believe there is a pudding in the refrigerator."

"No thank you." Tracy did not share the English passion for pudding.

He picked up her empty plate and carried it to the sink. Tracy followed with her silverware and glass and watched as he placed everything neatly on the drainboard. She waited, curious to see if he would attempt to wash up.

He didn't. He turned to her, and said, "Meg and Mr. Melbourne must have returned by now. Perhaps we should go back upstairs."

Tracy hesitated, then brought out the question she had been dying to ask for the last twenty minutes. "Before we do, my lord, I wonder if I could see that picture of Charles Oliver you mentioned."

He gave her a curious look. "Why on earth should you be interested in Charles?"

Tracy was not an actress for nothing. She laughed, and said lightly, "It's the Regency thing. I've grown rather interested in the period, and I'd find it fascinating to see a picture of the man who lived in this house at that time. But if it's going to be a bother, forget it. We can go upstairs."

"It's not a bother," he said. "You can see it if you like. Come this way."

Tracy followed him into a narrow hallway, which was closed off halfway down, and Tracy guessed that, like upstairs, only a portion of the basement was heated. He opened a door on the left side of the hall, flicked on a light, and motioned Tracy into his office.

It was a shabby and comfortable-looking room, with glass-fronted bookshelves, several file cabinets, an old leather sofa and two chairs, a large mahogany desk with a computer and a faded red-and-blue Oriental rug on the floor. Over the stone fireplace on the left wall hung the full-length portrait of a man in military uniform. Tracy knew him immediately. It was the man she had seen on the bridle path, the man she had seen in the drawing room with the girl who looked like her.

Charles Oliver had been painted full-length, wearing his uniform and posed against a backdrop of rocks and trees that suggested the landscape of the Iberian Peninsula. He was hatless, with a sword cradled in his arms and a cloak hanging dashingly off one shoulder. The embroidery and the gold buttons on his uniform were gorgeous. He stared out upon the room with a careless supremacy that was simply breathtaking.

"Lawrence did it," Harry said.

"He looks like a lord of the universe," Tracy said in a choked voice.

"He was," Harry replied. "He was born an Oliver, which meant he had a knowledge in his bones and blood and brain of his own superiority over 99 percent of the rest of the world." He turned to look at her. "That's what it was like to be an aristocrat in Britain during the last century, Miss Collins."

"You sound as if you wished it was still that way, my lord."

"It would be nice."

"He looks like you," Tracy said in a low voice.

"Yes. I know."

With the faces of the two men in front of her, Tracy could see that the resemblance between them was as uncanny as she had first thought. Charles's hair was a brighter gold, his nose was more aquiline, and his eyes were not quite as dark a brown. But the two men could certainly have been twins.

"Was he married?"

He gave a short laugh. "He was the Earl of Silverbridge. Of course he was married. He had two sons, the eldest of whom succeeded to the earldom after he died."

Tracy had several other questions she longed to ask: *Was his marriage happy? Did he have a young cousin he employed as governess for his children?* But she could hardly expect the present Lord Silverbridge to know the answers to those questions, and he would be exceedingly startled by her asking them.

They were standing side by side facing the picture, and even though Tracy's eyes were focused on the man in the portrait it was the man beside her whose physical presence she felt with an almost frightening intensity. She had a sudden, wild desire to throw herself into his arms, to feel the length of his body pressed against hers, to feel his mouth covering her own . . .

She closed her hands into tight fists, pressing her nails into her flesh.

"It's almost time for the news," he said. "We'd better be getting upstairs."

Tracy agreed, so shaken by her reaction to him that she didn't notice the sudden hoarseness that had come into his voice.

9

Meg and Jon were indeed in the morning room, and Tracy went to sit beside Jon on one of the sofas. Harry turned on the television and a BBC report of a meeting of the European Union that was taking place in Brussels came on. Ebony appeared out of nowhere, jumped on his lap, and he began to pet her as he watched the show.

Tracy could feel the tenseness in Jon's body as he sat beside her. She glanced at him once out of the side of her eyes and his facial expression was as rigid as the rest of him. *He really doesn't like Lord Silverbridge at all,* she thought.

When the program was over, Meg said, "Before I forget to tell you, Harry, Tony called. He's coming down tomorrow, and he's going to stay for a while."

Harry stopped petting Ebony. "What about his job?"

"He says they don't keep him on a schedule," Meg said airily. "He can do pretty much what he wants to do."

Ebony *meowed* loudly, and her owner went back to stroking her. "I must apologize, Mr. Melbourne, but I am afraid that you will have to share your bathroom with my younger brother while he is here."

"That is perfectly fine," Jon replied, but the stilted tone of his voice did not match his accommodating words.

The earl appeared to notice Jon's chilliness and actually made an effort to bridge it. "Would you care for a nightcap, Mr. Melbourne, Miss Collins?" he asked. "I can offer you sherry, brandy, or whiskey."

"I'm afraid that alcohol gives me a headache," Tracy said, "but please do go ahead without me."

"Mr. Melbourne?"

Jon glanced at Tracy, to see if she was going to leave. When it became apparent that she was not, he replied, "Thank you. Sherry would be nice."

Meg said, "I'll have brandy, Harry."

The earl's brows drew together as he regarded his young sister. Her returning blue stare was wide and innocent. After a moment, he shooed Ebony off his lap, stood up, went over to a beautiful cabinet of inlaid satinwood, took a key from his pocket, and bent to open the cabinet door. As he poured the wine and the brandy, Tracy's eyes moved irresistibly to the large oil painting that hung on the long wall between two windows. She got to her feet and went closer to examine it.

She was still standing there when Harry joined her, a glass of sherry in his hand. "I see you have found another of our family portraits, Miss Collins."

"Yes." She was looking at the full-length portraits of two teenage blond boys, with a sleek greyhound between them. The background scene was recognizably the lawn at Silverbridge.

"Those are Charles's two sons," her host informed her. "The one on the left, William, was actually the earl at the time the picture was done."

Tracy was acutely conscious of him next to her and stepped closer to the portrait to put more space between them. She gazed earnestly at the tall, slender, blue-eyed youngster who stood to the left of his brown-eyed brother.

From behind them, Jon said, "He seems rather young to be an earl."

"Yes." Lord Silverbridge turned to answer Jon. "His father was killed in a hunting accident when he was only thirty-four."

A stab of wild grief pierced through Tracy, totally surprising her. She closed her hands into fists and willed herself not to cry out.

What is the matter with me? she thought, half in anger and half in fear, as she stood, rigid and breathless in front of the portrait of Charles's sons.

Lord Silverbridge continued speaking to Jon. "Charles Oliver was the earl who lived here during the period you are supposedly filming. Miss Collins was curious about him, so I showed her a portrait I have in my office."

Before Jon could reply, Meg complained, "You hardly gave me any brandy, Harry."

"I gave you enough," he returned evenly. "You don't have the body weight to tolerate any more."

Tracy forced herself to turn away from what had become a blurry picture, blinked hard twice, and faced the group behind her. She breathed slowly in and out, unnerved by her emotional reaction to Charles's death.

Jon was still sitting on the sofa, holding an almost-finished glass of sherry; Harry was standing four feet from her, holding a full glass; and Meg was sitting on the edge of another sofa, her glass empty.

"You always blame everything on my being too thin," she said, her face flushed with anger. "You're always after me to eat and drink something disgusting. I should think you would be pleased to see me ask for more."

"Not for more brandy," he replied crisply. "Your body is already stressed enough; you don't need to be adding stimulants to it."

With quiet intensity, Meg said, "I hate you," jumped up from the sofa, and ran out of the room.

An embarrassed silence fell on the three left behind. Then Tracy said, "I believe I will follow Meg, if not in quite so dramatic a fashion. It was a long day and a long night."

Jon put down his half-finished sherry. "I'm tired as well," he said, and he and Tracy said good night and left the room.

"Perhaps we could have dinner together tomorrow night," Jon said, as they walked together down the corridor.

"I don't think it would be a good idea. Did you see that picture of us in the afternoon paper?"

"Yes. I didn't think it was so terrible. Even without makeup, you looked beautiful."

Tracy was annoyed. "That's not what I meant. Now there is going to be all sorts of speculation about you and me. If we're seen having dinner together, it will only fuel the fire."

"Would it be so very dreadful to have your name linked with mine?" he asked gently.

She sighed. "I don't know. Let me think about it, Jon."

"Certainly."

They said good night, and Tracy continued along the corridor to the door of her own room. As she put her hand on the doorknob, her pulses began to race.

Will they be inside?

Slowly, cautiously she pushed open the door. Inside there was only darkness. She left the door open and switched on a light.

No one was there.

Tracy didn't know if what she felt was relief or disappointment. She closed the door and walked all the way into the room.

What I have been seeing must be real, she thought. *I can't be manufacturing these apparitions out of my imagination. I saw that picture of Charles after I saw his ghost—or whatever it is that I have been seeing. And Ebony certainly knew that something was there in the drawing room.*

She continued to think as she methodically undressed and put on a pair of warm flannel pajamas. *I seem to have accessed the ghost of an old love story. The girl looks so much like me . . . Could that be the reason I can see these people and no one else can? Was I once that girl?*

She went over to the bed and pulled down the blankets. *This is ridiculous. I'm beginning to sound like*

Shirley MacLaine. Soon I'll be imagining I was Cleopatra, or something equally fantastic.

She climbed into the bed, which thankfully was made up with flannel sheets, and pulled the covers over her head in an effort to get warm. A half hour later her nose was poked out from beneath the covers and she was still wide-awake, her brain going over and over the few encounters she had had with the phantasmagoric Charles and Isabel.

A loud knock sounded on her bathroom door, causing her to sit bolt upright in bed. *It must be Meg,* she thought, staring at the closed door. She said nothing, hoping that the girl would go away. She was too tired to deal with Meg.

The knock came again, louder than before. "Are you awake, Tracy? Do you know your light is on?"

"*Damn,*" Tracy muttered. Then, resignedly, "Come in."

The bathroom door opened to reveal Meg clad in a sweatshirt, flannel pajama pants, and furry slippers. The loose clothes helped to conceal how thin she was, and her face was flushed with color. It took a moment for Tracy to realize that she was carrying the brandy bottle and two glasses.

"Look what I got." She giggled. "Harry forgot to re-lock the cabinet when he went downstairs to let out the dogs. Won't it be fun to get drunk together?"

From the giggle and the flush on her face, Tracy deduced that Meg had already sampled from the brandy bottle. She said calmly, "I don't drink, Meg. Alcohol gives me a headache. And what is your brother going to say when he finds that his brandy has disappeared?"

Meg pushed out her lower lip. "Don't be a shpoil-short, Tracy." She walked unevenly across the room and parked herself on Tracy's bed. She put the glasses down on the bedspread and giggled again. "Harry's always watching me. Thish time I fooled him."

"Meg," Tracy said gently, "why don't you put the brandy bottle back before your brother knows you took it?"

"No. No. No. Don't want to." Meg was shaking her head back and forth again and again and again. "I want us to drink it together." She splashed some brandy into one of the glasses, spilling half of it on the spread, and took a sip. "Aaahhh," she said. "Thash good."

Tracy crawled across the bed until she was beside Meg. As persuasively as she could, she said, "I'll tell you what, Meggie. Let's go back to your room. Okay?"

Meg blinked her glittering blue eyes. "We'll party there?"

Still in the same coaxing voice, Tracy said, "Give me the brandy bottle, and we'll walk to your room together."

"Okay. Okay." Meg relinquished the bottle to Tracy, slid off the bed, and immediately fell to her knees. She held her stomach and began to laugh.

The brandy bottle was about three-quarters full. Harry had been right, Tracy thought. It wouldn't take much to make Meg intoxicated.

Tracy put the bottle on the floor, bent to slip an arm around Meg's shoulders, and boosted her to her feet. "Come on, Meggie. Come with me."

Meg let Tracy begin to walk her across the room.

They had almost made it to the bathroom when Meg said, "Don't feel sho good."

Tracy practically shoved her into the bathroom and flipped open the toilet bowl. Meg immediately began to retch.

Half an hour later, after Tracy had cleaned Meg up and got her into bed, then cleaned up the bathroom as best she could, she took the brandy bottle back to the morning room. She would just leave it on top of the cabinet, she thought, so that Lord Silverbridge would know what had happened. She had no desire to discuss his sister's problems with him.

A small lamp was always kept lit at the top of the stairs, and it gave enough light for Tracy to see her way down the hall. It was dark in the morning room, but Tracy could make out the liquor cabinet, and she walked swiftly across the floor and placed the brandy bottle squarely on top of it. She had turned around to leave when a voice said, "Dare I hope that it was you who stole the brandy?"

Tracy jumped. "Good God!" She stared at the shadowy figure that had risen from an armchair and was now crossing the floor in her direction. "You almost gave me a heart attack, my lord!"

He stopped next to her. "Sorry. I didn't mean to frighten you. Did you get the brandy from Meg?"

Tracy's heart was racing, but it wasn't from being frightened. He was so close that she could feel him in all her nerve endings. She said, "Yes. She came to my room wanting to party. I don't think she drank very much."

"Is she all right?"

The light from the hall lamp was not bright enough to

allow her to distinguish his expression. His voice sounded edgy, she thought. She looked up into his shadowed face, and replied, "Yes. She threw up, so most of it is out of her stomach. She should be okay in the morning."

She saw his eyebrows draw together. "I hope to God she didn't throw up in your room."

The sound of his voice was doing funny things to her stomach. *What is wrong with me?* she thought desperately. She heard herself saying, "We made it to the bathroom in time."

I am wearing only thin pajamas and he is much too close. That's what's wrong with me. She tried to take a step back, but for some reason her legs didn't move.

He said, "I am so sorry that you were subjected to this unpleasantness, Miss Collins."

He was almost as tall as Scotty had been. Tracy's eyes were on a level with his mouth, and his lips were so perfectly cut they might have been chiseled in stone. She stared at his mouth and struggled to come up with a reply. Some part of her brain was still functioning because she managed to say, "No problem, my lord. And I won't mention what happened to anyone else."

"Thank you." His cool, clipped voice sounded deeper than usual.

All of a sudden the stillness that she had felt the first time she saw him seemed to settle over her, like a fleecy blanket. She raised her eyes to his and what she saw there made all of her insides clench. He bent his head, and she saw his beautiful mouth coming down toward hers, and she didn't move. He kissed her.

It was like coming home.

For a long while she stood perfectly still, and then she leaned against him, her arms encircled his waist, and she spread her hands flat against his back. The intensity of her response was dizzying. Everything inside her was quivering, and she could feel the liquid heat gushing through her loins. He could have carried her to the sofa and taken her, and she would have let him do it.

It was he who finally broke the kiss. He placed his hands on her shoulders and put her away from him.

Tracy had to force herself to let him go.

"Christ." His voice sounded as shaken as she felt. "I'm sorry. I shouldn't have done that."

She was incapable of saying a word.

"I apologize, Miss Collins," he said. "You must have had your fill of the Olivers tonight. I'll leave you to return to your bedroom. Good night."

Tracy watched him walk away in dumbfounded astonishment. No man had ever kissed her and walked away. Yet there he was, the mighty Lord Silverbridge, walking with measured steps toward his room.

Even though he was moving without haste, it suddenly occurred to Tracy that he had the look of a man who is running away.

To her great surprise, Tracy fell instantly asleep and did not awaken until just after sunup the following morning. The world outside her window looked fresh and new. The delicate, lacy canopies of new-budded trees cast their shade over the spring green lawn, and the ~und of birds floated to her ears.

~e impulse was irresistible. *I'm going out.*

She dressed in a pair of jeans from her suitcase, pulled on a sweater, and went along the corridor to the staircase. As she reached the ground floor, she met Harry emerging from the kitchen staircase. He was dressed in high black boots, fawn-colored breeches, and a gray sweater. His dogs were with him.

They stared at each other in shocked surprise. Tracy could feel her face color, which annoyed her no end.

He recovered first. "Miss Collins! What are you doing up so early?"

"I'm going for a walk," she said. Her voice was huskier than usual, and this annoyed her as well.

The dogs had sat on either side of their master and were regarding Tracy with peaceful brown eyes.

"It is a lovely morning," he agreed. "In fact, I was just going for a ride." A muscle jumped in his jaw. "Would you care to join me?"

The less time I spend in the company of this man, the safer I will be, Tracy thought.

"I'd love to," she heard herself saying. "I'll have to ride in jeans, though."

He looked down at the lace-up boots she had put on to protect her feet from the dew. "Jeans are fine, and your boots have a heel, so they're all right too."

"Great."

"Come along then," he said. "We'll have to get to the stable before the horses are grained, or you won't have anything to ride."

10

Why the hell did I ask her to ride with me?

Harry strode furiously along the path to the stable, his long legs eating up the ground, completely unaware that Tracy was having to half run to keep up with him.

She's trouble. The last thing in the world I need is to get involved with another high-profile diva.

He was not paying attention to her but knew instantly when she was no longer beside him. He stopped and turned to look for her.

She was standing on the path, her arms folded across her chest, her expression mutinous. "I'll meet you down there," she said. "I'm not in the mood for a race."

The gold streaks in her glorious hair glinted in the bright light of early morning. Her skin was flawless, and her dark blue crewneck sweater exactly matched her eyes. The curve of her mouth held a suggestion of great sweetness. Every time he looked at her he felt profoundly stirred.

They stood on the path, regarding each other, and all he could think about was kissing her. He cleared his throat, and said, "I'm sorry. I wasn't thinking. I'll walk slower."

She nodded, and they once more began to walk toward the stable. The spaniels, who had been scampering ahead of him and who had stopped when he did, started up again as well.

When they reached the stable most of the horses were chewing their breakfast hay in their stalls and Peter, one of his grooms, was saddling Pendleton up in the aisle.

"Who hasn't been grained yet?" Harry asked the boy.

"None of them, my lord. I was waiting for them to finish half of their hay."

"Good." Harry called to one of the young girls scrubbing water buckets. "Gloria, will you saddle up Maestro, please? Put Lady Margaret's saddle on him."

"Sure thing, my lord," came the cheerful reply and the tall, skinny teenager put down her bucket and went to bring a second horse out into the aisle.

He turned to Tracy. "Maestro is my hunter. He's very comfortable. He'll give you an easy ride."

"That's good," she replied with a crinkle of her charmingly tilted nose. "I'm afraid that my riding muscles are badly out of shape."

He nodded. "It's amazing, isn't it, how you can be in terrific shape in every way, but if you haven't ridden in a while, you'll still be sore. Riding just uses muscles that you don't use in any other activity."

"Don't remind me. Dave would have a heart attack if he knew I was doing this."

He said stiffly, "In that case, perhaps you oughtn't to come."

For the first time ever, she smiled at him. "But I want to. I have missed riding very much."

His stomach clenched. *Christ,* he thought. *What is going on here?*

At that moment, Peter led Pendleton into the stable yard, and Harry gratefully went to take his reins. He looked into his horse's soft, intelligent eyes and stroked his nose. "Good morning, little fellow."

Pen whuffled through his nose in response.

Tracy came to stand at his shoulder. "He's beautiful." She sounded as if she meant it.

Harry continued to stroke Pen's nose. "He's the smartest horse I've ever known. Everything he's accomplished he's done because of his brain. Once he understands what you want, he'll kill himself to get it right."

"He looks very happy."

She had said exactly the thing that he liked most to hear. "He deserves to be," he replied a little gruffly, and patted his beloved horse's satiny seal brown neck.

There was the *clap clap* sound of shod hooves on cobblestones, and Gloria brought Maestro to stand next to Pen. "My," Tracy said to the big gelding, "Aren't you handsome?"

Maestro pricked his ears forward and regarded his admirer regally. Tracy laughed and glanced at Harry. "He seems to be well accustomed to compliments."

He smiled in return. "That coat of his has always attracted attention."

Maestro was a chestnut with a particularly bright, almost copper-colored coat that gleamed with good health and good grooming. "You're a good match," Harry heard himself saying. "Two redheads."

She gave him a startled look, and he was annoyed with himself. *Why the hell did I say that? Now she'll think I'm flirting with her.*

She put her foot in the stirrup and swung up into the saddle—not an easy feat as Maestro was almost seventeen hands high. She picked up her reins and moved her leg out of the way for Gloria to adjust the stirrups from Meg's length to hers. Harry watched while she okayed the new length, approving of the way she sat, with her shoulders, hips, and knees all lined up correctly. Then he mounted Pendleton, who was a much smaller horse than Maestro, barely sixteen hands in height.

Tracy commented on this as they walked out of the stable yard. "somehow, I pictured Pendleton as being bigger."

"I know. It's always been a problem in the show ring because the judges like big horses. But the Lipizzaners of the Spanish Riding School in Vienna are not even as tall as he is."

"Really? I didn't know that. I've seen them in performance, and they look quite large."

"They have enormous presence—and so does Pen when he's in the ring." He leaned forward to pat his mount's arched neck.

They walked along for perhaps five minutes, Harry carefully checking to see how she handled Maestro, who had a tender mouth. By the time they reached the home woods he was satisfied that he could trust her not to inflict pain. As the horses stepped onto the familiar terrain of the bridle path, their ears pricked forward, and their pace quickened.

"What about a brisk trot to warm up?" Harry asked.

"I'd love it."

The dogs had already disappeared into the woods in search of fun, and now Pen began to trot along the dirt path, which was only wide enough for one horse. The way was clear, however. Harry always had the trees alongside the bridle paths pruned, so there was no danger of a rider being hit in the head by an overhanging branch.

The woodland flowers were everywhere, the bluebells and windflowers and cowslips splashing their bright colors across the green-brown forest floor. The air smelled fresh and new. It was Harry's favorite time of day, and he felt happy.

He pulled up at a place where the path turned down a sharp incline and turned to regard Tracy. Her hair was a windblown mass of curls, her eyes were sparkling, and her cheeks were flushed to an exquisite rose. "He's fabulous," she said, enthusiastically patting Maestro's neck. "Even out in the woods, he goes perfectly straight."

Harry felt a rush of pleasure. So she really did know something about horses. "All of my horses go straight. You can't achieve anything with a horse unless he goes forward and goes straight."

She regarded him ironically. "I told you I've read Podhajsky, my lord."

My God, he thought. *She really has read Podhajsky.* He said as matter-of-factly as he could, "We'll walk them down this hill and at the bottom there's a nice open stretch where we can canter."

"Great."

He whistled, and they waited for the dogs to join them, which they did with bright eyes, swishing tails, and coats tangled with burrs. Marshal and Millie charged down the hill, and the horses followed more slowly. At the bottom Harry turned right and entered into what appeared to be a long, broad alleyway, enclosed by arching green branches and dappled with sunlight. He heard Tracy's breath catch. "Oh," she said. "How beautiful."

"Are you ready to canter?" he asked.

"Absolutely."

This path was wide enough to accommodate two horses, and Maestro cantered easily next to Pendleton. Out of the side of his eye, Harry could see that Tracy rode beautifully, her hands in contact with Maestro's mouth, reassuring him that she was there, but never pulling.

A feeling of wild exaltation shot through him. *She can ride,* he thought. *She can really ride.*

He pulled up to a walk a short way before he knew the path would end, and Masetro slowed with Pen. Tracy turned around to look back down the long, tree-enclosed ride, and said fervently, "How wonderful to have access to a place like this. A private place where there are none of those ghastly all-terrain vehicles to scare the horses and the wildlife."

As she finished speaking the horses emerged from the woods onto the shore of a small lake, upon which two majestic swans and their family glided serenely. The dew on the meadow grass around the lake twinkled like diamonds in the sunlight, and a pair of thrushes were calling to each other from the woods on the other side.

Tracy let out her breath in a long, satisfied sigh.

He firmly squelched the smile that curved his mouth at her appreciative reaction.

"Does the lake belong to you, too, my lord?"

"Yes." He deliberately wasn't looking at her; instead he kept his eyes on the swans.

Her next question made him jerk his head around in surprise. "Is this part of the land that that Mauley person wants to make into a golf course?"

Every time he thought about the golf course, he felt grim. "I don't know if Mauley wants the lake or not," he replied. "I haven't bothered to look that closely at his proposal. I have no plans to sell any part of Silverbridge, and I wish he would get that through his head and leave me alone." He was sitting straight as a lance in his saddle and gestured to a dirt track that cut a swath through the marsh grass. "That path encircles the entire lake. Would you be up to a gallop?"

"Sure," she replied.

He whistled to the dogs, and they appeared from the woods and came running to stand by Pen's legs. "They love to run around the lake," Harry said, "and it's good exercise for them."

Without another word, he asked Pen for a gallop and the seal bay responded with a burst of speed. Maestro followed, and after him, the dogs. They galloped around the entire lake, with the scent of the May morning in their nostrils and the sound of birdsong in their ears. Harry finally pulled up at a place where a different path led off into the woods, turned to Tracy, and said, "This will take us home."

They walked single file for perhaps five minutes, with the dogs trailing after Tracy, then the path widened. "You can bring him up beside me now," Harry said over his shoulder.

When she had pulled alongside of him, and both horses were walking on a long rein, he heard himself say in an abrupt voice, "Everyone in my family thinks I'm crazy not to sell to Mauley. He's offered me an enormous sum of money."

She was looking between Maestro's ears, and her profile was one of the loveliest sights he had ever seen. She said, "As the old saying goes, money isn't everything."

"In today's day and age it is," he returned bitterly.

They walked on in silence until at last he could no longer stop himself from asking, "Do you think I'm crazy not to sell?"

"No." Her reply was immediate and definite. "If I had a place like this that had been in my family for centuries, I'd never sell it. I'd feel as if it was a sacred trust or something."

That was exactly how he felt himself. To test her he threw out one of the arguments he kept hearing from his family. "People don't live like this anymore. Well, perhaps they do in Saudi Arabia—or in Beverly Hills—but they don't here in Britain. We have the welfare state now."

She lifted a hand to smooth her hair back from her face. "There isn't anyplace like this in Saudi Arabia or Beverly Hills. What's so wonderful about Silverbridge is its sense of always having been here. I think it's something very special, that generation after generation of your family has grown up here and added their own bit of history to the house and the land."

He was surprised and profoundly moved that she should have such an insight. He said sternly, "That's what I think, too."

She shot him a questioning look. "After all, it's not as if you hoard all this beauty just for yourself. You open the house to the public, don't you?"

"Yes. It's part of the deal I made with the Inland Revenue when my father died. I turned over most of our valuable pictures to the National Trust to pay the death duties, and they allowed them to stay here at Silverbridge if I would open the house to the public. So for two months out of the year parties of day-trippers and Germans and Japanese and Americans come trooping through Silverbridge, oohing and aahing at the paintings and the furniture."

"My, my, my." She sounded amused. "You *are* a snob."

He set his mouth in a hard line. "If it's snobbish not to want to open a tea shop and a gift shop and sell postcards with pictures of the house, then I plead guilty."

Something rustled in the trees, and Marshal and Millie shot off in pursuit.

"The question is, can you afford to maintain your heritage without commercializing it?"

He opened his mouth to answer, then thought with horror, *Good God, was I really going to discuss my finances with this movie actress?* "Of course I can," he answered shortly.

At that moment they emerged from the woods, and in the distance he saw the stone stable, which to him was far more beautiful than any modern dwelling could ever be. His feelings momentarily breaking through his wall of reserve, he said, "My family doesn't understand. Silverbridge doesn't belong to them; it belongs to *me*. And I intend to keep it."

Four centuries of possessiveness sounded in the steely, unyielding notes of his voice.

When he turned to Tracy she was staring at him. He lifted a brow in inquiry, and she said breathlessly, "Do you know, for a moment there you looked exactly like that picture of Charles you have in your office?"

"Did I?" He took a deep breath and made himself relax. "Well, I'm quite sure that Charles wouldn't have sold Silverbridge either. Fortunately for him, he lived in a different world, and the issue never came up."

She returned somberly, "He couldn't have been that fortunate, my lord, if he died at thirty-four."

He stood in his stirrups, looking for his spaniels. When he didn't see them, he whistled. "True. He was killed right near the lake, you know."

"How did it happen?" Her voice was almost a whisper.

He whistled again, then turned to look at her. "He was out riding, just like we are, when a poacher must have mistaken him for something else."

She was looking straight ahead, and the line of her mouth looked ineffably sorrowful. "How terrible."

He found that he couldn't pull his eyes away from her mouth. "Yes, I've always thought so. Ironic, too. He had made it through a war and then, to be picked off in his own woods like that. . . ."

Her head turned and she looked directly at him. "I thought you said that no violent deaths had ever occurred at Silverbridge." She sounded as if she was accusing him. "Charles's death was certainly violent."

He dragged his eyes away from that tantalizing mouth. "Yes, I suppose it was."

"But no one has seen his ghost?"

Finally, the dogs came catapulting out of the woods, and he managed a shaky laugh. "You really are keen on ghosts, aren't you?"

Her chin came up. "There's a lot of evidence that they do exist."

"It depends on what you call 'evidence.' All I can tell you is that, fortunately or unfortunately, depending upon how you look at it, Silverbridge has been remarkably free of ghosts."

A flock of sparrows rose in the air from the grass on their left and the dogs gave chase.

Tracy asked, "Did they ever find out who shot Charles?"

He shook his head. "Not that I know. But it was a long time ago, and records get lost."

Tracy turned in her saddle so she could look back at the woods. "Well, I'm on your side about the land, my lord. I think it would be a sin to cut all that natural loveliness down to make a golf course."

He didn't like the pleasure he got from hearing her say she was on his side. He made his voice expressionless, and said, "Some people think golf courses are beautiful."

"They may be pretty, but they're unnatural. They don't shelter any wildlife or grow any food or have any viable ecosystem. They're only a playground for people who ride around in carts trying to hit a little white ball with a stick."

It amazed him that this American movie star should be the only person he knew who seemed to share his feelings. *Christ,* he thought with alarm. *I'd better watch out. The last thing I need is to get entangled with a movie star!*

11

The Honorable Anthony Oliver arrived at Silverbridge early that afternoon. Tracy met him as she and Meg were finishing lunch in the kitchen. Meg, who looked paler and even more fragile than usual after her evening's foray into the brandy bottle, had eaten exactly one quarter of a bowl of Mrs. Wilson's excellent vegetable soup. Tracy, on the other hand, had eaten two bowls, as well as some homemade bread. In fact, she was still nibbling on the bread while Meg was ignoring her almost-full bowl, when a flexible tenor voice said liltingly, "Mrs. Wilson! You've made soup. Surely this is my lucky day."

The stout, middle-aged woman at the sink turned around, a smile on her square, no-nonsense face. "Mr. Anthony! How grand to see you again!"

Tracy watched as the slim, athletic figure of Anthony Oliver swooped across the kitchen floor to catch Mrs. Wilson up in a hug.

"La, now, Mr. Anthony. Enough of your shenanigans," the woman scolded, as he set her back on her feet. But she was smiling.

"Hi, Tony," Meg said, her face brighter than it had been all day.

"Meggie, darling. How are you doing, sweetheart?"

Tracy watched curiously as Harry's younger brother crossed the kitchen to bestow a kiss on his sister. When he straightened up it was Tracy's turn to receive the radiance of his smile. "Miss Collins. How delightful to meet you. And I understand from Meg that we are fortunate enough to have you actually staying with us?"

He had Brad Pitt good looks, with a cap of silver-blond hair, sky-blue eyes, and chiseled features. He kept his hands on Meg's thin shoulders as he regarded Tracy.

"Yes, I am," she replied. She was not quite sure how to address him, so she asked, "Do I call you Lord Anthony?"

He laughed, his teeth very white against the golden tan of his skin. His classic features had none of the male toughness or arrogance that characterized Harry's. Everything about Tony was sunshine and charm.

"Alas, while the daughter of an earl is designated a *lady*, the son of an earl does not merit the title of *lord*," he replied. "I am merely an Honorable, to be addressed as Mr. Oliver." His blue eyes smiled cloudlessly. "But please do call me Tony."

"Where'd you get the tan?" Meg asked, twisting her head to look up at him.

"I was in Spain last week on business and I managed to get to the beach for a few hours," he replied carelessly.

"Would you care for some soup, Mr. Anthony?" the housekeeper asked.

"I should adore some soup." Tony pulled out the chair next to Meg and sat at the table. He glanced at his sister's bowl and a faint line marred the perfection of his forehead. "Eat some more, Meggie," he said.

"I'm not hungry," she replied sulkily. "I ate a big breakfast."

"And where was that, Lady Margaret?" Mrs. Wilson asked from her place in front of the stove. "It certainly wasn't here."

Meg slammed her hand on the table. "Leave me alone, all of you! Can't you talk about something other than my eating?" She jumped up and ran out of the kitchen.

In the ensuing silence, Mrs. Wilson brought a bowl of vegetable soup to the table and placed it in front of Tony. He looked at it, then looked up at the housekeeper. "Is she eating at all, Mrs. Wilson?"

The reply was grim. "A bit here and a bit there. His lordship has her going to some therapist over in Warkfield, but it don't seem to be helping much."

Tracy said quietly, "Anorexia is very difficult to treat."

"Are you familiar with the problem, Miss Collins?" Tony asked.

She finished her bread and wiped her fingers on a linen napkin. "We see quite a bit of it in America. Unfortunately."

He looked interested. "How is it treated in America?"

"The same way you treat it here, I imagine. It's a

mental disease, really, so psychotherapy is definitely called for."

"I'll have to talk to Harry." Tony's blue eyes were somber. "She's always been thin, but today her shoulders felt as sharp as blades under my fingers."

"His Lordship told me to leave food for her in the refrigerator, in case she might want to eat when no one's watching her. I do that, Mr. Anthony, but it's never touched," Mrs. Wilson contributed.

"Something has to be done." He shook his head. "What the hell is the matter with her? Why won't she eat?"

His concern for his sister was palpably genuine, and Tracy found herself warming to him. Since he had been so frank, she felt comfortable asking, "Is this a long-standing problem?"

He sighed and dipped a spoon into his soup. "Meg has been a problem ever since my mother died, which was three years ago. My mother never paid very much attention to her, so I don't really understand why she should have been knocked into such a tizzy. But she was, and she hasn't come out of it. Harry's had her in five different schools, and the last one said she couldn't come back unless she gained some weight."

"She wants attention is my guess," Mrs. Wilson said unsympathetically. "Starving herself is the way she's going about getting it."

That may well be true, Tracy thought, *but such drastic behavior is the sign of a deeply disturbed person.* "Your father is also deceased?" she asked Tony.

He nodded. "Papa died when Meg was eight."

Good grief, Tracy thought. *She lost both parents before she was fourteen. No wonder she's troubled.*

Tony said, with a clear desire to change the subject, "Tell me, Miss Collins, how is the movie progressing?"

"Very well, thank you," she returned briskly. "I believe we are on schedule, which is very important to the producer and director. Time is money, you know, and fortunately the weather has been cooperating."

The kitchen door opened and, even though Tracy's head was turned away from the door, she immediately knew who had come in. "Tony," Harry said. "I didn't know you'd arrived."

"I just got here." Tony had risen and was holding out his hand to his brother. "I'm going to stay for a few weeks. Did Meggie tell you?"

"Yes, she did." Harry looked as if he wanted to say something else, but then he glanced at Tracy and contented himself with shaking his brother's hand.

Don't air family business in front of strangers, Tracy thought cynically.

He said, "I was looking for Meg. I'm driving over to the point-to-point, and I wondered if she'd like to come."

"She was here, but she left in a huff," Tony said. "I made the mistake of urging her to eat. She's painfully thin, Harry. It can't be healthy."

"I know." Once again Harry shot Tracy a look. "I'll see if she's in her room."

Then, without speaking a single direct word to her, he left.

Tracy was furious. Not only was it inexcusably rude for him to ignore her in such a way, but they had just spent a delightful morning together. *I thought we were becoming friends,* she fumed. *Then he has the nerve to act as if I wasn't there.*

He had known she was there, though. Her presence was what had kept him from discussing family problems with Tony.

She went back upstairs to the morning room, sat in Harry's usual chair, and wondered what to do with herself for the rest of the afternoon.

I could go shopping, she thought unenthusiastically. Gail had rented a car so she could get back and forth from her B&B, and Tracy knew her secretary would be delighted to pick her up for a shopping expedition.

She was still debating with herself when Tony came into the room accompanied by a large, burly man whom Tracy recognized as Robin Mauley. Both men looked surprised to see her.

She produced her most bewitching smile and watched as their faces relaxed and they smiled back. "Am I in your way?" she asked lightly.

"Not at all, not at all," Mauley blustered. "You could never be in anyone's way, Miss Collins."

"How nice of you to say that," she returned pleasantly. "Have you gentlemen got together to discuss the golf course?"

Mauley's thick, bushy brows snapped together.

Tony said sharply, "What do you know about the golf course?"

"Oh dear." Tracy's lovely face looked distressed. "Have I said something I shouldn't? All I know is that Meg told me Mr. Mauley wanted to buy some Silverbridge land to build a golf course. Was it wrong of her to tell me that?"

The two men exchanged a glance, and Tony said, "Of course it wasn't wrong." He smiled ruefully. "The problem is that my brother is being stubborn and doesn't want to sell. Mr. Mauley and I have got together to see if we can come up with a persuasive enough argument to change his mind."

"Why do you want him to change his mind?" she asked ingenuously.

Tony took a seat on one of the sofas and gestured for Mauley to do the same. "Money," he replied succinctly. "Harry doesn't have the money to keep up this immense property. With the money he would get from Mauley, he could afford to maintain the house and expand the stables. Hell, he would be able to afford a new car! It's completely to his advantage to sell the land.

And I imagine that it would be to your advantage too, Tracy thought. *Some of Mauley's money would be bound to trickle down into your pockets.*

Tony said grimly. "I cannot believe that he is being so stubborn about property that is just farmland."

"At least farmland contributes to the common good," Tracy said. "It produces food."

"And a golf course produces exercise and enjoyment for thousands of people," Mauley returned swiftly. "It will contribute to the common good as well if not better than any farmland."

Tracy disguised her disagreement and rose gracefully to her feet. "Well, I'll leave you gentlemen to your discussion. I have shopping to do."

Both men had risen with her, and Robin Mauley

bared his small teeth. "Pleasure to have met you again, Miss Collins."

Tony said with an engaging smile, "I'll see you later."

Tracy shared a gracious smile between them and floated out into the foyer, where a worried frown creased her brow. There had been an air of conspiracy between the two men as they came into the room that she did not like.

Harry's bedroom door was half-open as usual, and she glanced back at the morning room to check if the men could see her. The sofa where both men were seated was out of her line of sight. Without stopping to think, she stepped into Harry's room and shamelessly prepared to eavesdrop.

Mauley's deep, gruff voice was easy to distinguish. "Percy isn't going to wait forever on this, Tony. If I can't tell him that I definitely have the land, he will look elsewhere to build his hotel. And that is something we don't want to happen. A hotel is a key part of my plan, and Percy Hotels are the best."

"I know," Tony replied. Tracy had to strain to hear his lighter voice. "Harry is just so goddamn stubborn. But I have a few ideas that might make him change his mind."

"I can stall Percy for a few more weeks, but not much beyond that," Mauley said warningly.

"Okay, okay. I'll see what I can do. And if you do get the land, our deal stands?"

"Absolutely, dear boy. Absolutely."

What deal? Tracy thought. But the men must have moved because their voices had become indistinguishable. She waited for a few more minutes, hoping that they would become audible once more, and while she waited she looked around the room.

It was a larger bedroom than hers, with an equally high ceiling and tall windows. The walls were painted Wedgewood blue, with the elegant moldings that divided the walls into squares and rectangles painted a contrasting white. Over the white marble fireplace hung a picture of horses on Newmarket Heath that Tracy was certain was an original Stubbs. Most of the furniture in the room was either Regency or French in style, from the blue silk chairs in front of the fireplace, to the small satinwood tables that flanked the fireplace, to the magnificent rosewood armoire. However, the blue-patterned carpet was definitely modern, as was the king-size bed, which was covered with a blue-and-white comforter.

A jet-black spot of fur was curled up in the middle of that comforter and Ebony was directing an outraged green glare at the intruder in her domain. "It's okay, little girl," Tracy said softly to the cat. "I'm not going to touch anything."

The room was neat, but there were definite signs that someone beside Ebony inhabited it. Reposing on the Louis XIV table in front of the window was a pile of loose change, a set of car keys, and a folded-up newspaper. A man's wool sweater was carelessly tossed on the bed and a pair of maroon slippers was on the floor. A book lay open and facedown on the bedside table, as if the reader had put it that way to mark his place before going to sleep. Before she could think better of her action, Tracy crossed the carpet on soundless feet to look at the book's title.

Wellington: The Years of the Sword. The author was Elizabeth Longford.

He was reading a biography of the Duke of Wellington, the British general who beat Napoleon at Waterloo.

Tracy felt a shiver go up her spine. *Charles fought under Wellington,* she thought.

There was the sound of a door closing in the corridor, and Tracy flew to conceal herself behind the door. *I hope to God it's not Harry,* she thought, and wondered why she had placed herself in such a potentially embarrassing situation for a man she heartily disliked. After a few minutes she peeked out into the hallway and saw no one. In five seconds flat she was inside the security of her own bedroom.

Tracy decided to get away from Silverbridge for the day and called Gail to make plans to go shopping. They were joined at the last minute by Jon Melbourne, who had finished his scheduled scenes and had reached the house just as Gail pulled up in a dark green Mercedes. When he heard that they were going shopping, he asked to come, as he needed to make some replacements to his burned-out wardrobe.

"I'm going to ask Dave to have the studio rent me a car, too," he said as he got into the backseat. Tracy had traded places with Gail and was at the wheel. "Driving in the country is easy. One really doesn't need a chauffeur."

"That was my feeling," Tracy said. She went down the drive for a hundred feet, then veered off onto a dirt road.

"Where are we going?" Jon asked, surprised.

"Meg told me there was a tradesman's entrance to the property at the end of this road," Tracy said. "I hope by using it to avoid that reptile Counes."

The entrance was only wide enough for a single car to pass through at a time, and the gate was closed. Gail got out and opened it, and Tracy drove through. There was no sign of Counes, so she headed the Mercedes toward Warkfield.

All three of them were successful in purchasing the things they needed, and Tracy found a beautiful silver cup to send to her sister as a christening present for the new baby. When they had finished shopping, Jon suggested that they drive to Myddelton for tea. "There's a charming old inn there that I think you would enjoy," he said. "And you might like to see Myddelton. We are going to be shooting there in a few weeks."

The day was still fine, and Tracy and Gail agreed that a side trip might be fun. When they arrived at the village, which did not include a house that had been built after the eighteenth century, they were enchanted.

"It's like a place out of time," Tracy said. "Like Brigadoon."

They had just finished tea at a timber-framed medieval inn and were standing in front of the fifteenth-century battlemented and pinnacled church of St. Stephen. A group of tourists nearby were staring at Tracy.

"Do people actually live here?" Tracy asked, turning to look down the street at the lichen-and-moss encrusted stone-slated roofs and gables that adorned the charming old houses.

"It *is* her," one of the tourists said loudly.

"Yes, people do live here," Jon returned. He glanced at the tourists. "May I suggest that we move along, ladies, before we are assaulted by requests for autographs."

Jon was familiar with Myddelton and played guide as the three of them walked around the village's four main streets, which were lined with timber-framed buildings with mullioned windows, seventeenth-century stone cottages, and elegant Georgian brick mansions. The tourist group followed them, and eventually Tracy did have to give autographs.

Why should these strangers have the right to interrupt my life just because they once bought a ticket to one of my movies? she thought as she signed her name on someone's National Trust brochure.

She knew the standard reply to that question by heart: *You're a public figure, Tracy. You gave up your right to privacy the moment you appeared on a movie screen.*

The problem was, she had never planned to be a public figure, and she didn't like it. She doubted that she ever would.

By the time they had finished touring, it was time for dinner, which they had in another old Myddelton inn, where once again Tracy had to sign autographs. It was nine o'clock when Gail finally dropped Tracy and Jon back at Silverbridge. They went up the stairs, and Tracy could not resist looking into the morning room to see if Harry was there. Jon followed her.

Harry and Tony were playing chess in front of the fire. Tracy looked at the two blond heads bent over the chessboard, one tawny and one sublimely fair, and felt a pain in her heart.

Shit. I have to get out of this house. I have to get away from him.

As she was thinking this, Harry's head turned toward the doorway. "I see you had a successful shopping expedition," he said, looking at the packages she was carrying.

"Yes, and Jon showed us around Myddelton Village, where we're going to film in a few weeks. It was very lovely." Tracy was relieved to hear that her voice was calm. Her heart certainly wasn't.

"Isn't Myddelton charming?" Tony said. "That's why the National Trust took it on, you know. It's so perfect."

"It's a fossil," Jon said flatly. "Your family killed it when you wouldn't allow any railroad lines to come through."

"A good thing too," Harry said, his voice very clipped. He was holding a knight in his hand. "The result is one of the most pleasing and individual places in all of England."

"It couldn't have been so pleasing to the people who saw their livelihoods disappear," Jon said.

Harry deliberately placed his knight on the chessboard, leaned back in his chair, and regarded Jon with an expression that Tracy could only term insufferable. "It probably wasn't pleasing to the slaves who built the pyramids, either, but the magnificent result of their labor has astounded and gratified people for centuries."

Tracy abruptly realized that Harry was being deliberately provoking.

Tony's light laugh cut through the tension. "Pay no

mind to my brother, Mr. Melbourne. He's a throwback to different times."

"If it's being a throwback not to want my acres of farmland turned into a golf course, then perhaps I am," Harry returned evenly.

For the briefest of moments, a cloud appeared in Tony's celestial blue eyes. Then they cleared, and he smiled. "See? He's incorrigible. Don't waste your breath trying to make him see reason, Mr. Melbourne."

"Good advice," Jon said tersely. "And now I will wish you all a good night. I have lines I must learn for tomorrow."

"So do I," Tracy said, deciding it would be wise to remove herself from Harry's dangerous presence.

As she was turning away, he said, "If you care to go to church in the morning, Miss Collins, I will be leaving at eight-thirty."

Tony groaned. "I hope you don't expect me to come with you."

Harry looked at his brother. "You most certainly will come with me. It won't be long before the neighborhood knows that you are home, and it won't look good if you don't come to church."

"Damn it, Harry. What do I care what the locals think?"

"You have a responsibility to set a good example," Harry said implacably.

"*Noblesse oblige* and all that," Jon said from the doorway.

Harry gave him a long level look. "Something like that."

Tracy, who had just decided it would be wisest to stay

away from him, heard herself say, "I'd like to go to church, my lord. Thank you."

He nodded.

Tracy shifted her packages from one arm to the other, said brightly, "Well, good night, again," and turned back into the foyer, leaving the two brothers to their chess game.

That night the Silverbridge stable burned down.

12

Tracy awoke to the sound of sirens. She sat bolt upright in bed, her heart pounding, and her first thought was, *Not again!* In ten seconds she had pulled on the fleece robe she had bought the day before and run out into the hallway. Meg was coming out her door at exactly the same time.

"What happened?" Tracy demanded.

"I don't know, but it sounded to me as if the engines went toward the stables," Meg replied.

"Oh no!" Tracy thought of all the beautiful horses living in the Silverbridge stable and went cold with horror. "I'm going to put on my sneakers and go down there. Perhaps I can help."

"Me too," Meg said.

It took less than a minute for Tracy to lace up her sneakers, then she met Meg in the corridor again, and the two of them raced toward the stables.

First they smelled the smoke. Then they heard the

high-pitched screams of horses in fear. Then they saw the flames. Tracy increased her speed and raced into the stable yard, which was a chaos of heat, loose horses wearing stable blankets, firemen, hoses, and spraying water. Harry and his assistant Ned Martin were trying to round up the horses to get them out of the firemen's way. This was proving rather difficult, however, as none of the horses were wearing halters.

Tracy immediately pulled the tie off of her fleece robe, slipped up behind one of the horses, spoke to him soothingly, and slid the tie around his neck. When he turned his head to look at her she realized she had caught Maestro.

"Where do you want him, my lord?" she called.

Harry was in the process of leading Pendleton out of the stable yard by his forelock. "In the first paddock," he shouted over his shoulder. "Follow me."

The fire lighted the whole area, enabling Tracy to see clearly as she led her horse after Harry and Pen. Maestro, thank God, was no trouble, walking eagerly after his stablemate. As soon as they had turned the horses loose in the paddock, Harry bolted the gate and said, "Thanks, but you shouldn't be here. It's dangerous."

He was wearing jeans and a T-shirt, and there was a streak of dirt across his left cheekbone. She could almost feel the intensity of his concentration as he surveyed the chaotic scene in the stable yard.

"Don't be an idiot," she returned. "You need all the help you can get."

Ned Martin was approaching them, leading a haltered Dylan, and Meg was following with another horse. Behind them the whole sky was brilliantly orange from the flames.

"I got the extra halters from the truck," Ned Martin said to Harry, motioning with his chin to the leather straps hanging from his shoulder. "Take them."

"Good thinking." As Harry grabbed the halters, Tracy said, "Give me one."

Without any noticeable hesitation, he tossed her a halter. "Let's go."

The two of them ran back to the stable yard to catch more horses.

By the time the red ball of the morning sun had arisen, the fire was out. Two horses had managed to slip away, but the rest of them were milling around in the first paddock. Harry was relieved that the escaped horses belonged to him, not to a client, and was confident that someone would find and return them. "The important thing is that they all got out of the stable," he said.

The stone shell of the stable still stood, but the roof and the whole of the inside was just charred wet rubble.

"Jesus, Harry," Ned Martin said as he stood in the stable yard regarding the smoldering pile. "Jesus." He sounded deeply shaken.

"At least it didn't spread," Harry returned grimly. "The fire department did a good job of containing it."

"How did it start?" Meg asked. The gray sweatshirt she wore over her flannel pajama pants was stained with the slobber of several horses.

"I don't know," Harry replied wearily. "We are always so careful of fire around the stable. Perhaps the fire department will be able to tell us something."

"I never let the grooms smoke in the stable," Ned said. "You know that, Harry."

"I know, Ned."

The firemen were still pouring water into the already-sodden building. "They're only making a bigger mess," Meg said fretfully. "Why don't they give it a rest?"

"They want to make certain that there are no sparks left," Harry returned. "We don't want it to start up again."

"It won't start again. There's nothing left to burn," Meg said bitterly.

It was true. Tracy felt infinite sadness looking at the wreck of what had once been a proud and beautiful building.

"I need some coffee," Harry said.

"I can brew you some if you don't feel like going all the way back to the house," Ned offered.

"Thanks," Harry said, and the four of them began to walk in the direction of the indoor riding ring, where Ned's apartment was located.

Tracy was pleasantly surprised by the living quarters that Harry provided for his assistant. The upstairs apartment had a big, bright modern kitchen, and the living room that they passed through was painted a pale yellow and was tastefully and comfortably furnished. She took a seat at the light wood kitchen table and watched as Ned measured coffee into his coffeemaker.

"I'd rather have tea," Meg said.

"That's easy," Ned replied, and filled a kettle at the sink.

Tracy had been running around so much with the horses that she had not realized how cold it was. Now that she was at rest, however, she began to feel chilled. She pulled her fleece robe closer around her and hoped that the coffee would not take long to make.

Harry must have seen her gesture, for he said, "Are you cold, Miss Collins?"

"A little, but the coffee will warm me up."

"It's just plain silly to go on calling Tracy *Miss Collins*, as if she was a stranger, Harry," Meg said. "After all, she's staying in our house, and she just helped you save your horses."

"True." Harry's dark eyes rested on Tracy's face. "But perhaps Miss Collins has other ideas."

Tracy felt his eyes touch her as if they had made actual physical contact. "I should be delighted if you would call me Tracy," she said as lightly as she could.

"Thank you." Why did his voice send such shivers along her nerves? "And you must call me Harry."

"Very well," Tracy said. "Harry."

For the briefest of moments they looked at each other, and something trembled in the air. Then Meg said, "Where are you going to put the horses, Harry? Have them live outside until you can rebuild?"

Ned placed a cup of coffee in front of his employer, and Harry drank half of it in one gulp. Then, "I can't do that," he replied. "The horses would survive just fine, but the owners will pull them out of training at Silverbridge before the end of the week if they don't have a stall."

Tracy said, "Rent the portable stalls they use at shows and put them in the indoor riding arena."

"That's a great idea," Meg said with enthusiasm.

"Yes, it is," Ned replied more slowly.

Apparently it was an idea that had also occurred to Harry. "It's a temporary solution, and I'll see about getting the stalls, but I am going to have to demonstrate that I am actively rebuilding the stable if I am to expect people to send their horses to me." He thrust his hand through his already-disordered hair. "The stable will have to be finished before winter."

His mouth was grim.

"Surely you have insurance," Tracy said.

A brief nod was his only response.

They all jumped as the knocker on Ned's front door sounded. He went to answer it and came back accompanied by one of the fire officers, who asked Harry, "May I speak to you privately, my lord?"

They went into the living room while Tracy, Meg, and Ned sat in tense silence in the kitchen, wondering what was being said.

When Harry rejoined them he was alone. He resumed his seat at the table and looked bleakly at the faces gathered around him. "The fire department thinks the fire was set," he said. "They found an empty can of kerosene in the rubble."

Tracy was suddenly terribly afraid.

"Couldn't it have been there for some other reason?" she asked quickly. "I know that at home we often used a kerosene heater in the barn when the farrier came."

"I never let kerosene within a hundred yards of my stable," Harry returned.

Ned's thin face looked strained. "Thank God for that monitor you had installed in my bedroom. The sound of the horses whinnying woke me up, but by the time I got to the stable the fire was already raging. If all of the stalls didn't have outside doors, the horses would have been incinerated."

"Thank God, indeed," Harry said. "And thank you, Ned. You were magnificent."

His words were quiet, but Ned's face flushed a bright red.

Meg was chewing on her hair. "Who would want to set fire to the stables? It doesn't make any sense."

"I can't answer that question, Meggie," Harry replied wearily. He pushed back his chair and stood up. "Thanks for the coffee, Ned." He glanced at the clock that hung on Ned's wall and looked at his sister. "If we hurry, we can still make church."

"Not me," she said positively. "I'm exhausted, and I'm going back to bed."

"All right." Tracy noticed that he didn't pressure her as he had pressured Tony. "I'm going, however. I seem to have a lot to pray about."

"I'll come with you, if I may," Tracy said.

He looked dubious. "It's already eight o'clock. Can you be ready by eight-thirty?"

Tracy looked down at her mud-splattered pajamas and fleece robe, which was anchored by a tie that had pieces of straw sticking off it. Her running shoes were also muddy, as were her sockless feet. "Sure," she said.

Meg said a little hesitantly, "Perhaps you're right, Harry. I suppose we do have some things to pray about."

He reached out to put an arm around his sister's frail shoulders. "Thanks, brat. You were a big help tonight."

Her thin face lit to beauty.

"I wonder where Tony is?" Meg asked, as they went down the stairs from Ned's apartment. "I know he sleeps like the dead, but those fire engines made a lot of noise."

"He's used to the racket of London," Harry said.

But Tracy, who had heard Tony's words to Mauley about finding a way to get Harry to change his mind about the golf course, was terribly afraid there might be another reason for Tony's absence.

𝓗arry's car was a Mercedes, but unlike the one that Gail had driven the day before, his was nine years old. He sat behind the driver's seat watching as his three passengers walked down the path from the house, although he looked at only one of them.

She was incredibly beautiful in a navy blue sheath dress that came just to the middle of her knees. Her matching shoes were high enough to be fashionable but not so high that they would look out of place in a country church. Her magnificent hair was still damp from the shower, and her deep blue eyes were like gemstones in the perfect setting of her face.

With considerable effort, he dragged his eyes away from her in order to get out of the car and open the door on the passenger side. She shot him a look as she slid past him and into the car.

It's not just me, he thought. *She feels it, too.*

Tony, who looked as if he had just stepped out of a tailor's shop on Savile Row, got into the backseat after Meg. "I just heard about the fire," he said soberly. "God, Harry, I am so sorry."

"No one was hurt," Harry returned expressionlessly. "We must be grateful for that."

"That stable was your pride and joy." Tony leaned forward to lay a brief hand on the shoulder of his brother's gray suit. "What rotten luck."

Harry, who had spent some of the happiest moments of his life in the Silverbridge stable, merely nodded, and said, "Yes."

"Would you mind very much going out by the tradesman's entrance?" Tracy asked. "A photographer who has been stalking me is parked outside the main gate."

"Stalking you?" Harry said sharply as he turned onto the road that led to the smaller gate.

"I call it that," she replied. "There seems to be nothing I can do about it, however. I did get a court order demanding that he keep a certain number of feet away from me, but he still follows me and photographs me. It's infuriating."

"The price of fame," Tony murmured.

"It's outrageous," Harry said with heartfelt sympathy. "Freedom of the press is all very well, but there should be some protection of personal privacy as well."

"I couldn't agree more," Tracy said. "But, in America, public figures don't seem to be entitled to any privacy at all. As I have discovered, to my sorrow."

The tradesman's exit was clear, and Harry turned the car in the direction of All Saints Church. He drove for a short time, then, from the backseat, he heard Meg say to Tony, "We could have used your help last night. I can't believe you slept through all that noise."

"I didn't hear a thing," he said apologetically. "I had

a headache last night, and I took some pills, and they always knock me out. I'm sorry."

"We managed without you," Harry returned as he pulled into the driveway of the parish church.

"We're fifteen minutes early," Tony complained. "Honestly, Harry, you're just like Papa, insisting that one arrive at church before everyone else."

Tracy swung her long, slim legs out of the car, and Harry could not help looking at them. "Your father sounds exactly like my father," she said. "He always herded us off to church *eons* before mass started. And if you were still combing your hair or something, he would invariably reply, 'When you get to the Pearly Gates, I hope Saint Peter doesn't say to you, "I'm too busy combing my hair right now to let you in. You'll have to step below."'" Her laugh was like the ringing of deep-toned bells. "Of course, there was no answer to *that.*"

Harry picked up on the mention of mass. "Are you Roman Catholic?"

"Yes. But I'm quite sure the Lord won't mind if I attend a Church of England service."

"All Saints is so High Church, it's probably more Catholic than most of the churches you go to," Tony said ironically.

They walked toward the front door of the familiar stone building, where for centuries the Oliver family had been baptized, married, and buried. "The church was built in the fourteenth and fifteenth centuries," Harry said to Tracy, who was walking by his side. "It's been the parish church for Silverbridge forever.

"Good morning, my lord." An elderly man was standing by the front door of the church, and he beamed as Harry came abreast of him.

"Good morning, Matthew," Harry replied. "How is your arthritis today?"

"None so bad, my lord, none so bad," the man replied.

Harry noticed that Matthew, who worked as the church's handyman, was staring at Tracy as if he had just seen a vision. She smiled at him, and said, "Good morning."

"Good morning, miss," he croaked.

"Perhaps it's a good thing that we did come early," Tony remarked from behind. "If we had to parade Tracy down the aisle when the church was full, we'd cause an uproar."

Tracy didn't even make a polite attempt to disavow Tony's statement. *She's a bloody movie star, for God's sake,* Harry thought. *I mustn't let myself forget that.*

He spoke to a few more people who were gathered in the vestibule, exchanging news about crops and weather, then they entered the main part of the church. Beside him he heard Tracy catch her breath.

Harry had always felt a strong connection to his parish church, and today he thought it was looking its best. The morning light streaming in through every window fell on Georgian woodwork, patched and bleached from years of use. The flagstones underfoot had been worn to unevenness by centuries of worshipers, and the paneled box pews in the front boasted their original hinges and locks. The pew that had belonged to his family for generations was directly below the splendid three-decker pulpit, and along the walls were memorials to various of his ancestors.

The church was already a quarter full, and all of the people dressed in their Sunday best gazed with fascination at Harry and his entourage as they walked past. He stood aside to let first Tony, then Meg, then Tracy enter the pew. He followed, closing the pew door and lifting somber eyes to the cross that was raised behind the altar. *Please, dear God,* he prayed, *let me be able to afford to rebuild the stable.*

He sat back, shut his eyes, and tried to let the peace of the church dispel the anxiety that had had his stomach twisted into a knot all morning.

All of Harry's childhood associations with All Saints had been positive. His first lessons had been given to him by the old rector, Dr. Warren, who had been like a second father to him. When his parents had sent him to Eton, he had fought against leaving the safety of the rectory library and Dr. Warren's gentle goodness. He had been packed off to school, of course, like every other English boy of his class, but it was Dr. Warren's compassionate morality that had stayed with him over the years.

Always remember, Harry, that the ends don't justify the means. He could almost hear Dr. Warren's precise scholarly voice speaking those words in his mind. *The greatest evil happens when men convince themselves that any behavior is acceptable as long as the end is desirable. That is never true.*

The somber words of the fire officer he had talked to earlier sounded in his mind: "I am very much afraid that the fire was deliberately set, my lord. There are signs that kerosene was used."

What kind of ends would justify burning a stable and perhaps incinerating ten innocent horses?

Money or revenge, he thought. Those were the main motives for arson.

Since he couldn't think of anyone who would want revenge against him, the answer had to be money. Could Mauley have set the fire as a way of forcing him to sell?

I am not selling my land, he thought with grim determination. *I have just put a fortune into repairing cottages and buying new machinery and more cattle. I understand land. I can make money out of farming. I am not selling it off to be a golf course.*

The organ in the back of the church sounded a sonorous, attention-getting chord, and the choirmaster announced the opening hymn. Everyone stood, the organ began to play, and Harry, along with the choir and the rest of the congregation, lifted his voice in the familiar words of praise. Then, from beside him, he heard a clear soprano voice join with his deeper baritone.

He felt strangely comforted to know that she was there.

13

When Tracy and the church party returned to Silverbridge, they found a striking young woman having coffee in the kitchen by herself. "My God, Harry," the visitor said, as he, Tracy, and Tony entered looking for some breakfast. "I've just been down to the stables. What a horror. Thank God you got all the horses out."

"We were very fortunate," Harry agreed. "Tracy, I'd like you to meet Gwen Mauley. Gwen, this is Tracy Collins."

Gwen's slanting green eyes regarded Tracy with a look that was not precisely welcoming. Robin Mauley's stunning daughter had short black hair, high slashing cheekbones, and a pointed chin. *She looks like a cat,* Tracy thought as she said politely, "So nice to meet you."

"How do you do," Gwen responded imperiously.

The spaniels had got off the sofa the moment that

Harry entered and now they followed him as he crossed to the almost-full coffeepot. "Thanks for making the coffee, Gwen," he said as he poured a cup. He lifted it and turned to face Tracy. "Coffee?"

"Yes, thank you very much."

He brought her the cup, and said, "Sit down. You must be starving. I'll scramble some eggs."

As Tracy took her seat, Gwen said suspiciously, "Did you go to church with Harry?"

Tracy lifted her brows to indicate her surprise at the tone of the other woman's voice, and said coolly, "Why, yes, I did."

Tony said, "We all went, Gwennie, dear. You know how patriarchal Harry can be about the things he considers his baronial duty. The peasants expect to see the lord of the manor at church and so, if you're staying in Harry's house, you get carted along as well."

Gwen snapped, "Tracy Collins isn't staying in this house."

Tracy frowned slightly and wondered what exactly was the nature of the relationship between Gwen and Harry.

Tony said innocently, "Oh didn't you know? Tracy has been staying with us ever since the Wiltshire Arms burned down."

Gwen's eyes opened wide. "The Wiltshire Arms burned down? Good God. Is everything around here going up in flames?"

"I hope not," Harry said. "Coffee, Tony? Do you want a refill, Gwen?"

Both said yes, and after Harry had poured the coffee

he went to the refrigerator and removed a bowl of eggs. The dogs followed at his feet, tails wagging hopefully.

"Are you really going to cook?" Gwen asked in surprise. "Where is Mrs. Wilson?"

"Sunday is her day off," he replied, "and yes, I am going to cook. I don't cook many things, but I do very good scrambled eggs. Now, who wants some?"

"I do," Tracy said immediately. "Do you have bread? Shall I make toast to go with the eggs?"

"A splendid idea," he replied. "The bread is in the bread box—over there."

Tracy's high heels clicked on the wood floor as she crossed to the bread box. Gwen remarked acidly and audibly to Tony, "She certainly seems to be making herself at home."

Tracy's back stiffened, and her eyes narrowed, always a dangerous sign.

Tony prudently changed the subject. "Harry didn't tell me you were coming today."

"I wasn't planning to," Gwen replied. "But the house party I was at was a perfect bore, so I left a day early." She turned her head to flash a smile at Harry. "I couldn't wait another moment to see what you thought of Dylan. Do you think he'll make a Grand Prix horse?"

"I have no doubt that, provided he stays sound, he will be a marvelous Grand Prix horse," Harry returned. He was scrambling eggs briskly with a fork. "He has incredible talent and, what is equally important, he likes to work. However did you manage to acquire such a gem?"

"An American rider had him, and you know the Americans. They all want big German warmbloods to ride." Gwen said this as calmly as if she herself had never ridden a warmblood. "I thought he had terrific gaits, so I made her an offer and she took it."

"You can't ride him like a warmblood," Harry warned. "You do realize that?"

"I think I know how to ride a horse by now, Harry," she said imperiously.

"Well, I think he's a great horse, a once-in-a-lifetime horse," Harry said as he poured the egg mixture into a pan. "You're very lucky, Gwen."

Gwen put her elbows on the table and cradled her pointed chin in her hands. "Yes, well what are you going to do with my once-in-a-lifetime horse now that your stable has burned down? I certainly don't want him living in a paddock."

Harry was now scrambling the eggs. "I am going to put up temporary stalls in the indoor riding school. The horses can stay there until I get the stable rebuilt."

Gwen's jet-black brows drew together. "I suppose that will be all right—as long as it's not for too long."

"The toast is ready," Tracy said as she lifted the bread out of the oven. "Shall I butter it while it's hot?"

"Do I detect a little hint?" Tony asked gravely.

She gave him a quick look and laughed. "You most certainly do. Like most Americans, I don't enjoy stone-cold toast—which is the way you English always seem to serve it."

"Go ahead and butter it," Harry said, "but before you do, let me have a slice for the dogs."

Tracy handed him one, which he broke in half and gave to the eager spaniels sitting at his feet. Next he gave Tony a commanding stare, and said, "Get out some plates, will you?"

"Where is Meg?" Gwen asked, as Tony put a plate in front of her. "Didn't she go to church with you?"

There was a beat of silence, then Harry said, "She did, but she didn't want any breakfast."

Gwen took her elbows off the table so Tony could give her some silverware. "Is that girl still starving herself? Really, Harry, you must do something about her. It's embarrassing to have a sister who looks like a skeleton."

"She is seeing a therapist," he replied woodenly as he removed the pan of eggs from the stove.

Tracy finished buttering the toast, piled it onto a plate, and brought it to the table, where Tony had finished setting out the plates and silverware. At the counter, Harry was scraping the eggs into a blue-and-white bowl.

"She needs to go into hospital," Gwen said. "One of those private treatment places where they brainwash you and force you to eat."

Harry said pleasantly, "I am Meg's legal guardian, Gwen, and I believe I am the best judge of what she needs and doesn't need."

"If you're not sending her to a private treatment program because you think you can't afford it, then maybe you better sell Daddy that land he wants," Gwen said.

"I can afford whatever Meg needs," Harry replied. He was eating hungrily.

"You're going to have to sell the land anyway," Tony said. "You'll need the money to rebuild the stable."

Harry helped himself to a slice of toast. "I have no intention of selling my land. The insurance will pay to rebuild the stable."

Tony looked skeptical. "Isn't the stable a listed historic building? Along with the house and the riding school?"

"Yes." Harry regarded his brother with a level stare.

"Doesn't that mean you have to restore it to the full level of its original condition."

A muscle jumped in Harry's jaw. "Yes."

Tony went on relentlessly. "Which means you would have had to have it insured at well over market value in order to cover the cost of rebuilding."

"Yes." Harry continued to hold his younger brother's eyes.

Tony raised an eyebrow. "Did you have it insured over market value?"

"I have the house insured for four times its market value," Harry replied. He broke eye contact with Tony and ate another forkful of eggs. "All of the outbuildings, including the stable, are insured at market value. It would have been prohibitively expensive to do otherwise."

A brief silence greeted this information.

Then Tony said, "In that case, the insurance money isn't going to be enough to rebuild the stable, not if you have to duplicate the original work."

Harry had finished his eggs, and he took a bite of toast. "I'll get a waiver from the local English Heritage officer."

"Not bloody likely," Tony replied.

Tracy had also been eating hungrily, but she looked up, and inquired, "What is an English Heritage officer?"

Tony answered. "An English Heritage officer is the vigilant guardian of any property that the state has declared to be a fixed and timeless piece of art. Tangentially, he has absolutely no interest in the needs of the family who happens to own said property." He turned to Harry. "Do you know it took the Alanbys *five years* to get approval for an addition to their kitchen?"

Harry shrugged.

"Bloody hell, Harry," Tony exploded. "Can't you see the writing on the wall? Take Mauley's offer, and you will have the money to rebuild the stable and make any repairs to the house that you desire. You will have the money to send Meg to the best sanitarium in the world. Christ, you'll have the money to buy yourself a new car! Why are you being so stubborn?"

Harry wiped his mouth with a napkin, and said evenly, "I inherited that land from my father, and I am going to guard it and improve it and pass it down to my son. And that is all I have to say on this matter—now or ever."

He pushed back his chair and stood up. "Would you like to ride Dylan, Gwen, and see how his training is coming along?"

"That's what I came to do," she replied, gesturing to her breeches and boots.

"I'll go change then. It won't take me long."

After the door closed behind Harry there was a short silence in the kitchen. Then Tony said, "Christ, but Harry can be a bloody mule."

Tracy began to gather the empty dishes.

Gwen made no motion to help. "Daddy says that Ambrose Percy will choose another location for his hotel if Daddy can't get the land soon."

Tracy carried the dishes to the sink, then returned to the table to collect the coffee cups. "Why doesn't your father just buy some other land?" she asked Gwen.

Gwen gave her the kind of look a very rude person might give a moron. "Because there *is* no other land that's equal to Silverbridge. That amount of suitable land, in a convenient location, is almost impossible to come by these days."

Tony chimed in. "And even after the sale, Harry would still have over twelve thousand acres! It's absurd for him to act as if he's being asked to sell the family heritage."

"I thought I understood that Mr. Mauley wants all the farmland." For some reason, Tracy felt impelled to defend Harry. "If your brother gives up his farms, then he will have no income."

Tony's eyes were bright with anger. "He won't need the bloody farm income! He'll have the money from Mauley, which he can invest." He looked from Tracy to Gwen. "Do you know that Harry has virtually no investments? There are some safe, low-return stocks that have been in the family for ages, but to all intents and purposes, today's economic race has left him behind. Fortunes have been made all over Britain, but, except for a few cases, not by the aristocracy. It's unbelievable, but Harry still believes in land over stocks."

Tracy had carried the cups to the sink and now she began to run the water. Tony said quickly, "You don't need to do that, Tracy."

"I'll just rinse them and put them in the dishwasher," she said. "I hate the thought of dirty dishes."

"American women are so housewifely," Gwen said. She did not mean her statement as a compliment.

"American women do everything well," Tracy returned condescendingly.

She wanted to remain in the room in order to overhear Tony and Gwen talk, so she reined in her strong desire to annihilate Gwen and held a plate under the faucet.

Gwen dropped her voice, and asked Tony, "Is he over the Dana Matthews scandal yet?"

"I think so." Tony had lowered his voice as well. "I'll never understand how he came to be involved with her in the first place. She was a cokehead. Of course, Harry didn't know that when he first started going out with her. Everyone else in town knew, but not Harry. Then she became so dependent on him that, when he did find out, he felt he couldn't desert her. It was the screaming-and-throwing tantrum she threw in Harrods that finished him off. It was in all the papers—you must have seen it."

"Of course I did."

"So, unfortunately, our chance to annex Dana and her fortune went down the tubes."

"*Our?*" Gwen drawled. "Were you looking to share in Dana's largesse?"

Tony said something that Tracy couldn't hear, and Gwen laughed. Then Tony said, "How about you, darling? Are you ready to move in now that Harry seems to have recovered from the Dana fiasco?"

"It might be fun to be a countess," Gwen said lightly.

Tracy felt such a surge of jealousy that she had to put down the cup she was holding because her hand was shaking.

My God, she thought. *How can I feel this way when I scarcely know the man?*

The legs of Gwen's chair scraped against the floor, and Tracy heard her get to her feet. "I'm going to use the loo before I go down to the stables."

Tony's voice resumed its normal volume. "We're going upstairs, Tracy. Do you want to come?"

What Tracy wanted was to scratch out Gwen Mauley's eyes. She said with a sufficient degree of calm, "I'll come when I finish the dishes."

"Suit yourself," Tony said. The kitchen door closed, and Tracy turned off the water and put the last dish in the dishwasher.

She had eavesdropped to find out if Tony would give away anything that might connect him to the stable fire. He hadn't, but what she had heard had been just as worrying. She had been upset by the conversation, and she was upset with herself for being upset.

What is it to me if Harry marries that evil woman? she thought angrily.

At that moment the kitchen door opened, and Meg walked in. "Tracy, I didn't know you were here," she said in surprise.

"I was just tidying up after breakfast," Tracy returned.

Meg had changed out of her church clothes and into her usual jeans and sweater. She wandered over to the sofa where the two spaniels were stretched out and sat down between them. "Poor Millie," she said, petting one of the silky heads and gazing into a pair of quiet brown eyes. "Did Harry desert you?"

Marshal, jealous of the attention his sister was getting, nudged her.

Tracy returned her apron to the cupboard. "He went upstairs to change into riding clothes. Gwen Mauley is here and wants to ride her horse. I expect he'll collect the dogs before he goes down to the stable."

A scowl descended over Meg's fine-boned face. "I don't like Gwen Mauley. She's after Harry."

"Surely it would be a suitable match for him," Tracy said. "Gwen likes horses, and she has money. What could be better?"

"She's a bitch. And she doesn't like me. I would hate it if she became my sister-in-law. She'd be even worse than Dana Matthews."

"You don't seem to like any of your brother's girlfriends," Tracy said.

"He was engaged once to Hilary Mortimer, and I liked her okay. But they had some kind of a falling-out and called it off." The sun was shining on Meg's silvery hair, which should have been beautiful but instead looked dull and lifeless. "He'd better get married soon, though. He's going to be thirty this year." She gave Tracy a wide-eyed look. "That's *old*."

To Tracy, at twenty-seven, thirty didn't seem old at all. It seemed, in fact, a perfect age. She casually leaned against the counter, and said, "There is quite an age difference between you and your brothers."

Meg bent her head to pet Millie again. "There's twelve years between me and Harry and nine years between me and Tony." Her voice sounded oddly gruff. "I was a surprise to my parents—and not a pleasant surprise either. My mother thought that she was finished with children, and then there I was." Meg ran Millie's silken ear through her fingers. "Not that I got in her way very much. When I was little she fobbed me off on a nanny, and when I was eight, I went away to school."

Tracy thought of her own cherished childhood and was appalled at the picture that Meg had painted. *No wonder the poor kid is anorexic,* she thought, and said, "I have never understood why the English send their children off to boarding school at such a young age. It seems so irresponsible to entrust the most formative years of your child's life to someone else."

Meg shrugged. "Everyone does it."

"We don't do it in America, thank goodness. At least, a few people do, I suppose, but never at the age of eight!"

"There was this mean girl in my dorm," Meg confided as she continued to stroke Millie's long ears. "She used to tell me scary stories and make me cry."

Tracy put down the sponge she had been holding. "It sounds ghastly."

"Oh, it toughened me up," Meg returned with a forced smile. "We Olivers come from tough stock, you know."

Tracy looked at the fragile wrists that protruded from Meg's sweater and went to sit next to the girl. The displaced Millie gave her an outraged look. Tracy put an arm around Meg and hugged her. "You're not tough at all, you're a sweetheart," she said warmly. "I wish I had a little sister like you."

Meg turned to look at her. "Do you really?"

"Absolutely."

A little color had flushed into the skin over Meg's sharp cheekbones. "I wish you were my sister, too."

"I'll tell you what," Tracy said. "Let's get Gail to pick us up and we can all three of us go out to lunch."

"But you just ate breakfast," Meg said in surprise.

Tracy smiled. "True. We'll give it another hour before we leave."

Meg looked at Tracy's long, elegant legs, which were encased in sheer panty hose ending in navy high-heeled shoes. "How do you stay so thin if you eat so much?"

Tracy thought a moment before she replied, "Do you really think I'm thin, Meg?"

Meg nodded emphatically. "Of course, You have a beautiful figure."

"Thank you." She hesitated, then went resolutely on, "You do realize, don't you, that you are much thinner than I am?"

"No," Meg said. "I'm fat. Mummy used to call me a dumpling."

What a dreadful woman her mother must have been, Tracy thought. She held out her bare right arm, and said, "Here, put your arm next to mine." After a moment, Meg slowly complied. "Now roll up your sweater sleeve." Meg shot her a suspicious look, but then she pushed up her beige wool sleeve, revealing an arm that was nothing more than a covering of flesh and blood vessels over bone.

"Look at our two arms, Meg," Tracy urged. "Your's is much thinner than mine."

"No it's not," Meg replied. "Look at all this fat." And

she pulled at the loose skin that had wrinkled in the crook of her arm.

"That's not fat," Tracy replied. "That's a sign that you have shrunk your body more than your skin can contract. Your skin is like an oversize sweater, with folds."

Meg jerked her sleeve down and averted her face. "I know what you're saying. You're saying that I'm anorexic. Well what if I am! I can't help it."

Tracy regarded Meg's sharp profile. "Perhaps you could help it a little," she said gently. "Do you think you could come out to lunch with Gail and me and eat something? It doesn't have to be very much, but something."

Meg's back was rigid, and Tracy thought she was going to say no. Then, "I suppose I could do that," she mumbled.

Relief surged through Tracy. "Wonderful. You know, if you *were* my little sister, I'd be very worried about you."

Meg was staring at her lace-up boots. "Harry worries about me. He doesn't know what to do, though."

Tracy reached out and gently smoothed Meg's hair back from her forehead. "Harry can't do anything, Meg. It's you who must save yourself."

Meg's head bent even lower, and in a gruff little voice she said, "I don't know if I want to."

Tracy's heart ached. "Then try to *pretend* that you want to. Okay? Will you do that for me?"

"Oh—all right." Meg lifted her head and said with feigned exasperation, "Anything is better than you nagging at me."

Tracy grinned. "I'm a great nagger. Just ask my mother." She patted Meg's knee then stood up.

"Uh-oh," Meg said.

Tracy looked at her. "What?"

Meg's eyes were dancing. "The back of your navy blue dress is covered with dog hairs."

Tracy turned around to look. "Yuck. It looks like I have more of their hair than they do." She gave an ineffective brush or two at the dress. "Oh well, a visit to the dry cleaner will fix it." She smiled. "Come along, Meg, and we'll go and call Gail."

14

$\mathcal{T}$racy was recognized in the restaurant and had to sign about a dozen autographs before she could eat. She did this with as much enthusiasm as a child who had been commanded to be polite by his parents while visiting a hated relative.

"Isn't that annoying, having people bother you like that?" Meg asked when the last autograph seeker had walked away.

"It's a pain in the ass," Tracy returned grimly.

Gail sighed.

Tracy glared. "I signed the stupid autographs, didn't I?"

"You were wonderful," Gail said expressionlessly.

Tracy turned to Meg. "Can you tell me why a person would want to have someone else's signature on a menu? Or a napkin? Or a piece of toilet paper? I can understand wanting an author's name on a book, or an artist's signature on a painting, but what the hell good is my signature on a napkin?"

Meg looked thoughtful. "I don't know, but people seem to like it."

"Well, I don't," Tracy said resentfully.

Meg was staring at her. "Don't you *like* being an actress, Tracy?"

"I like being an actress very much. It's why I accepted this role, because it's a challenge. What I don't like is being a movie star."

"Goodness," Meg said, wide-eyed.

"This is a running battle between Tracy and the rest of the world," Gail said. "She doesn't think her fans should have any part of her outside her movies, and they want to devour her whole."

"You could do what Harry does when obnoxious people try to cozy up to him because he's an earl," Meg said.

"What does Harry do?" Tracy asked curiously.

"He looks at them as though they were some kind of disgusting bug," Meg said. "Like this," and she made a face.

Tracy and Gail roared with laughter.

Meg laughed, too. "Well, he does it better than that."

A waiter stopped at their table, and said, "Are you ready to order, Miss Collins?"

"Yes," Tracy said. Both she and Gail ordered the pasta salad and Meg, after a noticeable hesitation, ordered the same thing. When the food came, Tracy tried hard not to watch Meg eat. Instead she and Gail kept up a series of reminiscences about past movies, most of them amusing. Meg seemed to enjoy listening and by the time the waiter came back to remove their plates,

Tracy was relieved to see that she had eaten some of her salad.

Prudently, she did not remark on this to Meg.

When they exited into the warm afternoon air, none of them felt like returning home.

"Nothing much is open on a Sunday, but we could go and look at the white horses," Meg suggested.

Tracy's attention was instantly caught. "What white horses? Lipizzaners?"

"No." Meg laughed. "I mean figures of horses that are carved into a chalk hillside. We have a number of them in Wiltshire, and they're super."

"Oh yes, I've seen pictures," Tracy said enthusiastically. "I'd love to see them."

"Okay," Meg said. "I'll be the navigator."

They had a delightful day, eating dinner out as well. Meg balked a bit at the suggestion of another meal, but when Tracy and Gail professed themselves to be starving, she went along. She only ordered a bowl of soup, however, and did not finish it.

Gail delivered Meg and Tracy back to Silverbridge at eight o'clock. "Oh, before I forget," Gail said, as Tracy opened the car door. "I spoke to Mel late last night. He's sending you a script he wants you to consider."

"Who is Mel?" Meg asked from the back seat.

"My agent," Tracy replied, and turned to Gail. "Who is the writer?"

"Seth Nagle." Gail named the screenwriter of one of Tracy's most successful movies. "And Harrison Ford is interested."

"He's old," the voice from the backseat pronounced.

Tracy laughed. "I'll look at the script," she told Gail, "but I've talked to Mel about the sameness of my last few roles, and he agreed to try to find me something different. Seth Nagle is more of the same."

"The movie you're doing now is different," Gail pointed out.

"I know," Tracy said. "And I love it."

"What time are you called for tomorrow?" Gail asked.

"I have to be in makeup at ten o'clock."

"Okay, I'll see you in your dressing room after that."

"Good." Tracy slid out of the car, and Meg did likewise. They both gave Gail a wave as she drove off.

Then Tracy turned to Meg. "I think I'll go down to the stable and walk off my dinner."

"Okay," Meg said. "I'm going upstairs. One of my favorite shows is coming on the telly."

Tracy was pleased not to have company and set briskly off in the direction of the stable path. She had changed after breakfast from her dress into wool slacks and a deep lavender cashmere sweater set, which had been warm enough during the day but felt a little thin in the chilly evening air. She did not turn back toward the house, however, but kept walking in the direction of the burned-down stable.

Harry was there, as she had hoped, leaning on a paddock railing and watching the horses as they munched on the hay that he had put out for them. Millie and Marshal were with him. Tracy counted the number of horses in the three paddocks as she approached.

"Hi," she said as she came up beside him.

"Hello," he returned, giving her a quick glance before returning his eyes to the horses.

Tracy crossed her arms against the evening breeze. "I see your two strays have been returned."

"Yes. Martin Chubb, one of my tenant farmers, found them eating in his hay pasture. He brought them back this afternoon."

Tracy regarded the ten horses, which were spread among the three paddocks according to sex. They all wore their turnout blankets, and their manes and tails had obviously been brushed. They seemed perfectly peaceful as they dipped their muzzles into their own individual hay piles, then lifted their heads to chew and look calmly around.

"Thank goodness it's a nice evening," Tracy said. "If they had to be out in the rain, they wouldn't be half as content."

"I know." His voice sounded preoccupied. "There's a horse show going on near Winchester today, and I managed to arrange for the company that they rented their portable stalls from to bring ten of them here tomorrow."

"That's great. You'll be more comfortable with them indoors."

All the while that she had been conducting this perfectly rational conversation, something completely irrational had been going on inside Tracy. Harry was standing at least two feet away from her, the sleeve of his jacket hadn't even brushed her arm, and yet she had never been more physically aware of a man in her entire life. Every nerve in her body was attuned to him: the slight stirring of his hair with the evening breeze, the flicker of his eyelashes, the tendons in his left hand as he rested it on the fence; all these affected her in a profound and disturbing way.

He asked abruptly, "Did Meg eat anything today?"

"A little. She had some pasta salad at lunch and a half a bowl of soup at dinner."

"That's good." He glanced over Tracy's shoulder as if he expected someone to be there. "Where is she? I thought she was your shadow."

"She wanted to watch a TV show."

"No, she didn't." He sounded very weary. "She wanted to go to her room to exercise off all of those calories she consumed today."

Tracy asked cautiously, "Just how dangerous is her physical condition?"

He rested his arm against the paddock fence and turned to face her. "It's not necessary for her to go into hospital—at least not yet. In fact, when I spoke to her therapist yesterday, she said that she saw some improvement. Evidently this movie has caught her interest, and one of the problems with anorexics is that they become so inner-directed that they lose interest in everything else. The therapist also told me that she feels Meg has developed a tie to you."

Tracy looked into his brown eyes, and a shiver ran up and down her spine. She cleared her throat and said, "If there is anything at all I can do to help, please let me know. Anorexia is a terrible disease, and I know it is difficult to treat."

"Thank you. I would ask you to continue to befriend her, if that wouldn't be too much of a burden. She trusts very few people, which is one of the problems that triggered this disorder."

"Of course I will continue to be her friend. It's not a burden at all; I like Meg."

"Thank you," he said quietly.

For the first time she noticed that he had a raw, ugly burn on the back of his hand.

"You should have a bandage on that so it won't get infected." And, without thinking, she reached for his hand, as if she would examine the burn more closely.

The moment she touched him, his hand turned and his fingers captured hers. In a rough voice he said, "That was a dangerous thing to do."

She yielded as soon as his lips touched hers, her whole body surrendering to him, relinquishing herself to his strength. All thought ceased. Everything was feeling: the taste of his mouth; the heady smell of his shaving lotion; the feel of his body against hers, a feeling that was wildly erotic, yet strangely safe. Tracy experienced all these things so intensely that she was dizzy with sensation and had to cling to him even more tightly to keep from falling.

At long last he lifted his head, but he didn't let her go. Instead he guided her head to his shoulder and buried his mouth in her hair. "Tracy," he said in a voice that sounded profoundly shaken.

She stretched her arms around his waist and held him tightly. For a moment out of time, they stood there in silence, locked in each other's arms.

They flew apart as soon as they heard the sound of the camera clicking. Tracy was horrified to see Jason

Counes standing about twenty feet away, his camera pointed in their direction.

Harry cursed and started toward him. Counes turned and fled. Harry went after him, and they both disappeared into the trees.

Tracy's heart was pounding. *That horrible, horrible man.* She wanted to kill him, and she was afraid that Harry felt the same way. She said out loud, "For God's sake, Harry, don't hurt him."

She shuddered to think what the newspapers would say if Jason got beaten up.

At last Harry came into view, walking out of the woods. There was a camera in his hands. She went to meet him.

"I got the little weasel's camera," he said when she reached him. He was white with fury. "I also told him what I'd do if I caught him trespassing on my land again. I hope he listened, because I meant it."

"That's the man who's been stalking me," Tracy said.

He nodded, glanced at his watch, and said curtly, "We should be getting back to the house. It will be dark shortly."

The incident with the camera had transformed him from lover into wary stranger. Tracy didn't know whether to be angry or sad. Without replying, she accompanied him back up the stable path. It was at the place where the road to the woods branched off that the dogs began to growl.

"What is it?" Harry said with a mixture of puzzlement and incipient alarm.

Tracy looked at the dogs, both of which were crouched into attack positions, hackles raised, their eyes fixed on a single spot. The deep growling noise they were making was hair-raising.

"What can they be seeing?" Harry asked, looking where the dogs were looking.

Tracy looked likewise, and on the path she saw a man and a woman locked in a passionate embrace. The man's hair was a lighter color than Harry's and the woman's a darker color than hers. Everything about their pose screamed desperation.

"You don't see anything?" she asked Harry cautiously.

"No, do you?"

When she didn't reply, he turned to the dogs. "Easy, Marshal. Easy, Millie. It's all right. There's nothing there."

Marshal gave a single sharp, threatening bark and moved forward. The bark caught Tracy's attention and she looked away from the couple on the path. Marshal's black-and-white spaniel body and raised floppy ears looked astonishingly wolflike. Then, between one moment and the next, he relaxed.

Instantly Tracy looked back to the spot where she had seen Charles and Isabel. No one was there.

Harry said, "There must have been an animal in the undergrowth, although they usually don't react so ferociously to prowling wildlife."

He didn't see them. Tracy looked at Harry in amazement as she realized that his eyes were sealed to the visions. In the same way, Charles's and Isabel's eyes evidently were sealed to the time period they had infringed upon.

Tracy was the only one able to see into both worlds.

The time barrier must be like one of those windows that functions as a real window on one side and a mirror on the other, she thought. *I am the only one on the window side. Everyone else sees only the mirrored reflection of their own world.*

"They seem fine now," Harry said, and started up the path again. She moved to join him, and together, yet apart, they continued toward the house.

Tracy went right to her room, closing the door and going to stand at the window, her forehead pressed against the glass.

Scotty, she thought. *What is happening to me? Why am I feeling this way about this particular man?*

She knew that if Harry had asked to come to her room, she would have said yes, and the possibility of that yes had turned her world upside down. The fact of the matter was, in this age where sex was regarded as free entertainment rather than a sign of commitment, Tracy had never slept with anyone in her life except Scotty.

Her Hollywood friends couldn't believe her prudery, and over the years she had developed an assortment of reasons to explain her behavior, both to others and to herself. She didn't want to get a sexually transmitted disease; she didn't want to get pregnant and no birth control method was foolproof; her Church taught that sex without marriage was a sin. All of these reasons she presented as perfectly legitimate motives to explain and justify her failing to fulfill what her friends called "her sexual needs."

The actual truth underlying her behavior was very simple: She hadn't been tempted.

Tracy had loved Scotty and had loved making love with him. They had laughed and loved and been intimate in every way possible, physically as well as emotionally. Every man she had met since his death had seemed a stranger, and she just could not bring herself to do with a stranger the things that she had done with Scotty.

Then this man had come along. And he was pushing Scotty aside.

She felt tears sting her eyes. *I don't even have your picture in my bedroom anymore.*

In fact, the Westport photography studio had kept the negatives of her wedding and had promised to make up a new picture and send it to her. But in the turmoil of emotion that was besetting her, all she could think of was that she wanted to look at Scotty at that moment, and she couldn't.

Could it be possible that there is a link between Harry and me that goes back in time?

But if that were so, if the visions were connected in some way to her and Harry, why did she see them and he did not?

Perhaps it was because she was more receptive to them, she thought. She remembered vividly the scoffing way he had treated her inquiries about ghosts, and thought that perhaps his own skepticism was acting as a barrier between him and whatever message Charles and Isabel were meant to convey.

She knocked on the bathroom door, to make certain that Meg wasn't there, and then she took a shower, blow-dried her hair, and put on her ivory satin pajamas. When she came out of the bathroom, she went to the window. She had just pushed aside the curtain to look out at the moonlit night, when her eye was caught by a shadowy figure walking around the corner of the house.

She threw up the window and leaned out in an effort to see who it was, but in the brief moment it took to do this, the figure had disappeared.

Tracy's heart began to drum. *What was that all about? Is someone sneaking around in the dark, planning another act of sabotage?*

Without further thought, she ran down the hall to the morning room to see if Harry was there. He was, and she blurted out what she had seen and what she feared.

"Stay here," he said. "I'll go look."

She went to the front window and looked out, and in a few moments she saw Harry come around the corner of the building. He was holding a flashlight, which he swiveled around the lawn, searching for anything that looked out of place. Apparently he found nothing, because he turned and started back in the direction of the side entrance. It was not long before Tracy heard his feet on the staircase.

"No sign of anyone," he said as he came into the room. "Perhaps you imagined it."

"I don't think so," Tracy said. She had left the front window and was standing in the middle of the morning room floor, her hands clasped together anxiously.

Harry's brown eyes moved from her mouth, to her breasts, to her hips. "Pretty pajamas," he said.

Tracy suddenly realized that he thought she had planned this scene in order to seduce him. Fury flooded through her. "I am so sorry I troubled you, my lord," she said in an acid voice. "I won't take any more of your precious time."

In order to get to the door she had to pass him, which she prepared to do with chin up and body rigid.

"Tracy," he said and reached a hand toward her satin-clad arm.

She wrenched it away from him. "Good night!" she said angrily, and then she was past him and on the way to the safety of her room.

15

When Tracy woke in the morning, her anger was gone and what was left was a determination to find out more about Charles and Isabel.

I need to see them again. I need to understand why they are appearing to me.

Perhaps the apparitions were simply to let her know about some previous link between her and Harry. Perhaps their purpose was to alert her to the fact that he was her destiny.

Her lips curved in a wry smile. *Destiny. How Scotty would laugh at me.*

She glanced at the alarm clock on her bedside table and saw that it wasn't due to ring for another hour. She debated about whether or not to stay in bed, and decided she was wide-awake and wouldn't get any more sleep. She stretched her arms over her head, yawned, turned off the alarm, got out of bed, and went into the bathroom.

It was while she was dressing that the idea occurred to her that she use the extra hour to explore the rest of the house. The apparitions seemed to appear in the same places where the initial action had occurred almost a century ago, and Tracy thought, *It's highly unlikely that Charles would have met the governess in the bedroom wing of the house. That is probably why I have never seen them in any of the rooms of the family apartment. I need to go into the public rooms—like the upstairs drawing room, where I once saw them.*

She zipped up her jeans, thrust her feet into leather moccasins, and checked the corridor to see if it was clear. It was, and she went purposefully to the door that connected the apartment to the upstairs drawing room, pushed it open, and went in.

This time the room was empty. Tracy crossed to a set of beautifully molded double doors, pushed them open, and for the first time she stepped into the part of Silverbridge where Charles had lived and that today was viewed only by the public two months out of the year.

A large, picture-lined foyer showed off a magnificently carved staircase that descended to the lower level. Tracy went downstairs slowly, glancing up once to admire the splendid crystal chandelier that hung over the staircase well.

On a later visit she would marvel at the collection of paintings that hung on the walls of Silverbridge: the set of four history paintings by Angelica Kauffmann in the staircase hall, the two Van Dykes in the library, the large Constable in one of the drawing rooms, the two Claude landscapes in the dining room, the Titian and the three Velázquez portraits in one salon, the two Turners in a

second and in another the full-length picture by
Reynolds over the fireplace which showed the Athenian
courtesan Thais urging Alexander the Great to burn the
Persian royal palace at Persepolis. On a later visit she
would marvel at the ceilings by Joseph Rose and Antonio Zucchi, the chimneypieces by Thomas Carter and
the hundred-year-old carpets by Aubusson. She would
admire the Chippendale furniture, the armorial trophies
on the walls of the entrance hall, the elegant frieze in the
staircase hall. But for the moment, the house was sec-
ondary in her thoughts. She was searching for Charles.

She found him in the library, standing in front of a
beautiful chimneypiece, which boasted two inset carved
marble panels. The woman with him was not Isabel,
however. She was older, with pale hair cut in the short
feathery style of the Regency, and she was wearing a
long blue empire-style dress. She was standing in front
of Charles, and the rigid set of her shoulders spoke of
anger.

"I want Isabel to leave," the woman said in a tight,
hard voice. "She can go to one of her other cousins."

Charles was dressed in a riding coat, which made his
shoulders look very broad, and the expression on his
face was wary as he regarded the woman who must be
his wife. "Why should she go, Caroline?" he asked in
well-acted surprise. "She's doing a wonderful job. The
children adore her."

"It's not the children's adoration that worries me," the
woman replied bitterly.

The wariness in his brown eyes deepened. "What do
you mean?"

The woman threw up her head. "You know perfectly

well what I mean, Charles. You are enamored of her! I will not be cheated on in my own house. Nor will I agree to a *menage à trois,* like poor Georgiana Devonshire was forced to do."

His face grew hard, the way Tracy had seen Harry's do. "You are being absurd, Caroline. And insulting. If you think that I would take advantage of a young girl living under my protection, you don't know me very well."

She narrowed her eyes in irony. "I rather think it is the other way around, Charles, and it's sweet, helpless little Isabel who is taking advantage of you."

"That's ridiculous." Now he was openly angry.

"No, it's not, only you're too besotted to see it. I want her out of this house, Charles. Do you hear me?" A note of incipient hysteria had crept into her voice.

His expression was grim. "She has nowhere to go!"

"That's not my concern. I took her in, gave her a home, entrusted her with my children, and she repays me by trying to steal my husband. Well, I won't have it, Charles. Get rid of her, or I'll throw her out myself." And on that note she turned away from him, went by Tracy, then out of the room.

Tracy felt her passing as a rush of cool air.

Left alone, Charles turned to face the fireplace. He put his hands on the mantelpiece and bowed his head. From where she stood, Tracy could see the tendons standing stark in his hands, so tightly was he gripping the wood.

She wondered what would happen if she spoke to him.

"Charles," she said softly.

There was no change in his posture.

She tried again, more sharply. "Charles!"

Still nothing. He couldn't see her, and he couldn't hear her either.

He stood thus for a long time, and Tracy stood watching him. Then he straightened away from the mantel and walked steadily toward the door. She watched as he went out and thought that she had been right about another thing. He did not walk with the catlike agility of Harry. He walked like a soldier.

Tracy reported to makeup a few minutes early, then went back to her dressing room to wait until she was called. As Gail had promised, she was already there with a stack of letters that needed Tracy's signature. As Tracy finished signing the last one, Gail said, "It seems strange to see you without Meg in tow."

Tracy glanced sharply at her secretary to see how she meant those words. Gail's face was not wearing the ironic look that Tracy knew all too well; instead, she looked grave. "Talk about the quintessential poor little rich kid," she said. "The things she let out yesterday about her childhood were enough to curdle my blood."

Tracy sighed. "When you are not loved when you are young, damage is done that is sometimes irreparable."

"We didn't have any money, but we all knew that we were loved," Gail replied. "I guess when you look at it that way, I was luckier than Meg."

"You were," Tracy agreed. "Her brother is sending her to a therapist, and the woman told him that having this movie on the property has been beneficial to Meg.

It's given her something to think about besides the scale."

"Ah yes," Gail said. "Her brother." She arched an eyebrow. "I presume you mean Lord Silverbridge and not the younger one?"

Tracy spread her skirts carefully and sat down on the chair in front of her mirror. "Lord Silverbridge is her guardian."

"He has something you rarely see in a man these days," Gail said. She was sitting on the sofa stuffing letters into envelopes.

"What do you mean?" Tracy asked curiously.

Gail looked up and frowned thoughtfully. "I can't say exactly. It's not that he's good-looking or sexy—though he is both of those things. But there are thousands of good-looking, sexy men in the world. It's . . . oh I don't know, but whatever it is, he has it."

"He's an earl," Tracy said.

"What does that have to do with it?" Gail went back to stuffing envelopes with the recently signed letters.

"Everything. He has always been absolutely sure of himself and his position in the world. It's part of who he is. He's an earl."

"That sounds very castelike," Gail said. She stuffed the last envelope and stacked them so she could put a rubber band around them.

"England is still a caste-ridden society," Tracy said. "Much more so than America."

A knock sounded on the trailer door, and a male voice called, "They're ready for you, Miss Collins."

"Thank you," she called back. She checked her

makeup in the mirror, picked up a sweater to wear over her light Regency dress, and went out the door.

The morning's shoot was of one of the most crucial scenes in the film. It came at the point when Martin is almost certain that his wife is betraying him with other men, and for the first time he verbalizes his suspicions. Julia denies his accusations vehemently, and the scene ends with a kiss that had been one of the central moments of the book and needed to be one of the central moments of the film.

Dave took them over the scene before they started. "Jon, this scene is very important for Martin. He is almost convinced by now that Julia is being unfaithful to him, but he is still very sexually attracted to her. He resents this attraction, he wants to break free of it, but he can't. This is the scene that shows all of his conflicts. He begins by accusing her, he grows angry as he listens to her deny his accusations, he wants to throw her out of his house and out of his life, but when she appeals to him physically, he can't resist her. His feelings at the end of the scene are frustration, desperation, and pure unadulterated lust. Do you have that?"

"Yes," Jon said.

The day was cloudy, the weather forecast was predicting rain in the afternoon, and Dave was anxious to get the shoot done before that happened. "All right, Tracy," he said. "This is a pivotal scene for your character as well. For the first time we see clearly that Julia is aware of her sexual power, and when she uses this power to quiet her husband's suspicions, the whole question of which of them is in control of the other comes to the fore."

"Yes," Tracy said. In fact, long before she had attended the first read-through of the script, Tracy had determined to play Julia as a young girl who had been awakened to passion by her husband and who gradually comes to realize the power her sexual magnetism gives her over men. In Tracy's view, Julia was innocent of the infidelity with which her husband charged her, but she was guilty of being a sexual tease.

And that was the tragedy, in Tracy's opinion. A young girl, a nineteenth-century young girl, brought up to consider herself powerless, a pawn of men, discovers that she possesses this marvelous power over the superior beings who have ruled her life. She exercises this power unwisely and thus brings about her own downfall.

The book and the film deliberately left Julia's culpability open to question. Was she or was she not guilty? But in Tracy's mind, Julia was an innocent who was destroyed not just by her husband, but by the society that had made her what she was.

"Great," Dave said. "Let's get rolling then."

They shot the scene once. From the first word that he spoke, Jon conveyed such a sense of barely controlled menace that Tracy could easily play off it. Confronted by an angry, threatening male, Julia would have instinctively reassured and placated. After her initial indignant denials of her husband's accusations, she would attempt to appease him by exercising the only power she had ever had over men.

"Truly, my lord," Tracy said in a soft, breathless voice, *"you* are the one that I love." She lifted her lashes, and the brief glimpse she had of Jon's angry face caused her to take one step away from him. Then, determined to be brave, she retraced that step and lifted her hand to touch his lapel. "I do not know why you should make these accusations against me." She allowed her eyes to fill with tears. "They hurt me."

Angrily, he thrust her hand from his lapel. "My words can't hurt you any more than your behavior has hurt me." His voice was deeply bitter.

Tracy blinked so that two tears would roll down her face. "You are my *husband,* my lord. You know well that I was innocent when I came to your bed. How can you believe that I would dishonor the vows that I made to you?"

Jon was looking at her with an expression of mixed bafflement and fury. She cupped his face in her hands and lifted her own face to him. "I would never betray you, my lord." She let her teeth rest on her lower lip, calling attention to the lushness of her mouth. "Truly," she breathed.

Jon gave a groan like a wounded animal, reached out, and crushed her to him. Then his mouth, hard, ravaging, punishing, came down on hers.

It was a frightening kiss, and when he finally released her, Tracy tasted blood. She backed away from him and lifted her hand to her mouth.

"How did you like that, madam?" Jon said dangerously. "Would you care to continue this encounter in our bedroom?"

Tracy's heart was pounding, and she stared at the blood that stained her fingers. That kiss had been much more than she expected.

I'm frightened, she thought. *I'm frightened, and my only safety lies in making him want me.*

With a barely concealed shiver, she stepped up to her husband, put her arms around his waist, and rested her head on his shoulder. "I'm sorry, my lord," she whispered. "I am so sorry that I have made you angry with me. I never meant to do that. I thought I was just being polite to those other men. There was nothing more than that, I promise you."

Jon's body felt rigid to her touch. She could not see the expression on his face that the camera was filming. Finally, in a strangled voice, he answered her. "Let's go upstairs."

"Cut," Dave called, "and print."

He was beaming as he approached his two lead actors. "That was great, absolutely great."

A makeup woman had brought Tracy a tissue, which she was holding to her cut lip. "It was certainly realistic," she said fervently. "You scared me half to death, Jon."

He still wore the look he had worn while shooting the scene. His voice was harsh as he answered, "I'm sorry I cut your lip. I didn't mean to."

"The cut lip is great," Dave enthused. He rubbed his hands together. "The first shedding of Julia's blood." He clapped Jon on the back and turned to Tracy. "You were marvelous, Tracy—innocent yet very sexy. Okay. Let's do it again."

As soon as he finished speaking, the rain began to fall. Tracy was relieved that she wasn't going to have to redo the scene. She did not want ever again to feel herself locked in Jon's steel-like embrace or be the subject of his ravishing kiss. The experience had been both scary and deeply repulsive.

Greg came up with a large golf umbrella and held it over her while Dave complained. "Damn, damn, damn. If the first take doesn't come out, we're going to have to do it all over again."

"I'll bet the scene is great the way we shot it," Tracy said.

Dave sighed. "I'll have to wait until I see the rushes tomorrow. This was the last scene in the garden. We're supposed to start filming in the house next." He sighed again. "Well, the rain has finished us out here. At least that will give us more time to get the house ready to begin filming there."

The rain was drumming hard on Tracy's umbrella. "What about the actors, Dave? Are we free for the afternoon?"

"Yes," Dave said. "But be ready to be called tomorrow. If I see a problem with today's filming when I view the rushes, I'll want to refilm the scene."

16

Gail was on the phone in the trailer when Tracy got back. She gave her secretary a brief wave, sat at her dressing table, and began to cream her face, all the while listening to Gail's half of the conversation.

"I don't see how Tracy is to do the *Letterman Show* when she's still filming in England, Mel," Gail said in a reasonable tone.

Tracy swung around in her chair and mouthed the words *NO LETTERMAN* at Gail. She hated to do the *Letterman Show*. He kept the temperature in his studio at a few degrees above freezing, which would have been okay if she could have worn wool slacks, a sweater, and long underwear. But the studio insisted that she look glamorous, which translated to "bare a lot of flesh," and the two times she had done the show she had frozen.

Still speaking reasonably, Gail said, "Yes, I know she has a film coming out at the end of June, and yes, I know that the studio expects her to promote it. But she can't be in two places at one time, Mel." Gail rolled her eyes at Tracy as she listened to Mel's reply. Then she put her hand over the mouthpiece, and said, "He wants you to fly to New York, do the show, and fly back to England the next day."

Tracy held out her hand. "Give me that phone."

Gail complied.

"Mel?" Tracy said. "Have you lost your mind? I am not crossing the Atlantic twice in two days!"

The reply came over the wire from California, "You can take the Concorde, babe."

"No, I cannot take the Concorde. The whole idea is ridiculous."

"Tracy." She always knew Mel was annoyed when he called her Tracy and not babe. "The studio expects you to promote this film. They expect it to be one of the blockbusters of the summer and, as its star, you have to do your part to publicize it."

"I know that, Mel." Her voice was steely. "And I will do *Leno* when I get back home. But I am not flying in and out to do the *Letterman Show*, which I hate."

"He has a lot of power."

"Screw his power," Tracy said. "And screw you, too, Mel."

Mel sighed. "All right. I'll beg off *Letterman*."

"Thank you."

"There's going to be some publicity about you coming from another source anyway. What's going on between you and the Earl of Silverbridge?"

"*What?*"

"I got a call from someone at the *Examiner*. Evidently Jason Counes has contacted them about some pictures with you and His Lordship. Kissing."

"Oh my God," Tracy moaned. "I thought Harry got those pictures away from him!"

"Aha! Then you *were* kissing Silverbridge!"

"Mel," Tracy said dangerously, "Jason Counes does not have any pictures. Lord Silverbridge took his camera away from him."

"He may have taken the camera, but Counes unloaded the film first."

"Shit," said Tracy.

Mel laughed.

"It's not funny! Lord Silverbridge will be horrified to find himself in a scandal sheet."

"It won't be the first time it's happened to him, babe," Mel replied. "And the publicity won't hurt you at all. An earl. My, my, my."

Tracy said tensely, "Can you contact Counes and buy the pictures from him?"

"Not likely. And if I do, he'll only give the *Examiner* a story about our buying the pictures. Or give me the negatives after he's had them copied."

There were tears of frustration and anger in Tracy's eyes. "There must be *something* we can do."

"Just ride out the storm, babe. Just ride out the storm."

"Thanks, you're a great help." She slammed the phone down, pulled the wide elastic band off her hair, and threw it across the room.

Gail looked at her in concern. Tracy had a temper, but it usually blew over quickly and never manifested itself in a physical way. Then Tracy turned back to her dressing table and lowered her face into her hands. "God," she said in muffled tones. "How am I going to tell Harry he is about to be featured in one of the worst newspapers in America?"

While Tracy was on the phone with Mel, Harry was approaching the outskirts of Warkfield with Meg in the car seat beside him. He was taking her to her appointment with Beth Carmichael, her therapist.

Meg was silent, but Harry scarcely noticed. He was too busy replaying in his mind his meeting with Tracy in the morning room the night before.

I insulted her, he thought. *She didn't like the way I looked at her.*

Harry was having an increasingly difficult time fitting Tracy into the category he had established for her in his mind. He was trying very hard to see her as a movie star, but the more time he spent with her, the more difficult it became for him to see her as anything but Tracy.

No other woman had had the impact upon him physically that she had. And there was something about her personality, an underlying sweetness all the trappings of Hollywood could not disguise, that stirred him enormously.

They had reached the top of the hill that led down into the town of Warkfield, and Harry glanced over at Meg. She smiled at him and he felt the protectiveness that she always evoked in him awake. She looked so terribly fragile.

"It's going well with Beth?" he asked.

She nodded. "I think so."

The car was gathering speed on the steep hill, and Harry put his foot on the brakes to slow it. His foot went right to the floor.

In the flash of a second, the situation presented itself to him. There was a line of cars at the bottom of the hill, waiting for the light to change, Meg was in the seat beside him, and he had no brakes.

"Meggie," he said, using the same tone of voice with which his ancestors had ordered men into battle. "Get into the backseat and put on the seat belt. Fast!"

Like a good soldier, Meg responded to his command and climbed over the seat into the back. "Okay!" she said. He put the car into a lower gear to slow it, and it did slow at first. But then it bucked and swerved and headed toward a truck that was parked next to the curb. Harry fought the steering wheel but could not get control of the car. His last thought before they crashed was, *Tracy.*

He woke up in the hospital with an IV in his arm, a bandage on his head, and a skull-splitting headache.

"What happened?" he asked the nurse who was doing something with the IV. His voice came out like a croak.

"You were in a car accident, my lord," she said soothingly. "You've a bad concussion, but you're going to be fine."

He had no memory of the crash. "Was I alone?"

"Lady Margaret was with you, my lord."

Christ. "Is she all right?"

"She is fine. In fact, she has been waiting for you to wake up so she can see you."

"Was anybody else hurt?"

"No, my lord, just you."

Well, that's something, he thought.

"My head hurts," he said.

"That's the concussion, my lord. The doctor wanted to know when you woke up, so I'll just go and get him, shall I?" She gave him a cheery smile and left the room.

Hell, Harry thought. *An auto accident. Why can't I remember?*

He was staring up at the ceiling, concentrating on enduring the pain in his head, when Meg appeared at his side. She was followed by Tracy.

Meg had initially tried to get hold of Tony, but hadn't been able to. Her next thought had been to try Tracy, and her call to Gail's cell phone had found Tracy in her dressing room taking off her makeup. Tracy had said she would come.

The twenty-minute ride to the hospital had been a nightmare for Tracy. She could not get out of her mind the words of Scotty's doctor when she had got to the hospital. *I'm so sorry, Mrs. Collins, but the fire was too intense for anyone to get to him.*

Harry can't be dead. She said it like a mantra the whole time she was parking the car and running to the hospital door. *Harry can't be dead. God wouldn't do this to me again. Harry can't be dead.*

A hospital administrator met her in the lobby and her first words were, "Is he alive?"

"Oh yes, Miss Collins, it's not as bad as that," the gray-suited man replied reassuringly.

She shut her eyes. *Thank you, God. Oh thank you, God.*

They had put Meg in a private waiting room, and when Tracy came in she jumped up and ran to her. "Tracy! Thank God you've come. I can't find out anything about Harry. They took him away as soon as the ambulance got to hospital. They finished checking me out an hour ago, but no one's told me anything about Harry!"

There were shadows like bruises under Meg's blue eyes. She looked incredibly fragile.

"Let's sit down, and you can tell me exactly what happened." Tracy said steadily. Meg followed her to the sofa, sat a trifle awkwardly, and recounted the whole ordeal, from the failing of the brakes to the crash.

"I . . . I think Harry hit his head on the steering wheel." Meg began to cry. "It was so scary. Harry was unconscious, and I thought I should get him out of the car in case it went on fire, but I couldn't budge him from behind the wheel. Then some men came running, and they did get him out. Then the ambulance came and brought us here."

At the mention of fire, Tracy felt sick to her stomach. She said unsteadily, "Did Harry wake up in the ambulance?"

"N . . . no," Meg said. Her tears were coming faster.

"They wheeled him away, and no one's told me what's happening."

"I'll go and find out right now," Tracy said. Then she reached out and put her hand on Meg's knee. "How about you, Meggie? Are you all right?"

"I have some bruised ribs from the seat belt, but otherwise I'm fine."

Tracy stood up. "Okay. Wait here."

She went to the nurses' station and, after a minute or two returned to tell Meg, "The doctor is coming to talk to us. Harry's conscious, Meg, so that's good news."

"Is he badly hurt?"

"I don't know the extent of his injuries. We'll have to wait for the doctor."

They had barely reestablished themselves upon the sofa before the door opened to admit a tall, rangy, middle-aged man with gray hair and washed-out blue eyes. He looked at Meg, and said immediately, "His Lordship is going to be fine, Lady Margaret. He has a concussion, and we want to keep him overnight, but nothing appears to be broken."

At this good news, Meg once more began to sob. "Oh thank God, thank God."

Tracy said, "I am Tracy Collins, Doctor, and I'm a friend of His Lordship. Is it possible for us to see him?"

The doctor nodded his stately gray head. "Certainly. As I said before, he has a concussion and should be quiet, so I would ask you not to stay for too long."

"I understand."

The three of them walked along a confusing maze of corridors until finally the doctor stopped outside a numbered door. "He's in here. I'll send a nurse to fetch you if you're too long."

Tracy nodded that she understood and motioned for Meg to precede her into the room. She waited until she heard Harry's voice before she herself slipped inside.

He had an IV in his arm and a bandage on his forehead and his eyes looked almost black in the pallor of his face. Meg was standing beside his bed saying, "*I'm* fine. It's you who are hurt, Harry."

"It's just a little bump on the head," he replied soothingly, and then he noticed that Tracy had come into the room. His concussion-dilated eyes met hers, and he said her name. He did not seem surprised to see her.

Her heart turned over in her breast. She walked to the bed and had to forcibly restrain herself from touching his hair. "Meg said your brakes failed."

"Yes." He frowned, and said fretfully, "I can't remember a damn thing, though."

Meg, who was standing on the opposite side of the bed from Tracy, said tearfully, "You made me get into the backseat, Harry. You saved my life. The f . . . front seat where I was s . . . sitting took the worst part of the crash."

Slowly he turned his eyes from Tracy to his sister. "You're sure you weren't hurt?"

"Just some bruised ribs from the seat belt."

He let out a slow careful breath. He had not yet moved his head. "Have you contacted Tony?" he asked his sister.

"No." Meg fished a tissue from her pocket and blew

her nose. "I called the house, but he wasn't there. So I called Tracy, and she came."

The dilated black eyes looked back at Tracy. "Thank you."

Tracy said, "If you don't mind, I'd like to find out where they took your car. I think a mechanic should go over it to see why the brakes failed."

His face didn't change. "Get Ian Poole to look at it. Meggie will give you his number."

Their eyes locked, and Tracy felt the connection between them so strongly that the sensation was almost physical.

"Don't worry," she said, answering what she was certain were his two main concerns. "I'll take care of Meg, and I'll get the car looked at. You, in the meanwhile, need to rest."

As if on cue, a nurse appeared at the doorway to announce bossily, "I'm afraid it's time for you to leave. His Lordship needs quiet."

"Good-bye, Harry," Meg said, bending down to give her brother a kiss on his cheek. "I'm so sorry that you're hurt."

"Get Tony to take you to see Beth tomorrow," he ordered. "I don't want you to fall into a funk about this, Meggie. It won't be good for your health."

She scowled. "I'll be fine."

"Promise me you will go to see Beth," he said.

She gave a loud, elaborate sigh. "Oh, all right. I'll go and see her. But I'm okay, really."

He nodded, and a deep line appeared between his brows, as if the slight movement had produced pain.

Tracy, abruptly deciding that she didn't care what

he would think, bent down and lightly kissed his hair above the bandage. It felt thick and soft under her lips.

And then the nurse was ushering her out the door.

$\mathcal{I}$t was when Meg winced as she got into the front seat of the Mercedes that Tracy realized she was in pain. "Are you certain you didn't break anything?"

"Yes. They took X rays."

Privately, Tracy thought it was a miracle that those fragile bones hadn't snapped right in two. "You were lucky," she said out loud.

Meg sniffled. "I keep thinking that if I hadn't been there, Harry could have put the car in low gear even sooner. He waited to make sure I was in the backseat."

Tracy had turned the engine on, but instead of driving off, she rested her arm along the back of the seat and looked at Meg. "Your life is very important to him. I think he demonstrated very clearly today just how much he loves you. And I think you owe it to him to try to get better."

Without waiting for an answer, she put both hands on the wheel and began to back out of the parking space.

Silence reigned as Tracy drove away from the hospital through the slanting rain. Then Meg said in a low voice, "What are you going to do about the car?"

"Find out from the police where it was taken and get it to this Ian Poole. Where can I find him?"

"Poole Garage is in Silverbridge village. Harry and Ian Poole are friends. Ian always looks after our cars."

"Then, when we get back to the house, I'll find out where the car is and call and ask Ian Poole to examine it. If he's the one who's supposedly taking care of it, I imagine he'd like to know how the brakes came to fail so catastrophically."

"It's an old car," Meg said. "Tony is always after Harry to get a new one."

"It's not *that* old, and it's a Mercedes. If it was properly looked after, the brakes shouldn't go like that."

"Well," Meg said, "they did."

"True." Tracy smiled reassuringly. "And we must be grateful that neither you nor Harry was seriously injured."

Meg said gloomily, "Now Harry *will* have to buy a new car, and that's an expense he wasn't counting on. I should have got Mrs. Wilson to drive me to see Beth."

"Meg, this accident was not your fault! If there was something wrong with the brakes, they would have failed the next time Harry took the car out, no matter where he was going and who he was with. And the resulting accident could have been much worse—perhaps even fatal. Please don't try to take the blame for this."

"I just feel guilty," Meg said in a small voice.

Tracy's own voice softened. "I know, and you have to try to overcome that feeling if you want to get better. You are a lovely young woman, and your brother was willing to risk his life for you because he loves you. And he loves you because you are worth loving. The accident happened because the brakes failed, not because of anything you did. Keep telling yourself that, Meggie, because it's true."

In the same small voice, Meg replied, "I'll try."

When Tracy and Meg arrived back at Silverbridge it was to find the first floor of the mansion overrun by movie people. Scaffolding was being erected, and lights and cameras were being positioned. Meg was intrigued by the transformation and went to take a look around all of the rooms while Tracy went upstairs to use the telephone. She had just finished making arrangements with Ian Poole to have Harry's car towed to his garage, when Tony came in.

He smiled at Tracy. She had not turned on any lamps and, with his silver-blond hair, his golden tan, and his drop-dead good looks, he looked like a ray of sunshine in the gloomy morning room. "Were you washed out of your shoot?" he asked.

"We got one print in before the rains came," she replied. She replaced the phone book she had been using in a drawer of the antique French desk upon which the telephone stood. "Have you heard about the accident?"

His blue eyes clouded slightly. "Accident? What accident?"

"Harry and Meg were in a car crash this afternoon."

She could have sworn his surprise and concern were genuine. "Are they hurt?"

"Harry's in the hospital with a concussion, and Meg has some bruised ribs."

"My God." He took a few steps closer to her. "What happened?"

As Tracy recounted the scenario of Harry's accident, she watched Tony's face. Nothing on that perfect facade seemed amiss. He looked genuinely concerned, and the questions he asked were legitimate and intelligent.

Finally, "I don't know why Harry insisted on hanging on to that ancient car," he said with exasperation.

"Meg says he doesn't have the money to buy a new one," Tracy replied.

"Meg may buy that story, but I don't. He always has the money to buy a new horse." His lips set into a hard line, and for a brief moment he resembled his brother. "If he would only be sensible and take Robin Mauley's offer, he would have enough money to buy himself a dozen horses and a brand-new car as well!"

Tracy watched carefully as she said, "He wants to keep his land."

"I know." An expression of contempt flitted across Tony's perfectly tanned face. "Harry is an anachronism. He still thinks land is important. Well, it's not. The house is but the acreage is negligible. The days of the great land-owning aristocrat are long over—Harry just hasn't tumbled to that fact yet."

Before Tracy could form a reply, Meg came into the room. "Tony!" she cried. "Did Tracy tell you about the accident?"

He turned to her. "Yes, she did. Poor little Meggie. How are your ribs feeling?"

"They hurt, but I don't think they hurt as much as Harry's head. He looked white as a sheet, Tony."

Tony did not look overly worried. "He'll be fine, Meggie. Harry has a hard head." There was a moment of silence before he added sardonically, "As I have discovered many times, to my sorrow."

"Tracy's having the car checked by Ian Poole to see why the brakes failed," Meg said.

No trace of alarm showed in Tony's bearing. Instead he raised his brows, and asked Tracy, "Is that useful? After all, Ian is the one who maintained the car. If he didn't pick up that the brakes needed replacing, he's hardly going to come out and blame himself."

Tracy had thought of that, but she was willing to bet that Ian Poole wasn't to blame for Harry's accident. "We'll wait and see what he has to say."

Tony shrugged. "Suit yourself." And he exited gracefully in the direction of his room.

17

$\mathcal{H}$arry's head still ached when he awoke the following morning, although the ringing in his ears had subsided somewhat. He drank some tea for breakfast but refused the food. All he wanted was to get out of the hospital.

"The doctor will be in shortly, Your Lordship," the nurse told him. "In the meanwhile, it will be best for you to remain quiet."

Harry bit back a sarcastic reply. *She's only doing her job. Be patient.* Out loud he said, "Is this telephone hooked up?"

"Yes, my lord, it is."

"Good. I have a call to make."

The expression on the thin, middle-aged face of the nurse said clearly that she did not approve. Rank had its advantages, however, and she didn't quite have the nerve to tell the Earl of Silverbridge that he couldn't use the telephone.

Harry had a difficult time reading the numbers on the phone. They didn't seem to be staying still and had an annoying habit of dissolving as he tried to focus on them. Eventually, however, he managed to dial the number he wanted. The phone was picked up on the fourth ring.

"Hello," Harry said. "This is Silverbridge. Is Ian there?"

A young male voice answered, "Yes, my lord. I'll fetch him right away."

Ian must have been under a car or something because it took him almost five minutes to get to the phone. When Harry heard his familiar voice, he closed his eyes. He had to know what had happened to the car, but he was afraid to hear it. "Did you get a chance to look at the car, Ian?" he asked steadily.

"I did," the mechanic said. "That was no accident, Harry. The brake lines were cut."

Why am I not surprised?

"How can you be sure?"

"First of all, I maintained that car, and I would have noticed if the brake lines were wearing. Second, they weren't shredded and frayed, the way they would have been through natural deterioration. The cuts were clean, as if done with a knife. I expect whoever did this didn't slice all the way through, just enough to ensure that the lines would eventually blow when you applied the brakes."

Harry's headache seemed to have doubled in intensity. "I see."

"What do you want me to do?"

He breathed carefully in and out. "At the moment,

nothing. This is something I'm going to have to take care of myself."

Ian was doubtful. "Are you sure? It looks to me as if someone just tried to kill you."

"I'll take care of it," Harry repeated. "How about the car, Ian? Is it salvageable?"

"No, I'm afraid it's not. The cost of repairing it wouldn't be worth the money."

"That's what I was afraid of," Harry replied gloomily.

After another brief exchange, he rang off, rested his aching head against his pillow, stared at a long crack in the ceiling, and thought about his situation. Someone had burned down his stable, and someone had cut the brake lines on his car. The probability was that the same person was responsible for both acts of sabotage. It was hard enough to imagine that he had one enemy, let alone two.

It must be connected to the sale of the land, he thought. *First Mauley had the stable burned down, so that I would need money immediately. Then, when that didn't work, he tried to do away with me altogether. If I die, Tony will be the earl, and Tony would sell the land to Mauley in a shot.*

It was hard to believe that a reputable real estate magnate such as Robin Mauley would go to such drastic lengths to get his hands on Silverbridge land. But Harry couldn't think of any other motive for the acts of sabotage that had occurred within two days of each other. At that moment, the partially closed door to his room was pushed open, and Tracy walked in. Harry's heart lifted as he looked at her. Once more he felt the feather-light touch of her lips on his hair last night.

He frowned, and said gruffly, "What are you doing here?"

"I dropped Meg at her therapist and thought I'd kill the hour by checking on you. How are you feeling this morning?"

She was dressed in jeans, boots, and a blue sweater, her hair was floating around her shoulders, and Harry thought she was the most beautiful sight he had ever beheld. He said, "I'm all right. Why aren't you filming?"

"The set won't be ready until this afternoon, so I volunteered to drive Meg. Tony had a meeting of some sort to go to."

This was excellent news. "Then I'll catch a ride home with you, if you don't mind. I'd rather not wait for Tony."

She frowned. "You look dreadful. You belong in the hospital for at least another day."

It was nice to have her worry about him. "I have a headache, that's all. I can recuperate at home just as well as I can in hospital."

There was a little silence as she looked at him. "Perhaps you can recuperate," she said somberly, "but will you be safe?"

He didn't want to answer that.

She wouldn't let it drop. "I had Ian Poole go over the car. Have you heard anything from him yet?"

He debated about how he should answer, and said reluctantly, "I talked to him just a few minutes ago."

"What did he say?"

A muscle tightened in his jaw. "He said that it looked like the brake lines had been cut."

"Oh, my God." She had gone very pale.

"Perhaps you really did see someone prowling around the other night," he said.

Her eyes flashed. "I told you that I did, but you thought I was making it up."

"I'm sorry, Tracy. And I'm sorry I was so rude that night."

She looked at him with uncertainty. His head was killing him, and all he wanted was to kiss her.

"You and I got off on the wrong foot," he said seriously. "Do you think we could start again?"

She looked at him searchingly, then said, "I'm willing if you are."

A brisk voice said, "Good morning, my lord. How are we feeling today?"

It was a different doctor from the previous night, and Harry replied evenly, "*We* are feeling quite well, thank you. We have a slight headache but no ringing in our ears."

Tracy stifled a giggle.

The new doctor, who was as portly and short as the one last night had been tall and elegant, came over to look in his eyes with a pencil light. "Still some dilation," he said. "Now, if you would allow me to check your blood pressure, my lord?"

He wrapped the cuff around Harry's arm and pumped. "Hmmm," he said as he read the dial.

Harry said crisply, "I'm sure my blood pressure is all right. It always is. I wish to check out of hospital as soon as possible and go home. Would you please arrange matters for me?"

Centuries of command sounded in his voice, and the doctor responded as Harry had expected. "If you insist, my lord. It is very important for you to remain quiet, however. A concussion is a serious matter."

"Yes, yes, I understand." Evidently his irritable reply did not reassure either the doctor or Tracy, because they both frowned at him. He offered a huge concession: "I will keep to the house for the rest of the day."

"You will keep to your bed for the rest of today, and for tomorrow as well, my lord," the doctor said.

"Oh, all right," he replied, having no intention of doing as instructed. "Just get me out of this place. I don't like the smell in here."

The doctor looked affronted. "This hospital is very clean, my lord."

"I know. It's the smell of all the cleaning agents that puts me off."

Tracy smothered a smile, and said severely, "Behave yourself, my lord." She turned to the doctor. "Are you certain it's wise to release Lord Silverbridge? As you just said, a concussion is a serious matter."

Harry scowled. *Whose side is she on here?*

"I own, I would prefer him to remain," the doctor said.

Harry said, his voice very clipped, "I am not staying in hospital. And I want my clothes. Now, if you please."

"Very well, my lord, if you insist," the doctor said reluctantly. "I'll have a nurse bring your things." He went out.

Tracy said, "I think this is a mistake."

He said huffily, "I think I am the best judge of how I feel."

The nurse came in the door with his clothes.

Half an hour later, Harry was installed in the front

seat of Gail's rented Mercedes. He was feeling extremely seedy, which he endeavored to hide from Tracy.

"We have to pick up Meg," she said.

"Yes, I know."

"You should have stayed in the hospital. You look
awful."

He felt awful, which made him angry. "When I want
your opinion, I'll ask for it."

Her mouth tightened but she did not reply. He
watched as she drove through the narrow city streets
and approved of the way she handled a car. When she
pulled up in front of a red brick Georgian-style building,
Meg came running from the porch. "Harry!" she said
when she saw who was sitting in the front seat. "How
super. Are you feeling okay?"

"I am perfectly fine," he answered over the pounding
in his head.

Tracy said calmly, "Your brother is miserable, Meg,
but he insisted upon leaving the hospital. As soon as he
gets home he is getting into his own bed and staying
there for the rest of the day."

"Bossy little thing, aren't you?" he muttered.

"You don't know the half of it," she replied.

He thought of a few things to say to put her in her
place, but felt too rotten to make the attempt.

By the time they reached Silverbridge, he was extremely grateful to crawl into his own bed.

The film company was to shoot a scene in the staircase hall that afternoon, and Tracy had to rush to
makeup as soon as she returned to Silverbridge. Finally,

dressed in costume and made up correctly, she joined
Jon in the front hallway to wait while the lighting crew
put the finishing touches to the set.

Jon glanced at her. "I looked for you earlier."

"I drove Meg into Warkfield this morning."

He shifted on his feet. "I heard that she and Silverbridge were in an accident yesterday. Is she all right?"

"Yes. He had to spend the night in the hospital, but
we brought him back with us today."

There was a brief silence, then Jon said quietly, "I
don't mean to intrude into your business, Tracy, but I
like you very much, and I would hate to see you hurt."

Tracy felt herself stiffen. "Thank you, Jon, but I am
not going to get hurt."

"It seems to me that you may be falling for Silverbridge," he continued, his expression very grave, "and
that's a mistake."

She started to deny any feelings for Harry, then
changed her mind and asked, "Why?"

One of the lighting crew shouted, "Move that spot six
inches to the left."

"He's like the rest of the aristocracy," Jon said bitterly. "He does what he wants and be damned to anyone
else. Take the Dana Matthews case, for example. She
committed suicide because of him."

Tracy thought that she was seeing firsthand an example of the caste system she had spoken about to Gail.
Jon obviously disliked Harry because he was upper-
class. She said quietly, "Dana was a drug addict, Jon.
She overdosed."

"She overdosed and then she called him for help and
he refused to come to her. It was in all the papers."

That can't be true, she thought.

"Look," Jon went on, "I don't give a damn about Silverbridge, but I do give a damn about you. Just be careful with him, will you? Don't let your heart get involved."

It's too late for a warning, Jon, Tracy thought. She looked around the lovely room in which they stood. *Perhaps it was always too late.*

"I'll keep your words in mind," she said.

He nodded. "Good."

"That's it everybody," the lighting gaffer called. "We're ready to go."

"Excellent," Dave said.

"Actors on the set," Greg called, and Tracy and Jon went to take their places.

When the afternoon's filming was done, Tracy went to have dinner with the crew, her mind unpleasantly preoccupied with what Jon had told her.

Why didn't Harry go to her?

The question haunted her mind the entire time she and Jon were eating dinner with the rest of the film crew in the catering bus. She was quiet enough to draw a remark from Liza Moran.

"Cat got your tongue, Tracy?" the older actress asked in an acid tone.

Tracy had little use for Liza Moran. The woman had the inclinations and morals of a bitch in heat, and more than once the rest of them had been kept waiting because Liza was shacked up with some man and no one could find her. Sally Walsh, the associate producer, was taking bets that Liza would get through every capable man on the set by the time the filming ended.

Tracy replied, "No. It's perfectly intact. Would you care to see it?"

"I think I can manage to live without a view of your tongue," Liza said in the same acid voice as before.

"Really?" Tracy's voice was sweet. "You're always so interested in me and in everything I do, that I thought perhaps you'd be interested in my tongue as well."

Several people at the table laughed. Liza had been trying to discompose Tracy ever since the filming started, and so far Tracy had got the best of her every time.

Tactfully, Jon began to talk to Tracy about a review he had seen of a new London play in the *Times* that morning. He had an amusing story to tell about one of the stars of the play, and Tracy dutifully laughed in response, but her heart wasn't in it.

They didn't finish filming until eleven and, when Tracy was finally free, she went up the main staircase in order to cut through the upstairs drawing room to the family apartment. She was exhausted and depressed and thinking about bed and not ghosts when she pushed open the drawing room door and stepped inside.

The room was in deep shadow, except for a single candle burning on one of the Chippendale side tables. It was a moment before Tracy's eyes adjusted and she saw the couple seated together in the Queen Anne wing chair next to the table with the candle. Charles was still dressed in his dinner clothes, but Isabel wore a blue velvet robe and bedroom slippers. Her long auburn hair was tied back with a ribbon, as if that was how she wore it to bed. She was sitting on his lap, with her cheek buried in his shoulder. His hand was gently stroking the hair away from her brow.

"Caroline has a perfect right to want me gone," she said in a voice that ached with unshed tears. "It isn't fair to be angry with her, Charles."

"Perhaps not." His curt tone dismissed Caroline. "Perhaps she has even done me a favor by forcing my hand." For a moment his hand gently cupped the back of her head, commanding attention. "Now listen closely, love. This is what we are going to do. I sent Rupert to Southampton this afternoon to buy you a ticket on a ship to Boston. I have a family connection there with whom you can stay while you wait for me to join you."

At that, she straightened up and looked into his face. "No, Charles. I will go to America if that is what you want, but your place is here." Her husky voice sounded very firm. "I won't take you away from your home and your family."

There was a long silence as their eyes held. Tracy stood so quietly that she scarcely breathed. At last he said, "I am not a sentimental man, Isabel. Don't think that I am making some grand, unthinking, romantic gesture that I will one day come to regret. It's quite the contrary, in fact. I am ruthlessly putting my own personal happiness above my home and my family. This is a deliberate choice, and one that you must allow me to make."

His voice was very quiet and very sober, and his dark eyes seemed to be boring into her soul. After a moment her neck bowed in surrender, like the graceful stem of a lily, and her head came to rest once more on his shoulder. He cupped her nape with his hand and said, "When I came back from the war and found you here . . . it was as if I had found a part of myself that had been missing all my life. I knew it immediately. Caroline, the children—they seemed like wraiths to me. All I could see was you."

Isabel's husky voice drifted to Tracy's ears. "I know. I felt the same way."

He rested his cheek against her hair. "When I am with you, I am at peace. If I let you go, I will never be at peace again."

The candlelight glittered on the signet ring he wore on his right hand. The ring looked familiar and Tracy abruptly realized that Harry wore that exact same ring.

Charles was going on in a ruminative voice, "Perhaps if I hadn't been to war and seen so many men die, I would be less ruthless. But I know how brief life can be, and I don't want to spend the rest of mine regretting your loss."

A draft caused the single candle to flicker momentarily, putting the couple in shadow, but then it steadied, and Tracy could see them again. Isabel said, "What about your children?"

His face took on what Tracy was beginning to think of as its commander in chief expression. "I will appoint my cousin George to act as trustee for William. George acted for me at Silverbridge during the war, and he knows the estate as well as I do. There will be ample money to take care of the boys and Caroline; they will lack for nothing."

His imperious tone made it clear that he considered

that particular subject closed. But Isabel wouldn't let it drop. "They will lack a father," she said softly.

His response was final. "They would lack a father even if I remained. My body might be here at Silverbridge, but my heart would be dead."

She raised her face, and for the first time Tracy saw the tears sparkling on her cheeks. "But Charles—what will you *do* in America? I simply cannot imagine you anywhere but here."

His reply was supremely confident. "I shall amass a fortune and build a magnificent home for you and for our children."

After a moment, she laughed shakily. "You probably will."

He smiled and ran a gentle finger down her nose. "Of course I will." His face sobered. "We may not be able to marry, Isabel. It will be up to Caroline to decide whether she wants to divorce me or not; I won't force that issue. But in a new country no one need know about my previous marital situation. There is no reason for you not to have all the respect and status due to my wife."

Again that note of confidence sounded clearly in his voice.

Isabel sighed. "I shouldn't let you do this, but I love you too much to stop you."

"You couldn't stop me, even if you wanted to," he replied with a trace of amusement.

She straightened away from him. "I could refuse to go to Boston. That would stop you."

His amusement deepened. "I'd kidnap you."

"You wouldn't dare," she returned snappily.

His kissed her forehead. "Let's not argue, my love.

We can't keep having midnight meetings like this, and I need to make certain that you understand what you are to do."

Her momentary indignation died. "I'm listening."

"I told my secretary to book you on a ship to Boston. I also gave him a letter to my cousin, Stephen Oliver, with instructions to send it on the next available ship going to America. Stephen should receive it before you arrive."

"Do you know this cousin, Charles?" Isabel asked in a muted voice.

The candlelight glimmered on his golden hair as he shook his head. "I have never met him. His branch of the family has been in America since before the colonies revolted. But he has a successful shipping business in Boston, and we have had cause to correspond on a number of occasions. I know he will keep you safely until such time as I can join you."

Worry was clearly visible on Isabel's face, but all she said was, "All right."

"Do not concern yourself about Stephen Oliver," Charles ordered. "I have further instructed Rupert to buy a ticket for himself so that he may accompany you to Boston. Once you have arrived in that city, he will open up a bank account for you, so you will not be dependent upon Stephen."

"You don't have to send poor Mr. Holt with me, Charles," Isabel protested. "I shall do perfectly fine on my own."

His face took on its commander in chief expression. "You are not traveling on a ship to America without an escort."

Evidently Isabel recognized that expression as well as Tracy, for she ceased to protest, and asked instead, "How long will it be before you can join me?"

"Two months, I should think. I have a great many legal ends to tie up here before I can get away."

She cupped his face in her hands and looked into his eyes. "Are you certain that you want to do this?"

His expression was perfectly sober as he replied, "More certain than I have been of anything in my life."

He pulled her close and buried his lips in her hair. Like a sleeper in a daze, Tracy walked quietly to the other door, let herself into the family apartment, and left them there, alone.

18

Tracy's mind was so agitated by what she had heard and seen that day that she didn't expect to get much sleep. In fact, her last though before she fell asleep was, *I'm going to be awake all night.*

The next thing she knew, it was morning.

She peeked through the narrow opening in Harry's door on her way down to breakfast and saw a heap of blankets from which protruded a tangle of tawny hair. Her fingers itched to smooth that hair away from his face, but the small black head that was resting on the pillow next to his clearly had other thoughts. Ebony's hostile green stare bore an unmistakable message: *Go away.*

Tracy went on down the stairs to the kitchen, where she was surprised to find Tony, dressed in another Savile Row suit with a gray silk tie, drinking coffee at the table. "You're up early," Tracy said.

"I have a breakfast appointment with a client," he

replied, politely standing as she came in. "But I simply cannot leave the house without a cup of coffee, so I made a pot. Help yourself."

"Thank you." Tracy poured herself some and leaned against the counter, her eyes on Tony, who had sat back down at the table. His blue eyes glimmered a little as he regarded her.

"Congratulations," he said. "It's quite a feat to appear *sans* makeup in the morning and still manage to look beautiful."

Tracy ignored the compliment, watched him closely, and said, "Did you know that someone tampered with the brakes on Harry's car? That's why they failed, and he had that horrible accident."

Tony's look of incredulity could not be faulted. "Someone tampered with the brakes? Are you sure, Tracy? Why on earth would anyone want to do such a thing?"

"I was hoping you might be able to answer that question."

His incredulity deepened. "Me? Why should you think that?"

"You're his brother."

"I'm his brother, not his keeper." His expression suddenly changed. "Who told you that the brakes were tampered with, anyway? Was it by any chance Ian Poole?"

Tracy took a swallow of coffee. "Yes."

Tony snorted. "Well, there you have it, then. Ian is covering his own backside. He's the one who maintained that car, and he obviously missed the fact that the brakes needed replacing. He's not about to admit that, however, so he came up with this story about the brakes being tampered with."

Tracy said steadily, "Harry believes him."

Another snort. "Of course he does. Ian is one of Harry's inner circle of magic friends who can do no wrong."

Tracy took another sip of coffee and regarded Tony over the rim of the cup. "The fire marshal thought that the stable fire had been set. Doesn't it seem a little odd that two suspicious 'accidents' should occur within such a short space of time?"

Tony wiped his mouth with a linen napkin. "The fire marshal's investigation has turned up no proof of arson. From what Harry told me, he based his suspicion on an empty kerosene can he found in the stable. I shouldn't be at all surprised if Ned Martin didn't have a small kerosene heater that he uses when he has to be in the stable at night. No doubt he, or somebody else, was careless, and the kerosene caught on fire."

"Harry said he doesn't allow any flammable liquid near the barn."

"He told that to the fire marshal, too." Tony put the napkin down on the table. "And Ned Martin is another one of Harry's inner circle, so it would never occur to my brother to question him. But the fire marshal could find nothing else to indicate that the fire had been deliberately set, and he has ruled it an accident."

Tony seemed to be sincere, but Tracy knew that a good actor could play any scene with conviction. She said, "You don't seem very impressed by your brother's friends."

Tony leaned back in his chair. "Loyalty is all very

well, but Harry carries it to extremes. And I question the wisdom of making friends outside one's class. People like Ian Poole and Ned Martin look at Harry as a source of income. The more they can get out of him, the better. He doesn't have enough money to buy a new car, but I know for a fact that he lent Ian the money to start his garage. And Ian has yet to pay him back."

There it was again, the class thing. Tracy said defensively, "I think loyalty and generosity are admirable qualities."

"Yes—in a dog!" Tony retorted. "A man should have more discrimination about whom he trusts. Please don't get me wrong, Miss Collins. I love Harry. It's because I love him that I hate to see him always scraping for money. If he would only sell Mauley the land, he would be fixed for life. And Silverbridge would still be one of the premier estates in the country. In fact, once Harry had the money to bring back the gardens and make the necessary repairs to the buildings, it would be one of the most beautiful homes in all of England."

"He likes farming, though," Tracy said. "If he sold all his farmland, he would be out of a job."

Something sparked in Tony's blue eyes. "You appear to understand him very well."

Tracy didn't know what to answer.

Tony grinned. "Well, good for Harry. You are a definite improvement on Dana Matthews. She had money, but she was nuts. And Harry's other serious girlfriend came from one of England's best families, but her father is even more broke than Harry. He came to his senses a month before the wedding and called it off. You, on the other hand, are beautiful, presentable, and rich. Perhaps Harry has finally got himself on track." He stood up.

Tracy wanted to smack him. "Do you mean to be insulting, or are you just dense?"

"And you're smart, too," Tony said approvingly. Don't get me wrong, Miss Collins. I'm in your corner all the way."

He crossed to the door but before he left he turned to say one more thing: "Try to persuade him to sell that property, will you?"

Then he was gone.

Harry arrived in the kitchen a half an hour after Tracy had gone. He still had a headache, but he had treated it with aspirin and thought that he would be all right as long as he didn't try to ride.

He was disappointed to have missed Tracy but surprised and pleased to find Meg in the kitchen when he came in. She was seated at the table with a bowl of cereal in front of her, and either she had only taken a small amount of cornflakes or she had actually eaten some.

"Good morning, my lord," Mrs. Wilson said after the dogs had given him a much noisier greeting. "Scrambled eggs, bacon, and fried tomato?"

It was his usual breakfast, but for some reason his stomach rejected the idea of all that food. "No thanks, Mrs. Wilson. I'll just have some toast."

"You look awfully pale, Harry," Meg said. "Are you sure you're well enough to get up?"

"I'm fine," he replied.

She gave him a skeptical look but said nothing. Instead she dipped her spoon into her cereal, filled it with cornflakes, and ate them.

Thank you, God, Harry thought.

"You don't have to look at me like that," Meg said.

Mrs. Wilson brought him a cup of coffee, and he joined Meg at the table. Instead of returning to their sofa, Marshal and Millie sat on either side of him, ears lifted expectantly.

Mrs. Wilson brought a plate of cinnamon raisin toast to the table, and Harry gave half a slice to each of the spaniels.

"You spoil those dogs something fierce, my lord," Mrs. Wilson said.

"A child or an animal that isn't spoiled isn't loved," Harry returned peaceably, and took a bite of the toast he had left.

"*I* wasn't spoiled," Meg said defiantly.

Harry looked at his sister's set face and felt a pain in his heart. "I spoil you," he said. "Look at how I'm letting you lie about, no school, no job. All you do all day is watch the movie being filmed. If that isn't spoiling you, I don't know what is."

"I'm sick, that's why I'm not in school," Meg shot back. "No school will take me. They're all afraid I'm going to die."

She looked so fragile in her brave blue sweater. He reached out and took her hand. It was like holding a bundle of bones. "Don't die, Meggie. It would break my heart to lose you. I'm sorry that I didn't pay more attention to you when you were little. But I love you, and I want you to get better."

Meg had dropped her eyes when he said he was sorry, but she raised them again when he had finished speaking and gave him such a timid, hopeful look that it made him feel like crying. "Do you really love me, Harry?"

He raised her hand to his lips and kissed it. "I love you very much. You're my sister, Meg. I would do anything in the world to help you."

She said, "Would you come with me today to watch the filming?"

He had a million things he needed to do and another million things that he wanted to do. He looked into her hopeful eyes, and said, "Of course I will."

The lighting and set crews were setting up in the drawing room and wouldn't be ready to film until after lunch, so Harry used the time to go down to the stables. A sense of familiar contentment came over him as he came into view of the horses turned out in their paddocks. Pendleton had seen him coming and was waiting at the fence for his usual tribute. Harry produced the expected sugar cube from his pocket, rubbed his horse's forehead, straightened his forelock, and proceeded to the riding ring, where Ned was riding Lady Anisdale's mare, Marita.

Marita was a three-day-event horse that Maria Anisdale had sent to Harry for training. The mare did very well in the cross-country and stadium-jumping components of the event, but she had been losing points on the dressage test.

He stood for a few moments in silence, watching as the mare cantered a twenty-meter circle. "Bring her shoulders in a little more," he said, then watched in silence once again. "She's looking much better," he said at last. "She's really reaching under with that inside leg."

Ned brought the mare down to a trot and then to a walk. He stopped in front of Harry, who bestowed a pat on Marita's sweaty chestnut neck, and said, "She's leaving next week, so that will be one less horse for us to worry about."

Ned unbuckled his helmet and took it off, baring his curly brown head to the cloudy sky. "Have you spoken to the insurance company?"

"Yes," Harry replied, his voice more clipped than usual, "and they are going to drag their heels because the fire may have been arson. In fact, I got the distinct impression that they thought I might have set it myself."

"That's just ridiculous," Ned said heatedly. "Why would you burn down your own stable, a listed historic building?"

"An excellent question and one that I have charged my solicitor to bring up with the insurance company. I don't have the patience to deal with them. The fellow I talked to on the phone made me so angry that I hung up on him."

Ned grinned. "Better to hang up than to tell them what you think of them." He swung down from the saddle. "It will work out, Harry." He regarded his employer with concern. "How are you feeling? Are you sure you shouldn't stay in bed? I heard you had a bad concussion." His hazel eyes narrowed as he assessed Harry's face. "You're much too pale."

Harry scowled. "I'm all right."

Inside the ring, Ned began to lead the mare in a ten-meter circle to cool her down. Harry rested his arms on the fence, and said calmly, "Ian Poole told me that the accident happened because someone cut my brake lines."

Ned stopped in his tracks, and the mare stopped with him. "Are you serious?"

"Ian was quite serious. There's no doubt about it, apparently. The car was in for work three weeks ago and Ian checked the brakes and they were fine. He also said that he looked at them after the accident and they weren't frayed, as they would have been from wear. They were cut quite cleanly."

"My God." Marita nudged Ned's shoulder and he ignored her. "Have you told the police?"

"Not yet."

"You have to tell them, Harry. It sounds as if someone is out to get you." He pushed a curling lock of hair off his forehead. "But *who?*" He shook his head in bewilderment. "You don't have enemies. I don't get it."

Harry said jokingly, "I can't even suspect any of my competitors. They all know that I am retiring Pendleton and that I'm out of competition until another of my horses moves to Grand Prix."

"It's not funny, Harry!" Ned exploded. "You've got to do something. You just can't sit around waiting for this maniac to strike again."

The mare blew impatiently out her nose, and Ned began to walk her in a circle once again.

Harry said, "What do you suggest I do?"

"Go to the police," Ned replied promptly.

Harry's negative headshake was firm. "The police will be as clueless as we are. In fact, if they're brought in, they might just scare the bastard away." His face hardened. "I don't want that. I want to find out who burned my stable. And I *will* find out, Ned. I swear it."

Ned said in a strange voice, "Surely the attack on your life is more important than the attack on the stable."

Harry made an impatient gesture. "I want you to be extra vigilant, Ned. The horses may be the next targets."

"All right. I'll sleep downstairs, where they are stabled."

"Keep your hunting rifle by you."

The two men looked at each other. "Jesus, Harry, I can't believe this is happening. With all the bastards in the world, why would someone want to pick on you?"

Because I own Silverbridge and someone else wants it.

He didn't say the words, however. He had no proof of anything, only a suspicion. He contented himself by repeating, "I don't know, Ned, but I am damn well going to find out."

19

Meg wanted Harry to have lunch with the crew in the catering truck. "It's fun, Harry," she said as she met him on the front lawn. "You should make an effort to meet these people. You don't want them to think you're a snob, do you?"

He had absolutely no interest in what the film people thought of him, but he did care about his sister. "I'll eat if you promise you'll eat something, too," he said.

"Done!"

"And I don't just mean a half a cup of soup, Meg. I mean something substantial."

Her eyes sparked with anger. "What do you mean by substantial? I'm not eating red meat!"

"I don't care what you eat: pasta, a sandwich, chicken salad . . . so long as it's solid food. Do we have a deal?"

"That's blackmail," she protested.

He touched her nose and smiled. "I know."

Reluctantly, she smiled back. "Okay, we have a deal."

Harry hoped fervently that Tracy would be at lunch. If he could look at her, talk to her, then having to be polite to a group of people he didn't know wouldn't seem quite so horribly tedious.

His eyes found her the moment he stepped into the bus carrying his plate of food. *It's like a magnet finding true north,* he thought wryly. She couldn't be anywhere within his vicinity without his knowing it immediately.

"Hi, everybody," Meg said. "This is my brother Lord Silverbridge. He's come to join us for lunch today."

The look she gave him was so full of happiness and pride that he was determined to be as charming as he knew how to be. He smiled at the faces around the table, and said, with just the right touch of deprecation, "Hello. I'm sorry I've been so busy lately that I haven't had a chance to stop by and meet you."

A jumble of voices answered, "Glad to have you, my lord," and "Welcome to the crazy house," along with an assortment of other greetings.

Unfortunately, the seats on either side of Tracy were taken, but the person who was sitting across from her stood up, and said, "I've finished, my lord, if you'd like my place."

Harry gave this generous soul a heartfelt, "Thanks."

Meg went to take the empty seat one chair away from him, and he put his food on the table, sat down, and looked at Tracy.

"Are you sure you should be here?" she asked. "You're awfully pale."

He was getting sick of hearing how pale he was. "I'm fine."

Jonathan Melbourne was sitting on Tracy's left and

he said with a challenging note in his resonant voice, "Slumming, my lord?"

Harry met the actor's angry hazel eyes and thought he knew what was bothering him. Jon probably had an interest in Tracy himself, and he didn't like the possibility of an aristocratic rival.

Tough luck, old man, Harry thought, and gave him a sunny smile. "Not at all. Meg has told me that both the food and the company are excellent, and I came to sample some of both."

Tracy looked at his plate, which contained a small amount of pasta and a green salad. "You're not eating very much."

She sounded faintly maternal, which in any other woman would have annoyed the hell out of him. In her he found it enchanting.

He shrugged. "I'm not very hungry." He glanced at his sister. "Would you like to introduce me around the table, Meggie?"

She looked radiant. "Of course." She turned immediately to the person next to her, and said, "This is Liza Moran, one of the actresses."

Liza Moran looked thirty, was probably forty, and was looking at him in a way that he found all too familiar. Normally he would have frozen her right out, but he had sworn to be charming, so he smiled, and said, "How do you do."

"It's a pleasure to meet you, Lord Silverbridge." Her voice was husky, and the hunting look in her eyes became even more pronounced.

Meg was saying, "And this is Kim Hamilton, the script supervisor."

Kim wore a twin set and a tweed skirt, and Harry said apologetically, "I must confess to complete ignorance about filmmaking, Ms. Hamilton. Perhaps you wouldn't mind telling me what it is a script supervisor does?"

Kim was delighted to enlighten him, and then Meg went around the rest of the table introducing an assortment of actors and actresses as well as people who bore such peculiar titles as focus puller and grip and lighting gaffer.

It might have actually been a pleasant lunch if not for Liza Moran, who kept throwing out lures to him. She was not subtle, and he did his best to parry her remarks. He had never been able to stand her kind of woman, and it was even worse having to endure her in the presence of Tracy, who spent most of the lunch ignoring Harry and chatting with Jon Melbourne.

She's not fooling me, Harry told himself. *She's as aware of me as I am of her.*

He tried an experiment. He focused his mind and thought, *Tracy, look at me.*

He was profoundly shaken when, almost instantly, her eyes turned away from Jon's and met his.

By the time Harry went into the house to watch the filming, his head was pounding. He made a trip upstairs to his bathroom to swallow three more aspirin, but he was feeling pretty ragged when he joined Meg in the staircase hall.

The scene for the day's shooting was the great salon. The room had been built as a chapel, but in the eighteenth century the residing earl had turned it into a huge state reception room, adding a projection bay to the south with a Venetian window. It was an elegant, stylish, and beautiful room, with pale blue damask walls, matching silk draperies, and priceless Chippendale furniture. The intricate carpet, which mirrored the ceiling's design, had been taken up, baring the inlaid wood floor, which the film company had cleaned up and buffed till it glowed. Antonio Zucchi had painted the ceiling roundels with the seasons and mythological scenes; Thomas Carter had carved the chimneypiece; and Matthew Boulton had produced the tall candelabra, which stood in the four corners of the salon. Two Van Dyke portraits, two landscapes by Claude, a Gainsborough portrait of Harry's great-great-grandmother, all of which he had given to the National Trust to help pay off the death duties on his father's estate, decorated the blue damask walls, along with a large, baroque-style gilt mirror and the room's *pièce de résistance,* a painting of Silverbridge done in the eighteenth century by Canaletto. Harry had fought to hang on to this last painting, which had been valued at ten million pounds, and he had won.

The paintings on the north wall had been removed, and the wall was completely covered with a drop cloth, with scaffolding erected in front of it. The scaffolding was awash with lights and cameras. The big crystal chandelier in the middle of the ceiling, which had been wired for electricity years before, had been taken down and in its place hung an old-fashioned candelit chandelier, which Harry didn't recognize. Blackout curtains had been hung behind all of the windows.

The room was crowded with cameras and sound equipment and, looking at the mass of cables and equipment, Harry understood why the film crew had been so delighted with the enormous Silverbridge salon.

"They're filming the ball scene," Meg said into his ear, and he nodded very slightly. The aspirin had not yet begun to work on his headache.

"That's it, we're ready," the man who was in charge of the lights called.

"Great," Dave Michaels said. "Greg, will you call the cast?"

A tall thin young man with a ponytail passed in front of Harry and walked toward the front drawing room. Very shortly, groups of people clad in period costume began to flow into the salon. To Harry's complete surprise, he found that he recognized a number of them.

"Come to watch us, eh, my lord?" asked the wife of one of his tenant farmers.

Harry's jaw dropped as he placed the face under the brown wig. "Good God. Elsie. What are you doing dressed up in that rig?"

The high-colored face of Elsie Morton beamed. "I'm in the movie, my lord. The film company put a notice up in the village asking for extras, and here I am!"

As Elsie moved into the salon, the woman who seemed to be in charge asked loudly, "Have all the dancers been fitted out with microphones?"

"That's Jill Brown, the choreographer," Meg told her brother. "Michael Hudson, the sound director, wanted to film the dancing along with the dialogue, so Jill had to fit each of the actors with microphones that will play the music in their ears so they can keep time. Then Michael will record the dialogue and the dance music on separate tracks."

He looked at her in wonder. "You really have learned a lot about this, Meggie."

Her smile was brilliant. "I think it's fascinating."

While they were speaking, an eight-piece orchestra had come in and taken its place in front of the Gainsborough portrait. The choreographer began to arrange the dancers in front of the Canaletto, the men lined up facing the women. Dave Michaels said from his position behind one of the cameras, "Where are Tracy and Jon?"

"Greg went to get them," someone called. "They should be here in a moment."

Jon Melbourne's voice said, "We're here now," and he brushed past Harry, followed more sedately by Tracy, who looked surprised to see him.

Harry had never yet seen her in costume, and as he looked back at her, it was as if the bottom dropped out of his stomach. She wore an empire-style ice-blue satin ball gown, cut low enough to show the swell of her breasts. Her hair was her own, drawn into a topknot of golden auburn ringlets, with two wispy ringlets allowed to fall over her ears. Around her slender neck she wore a simple strand of pearls, and in her ears a pair of plain pearl earrings. A single white rose was tucked into her hair.

Meg said enthusiastically, "You look gorgeous, Tracy."

"Thank you." Her surprised look died, her eyes narrowed, and she said to Harry, "You should be in bed."

And you should be there with me. He said those words to her in his mind. Out loud, he replied, "I'm fine."

Even to his own ears his voice sounded hoarse—and

not because of the headache. *I could be on my deathbed, and she would stir me,* he thought with wonder.

She had colored up, an odd response to his spoken words. Then Dave impatiently called her name, and she had to go and take her place beside Jon in the midst of the dancers.

"Jill," Dave said, and the choreographer stepped forward to talk to her troops.

"All right, everyone. As you know, this is a very complicated scene. We are doing a progressive dance in which each couple has to go right from one end of this huge room to the other, which takes a long time. We'll cut to Martin and Julia for the dialogue when they are halfway down the line." She looked up and down the lines of men and women. "Is everyone's microphone working?"

"Yes," the dancers chorused back.

"All right. Let's rehearse it, please."

The musicians picked up their instruments, which they pretended to play, the line of women curtsied to the line of men, who bowed back, and the dance began in eerie silence.

They rehearsed it three times, and while the rehearsal was going on, Meg told Harry that this ballroom scene came at the beginning of the film. "Tracy's character, Julia, is supposedly visiting in the neighborhood and has come as a guest to the ball," she explained. "The moment he lays eyes upon her, Jon's character, Martin, is bewitched. He asks her to dance, and sexual sparks fly."

Harry watched the rehearsal and was surprised and a little disturbed by the potent sexual attraction that Jon was able to generate just by looking at Tracy's pearl-encircled throat. Tracy herself looked very young and vulnerable as she went up the line holding hands with Jon, and the dazzled expression on her face as she returned his smile portrayed perfectly the young, inexperienced, susceptible girl that Julia was at this early point in the movie.

An interruption occurred just as the mikes were to be turned on and the film to roll. One of the crew members rushed out of the room, and a moment later, Greg was at Meg's side.

"Nancy is sick, and Dave wants to know if you could handle her job for this shoot," he said.

Meg's face looked illuminated. "Of course." She turned to her brother, and said authoritatively, "You can sit in that chair, Harry, and you'll be out of everyone's way."

As Meg hustled off, Harry took the seat she had indicated. Shortly after that, the director called, "Action," and the actual filming began.

The aspirin had reduced Harry's headache to a dull pounding, but he was feeling dizzy and clammy, and the heat from the lights was making him sweat. This was his condition when he experienced what had to be the most bizarre moment of his entire life.

It occurred at a point in the dance when each pair of partners had clasped their hands, raised their arms high, and were moving around each other rather the way carousel horses go around on a carousel. Harry had watched Tracy perform this movement during rehearsals, and as he focused his eyes in her direction, he expected to see her innocently wondering face gazing at Jon as they circled their mutually clasped hands.

But the man he saw dancing with Tracy now was taller than Jon, and his hair was blond, not brown. Harry looked at him, and for the second time that afternoon felt his stomach drop. The man was himself.

He shook his head to clear it, further aggravating the pounding in his head, but when he looked again he still saw himself holding Tracy's hand. Fighting down a feeling of rising nausea, he looked at the other people on the dance floor, and it was then that he realized that the lights and sound equipment had vanished.

Dots danced in front of his eyes, and he blinked hard. He blinked again, the scene cleared, and once again he was able to see the blond man and auburn-haired woman who were holding hands and looking at each other as if no one else existed in the world. He recognized that the girl wasn't Tracy first. She wore a blue dress, but her nose was straight, not tilted, and her hair was purely auburn, with none of the gold threads that made Tracy's so extraordinary. Nor was she as tall as Tracy.

His eyes went to the girl's partner, and it was then that Harry realized that he was looking at the man who had posed for the portrait of Charles Oliver that hung in his office.

Dots obscured his vision once again and he had to lower his head to keep from passing out. His head had began to pound in rhythm with the beat of his heart. *Jesus,* he thought. *What's wrong with me? Now I'm hallucinating.*

He looked once more at the dance floor and still the

couple remained, misty now as his eyesight deteriorated, but oddly full of life. He didn't break contact with them until he realized that unless he left instantly, he would be sick all over the restored wood floor of the salon.

———

20

When Meg discovered that Harry was missing, she went looking for him, annoyed that he had not stayed for the entire filming session. She found him in his room, lying on his bed, which immediately dissipated her annoyance and sent a chill of fear through her.

"Harry?" She walked to the bedside and looked down at him. "Are you all right?"

He was still dressed, lying on his back on top of the bedspread with his eyes closed. When she spoke, he opened them so they formed two dark slits. "I have a really rotten headache," he said. "I think I need a better pain medication than aspirin. Do you think you could call Webster, Meggie, and see if you could get him to prescribe something?"

"Of course," she replied immediately. "I'll do it right now."

He looks terrible, she thought worriedly as she ran to

the phone in the morning room. *I shouldn't have asked him to go to the filming. He should have been in bed.*

She dialed the London number of their private doctor, only to learn that he was at his Wiltshire home for the week. This was usually good news, as Dr. Webster lived only ten miles from Silverbridge. Meg called the Wiltshire number and Dr. Webster himself answered the phone.

"Lady Margaret," he said warmly when she had identified herself. "How are you going along?"

Harry had originally taken her to Dr. Webster for treatment of her problem, but the doctor had referred her to a specialist. "I'm doing very well, thank you. But Harry has a terrible headache, Dr. Webster, and he needs some pain medication."

"Harry doesn't get headaches," Dr. Webster replied instantly.

Meg explained about the accident and the concussion. "I think he probably overdid it today," she ended. "He should have stayed in bed."

"What was the name of the doctor who saw him in hospital?"

Meg didn't know.

"It doesn't matter. I'll call over there and find out. I'll ring you back after I've spoken to him."

Clearly, Dr. Webster wasn't going to prescribe anything for Harry until he had more information about his injury. Meg said good-bye and reluctantly went back to tell Harry that he was going to have to wait for his pain medication.

His tawny hair looked darker than usual against the white pillow, and there were dark shadows, like bruises, under his eyes. Once more Meg felt a shiver of fear. She never remembered Harry being sick. "Harry," she said softly, "Dr. Webster is going to ring back within the hour with a prescription."

The eyes he turned on her looked black not brown. "Thanks, Meggie."

Ebony's small, square face lifted from her own pillow next to Harry's, and she growled. Clearly she sensed there was something wrong with Harry and was protecting him.

Dr. Webster called back within twenty minutes to say that Harry had a very severe concussion and should not have been released from hospital. "What was he doing to bring this headache on, Lady Margaret?" he demanded. When Meg explained that he had been to the stables and had spent the afternoon watching the filming, Dr. Webster hit the roof.

"I wish that man would take half as good care of himself as he does of those precious horses of his! Concussions are a serious matter, Lady Margaret. If they are not treated seriously they can lead to permanent brain damage—even death."

Icy cold fingers gripped Meg's heart. If something should happen to Harry . . .

"I want him back in hospital, where he can't hurt himself," Dr. Webster said.

"I don't think he'll go," Meg said faintly.

"I'll come myself to collect him," the doctor snapped. "Tell him I'll put him on a drip for the pain when I get him to hospital, but if he refuses to go then I wash my hands of him."

"A . . . all right," Meg said.

"I'll be at Silverbridge in a half an hour."

"All right."

"Good-bye, Lady Margaret."

"Just a moment!" Meg said hurriedly. "I'll leave the door open for you, Dr. Webster. Would you mind letting yourself in?"

"Not at all."

Meg hung up the phone, turned, and saw Tony standing in the doorway.

"What's going on?" he asked. "Where won't Harry go?"

"Oh, Tony." Meg was enormously grateful to have someone to share her burden. "Dr. Webster is coming out here to take Harry back to hospital, and I know Harry isn't going to want to go. But he got up today and was all over the place and now he has a terrible headache and Dr. Webster said he could die if he doesn't give his concussion time to heal!"

Tony held up one elegant hand. "Whoa, Meggie. Calm down. I'm quite sure that Harry isn't going to die."

"It's all my fault," Meg said tragically as she approached her brother. "I was the one who persuaded him to come to the filming this afternoon when he should have been in bed."

"If he hadn't been at the filming, you can be sure he would have been somewhere else," Tony said. "Harry isn't the type to stay quietly in bed."

Meg stopped in front of Tony. "That's why the doctor wants him back in hospital. Will you come with me to talk to him?" Her blue eyes pleaded. "He's not going to listen to me, I know he isn't."

"What makes you think he'll listen to me?" Tony said

with a trace of bitterness. "He never has yet." However, he accompanied Meg to Harry's bedroom and went in with her to break the news to their elder brother.

Harry regarded them from under the shadow of the arm he had flung across his forehead, and said flatly, "I'm not going back to hospital."

"But Dr. Webster is coming out here to get you," Meg wailed.

"Then he will have made a trip for nothing. All I need are some painkillers and rest, and I can get both of those things right here at home."

Tony said, "I know hospital is a bore, old man, but you really do look wretched. You're as white as your sheets, you know."

Harry shut his eyes. "I feel much too wretched to get into a car and make a half hour trip to the hospital."

Meg said, "Harry, Dr. Webster said you could have permanent brain damage if you don't rest. You could even die!"

Harry spoke with his eyes still closed. "He was trying to scare you, Meggie. People don't die from concussions."

"I think you're being egotistical and stubborn," Tony said brutally, "but then again, what's new about that?"

"Harry is not egotistical and stubborn!" Meg shot back in defense of her eldest brother.

"He isn't?" Tony elevated a single perfectly groomed eyebrow. "Then why won't he sell Mauley the land he wants?"

Harry's eyes opened to narrow slits. "Because I'd rather the land be used for cattle than for golfers."

Tony moved closer to the bed. "No, it's because you

have this *idée fixe* about not going down in history as
the earl who sold off Silverbridge's farms. It's all about
ego, Harry, and nothing else."

Harry moved his protective arm to cover his eyes.
"Go away, both of you, and when Webster shows up,
make him give you some painkillers for me. I don't
want to see him."

"You're the earl," Tony said sarcastically. "We bow
to your command. As always."

Meg thought Tony was giving up much too easily and
shot him a furious look. "Please see Dr. Webster,
Harry," she said pleadingly. "I'm worried about you."

"I'll be fine." His eyes were still hidden under his
arm. "Just get the painkillers."

Meg looked at his white face on the pillow, then
turned to look at Tony. He jerked his head in the direction of the door, and reluctantly she followed him out.

"As always, Harry refuses to do the sensible thing,"
he said bitterly after they had closed the bedroom door
behind them. "I don't know why we keep thinking that
he will."

"How can I tell Dr. Webster, after he's come all this
way, that he can't see Harry?" Meg fretted.

"Let Harry deal with him," Tony recommended.
"He's the one who's giving all the commands."

"You mean I should take him to Harry's bedroom
after Harry said not to?" Meg sounded aghast at the very
thought.

Tony rolled his eyes and said impatiently, "Do what
you want to do. Now, if you'll excuse me, I need to
dress. I have a dinner date in Warkfield."

Meg stood indecisively in the hallway as Tony went

into his room. There was little point in going back to
plead with Harry. She was only his little sister, and
clearly he was not going to listen to her.

Who would he listen to?

Tracy. The name flashed like a lightbulb in Meg's
mind. She didn't stop to think why she would go to
someone both she and Harry had known for so short a
time. She acted purely on instinct and raced all the way
to Tracy's trailer, praying that she would be there.

She was. When Meg burst in, Tracy was sitting at her
dressing table removing her makeup. She was alone;
there was no sign of Gail.

"Tracy," Meg said tensely as she closed the door behind her. "Harry is sick and the doctor wants to take him
to hospital and he doesn't want to go."

Tracy swung around on her chair. Her hair was tied
back, and her face glistened with the cold cream with
which she was taking off her makeup. "What's wrong?"

Meg came closer. "He's in bed with a horrible
headache. Dr. Webster is furious that he didn't stay in
bed today as he said he would."

"I knew he shouldn't be up," Tracy said grimly. "He
looked awful."

"It's all my fault," Meg said despairingly. "I asked
him to come to lunch and then go to the filming. And
now the doctor says that he could die!"

Tracy stood up and said, even more grimly than before, "He's not going to die, Meggie. I'll see to that.
Wait a moment while I get into my jeans, and I'll come
with you."

It took Tracy four minutes to wipe the cream from her
face and get dressed. Then she and Meg exited the

trailer and turned their hurried footsteps in the direction of the house. They had gone about forty feet when they ran into Jon.

"What's wrong?" he asked, scanning their worried faces.

"My brother Harry is sick," Meg said. "Tracy is going to try to convince him to let the doctor take him to hospital."

"Sick?" Jon repeated. "We just saw him at lunch. What's wrong?"

"I don't have time to stand here chatting with you, Jon," Tracy said crisply. "Come on, Meg," and the two young women began to jog across the grass. After a moment of indecision, Jon followed them.

Meg knew she had done the right thing in fetching Tracy the moment she saw Harry's face. Drawn with pain though it was, a look came over it that had not been there before. Tracy said, "Bad headache?"

"Mmm."

It was as though even talking hurt his head.

"The doctor will be here soon to take you to the hospital," Tracy said. "He'll give you something for the pain once you get there."

His mouth took on the stubborn look that his family was all too familiar with. "I am not going to hospital."

"Why not?" Tracy asked, her tone dangerous.

"Because I'm not."

A male voice said authoritatively from the doorway, "Oh yes you are."

Meg turned and gave Dr. Webster a nervous smile. "Thank you for coming, Dr. Webster."

"You have wasted a trip, James," Harry said. "I am not going to hospital."

Webster, who had been Harry's doctor since he set the broken arm Harry had got playing rugby at Eton, walked over to the bed. He was a silver-haired man of about fifty, and he looked like the prosperous practitioner that he was.

"You have a severe concussion, Harry," he said gravely. "The hospital had no business releasing you."

Tracy held out her hand. "Harry intimidated the doctor. How do you do, Dr. Webster. I am Tracy Collins."

Webster's face took on the slightly fatuous look that Meg had noticed all men wore when they looked at Tracy. "How do you do, Miss Collins."

She smiled, and the fatuous look deepened. Meg thought enviously that even with no makeup and her hair scraped back into a ponytail, she looked beautiful. She said pleasantly, "I believe that you actually have *two* patients in this room, Harry and Meg. Isn't that so Dr. Webster?"

"Lady Margaret is currently being seen by a specialist, but I am certainly her family doctor," Webster returned cautiously.

Meg had stiffed at the mention of her name, and she trained wary eyes on Tracy's face.

Tracy said, "Well, I have a suggestion that I think would benefit them both." Her dark blue eyes focused on Meg. "You want Harry to go to the hospital. Isn't that right, Meg?"

"Y—es," Meg said carefully.

Tracy looked down at Harry. "And you want Meg to eat normally. Correct?"

Lines of pain bracketed his mouth. "Yes," he agreed grimly.

Tracy said to the doctor, "So what if we do a deal? Harry agrees to go to the hospital if Meg agrees to eat three meals a day while he's gone."

"That's blackmail," Meg said hotly.

Tracy looked at Harry. "Maybe."

Everyone looked at Harry, who was regarding Tracy with that grimness still around his mouth. "I hate hospitals."

"I know you do," she replied matter-of-factly. "But we can't trust you to remain in bed if you stay home."

Meg waited for Harry to explode. He didn't. Instead he turned his eyes to her. "What do you think, Meg? Will you agree to this bargain?"

"But you don't want to go to hospital," she blurted.

"No, but even more than not wanting to go to hospital, I want you to eat. So if you will agree to this . . . blackmail"—here he shot Tracy a look—"then I will too."

Meg clenched her fists, rigid with the battle that was going on inside between the part of her that wanted to get well and the part of her that needed her illness and didn't want to give it up. It was the pain on Harry's face that decided her. "Okay," she said. "I'll agree."

"Good." Tracy turned to the doctor. "I really think he should have some painkillers before he gets into your car."

The doctor placed his black leather case on a table. "I'll give him a shot right now."

At that point, the door opened and Tony looked into the bedroom. He was dressed in one of his expensive, perfectly tailored suits, and a look of surprise crossed his face when he saw Dr. Webster. "What's going on?" he asked.

"I'm taking your brother to hospital," the doctor replied as he extracted a syringe from his bag. "He has a concussion, and he must be kept quiet."

Tony leaned against the door. "Bravo, Doctor. You have done what no one else could do. I was sure you'd have to knock Harry out to get him into hospital again."

"You can thank Miss Collins for changing his mind." The doctor was filling the syringe with a clear fluid.

Tony looked at Tracy and gave her a mocking smile. "Harry has always been a sucker for redheads."

Meg said, "Don't be an ass, Tony. Tracy got us to agree to double blackmail: Harry is going to hospital, and I have promised to eat three meals a day while he is gone."

Tracy said, "I really object to being called a blackmailer."

"It sounds like blackmail to me," Tony retorted. He grinned. "But it's brilliant blackmail, Tracy. Congratulations."

"Thank you," she returned.

"All right now, Harry." Dr. Webster was approaching the bed with his syringe. "This should work almost immediately, then we can get you downstairs and into the car."

"You can shoot it right into my head if that will help," Harry said.

Tony winced.

"Your arm will do admirably." He pushed Harry's cotton shirtsleeve up, revealing a well-muscled upper arm.

Tony said, "I say, if you don't need me here, I think I'll be running along. Got a dinner date I'm already late for."

"Go right ahead," Dr. Webster said, the needle poised over Harry's arm. As the needle plunged into flesh, Tony hurriedly left the room, Tracy averted her eyes, and Meg watched.

After he had emptied the syringe and removed the needle, the doctor turned, and said, "Lady Margaret, perhaps you could pack a bag for your brother."

Tracy said to Harry, "Do you want Meg and me to go with you?"

"No." Harry's reply was uncompromising.

"Okay." Tracy gracefully acceded to his wishes. "We'll come to see you tomorrow."

"Um," he said.

"All right, let's get him out of bed before the Demerol puts him to sleep," the doctor said.

Ten minutes later, Harry was sitting in the front seat of the doctor's BMW. Tracy and Meg watched as the car drove off, then went back into the house.

21

By the time Harry reached the hospital, his head was still pounding, but the shot had made him drowsy. Dr. Webster pulled up in the parking lot right across from the hospital building and came around to help him out of the car.

"Don't need help," Harry said fretfully, and attempted to stand up on his own.

The ground swayed under his feet, and he felt Webster's arm come around him. "Don't be an ass," the doctor said. "You're knocked out from the Demerol." Together the two men began to walk across the hospital driveway to the front door.

Harry was too groggy to understand exactly what happened next. All he knew was that he heard the screech of tires, and then he was lying sprawled between two parked cars, with Webster on top of him.

The doctor jumped to his feet, pulled open a car door,

and leaned on the horn. Almost immediately, two security men came running down the hospital steps.

The rest of the night would always remain a blur to Harry. He remembered getting into a wheelchair, but he didn't remember the trip from the front door to the hospital bed. He did remember asking Webster, while an IV was being put into his arm, "What happened out there?" and he thought the doctor replied, "Someone tried to run us down."

Then he knew nothing.

Dr. Webster called Silverbridge from the nurses' station once Harry was asleep. When Meg answered the phone, he asked for Tony. When he learned that Tony still wasn't home, he hesitated, then asked for Tracy. Briefly he recounted to her the car incident and recommended that she get someone to keep an eye on Harry while he was in hospital.

As he was walking out to his car, he tried to figure out why he had confided Harry's plight to Tracy Collins.

I didn't want to put this burden on Meg, and Miss Collins was the only adult in the house.

But she's not there as a friend, she's only there because of the movie.

Still . . .

There was no question that, during the brief time he had spent with Tracy and Harry, he had received the unmistakable impression that they were somehow connected. It wasn't in anything they had said. It was just an impression, but it was very strong—so strong that he had turned to her as the logical person to keep Harry safe. It might sound crazy, he decided, but he felt confident that he had made the right decision.

Tracy put down the telephone and turned to Meg, who was regarding her anxiously. "What was that all about?" she asked.

Tracy debated whether or not to tell Meg. Obviously Dr. Webster did not think she should be told, or he would have done it himself. Would the news that her brother's life was in danger overload her fragile grasp on health, or would it perhaps shock her out of her obsession with her illness?

It could go either way, and Tracy thought it would be best to wait. The words, once spoken, could not be recalled. So she said, "Dr. Webster wants us to put someone on with Harry full-time, to make sure he stays in bed."

"A nurse, do you mean?"

The two of them were standing in the morning room next to the telephone. Tracy said, "I doubt that a nurse would be sufficiently intimidating for Harry. I'm thinking we'd do better with a security person."

"We could call Tom Edsel," Meg said. "He's a private detective in Warkfield, and I remember that he did a job for Harry last summer."

"He sounds perfect." Tracy turned back to the telephone. "I'll get on to him right away."

"It's late," Meg protested. "He won't be at his office. Better to call him in the morning."

Tracy thought about Harry lying helpless in drugged

sleep, and said, "I'll call him at home. Where's the phone book?"

Meg found the number for her, and Tracy called. By the time she hung up, she had arranged for someone to go to the hospital right away to be with Harry, and for regular shifts to be set up for as long as necessary.

Meg was clearly puzzled by how adamant Tracy was about having a person go directly to the hospital, but Tracy didn't try to explain any more than she already had. Instead she said, "It's late, and we should go to bed. I'll take you in to see your brother tomorrow."

A bewildered Meg followed Tracy down the corridor to their respective bedrooms.

Tracy might have recommended sleep to Meg, but once she herself was in bed, sleep was hard to come by. Every time she closed her eyes, she saw the image of a car bursting out of a dark night and hurtling toward Harry.

If something should happen to him . . . She thought once again of Scotty, and the anguish she had known when she lost him. *I can't bear it again. Not Harry. Please God, not Harry.*

The way to keep him safe was to discover who was behind his "accidents." Tracy fought down her terror and tried to look at the situation logically.

Somebody knew he was going to be in the hospital parking lot at that particular time, she thought. *If I can narrow down just who had that information, then perhaps I'll have the culprit.*

She thought back to the scene in Harry's room and visualized all those who had been present: herself, Meg, Dr. Webster, and Tony.

Tony, she thought. *Tony was in Harry's bedroom, and he left when Harry was getting the shot of Demerol. He had enough time to get to the hospital before Harry and try to run him down.*

There was something about Tony that Tracy distrusted, but she found it difficult to believe that he was capable of cold-bloodedly murdering his brother.

He would have to be desperate to do such a thing. She stared at the ceiling and thought about the things that could make a man desperate. *Perhaps he has huge gambling debts. If he became the earl, he could get a large amount of money by selling Mauley the Silverbridge land he wants.*

Tracy frowned into the dark. *Maybe I should have Tony investigated.*

The more she thought about the idea, the more she liked it. Its only flaw was her realization that Harry probably wouldn't like it at all.

I won't tell him, Tracy decided. *If Tony is clean, then Harry will never have to know about it.*

She felt better once she had come up with a course of action and snuggled her cheek into her pillow. *I'll get Gail to find someone in the morning,* she thought, and finally went to sleep.

Tracy called Gail before she went down to breakfast and made arrangements to hire a private investigator. She was due in makeup at nine, and it was a little after eight when she walked into the Silverbridge kitchen and found Gwen Mauley sitting at the table drinking coffee.

"Good morning, miss." The housekeeper greeted Tracy with a friendly smile. "The usual?"

"Yes, thank you, Mrs. Wilson."

Marshal and Millie had gotten off the sofa when Tracy came in, but once they saw she wasn't Harry, they both climbed mournfully back into their nests. Tracy turned her attention to Gwen, who looked very striking clad in black breeches with a full leather seat, black high boots, and a white turtleneck sweater. "Good morning," she said.

Gwen didn't bother to return the greeting. "Harry and I had a lesson scheduled this morning, and I went to the stable but he wasn't there. Mrs. Wilson tells me that he's got a concussion and is supposed to stay in bed." Gwen drummed long, blood-red fingernails on the table. "If he's in bed, I want to know who is riding my horse."

Tracy took a seat across the table from Gwen. "I'm quite certain that Harry has made arrangements for your horse to be ridden."

Gwen's voice sounded edgy. "Yes, and I'm sure those arrangements were for Ned to ride him. I don't have anything against Ned, but he's not Harry. It's Harry I paid for, and Harry I want. He has a magic touch with horses."

Tracy looked into Gwen's green eyes and thought, *Spoiled brat.* "I'm afraid that he won't be able to train your horse for a few days at least," she said coolly. "He's in the hospital."

Gwen turned her green glare on the housekeeper, who was approaching with Tracy's fruit and cereal. "Mrs. Wilson told me he just had a concussion! Athletes get concussions all the time, and it doesn't stop them."

With difficulty, Tracy restrained herself from throwing her cornflakes into Gwen's face. Instead she said crisply, "Harry has a severe concussion, and the doctor put him in the hospital to make certain he remains quiet."

Gwen slammed her coffee cup into its saucer. "That's just great. I'm signed up for a show next week, and now Dylan won't be ready."

"Perhaps you could work with him yourself," Tracy suggested.

Gwen's eyes shot green sparks. She looked like a cat about to spit. "That's the problem. That's why I brought him to Harry. I can't work with him by myself." She stared angrily at her empty coffee cup, and said, "I'd like more coffee."

The housekeeper replied without expression, "Certainly, Miss Mauley."

Tracy speared a piece of melon with her fork, and asked, "Why can't you work with Dylan on your own?"

The housekeeper poured more coffee in Gwen's cup and put a fresh cup in front of Tracy.

Gwen said bitterly, "Because I don't think he likes me."

Tracy took a bracing swallow of black coffee. "Why do you say that?"

Gwen exploded. "Because he won't obey me! Every time I ask for something, all I get is backing and bucking and . . . and . . . resistance! He goes like a charm for Harry, but whenever I get on, he turns into a pig."

"Maybe you just need to spend more time with him," Tracy said.

Gwen leaned forward and glared at Tracy. "Let me tell you something, Miss Collins. I am an excellent rider. I have ridden and I have won at Grand Prix level in many well-known shows. There is nothing wrong with my riding. It's the bloody horse that's the problem."

Tracy remembered the words of her old riding instructor, *Beware of the rider who blames his horse and not himself.* She ate a strawberry and inquired mildly, "What does Harry say?"

"Hah!" Gwen folded her arms defensively across her chest. "He keeps telling me that Dylan is a Thoroughbred and that I can't ride him the same way that I ride my warmbloods. "'Be tactful,' he tells me." She did a fair imitation of Harry's clipped, upper-class voice. " 'Don't demand. Ask' " Gwen snorted. "When I tell a horse to do a canter pirouette, I expect him to do it! I'm not going to waste my time coaxing him."

"Thoroughbreds do have to be ridden with a light touch," Tracy said.

Gwen's glare increased in intensity. "I ride the way I ride. If that doesn't suit the horse, then I'll get rid of him."

Tracy's heart leaped when she heard those words. "Do you mean that?"

"Yes. I do. I went over to Germany on Tuesday and saw a magnificent black Hanoverian—that I can ride just fine! I've decided I'm going to sell Dylan and buy the Hanoverian. But I wanted to take Dylan to this show to shop him around."

Tracy said, "I'll buy him from you."

Gwen stared in astonishment. "You?"

"Yes." Tracy smiled pleasantly. "I've always been interested in dressage, and I grew up riding Thoroughbreds. I think Dylan would suit me very well."

Gwen's eyes narrowed. "Do you think this is a way to cozy up to Harry? Do you have a fancy to be a countess, Miss Collins?"

Tracy said, "How much do you want for him?"

"I'm asking forty thousand pounds for him."

It was far too much money. Tracy knew it, and Gwen did, too. "I'll give you twenty- five," Tracy said.

"Thirty-five," Gwen came back.

"Thirty," said Tracy.

"Thirty-two and we have a deal."

"Done," Tracy said. "How soon can I have him?"

"You can have him today, as far as I'm concerned," Gwen said. "I've already got a bid on the Hanoverian."

"I'll write you a check, but I'll want all of his papers."

"They're in my London flat. I'll have them by tomorrow."

"Fine."

Gwen's eyes narrowed again. "His board and his training fees are due on Monday."

"How much are they"?

The sum she named caused Tracy's eyes to widen. *Harry certainly doesn't undervalue himself,* she thought with a trace of amusement.

Gwen stood up. "Well, I wish you luck with Dylan. But I wouldn't count on making any points with Harry for buying him." There was a distinct note of warning in her voice.

A thought struck Tracy. "How long have you been in Wiltshire?"

"I came yesterday." Gwen's voice took on a tinge of sarcasm. "I was expecting to have a lesson this morning."

Tracy tried to think of how she could phrase her next question so it didn't sound nosy. There wasn't any way, she decided, so she came right out and asked, "Was your father at home last night?"

Gwen had bent to pick up her purse, and she stared at Tracy with open suspicion. "Why do you ask?"

Inspiration struck. "It's just that Tony had a dinner engagement last night and I wondered if he might be meeting your father. That's all."

"What business is it of yours who Tony has dinner with?"

Tracy said bluntly, "Was he having dinner with you?"

Gwen sat back down. "I thought it was Harry you were interested in, not Tony."

Tracy lowered her lashes to hide her eyes. "Harry is a great guy, but he's devoted beyond all reason to this mausoleum of a house. And he wants to be a farmer! Tony doesn't have the same . . . encumbrances." She lifted her lashes and treated Gwen to a gaze of great innocence. "I was just wondering if Tony was free."

"Are you asking if I have any claim to him?"

"Well . . . yes."

"I don't," Gwen said briefly. "He has a business relationship with my family, that's all."

"The golf course?"

"Yes, the golf course."

Tracy did her wide-eyed innocent look again. "But what relationship does Tony have to the golf course? He doesn't own the property; Harry does."

"Tony is going to manage it. Actually, he's going to manage the whole property, the hotel as well as the golf course. He'll be great at it. Tony can charm the skin off a snake."

Tracy produced a dewy-eyed smile. "Yes he can, can't he? So he was having dinner with your father and not you last night?"

"That's right."

Tracy racked her brain to see if there was any way she could reasonably ask if Tony had been late for the restaurant reservation. Before she could come up with a reason, however, Gwen stood up once more. "I'll call you tomorrow, when I have Dylan's papers, and we can get together to do the sale."

"Great," Tracy said. "I'll be tied up filming but leave a message with my secretary and I'll get back to you."

Gwen opened her purse and took out a small notebook and a pen. "What's her number?"

Tracy recited Gail's number and Gwen wrote it down. She returned the pen and notebook to her purse, then, without saying anything further, she left.

From her position in front of the sink, Mrs. Wilson said, "Would you care for more coffee, miss?"

The warmth that had heretofore been in her voice when she addressed Tracy was gone. In its place Tracy detected a distinct chill. Clearly Mrs. Wilson had listened to the conversation between Tracy and Gwen and did not approve of it.

"No thank you, Mrs. Wilson," Tracy said mildly.

At that point, Meg came in the kitchen door. She marched to the table, sat down, and said to Mrs. Wilson, with a trace of defiance, "I'll have a dish of fruit and a bowl of cornflakes, Mrs. Wilson."

The housekeeper turned sharply in surprise, saw Tracy's warning gaze and infinitesimal headshake, and stopped what she was going to say. "Very well, Lady Margaret. I'll bring them right away."

The dogs came over to Meg and nudged her. "Poor babies. They miss Harry dreadfully when he's not here." She looked up from petting Millie, and asked, "You said we can go to see him in hospital today, remember?"

"Yes, but I can't go until this evening." Tracy ate a spoonful of cornflakes. "I have to work all day."

A grin lit Meg's waiflike face. "I have to work, too. Dave asked me to stand in for Nancy again. She's still sick."

Tracy raised an eyebrow. "If this keeps on, you'll have to demand a paycheck."

Meg shook her head. "It's so much fun. I can't imagine getting paid for something that's so much fun."

"You're good at it," Tracy said. And it was true. The continuity supervisor's job was to make certain that the costumes and props remained in continuity with the script. If a particular ornament had been on a table in a previous scene, then it was the continuity supervisor's job to make certain that that same ornament was in the exact same position for a second shoot.

Dave had given Nancy's notebook to Meg, but it was a daunting task to pick up in the middle of a movie with someone else's notes.

"I'm surprised Dave asked you to do the job," Tracy said frankly. "You've had no experience."

"He says I have a good eye," Meg said with pride. "I've been kind of shadowing Nancy, and the other day I picked out that the magnifying glass was in the wrong place on the desk."

Tracy smiled warmly. "Good for you. Perhaps you've found a career, Meg. The money for a continuity supervisor is quite decent."

Meg's sharp-boned face looked radiant. "Do you really think I could do this job?"

"You *are* doing it," Tracy pointed out.

"Here you are, Lady Margaret," the housekeeper said as she put Meg's fruit and cornflakes on the table.

Meg looked at them as if she was afraid they might jump out of their bowls and bite her. Tracy said reasonably, "If you are to do this job, you need energy. If you want energy, you must eat. This is less food than I eat for breakfast. It's not too much for you."

Meg was chewing nervously on her hair. "If I eat this much food, I'll get fat."

"I think I can safely promise you, Meg, that you'll never be fat." Tracy reached over to touch Meg's hand. "But you will gain weight. You *need* to gain weight. Every doctor you've ever seen has told you that, and it's true."

"I know," Meg muttered. She had not yet picked up her spoon.

"I'm not going to sit here and monitor you," Tracy

said, standing up. "I trust you to uphold your end of the bargain, just as Harry has upheld his."

"All right!" Meg shouted. "I'll eat the bloody food! Will that satisfy you?"

"Yes, it will," Tracy replied.

As she left the room she heard Meg saying, "I have to work today, Mrs. Wilson. Do you think you could find the time to take the dogs for a walk?"

Tracy smiled at the note of pride she heard in Meg's voice.

22

When Harry awoke the following morning and found a large muscular stranger sitting by his bed reading a newspaper, he demanded to know who the person was. When he learned that someone had hired Tom Edsel investigations to baby-sit him, he blew up.

A call to Tom Edsel produced the information that Tracy Collins had hired him the previous evening after an attempt on Harry's life. When Harry tried to dismiss the agency, he was told that only Tracy Collins could do that.

Harry put in a call to Tracy, but she was filming. He tried again later, with the same result. By the time she and Meg showed up at the hospital at six o'clock, he was fuming.

His current baby-sitter stopped reading the newspaper aloud to him as Tracy and Meg came into the room. "Thanks, George," Harry said. "Would you mind waiting outside while I visit with Miss Collins and my sister?"

"Sure."

Harry waited for the door to close behind George before glaring at Tracy. "Why the hell did you hire Edsel? I don't need to be guarded, for God's sake!"

When Tracy did not immediately reply, Meg said, "Dr. Webster wants to make sure you stay in bed, Harry. He recommended that we hire someone to sit with you." She smiled brightly. "This way, if you want anything, you won't have to get up to get it for yourself. And if you can't read yet, you have someone to read to you."

Harry looked into Meg's innocent eyes and realized that she had not been informed about last night. Nor had he told her about the brakes being tampered with.

Damn. How could he yell at Tracy with Meg in the room?

Tracy said, "Meg, I left my sweater in the car. Would you mind terribly getting it for me?"

Meg looked from Tracy to Harry, then back again to Tracy. She smiled. "I wouldn't mind at all."

As soon as Meg was out of the room, Harry proceeded to tell Tracy, in great detail, exactly what he thought of her hiring Edsel investigations.

She stood there, looking like an angel, and listened. When he had finally finished, she said, "It's no good, Harry. I'm not taking Edsel off the case."

He couldn't believe what he had heard. "Didn't you hear what I just said?"

"I heard every word of it, and I'm sorry that your male ego is hurt, but someone has twice tried to kill you, and the chances are very good that he'll try again. You are helpless in a hospital bed. You need a guard."

He glared. "I am not helpless!"

"You have nothing to protect yourself with. And when you're asleep, you're doubly vulnerable."

He had no answer to this, so he said stubbornly, "I don't want a guard. I mean it, Tracy. Call them off."

"I can't," she said.

He glared again. "What do you mean, you can't?"

"I mean that I can't take the chance of losing you. I couldn't bear it." Her voice trembled, and she steadied it. "I'm so scared, Harry. Please don't be a bull about this. Let the guards stay."

How had they got to this point? Harry wondered. He had kissed her twice, and she felt she had the right to make decisions about his life. Even more strange was that he felt that way, too.

"I'm not paying Edsel for guards," he said.

"You don't have to. I'm the one who employed him."

He didn't want her paying Edsel on his behalf. "Shit," he muttered in frustration.

Then she said something that completely distracted him from the issue he had been stewing about all day.

"Would you mind terribly if I kissed you?"

He stared at her. "No," he croaked. "Not at all."

She came to the side of the bed where he was not hooked up to an IV, bent, and touched her lips to his.

It was the same way it had been the other two times they had kissed. Part of him wanted her so badly that he wanted to rip off her clothes, push her down, and take her; the other part wanted to go on kissing her forever, to cherish her, be kind to her, worship her.

"Oh dear," Meg's voice said. "Perhaps I should go back out to the car."

Tracy straightened up, and they both looked at Meg, who was grinning.

Tracy said, "Oh, good, you've got my sweater."

Meg handed it to her, then looked accusingly at Harry. "I was talking to George, and he said he's here because someone tried to kill you. Is that true, Harry?"

Well there goes all our care to keep Meg out of this, he thought grimly.

He glanced at Tracy and read clearly in her eyes that she was going to leave him to handle this.

Harry said, "I didn't want you to know, Meggie. I didn't want you worried." He shot a look at Tracy. "This is what comes of hiring outsiders. They blab things they shouldn't."

Meg said indignantly, "I'm not a child, Harry. If you are in danger, I think I should know about it." She came to stand at the foot of the bed and put her hands on the iron footboard. "Was our accident part of this?"

He sighed. "Yes. Ian told me that the brake lines on the car were cut."

One of Meg's hands went to her mouth.

Tracy said, "When Dr. Webster called last night, it was to tell me that someone had tried to run him and Harry down in the parking lot. That's why I got the guards, Meg. Not to keep Harry in bed."

"You should have told me," Meg said passionately.

"Yes," Tracy said. "I think I should have."

Meg turned back to her brother. "Well, I hope you're keeping the guards at least!"

He looked from Meg to Tracy, then said gloomily, "Oh all right."

Both women smiled at him as if he had given them a precious gift.

Dr. Webster kept Harry in the hospital over the weekend, and on Monday Tony brought him home. Tracy finished filming at seven, removed her costume and makeup in record time, and almost ran up the stairs to the family apartment in order to see him. Angry male voices coming from the morning room stopped her at the top of the steps.

Harry's voice was at its most clipped. "Tony, you have been at me all day about this, and I'm sick of it. I understand that it would be a great opportunity for you to manage the golf course property, but I'm not willing to sacrifice eight thousand acres of farmland in order to give you that opportunity."

Tony sounded both angry and frustrated. "You're not sacrificing it, for God's sake. You'll be making a bloody fortune out of it."

"I'm not selling," Harry said implacably.

"Trying to raise beef cattle in this environment is crazy! Look what happened last year, when so many farmers lost whole herds to foot-and-mouth disease."

"I didn't lose my cattle."

"You were lucky," Tony shot back. "But you still can't export your beef, and who's to say that you'll be lucky again the next time?"

There was a short silence, then Harry said, "Do you

need a loan, Tony? I'm a little tight, but perhaps I can come up with something."

"No, I do not need a loan! I am making decent money, thank you, but the amount I make is nothing compared to what I could be making at the golf club."

"Well find another golf club, then," Harry said harshly, "because this one isn't going to be built."

Tony came striding out of the morning room, his face white and pinched-looking as he brushed by Tracy without acknowledging her. She watched his slim back disappear below, then turned toward the morning room, wiping the worried frown from her brow as she went.

Harry was sitting in his favorite chair, with the dogs curled into two content black-and-white balls at his feet.

"However did Millie and Marshal earn the right to come upstairs?" she asked lightly as she crossed the floor.

His dark eyes sparkled as he watched her approach. "I didn't want to spend the day downstairs, and they were desperate to be with me, so I brought them up."

Tracy stopped to pick up a leather ottoman. "What about Ebony?"

"Her royal nose is royally out of joint, but she'll get over it."

Tracy plunked the ottoman next to his chair and sat down. His hair seemed to have grown longer while he was in the hospital, and she wanted more than anything to run her fingers through it. She said, "How are you feeling?"

"Fine." His dark eyes were fastened on her face.

"Well that's certainly enlightening."

He raised an impatient eyebrow. "What do you want me to say?"

She made her voice sound dispassionate. "Do you still have a headache?"

"Minor."

"Any more double vision?"

"No."

"Any ringing in the ears?"

"No."

Dizziness?"

"No."

She was silent, and he said ironically, "Is that it, Dr. Collins? No more questions about my health?"

She shook her head. For the first time in years, she was actually feeling shy. It was a disturbing feeling, and she didn't know what to say.

He said, "Do you know, I rather think I love you."

She stared at him. His voice had sounded matter-of-fact and detached, but the expression in his eyes said something else. She swallowed. "I thought you didn't like me."

"I tried not to like you. I didn't want to get involved with a movie star. But I couldn't help myself."

With horror, she recalled Mel's news about Counes and the picture he had taken of her and Harry. She said in a rush, "Oh my God, Harry, I have something terrible to tell you."

His golden brown brows drew together. "What?"

"Do you remember when that weasel Counes took a picture of us kissing?"

"Yes."

"Well, he's sold it to one of the worst scandal sheets in America."

His frown deepened. "He can't have. I took his camera away."

"Evidently he removed the film before you got to the camera."

He just looked at her.

"I'm so sorry," she said. "I know how you loathe publicity. I asked my agent to try to buy the pictures before they got into the paper, but he said it would be impossible."

He still didn't say anything.

"Harry?" She put her hand on his arm and slightly shook it. "Did you get it? You and I are going to be on display to every supermarket shopper in America!"

He said calmly, "Well, if everyone is going to think we're an item, then maybe we should *be* an item."

She had expected him to hit the roof, and his calm reception of her news floored her. Then his words registered in her brain.

"Do you think so?" she asked shakily.

"I definitely do."

She thought of one other thing she needed to tell him before she answered. "I think you should know . . ." She bit her lip.

He covered her hand with his and asked gently. "What should I know?"

She looked not into his eyes but at their joined hands as she replied with difficulty, "I haven't made love with anyone since Scotty died." She felt his hand stiffen, and continued breathlessly. "I'm telling you this because I don't want you to think that what I feel for you is . . . trivial."

"Scotty?" His voice was very quiet. "Who is Scotty?"

Her eyes flew upward. "Oh, don't you know? Scotty was my husband."

The lines of his cheekbones looked very hard, as if the skin had tightened over them. "No, I didn't know. What happened?"

"As I just said, he died. I was twenty and he was twenty-one when we married. He was killed in a car crash a few months after the wedding."

Something moved behind his eyes. "You were twenty?"

"Yes."

"And you haven't made love with anyone since?"

"No."

"You must have loved him a great deal."

"Yes, I did."

He said, his voice very clipped, "Why me? After all these years, Tracy, why me?"

She replied honestly, "Because I feel a connection to you that I have never felt with any other man."

He looked into her eyes. "Not even your husband?"

Slowly she shook her head. "Scotty and I grew up together. He was my best friend before he became my husband. But this thing between us is . . . different."

The tightness across his cheekbones relaxed infinitesimally. "Yes," he said. "I know."

Should I tell him about Charles and Isabel? she thought.

She had actually decided that she would, and was opening her lips to speak, when he said, "This may sound nauseatingly sentimental, but I think I have been looking for you all of my life."

He lifted her hand to his lips and kissed it.

She felt that kiss all the way down in her stomach. "I suppose we shouldn't care what other people think. It's only us who matter."

He smiled. "That's right."

A door slammed somewhere, and Tracy retrieved her hand from Harry's grasp. A moment later, Meg came into the morning room. "Ebony is sitting in your doorway, Harry, and she's definitely not happy. She yowled at me when I went by."

"She's upset because I let the dogs come upstairs. She'll get over it."

Meg looked at the spaniels and laughed. "They look so smug."

"You, on the other hand, look very pretty," he said.

Meg glanced cautiously down at her stomach. "My jeans are getting tight."

"You'll have to go shopping, then, and buy bigger ones."

"A bigger size?" Meg's eyes looked huge.

"That's what getting better is all about, Meggie. More weight and bigger sizes. You know that."

"I suppose," she muttered, looking unhappy.

Tracy said, "I understand that Nancy is coming back to work tomorrow, Meg."

"Yes."

"Then I suppose that means you're out of a job," Harry said.

Meg's face brightened, and for a moment she really

did look pretty. "Dave asked me if I would like to work with Nancy. He said I had a terrific eye for detail."

Tracy said quickly, before Harry could object, "Meg, how wonderful. I'll bet you don't realize what a compliment that is." She shot Harry a warning look.

After a moment, he said, "You were always an observant kid. I remember you were always the first one to notice if there were any strange lumps or bumps on any of the animals."

"That's true," Meg said. Her eyes were shining.

"Speaking of animals," Tracy said to Harry, "you must remind me to write you a check for Dylan's board and training. I understand it's due today."

His dark blond brows snapped together. "What the devil are you talking about? You don't pay Dylan's fees."

"I do now," she replied calmly. "I bought him last Friday from Gwen Mauley."

He looked stunned. "You *bought* him?"

"That's right. She was here Thursday morning for a lesson with you, and she was very upset to learn that you were out of commission. Apparently she had seen a horse in Germany she liked, and she had decided to sell Dylan. I said I would buy him."

He sat up straight, his eyes looking very dark. "What the hell are you going to do with Dylan?"

"I'm going to leave him here with you for training. I have to learn how to ride dressage before I can ride him myself. In fact, I was hoping you would give me lessons on Pendleton."

He frowned. "What did you pay for him?"

She was sitting on the ottoman next to his chair, and

their faces were very close. "Thirty-two thousand pounds."

He shook his head. "That's too much. Gwen is taking advantage of you."

"Well, you certainly charge top dollar for your services," Tracy retorted. "You can't blame Gwen for wanting to make money on Dylan!"

"I doubled my fees for Gwen," he said. "And the horse isn't worth thirty-two thousand pounds, Tracy."

"You said he was a once-in-a-lifetime horse."

"He *wlll* be. He isn't yet."

"Well, then, you will just have to work with him until he *is* worth thirty-two thousand pounds. Besides, I have no intention of selling him. I'm going to keep him."

He ran his hand through his hair. "This is crazy."

"I think it's great," Meg countered.

Tracy said, "Unfortunately, I can't take lessons while I'm shooting the movie. Insurance stipulations—no dangerous activities."

"Riding Pen isn't dangerous," Meg said indignantly.

"You're hardly a beginner," Harry said.

"I doubt that that will make any difference to the movie's insurance company," Tracy pointed out.

"Oh Harry!" Meg said, as if she had just remembered something. "What did the English Heritage office say about rebuilding the stable?"

"I haven't heard from English Heritage."

"There was a letter for you."

"I never got it."

Meg frowned. "It came the day after you went back into hospital, and we decided to wait until you were feeling better before we gave it to you. I put it in your room, on the mantel, so you'd see it when you came home."

"I didn't look on the mantel," Harry said irritably. "And I wish people wouldn't do things they think are for my own good."

"Shall I go and get it for you?" Meg said.

"Yes."

While she was gone Tracy said neutrally, "It was Meg's idea to hold the letter until you got home. I think it's a good sign that she's thinking of other people and not just herself."

Harry asked in a tight voice, "Did Howles—he's the English Heritage officer—call here by any chance?"

"Not that I know of."

"I don't have a good feeling about this," he said.

Meg came back into the room with an envelope in her hand. She gave it to Harry who ripped it open with his forefinger. He unfolded the linen paper, with its official letterhead, and stared at the print. When he had finished reading, he refolded the letter and put it back into the envelope.

"Well?" Meg said impatiently.

Tracy knew what the answer was before he spoke. She could read it on his face.

"I have to rebuild the stable with original materials," he said.

"Oh no!" Meg sat cross-legged on the floor in front of Harry's chair and looked up at him. "That's so unfair!"

"I talked to that fellow Howles myself, and I thought I had him convinced to let me rebuild with modern building materials." Harry crushed the envelope in his hand. "What the hell could have made him change his mind?"

"A large bribe, perhaps," Tracy said.

Harry and Meg stared at her.

"Don't look so shocked," she told them. "It happens in the States all the time when big real estate transactions take place. I'm quite sure it happens here in Britain, too."

"Mauley," Harry said.

"It wouldn't surprise me," she returned. "*Someone* burned your stable down, Harry, and the only purpose I can see for doing that would be to put you in so much debt that you had to sell those eight thousand acres. The more you have to pay to rebuild the stable, the greater your debt will be."

"Shit," said Meg.

"I couldn't agree more," Harry said bitterly.

"What will you do? Will you sell him the land?" Meg asked.

He replied very calmly, "I will sell every last painting and piece of furniture in this house before I sell that land to Robin Mauley."

Tracy and Meg exchanged glances but did not reply.

Harry stood up. "If you'll excuse me, I'm going to go to my office for a while."

Don't give yourself a headache poring over figures. Tracy almost said the words but bit them back in time. She and Meg sat in somber silence as Harry left the room, followed by his faithful spaniels.

Harry had not returned by the time the news was over, and Tracy went to bed wondering if he would come to her. She showered, put on some perfume, and got into bed with a book, which she stared at but didn't read.

She thought of Scotty. Would he understand what she was about to do? The answer was immediate, *Hell, yes.*

She smiled. She had not been celibate for so many years because she feared Scotty's displeasure. She thought of Harry's words: *I think I have been looking for you all of my life.*

It's the same for me, she thought with wonderment. *It's the same for me.*

Restlessly, she put her book back on the bedside table and went to look out of the window. She was still there when a soft knock came on her door. Breathlessly, she called, "Come in."

The door opened and Harry was there.

23

He was dressed in the same casual pants and shirt he had worn in the morning room, but he had removed his jacket and his shoes. He looked at her, and said, "Do you have any idea how beautiful you are?"

Her cloud of auburn hair was floating around her shoulders, and her eyes burned like sapphires in the moon-bleached purity of her face. The color of her satin pajamas exactly matched the silk of the drapes, which framed her like a portrait in ivory.

"Lots of women are beautiful," she replied gravely. "Hollywood is loaded with them."

He shook his head. "Not like you." He locked the door behind him, then turned back, and repeated softly. "Not like you."

She stood as if in a trance and watched him approach. Then he was standing in front of her. He cradled her jaw with gentle fingers, tilted her face, and kissed her. He kissed her and kissed her and went on kissing her and Tracy's arms came up to hold him close while she kissed him back.

The thin pajamas she wore were no barrier against him. She could feel the hard strength of his body as it pressed against hers, and she melted into him. Her head fell back on his shoulder, and she opened her mouth. She felt the urgency of his desire, and held him even closer.

Finally, his mouth lifted, and he murmured in her ear, "Let's go to bed."

"Okay," she whispered back, and he took her hand and led her toward the turned-down bed.

Nothing felt awkward, nothing felt wrong. Lying back on the bed, she pulled his shirt out from his waistband, slipped her hands under the soft cotton, and ran them up and down his rib cage. He was slim, but when she moved her hands to his back she could feel the strength of the muscles there. Her heart was beating so hard that it was making her breasts quiver, a fact he must have noticed since he had unbuttoned her pajama top and was kissing them.

It was not a long, exquisitely drawn-out lovemaking. She wanted him quite as badly as he wanted her and, once he realized that, he did not waste much time. His initial possession was hard and urgent, but once he was deep inside of her a sense of great stillness washed over them both. They lay there, joined together, and looked into each other's eyes.

"Tracy." He said her name as if discovering it for the first time. His brown eyes, which had been narrowed with passion a moment before, looked luminous. "This is what I have been waiting for."

She felt him so intensely, felt him inside of her, felt his weight on her, felt his wonderment at what was happening between them, and she was filled with happiness. "I know," she whispered back.

Slowly the luminous look disappeared, replaced by the narrow-eyed intentness of passion. "Are you okay?" he asked.

"I'm wonderful," she replied.

"Thank God." As he drove into her she could feel herself opening to him. Her body put no barriers in his way, yielding generously to his possession, surrendering, welcoming, passionate. When climax came, and her whole being was shuddering with pleasure, the name that she called out was *Harry*.

He kissed her mouth very gently, and she turned her cheek into his shoulder and closed her eyes. It was a long time before either of them stirred, and then it was he who made the first move. "I'm too heavy for you," he said, and rolled onto his side so that he was facing her. She looked into the face on the pillow next to hers, at the thick, tousled, silky hair, the long-lashed brown eyes, the lines of the beautiful mouth, and thought, *I love him.*

He sighed and reached out to trace her cheekbone with a gentle finger. "Do you want me to go back to my own bed?"

"No. Stay here."

He buried his lips in her hair. "You won't have to ask me twice."

*   *   *

𝒥racy woke with the sense that someone was looking at her. She opened her eyes, turned her head, and saw Harry. He was lying propped on his elbows, his shoulders bare above the quilt, a strand of tawny hair caught in his eyelashes, the shadow of a golden beard on his cheeks and jaw.

"Good morning," Tracy said, reaching out to brush the strand of hair away from his lashes.

"Good morning," he replied.

He shifted a little so he could reach her nose with a kiss. "It's five o'clock and we don't have to get up for at least an hour."

Tracy's lips curved. She was totally awake, every nerve in her body attuned to every sinew and muscle in his. "How nice. Do you have any ideas about how we could pass the time?"

"Yes." His voice was clipped, his face hard and concentrated. He pulled her toward him, and their mouths met.

How can a kiss be hard and soft, cool and burning, all at the same time? If Tracy has been capable of thinking, that was what she would have thought. But rational thought was far away; all she knew was feeling. Her fingers roamed all over his lean-muscled body, with its English-fair skin, learning him by touch the way a blind person would search out Braille.

"I thought about you every minute I was in the hospital," he muttered as his mouth moved from her breasts down toward her long, lovely waist.

"Harry." It was the only word she was capable of uttering. Her fingers found a ridge of scar tissue on his left shoulder and traced it with attentive precision. His hands and his mouth were moving all over her body, claiming every part of her, making her his. She held on to him as he entered her, opening herself even as her tense fingers bit into the strong muscles of his back. She gave a single, sharp cry as he slid home.

Harry. No other word, no other name, was in her mind. She arched up toward him, holding on desperately as he drove into her. Back and forth, back and forth, and each stroke softened her, opened her, until the river of her response crested and poured through her in an overwhelming flood of sexual pleasure.

They lay pressed together afterward, and, even though they had physically disconnected, still Tracy felt such unison with him, such peace. She felt . . . healed.

He shifted a little to bring their bodies into even closer contact, and she rested her hand on his head, possessively burying her fingers in his hair. "I love you so much," he said, touching her throat with his lips.

"I love you, too," she replied. His hair under her fingers felt absurdly silky, like a little boy's, and she though of Charles and his bright, glossy hair and wide-spaced dark eyes.

I wonder if this was what he wanted? she thought. *Is this joining of Harry and me the way for him and Isabel to rise above the lost years, the anguish of separation? Will they rest in peace at last?*

Harry said, "You smell so good, like the old-fashioned roses I have in my garden."

"It's a special perfume I have made up just for me. I love roses."

He lifted his head so he could look into her face. "Do

you find this at all peculiar? This intense attachment when we have known each other for so short a time?"

"I don't find it peculiar at all," she said.

A faint line appeared between his eyebrows. "Neither do I. And that, perhaps, is the most peculiar thing of all."

She hesitated, then brought out the question that she had wanted to ask him since before he went into the hospital. "Harry . . . Jon said something that bothered me, and I wish you would clear it up."

"What did lover-boy say?" His voice was heavily sarcastic.

"He said that Dana Matthews called you for help on the night she overdosed, and that you refused to go to her."

"And do you believe him?" he asked neutrally.

"I think that perhaps there was a phone call made, but it was not as Jon interpreted."

He rolled onto his back and stared at the ceiling. "You're right, she did call me, but I wasn't home. I was out walking. By myself." He shot her a look. "Needless to say, there were many people who chose to disbelieve me and think that I ignored her cry for help. It made for a good newspaper story."

"Oh Harry." She rose onto her elbow so she could look into his face. "I'm so sorry. It must have been terrible for you to hear her words and know that you were too late to save her."

Two lines bracketed his mouth. "It was the most pitiable message, Tracy. I raced to her house as soon as I heard it, but she was already in a coma. I drove her right to hospital, and they worked over her for a half an hour or so, but it was too late. She died."

"I am so sorry."

The lines at the corners of his mouth deepened. "It didn't help that she left me a wad of money. You can imagine how that made me look—I don't get to her house until an hour after her phone call, and she leaves me money. The scandal sheets had open season with that one."

"What did you do with the money?" she asked softly. "Donate it to charity?"

The bitter look left his face. "Thank you, darling. Yes. I donated it to several drug-rehabilitation programs."

"I just wanted to know, Harry. Jon made the story sound nasty when he told me, and I just wanted to find out the truth."

"Well now you know."

"Now I know. But I still loved you even when I didn't know."

He looked at her somberly. "Dana had auburn hair and a great smile. I think I mistook her for you."

They looked into each other's eyes, and both of them thought of the ghosts they had seen, but neither one of them said anything.

$\mathcal{H}$arry left at six o'clock, with great reluctance, and Tracy took a shower and dressed in jeans and sweater. They were shooting the second ball scene, and she was called for ten, which meant she had to be in makeup by eight. It would take almost an hour just to do her hair.

She still had not got her new wedding picture, and all

her albums were at home, but her sister had sent her a snapshot, and now she took it out of the drawer, sat on the bed, and looked at it. It was a picture of a young man in a basketball uniform. His eyes and every strand of his wiry dark hair looked electric with joy. She had taken the photo on the day Scotty had signed a letter of intent to play basketball for the University of Connecticut.

"I haven't forgotten you," she said softly to the photograph in her hand. "I will never forget you. But I have a new love, Scotty, and I'm so very happy."

There was no dimming of the incandescent happiness in the young face she was looking at. Some words of familiar poetry drifted into her mind: *Ah that it were possible to undo things done, / To call back yesterday.*

How many times since Scotty had died had she thought of those lines? If only . . . if only . . . if only she could roll back time to before the accident. If only she were able to put out her hand, to stop from happening those few terrible seconds when her entire world had been shattered. *Ah that it were possible . . .*

She had never doubted that, if she were given the chance to call back yesterday, she would do it in a flash. To have Scotty back, she gladly would have wiped away all of her success as a movie star, would gladly have become the obscure high school teacher she had always thought she would be.

But would she do it now? Would she call back yesterday if it meant she would never meet Harry?

Her mind shied away from the question the way a dreamer's mind shies away from the endless fall into the abyss. *I can't think about that. It's stupid to think about that. I don't have to choose between them. It's stupid to torment myself with choices that don't have to be made.*

Scotty continued to smile up at her, and other lines of poetry came into her head: *Golden lads and girls all must, / As chimney-sweepers, come to dust.*

It was true, she thought. Scotty and Charles, golden lads both, were dead. And in the ineluctable progression of time, she and Harry would one day follow them into the darkness.

But not now, she thought. She felt her blood running strongly, mounting like sap in a tree, felt the beating of her heart, of her pulses. *Now is our time,* she thought. *Now is the time for us to "roll all of our strength and all of our sweetness up into one ball."*

Slowly her eyes returned to Scotty's face. *Go ahead,* his brilliant light-filled eyes seemed to be saying to her. *Grab happiness while you can, Trace. Don't worry about me.*

She stood up and, with the picture still in her hand, crossed to the window. A shock ran through her as she saw the carriage drawn by four black horses standing in front of the house. As she watched, wide-eyed and with racing heart, a man dressed in a long, caped coat stepped out and went down the steps that had been set for him by a footman. For a wild moment she thought the film company must be shooting a scene from the picture, but then she realized that there were no cameras, no microphones, no people except for this single man getting out of the carriage, and the attending footman.

"Jeremy!" She heard the name called because she had opened the window slightly before her shower. A woman dressed in a long blue afternoon dress and wearing a shawl around her shoulders came into Tracy's sight at the bottom of the stairs. "I am so glad that you have come!"

The man kissed the woman on the cheek in an unmistakably brotherly fashion, and said, in the English accent used by Charles, "What the devil has happened, Caroline, to cause you to send me such a message?"

"Come into the house and I will tell you," Charles's wife replied.

As Tracy watched, the brother and sister disappeared from her view on their way into the house, and the coach vanished in the direction of the stables.

Tracy put her hand over her pounding heart. *I'm afraid,* she thought. *I'm so afraid. What do all of these visions mean? Have they something to do with the fact that someone is trying to kill Harry?*

Before Tracy left for her appointment in makeup, she called Gail with new instructions for the private detective. "See if he can find out if money was transferred from Robin Mauley's account into the account of a man named Howles, who works for English Heritage," she said, and Gail promised she would relay the order.

The morning's filming went badly. At first they were delayed because Greg couldn't find Liza Moran, who was needed for the shoot.

"Did you check her dressing room?" Dave asked his assistant director tensely.

"I did," Greg replied. "The door was closed, but I knocked several times, and there was no answer."

"Did you hear anything inside?" Dave said.

Greg lifted his brows. "I thought I did, but no one answered my knock. I could hardly burst in on her, now could I?"

Tracy got up from her chair. She didn't want to be delayed, she wanted to finish early so she could spend some time with Harry. And she was sick to death of Liza Moran. "Perhaps you can't, Greg, but I can," she said ominously.

Everyone on the set stared at her.

"I'm fed up with Miss Moran and her nymphomaniac ways," Tracy announced. "I don't care what she does on her own time, but this is the third time I have been kept waiting while she indulges herself, and I've had it." She looked at Dave. "I'll get her."

Speechless, he nodded.

As Tracy stalked off, Greg said to the electrician standing next to him, "I almost pity Liza when Tracy lights into her."

Liza's trailer door was still closed when Tracy reached it, and she ruthlessly pulled it open and went through. Inside, Liza was standing by the clothes rack, pulling her costume over her head. A young man was seated on the couch lacing up a pair of sneakers. Tracy said, her voice like ice, "We have been waiting for you for fifteen minutes already."

Liza's face emerged from her dress, and she stared at Tracy in stunned amazement. "What are you doing here?"

The young man, whom Tracy recognized as being one of the catering staff, charged by her with one sneaker still untied and his shirt still open. He left the door open behind him.

In the same icy voice, Tracy said, "Since you didn't respond to Greg's call, I thought you might respond to mine." She looked with disgust at Liza's mouth. "Your makeup is smudged. It will have to be fixed."

Liza had finally pulled herself together. "How dare you," she shouted. "How dare you walk uninvited into my dressing room. Who the hell do you think you are?"

Tracy's eyes narrowed. "I'll tell you who I am. I am Tracy Collins, and I do not like to be kept waiting while one of the cast members is screwing the caterers. So— this is the last time this will happen, Liza, or you will never work on one of my pictures, or my friends' pictures, again." Her eyes narrowed a fraction more. "And I mean never."

Liza looked furious, but she was afraid of Tracy's power and tried to be conciliatory. "Sorry," she muttered. "I didn't realize what time it was."

"In the future make sure that you do," Tracy said grimly. "Now, go over to makeup, get fixed up, and report to the set." She turned her back on the seething Liza and went out of the trailer.

When Liza finally arrived on the set, she was looking subdued. "I'm sorry," she said to Dave. "I didn't have my watch on. It won't happen again."

They started filming and, for the first time since the movie had started, Jon was distracted. He missed his lines in all of the first seven takes, almost, but not quite, causing Dave to blow up in a rage. Finally, Jon got them right, and Dave called, "*Print*," but Tracy knew, and Dave knew, and Jon had to know as well, that it was not his best work. It was good. Jon could sleepwalk through a role, and it would still be good. But his performance lacked the intensity of his earlier work.

At lunch break, Tracy called Gail, who put her in touch with Mark Sanderson, the private detective she had hired. "As far as I can see, Miss Collins, the Honorable Anthony Oliver is clean," the detective reported over the phone. "His lifestyle is certainly above his income, and he has a big credit-card debt, but nobody is after him to pay up. There's no doubt that additional money would be welcome, but he's not pushed to the wall, if that's what you wanted to know."

"Yes," Tracy said. "That was what I was wondering, Mr. Sanderson. Did my secretary speak to you about possibly tracing a bribe?"

"She did. It's rather a delicate operation, and I'm not sure if I can do it. Mauley is a big name."

"I will be willing to pay extra if you can manage it," Tracy said.

"All right, I'll get on it immediately then."

As Tracy hung up, she didn't know whether to feel relieved or disappointed. On the one hand, she didn't want to have to face Harry with the news that his own brother was scheming against him, but on the other hand, it would be an enormous relief to have a culprit so she could stop being terrified for Harry's safety.

She was free after lunch. They had finished with the scenes in the drawing room and were moving into the magnificent bedchamber that had once belonged to the resident Earl of Silverbridge. It would take at least the afternoon to light the set, and her stand-in would substitute for her when they needed a body to pose for the technicians.

Tracy was hungry and was trying to decide if she wanted to eat first or get her makeup and costume off first, when Jon came up to her, and said, "Finally, we're both free at the same time! Will you have dinner with me tonight, Tracy? I understand there's an excellent restaurant in the village."

She looked into his face and saw that he was trying to disguise his hopefulness. "I don't think so, Jon," she said gently. "I rather promised Meg that I would go shopping with her this afternoon, and I don't know when we'll be back."

His hazel eyes looked very green against the lawn that stretched out behind him. "I'll wait for you. We won't need a reservation in the middle of the week."

"I'd rather not. If I can get Meg to eat out, I will. It's good for her to be forced to eat from a menu." To soften her rejection she reached out and touched him on the arm. "I'm sure you understand."

An emotion that might have been anger flickered behind Jon's eyes. "You really have fallen for him, haven't you?"

Tracy waited a moment before replying in an expressionless voice, "What do you mean?"

He shook his dark head impatiently. "Don't play games, Tracy, you know what I mean. You've fallen for Silverbridge."

Tracy let another pause develop while she thought about the best way to respond to this comment. At last she decided on honesty. "Yes, I'm afraid I have, Jon. I've fallen rather hard, as a matter of fact. So you see,

I'm just not interested in spending time with other men right now."

He crossed his arms over his burly chest. "I suppose I can't blame you. He has everything going for him: an ancient title, a fabulous house, money, looks, charm. Why wouldn't you fall for him?"

He was making her attraction to Harry sound so superficial, but she shut her mouth on her initial impulse, which was to inform Jon that Harry was a farmer with much less money than Jon himself, and said instead, "Neatly put."

The tautness of his facial muscles relaxed at this forthright reply, and he forced a smile. "Well, you know I don't approve, but I most certainly do understand. However, if something should ever happen, and you need a friend, please know that I will be here for you."

Tracy tilted her head fractionally. "What could possibly happen?"

"He could dump you, my dear." Jon's tone was dry. "Shocking as that thought may be, it's happened to other beautiful young women who became involved with Silverbridge."

Tracy forced herself to maintain a pleasant expression. "That is kind of you, Jon, but I don't think I need to worry."

He patted her shoulder. "That's what they all say, my dear. But I promise faithfully that I won't say *I told you so.*"

And on that less-than-encouraging note, he walked away.

24

Harry sat in the morning room waiting for the six o'clock news to start. Ebony was draped across his lap, purring with pleasure as he petted her, and he was staring at the empty screen going over in his mind his afternoon interview with the local English Heritage officer.

"English Heritage believes that it is the *tout ensemble* of the English country house that defines its contribution to art history," the obnoxious young man with the Midlands accent and dreadful tie had said. "This includes the furnished house with its collections as well as its garden, green park, woods and, in the case of Silverbridge, stables."

"I can rebuild the stables to *look* authentic," Harry had said. "But surely you must see that the cost of the original materials is prohibitive—not to mention the exorbitant fees I would have to pay to the skilled craftsmen who know how to work with those materials."

"I understand and sympathize with your predicament, Lord Silverbridge." The Howles fellow had actually made an attempt to look down his nose at Harry. "But you should have had the stables insured for the correct amount of money to allow you to rebuild in the original style. Unfortunately, you did not do that, and now you must deal with the consequences."

Harry had made a heroic effort to hold on to his temper. "I've got the house insured for four times its market value. Do you know the cost of that kind of insurance?"

"The cost of insurance is not my concern, my lord. My concern is the preservation of England's great heritage." The young man had fingered his dreadful tie. "The fact that you underinsured your stable cannot be allowed to figure into my decision on this matter. My mission is to protect our heritage."

"Silverbride is *my* heritage, not yours," Harry had replied grimly. "And this is not the tune you were singing the last time I spoke to you. In fact, you led me to believe that there would be no problem with my rebuilding the stable with modern materials as long as I kept the appearance correct."

Howles's superior expression disappeared. "I have since changed my mind."

"And may I ask what caused you to change it?"

The young man gave an elaborate shrug. "You are a very persuasive man, my lord. When I was out from under the influence of your charismatic personality, I realized that I had made a mistake."

Suddenly Harry had had enough. "That's not the only mistake you have made, Howles." He stood up. "That tie of yours is an affront to good taste everywhere. How the devil the government could put a man like you in charge of 'England's Heritage' will always remain a mystery to me."

He had exited upon that note, and now he wondered if he should have remained to further exercise his "charismatic personality" upon the obnoxious Howles.

It would have been a waste of time, he decided. *I'm beginning to think that Tracy might be right and there was a bribe involved in Howles's change of mind.*

"This whole thing stinks, Eb," he said out loud, one long finger caressing his cat's small skull.

Ebony purred louder.

Harry glanced at his watch, saw that it was time for the news to begin and shooed Ebony off his lap so he could turn on the television. As soon as he stood up the telephone rang. He let it ring twice, hoping that Mrs. Wilson would pick it up, then when it rang a third time he went to answer it himself.

A man's voice with a thick Scots accent said in his ear, "Is this Lord Silverbridge?"

Harry frowned. "Yes. Who is this?"

"Tracy Collins asked me to call you, my lord, and ask you to meet her by the lake on your property as soon as possible. She said she had something important to show you."

"Who is this?" Harry demanded again.

"Just a local shopkeeper, my lord, doing as Miss Collins asked. Good-bye."

Harry stared at the phone, which had been disconnected.

A local shopkeeper. He knew that Tracy had taken

Meg shopping for new clothes, but why hadn't she called him herself? This phone call suggested that she had been in a great hurry.

What can she want to show me? And who the hell is this Scottish shopkeeper?

He ran down two flights of stairs to collect the dogs. Neither Mrs. Wilson nor Marshal and Millie were in the kitchen, however. The housekeeper had probably taken the spaniels out for a walk. He made a quick decision not to search for them, but went into his office, grabbed a rifle from its glass cabinet, loaded it, and headed in the direction of the lake.

Clouds had come in during the course of the afternoon, bringing an early twilight. Harry jogged steadily along the garden path, the rifle grasped firmly in his hand, feeling a sense of inexplicable urgency. He turned onto the path that would bring him to the woods, ignoring the headache that the exertion of jogging was bringing on.

He didn't use the bridle path but took the deer trails, and even so, it was half an hour before he reached the lake. A flock of blackbirds rose from the grass and flew away as he burst out of the tree cover, but, aside from the birds and the swans floating downstream, the lakeshore was empty of life.

"Tracy," he called. "Are you here?"

A distant birdcall was his only reply.

The skin on the back of Harry's neck prickled, and a thought flashed through his brain, *I'd better get under cover.*

Before he could translate this thought into action, however, two things occurred simultaneously. Someone shoved him from behind, causing him to fall sprawling to the ground, and a rifle bullet blasted over his head as he fell.

Shit, Harry thought as he lifted his face out of the prickly grass. Another rifle shot rang out, and this bullet whistled close to his ear. "Get out of here," he shouted to whoever had pushed him, got to his feet and dived into the woods.

A third bullet exploded, then everything was quiet except for the hammering of Harry's heart. *I should have brought the dogs,* he thought.

"I have a gun, too!" he shouted in the direction of the shot. He fired his own rifle into the air. "Come and get me, you cowardly bastard."

He heard a faint rustling in the distance, but it could have been deer spooked by the sound of shooting. Adrenaline was pumping through his bloodstream, and he scarcely noticed the pain in his head. His eyes searched the woods he knew so well, the woods he had hunted since he was a boy, but all was quiet. He picked up a rock and threw it, waiting to see if the noise and motion would draw another rifle shot. Nothing.

Bastard, Harry thought disgustedly. *He's not going to show himself. He's going to run away.* His finger curved around the trigger of his rifle. *Damn!*

He waited for half an hour and during that time saw no sign of either the shooter or the person who had pushed him. It was as if both of them had dissolved into the English twilight. Finally, he decided to return to the house.

By the time he let himself in the side door, his adrenaline rush had subsided and his head was pounding. He went downstairs to his office to return his rifle to its cabinet and found Tracy and Meg sitting at the kitchen table eating dinner.

"Harry! Where have you been?" Meg demanded. Her eyes focused on the gun that was still in his hand. "Were you out shooting?"

"Actually, I was the one being shot at," he returned.

Tracy went perfectly white.

Meg's blue eyes seemed to engulf her face.

Damn, Harry thought. *It's this bloody headache. I'm not thinking straight. Why the hell did I blurt that out?*

"Someone tried to shoot you?" Tracy said.

Her eyes were midnight blue in her pale face. Meg looked petrified.

"Hell," Harry said. He closed his eyes for a moment. "I should have kept my mouth shut."

All he wanted to do at the moment was go upstairs, take some painkillers, and get into bed. But he couldn't walk out and leave them looking like this. "I'm fine," he said. "It was probably just a poacher."

"Then why do you have a gun?" Tracy asked.

"Like Meg said, I was out shooting." He rubbed his forehead and avoided meeting those too-knowing blue eyes.

"And you gave yourself a headache," she said flatly.

"I'm afraid I did. So, if you don't mind, I'll put this gun away and go upstairs to rest."

"Don't you want some dinner, Harry?" Meg asked.

"No, thank you, Meggie," Harry replied.

He put the gun away, but when he returned to the bottom of the staircase, Tracy was waiting for him. "You can tell me what happened while you take some medication and get into bed."

"I've already told you what happened, and I don't need you to put me to bed," he responded.

She didn't answer, just turned and went up the stairs. He sighed and followed.

Ebony was parked in the middle of his bed, and when she saw Tracy, she arose, tail standing straight up, and glared at the intruder.

"Go take a pill," Tracy told him.

He went into his bathroom, shook two prescription pills from a plastic bottle, and washed them down with water. When he returned to the bedroom, Tracy was sitting in one of his fireside chairs, and she and Ebony were regarding each other warily. He went to take the other chair, and Ebony immediately came to claim her spot on his lap. He automatically began to pet her.

"Tell me everything," Tracy said.

He told her about the phone call and his trip to the woods and the shots. "Someone set me up, obviously. Good thing I had the forethought to bring a gun with me; otherwise, I would have been a sitting duck."

"You shouldn't have gone in the first place."

"Obviously I had to go. The call might have been authentic."

She pushed a lock of hair behind her ear, and he thought, watching the movement of her wrist and forearm, that she was the most graceful woman he had ever seen. She said, "Was it just luck that caused that first shot to miss you? Or did something else happen?"

Thud, thud, thud, went the pain in his head.

"What else could have happened?" he asked.

"I'm asking you. It just seems to me that if someone went to such trouble to set you up, he would have been certain he could make his shot."

His hand stilled on Ebony's fur. He looked at Tracy, and for the first time he fully understood that he was incapable of lying to Tracy. There was some link between them that made it impossible.

Moaw!

His hand began to stroke Ebony again, and he said to Tracy, "A very odd thing happened, so odd that I can scarcely believe it myself."

She nodded, as if this was the reply she had expected.

"Someone pushed me. It happened a split second before I heard the shot. I fell flat on my face, and the bullet went over my head."

Silence fell as she reflected on this disclosure. Then she said quietly, "Do you know who pushed you, Harry?"

He shook his head. "That's what is so weird. Whoever it was disappeared. I never saw him, and I never heard him. There was only the push."

"Do you think it was a man who pushed you?"

"From the strength of that push? Yes, I'm sure it was a man."

He had not switched on a lamp, but her skin glowed like pure porcelain in the dimness. She said, a little tentatively, "Harry . . . I can't help thinking that Charles was shot to death in those very same woods."

For some reason, his heart began to race. He said between his teeth, "What does that have to do with anything?"

She leaned toward him, hands loosely clasped on her

lap. "I know you've said there are no ghosts at Silverbridge, but maybe you're wrong, Harry. Maybe there is a ghost here, a benign ghost, and he saved you from the same tragedy that happened to him."

His heart beat faster, and the pounding of the headache beat with it. "Are you saying that the *ghost of Charles* saved my life?"

Her white teeth sank into her lower lip. "I suppose it sounds silly."

Ghost of Charles, ghost of Charles, the words thudded in his brain to the rhythm of his heartbeat and his headache. "It sounds more than silly," he said. "It sounds insane."

She smoothed a crease from her camel-colored slacks. "It may sound that way, but that doesn't mean it didn't happen."

Unwillingly his mind returned to the afternoon when he had been watching the filming and a scene from the past had interposed itself upon the present. He saw again Charles's golden head as he bent to say something to the auburn-haired girl in the white dress he was dancing with.

He looked into Tracy's eyes, and demanded, "Have you seen something?"

She stared back at him, then she nodded.

He swallowed. "Are you serious?"

"Very serious. I began to see them as soon as I arrived at Silverbridge."

"See whom?"

"Charles and Isabel."

He inhaled deeply. "Who the hell is Isabel?"

"She was governess to Charles's children. She looked

very much like me, just as you look very much like Charles."

That image of the girl in the white dress floated into his mind once more. He said roughly, "I can't believe we are actually sitting here talking about ghosts."

"I know." Her expression was somber. "But I also know what I have seen, Harry. I saw Charles's ghost before I saw his portrait in your office, and the image I saw looked exactly the same as the portrait. How could I have known how he looked if I had never seen a picture of him?"

Thud, thud, went his head. "I don't know."

"I've seen them a number of times," she said, leaning forward. "It's almost as if they're enacting a little play for me. Charles was in love with Isabel, and his wife found out and said Isabel had to leave. Charles made plans to send her to stay with a cousin in America. He was going to follow her, but he was killed before he could do so."

He said slowly, "Isabel's hair didn't have any gold in it, and her nose was straight."

Her eyes widened. "Yes." Her hands tightened into fists. "You *have* seen something, then!"

"Jesus," he said. "This is unbelievable."

"Tell me what you saw."

He told her about the dancing scene, and when he had finished they stared at each other in silence. At last Tracy said in a small voice, "When I first saw you, I felt as if I knew you."

"Yes," he said. "I felt the same."

She drew herself up, as if preparing for battle. "What do you think it means, Harry?"

"I don't know. It's . . . creepy."

"I think it's happening for a purpose. I think that once we find out who killed Charles, we will know who is trying to kill you."

"Jesus," he said again.

"I think that Charles and Isabel are trying to help us have the happy ending that they were denied."

He stared at her, and said slowly, "I have never believed in ghosts."

"I never did either, until I saw them," she returned. *Thud, thud, thud.* "I suppose it is difficult to deny something we both have seen."

She nodded solemnly.

"Somebody did push me," he reiterated. "I'm not mistaken about that. I can still feel the hand on my back."

Abruptly Tracy stood up. "You look like a ghost yourself." She came over to his chair, bent, and kissed his forehead. "Go to bed. We'll worry about this in the morning."

He turned his head and buried his face between her breasts. "Tracy," he said.

She enclosed him in her arms. "I love you," she replied. "I love you, and we will figure this mess out together."

He shuddered. "God, I hope so."

Her breasts were so soft. She smelled of roses. "Don't leave," he said.

Ebony had leaped off Harry's lap when Tracy approached, and she jumped on the bed and gave one sharp *moaw*.

Tracy laughed. "Ebony's just given me my marching

orders, and she's right. You need to sleep. We'll talk again in the morning."

"Who said anything about talking?" he muttered. But the pills were beginning to work. The thudding in his head was lessening, and his eyelids were feeling very heavy.

"Good night," Tracy said, placed a kiss on the top of his aching head, disengaged herself, and went to the door.

Within minutes, Harry and Ebony were asleep.

25

When Harry awoke the following morning, his clock told him it was too late to pay a visit to Tracy. Muttering to himself in frustration, he dressed and was about to go downstairs for breakfast when someone knocked on his door. It was Tony.

"May I speak to you, Harry?"

He looked at his younger brother, who was dressed in perfectly cut tan pants and a sky-blue sweater, and said, "I need a cup of coffee, first. Come downstairs with me. We can talk in my office."

He collected his coffee from the kitchen, which was empty except for Mrs. Wilson and the dogs, and led Tony into his office. He took a seat at his desk, so he was facing the portrait of Charles, and Tony sat in the old leather chair on the other side of the desk. Millie and Marshal took up their usual postures on either side of him.

Harry took a sip. "I hope you aren't going to start again about that bloody golf course."

"This is the last time, Harry." There was an unusually grim line around Tony's flexible mouth. "If you don't agree to sell now, Percy is going to pull out of the deal and build his hotel somewhere else."

"Good. That should get Mauley off my back." Harry took another sip.

Tony slowly shook his head. "I don't get you, Harry. I really don't. You don't have the money to rebuild the stable according to English Heritage specifications. You don't have the money to buy a new car. And yet, you turn your back on a fortune. It doesn't make sense to me."

Harry leaned back in his chair and said mildly, "How did you know about the E.H. specifications?"

"You told me."

"No, I did not."

Tony shrugged. "Well then, I must have heard it from Meg."

Harry put his coffee cup down on the desk and asked bluntly, "Tony, did Mauley bribe that wretched Howles to force me to rebuild with the original materials?"

Tony's eyes were perfectly blank. "What an extraordinary question. Of course not. Mauley is a respectable businessman, not a crook." He shifted in his chair. "Besides, I didn't think one could bribe an E.H. officer. They're all so bloody self-righteous."

"I didn't know you had ever had any dealings with them."

"I know about them from you." Tony's eyes blazed momentarily bluer. "Good God, Harry, next you'll be accusing Mauley of burning down your stable!"

Harry returned calmly, "Someone did, and Mauley is

the only person I can think of who might profit from the fire."

Tony's eyes flattened, and his voice grew colder. "I sincerely hope you are not including me in this accusation?"

Harry steepled his fingers and regarded them with interest. "Something very unpleasant is going on, Tony. Besides the stable fire, there have been three attempts on my life."

Tony jumped to his feet. "On your *life*? Good God, Harry, I don't believe this! Now you're accusing me and Mauley of trying to murder you?" Tony moved behind the leather chair, as if to use it as a shield against Harry, and rested his hands on its back.

Harry looked up from his fingers. "Someone is."

"Well it's not me!" Tony's jaw jutted out. "It's true that I want you to sell the land, but I'm not prepared to kill you in order to get it. What the hell were these attempts anyway? I know you think someone fiddled with your brakes, but I'm not ready to buy that story. I think Ian is covering his own backside."

"Someone tried to run me down in the hospital parking lot. That was the second attempt. The third came when someone lured me out to the lake with a fake message from Tracy and almost succeeded in shooting me."

"Are you serious?" Tony looked shocked.

"Unfortunately, yes." Harry flattened his hands on the desk and leaned toward his brother. "I can't prove anything about the murder attempts, but, if I can prove that Mauley bribed the E.H. officer, then I think I can get the Secretary of State for the Environment to reverse

Howles's ruling about rebuilding. Will you help me do that, Tony?"

Tony thrust his fingers through his perfectly brushed hair. "Let me be clear about this. You're asking me to help you catch Mauley out in a bribe? I'm working for him, for God's sake!"

Harry lifted an eyebrow. "I didn't know you were on salary already."

"Well I am," Tony snapped. "And I hardly think it's ethical for me to set traps for my employer." He paused. "Besides, I don't believe that Mauley bribed anyone."

"I think he did. And I hardly think it is ethical for your employer to try to bankrupt me in order to get his greedy hands on my land," Harry flung back.

Tony's finger gripped the chair back so tightly that they showed white. "This discussion is going nowhere. Keep your damn land, Harry. Much good may it do you."

He strode to the door and was on the verge of going out when Harry said, "You'd better rebrush your hair. You mussed it when you ran your fingers through it."

Tony glared at him and slammed the door.

Harry sat sipping his coffee and looking at the portrait of Charles. "What do you think?" he said out loud. "Is my own brother trying to do away with me?"

No, he's not. He answered his own question in his mind. *I can picture Tony bribing the E.H. officer; I can perhaps even picture him burning the stable. But I can't picture him disabling my brakes, or trying to run me down in the hospital parking lot, or shooting at me in the woods.*

"I think Tony is in the clear," he said out loud to

Charles. "Mauley must be acting on his own." He tried to push out of his mind the thought that if Mauley were indeed behind his problems, then the real estate mogul would have needed an assistant. One could hardly imagine Mauley creeping around in the woods with a rifle.

He hired someone, Harry thought. *He would need someone from Silverbridge to do his dirty work.*

The dregs in his coffee cup were stone cold, and he had come no closer to an answer when he got up and went back into the kitchen for breakfast.

That day the film company was shooting the final scene in the earl's bedchamber. It was Tracy's death scene, the scene where Martin, at the end of his rope, feels the only thing he can do to save his honor and his sanity is to murder his beautiful young wife.

The set was ready when Tracy came into the room wearing a long ivory silk nightgown, cut to show a lot of cleavage. The lights along one wall were trained on a beautifully carved four-poster covered in a gold-embroidered spread, which had been turned down in readiness for her. A chaise lounge covered in the same material as the spread stood near the window, along with an elegant little writing table; and two upholstered chairs, with a tea table between them, were set in front of the alabaster fireplace. Over the mantel hung a Titian portrait of the Contessa de Alfori, who Meg had once said was her distant ancestress.

It was a large, open room for a bedroom, but all the equipment made it seem smaller.

"All right, Tracy," Dave said. "If you would get into the bed, Ivan will check the lighting."

Tracy went over to the bed, stepped out of her loafers, and slipped in between the fine cotton sheets. Someone dashed over to remove the offensively muddy modern footgear.

"Lie back against the pillows, please," the photography director instructed from his place behind one of the cameras.

Tracy complied, resting her head against the lace-embroidered down pillows behind her.

"Fix her hair," Dave said.

The hairdresser came forward and spread Tracy's loose hair so that it haloed her head. "Like that, Dave?" she asked.

"Perfect," the director replied. He looked around, and asked, "Are both cameras loaded?"

"I've already told you six times, Dave," the cameraman replied patiently. "Both cameras are loaded and ready."

Dave's foot was tapping rhythmically. This was *the* crucial scene, the one that must elicit the tragic emotions of pity and fear from the audience, and he very much wanted to do it in one shoot, while his actors were still fresh. "Now all we need is Jon," he said impatiently.

"I'm here." At that moment, Jon came into the room wearing his costume: a ruffled dress shirt, which was open to bare his burly chest, and a pair of tight black satin knee breeches. His hair had been brushed so that a curl fell forward over his forehead, and he looked dashingly Byronic and very sexy.

Everyone on the set knew that this was Jon's scene. Tracy's job was to look helpless, and bewildered, and, at last, when she realized what he was going to do, terrified.

"Clear the set," Dave said. He wanted all extraneous personnel out of the way so that his actors' concentration would be at its peak. Jon positioned himself on the mark at the door, Tracy turned her face on the pillow and closed her eyes, and Dave said, "Roll."

Jon came in the bedroom door.

His first line was a deliberate reference to *Othello*, which had been in the novel. "Put out the light"—he looked at the candle in his hand—"and then put out the light." He came to a halt next to the bed and stared down into Tracy's sleeping face.

This was the cue for Tracy to open her eyes and regard him drowsily. "You have not yet undressed, my lord. Are you not coming to bed?"

He reached out and touched her cheek, and for the first time Tracy felt a real shiver of fear. The hazel eyes looking at her had turned a darkish green.

How did his eyes get so green? Is he wearing contacts? Tracy thought nervously.

The camera came in closer to catch her face.

"You are not asleep . . . yet?" Jon asked.

"No." Tracy's voice came out slightly breathless. "I was waiting for you, my lord."

Jon's hand moved to caress her long, bare throat. "So fair," he said. "So fair and soft and fragile."

Tracy struggled to sit up against the pillows. "Is something wrong, my lord?"

"Why would you say that, my love?" His voice was

gentle and caressing, in complete contrast to the look in his eyes.

Tiger eyes, Tracy thought. She had planned not to show fear until the end of the scene, but now her heart began to hammer in her chest.

"You seem . . . s-strange," she said.

The tiger eyes stared into hers, uncivilized, untamed, ferocious, cruel. Tracy instinctively glanced toward Dave for reassurance, but there was no alarm on his face. In the finished movie that look of hers would seem like a cry for help.

As the scene continued, the tiger Jon was harboring within came ever closer to the surface, pacing and lashing its tail in fury as Tracy tried in vain to placate him. She had little difficulty projecting her emotions; she had forgotten about the cameras and the mikes and was caught up in the terror of what was happening to Julia, sweet, harmless Julia, who hadn't realized what a perilous beast her innocent flirtations would make of her husband.

Inexorably, the scene marched on, Tracy pleading her innocence, Jon growing more and more brutal as he charged her with the long list of supposed betrayals that had been destroying his mind. Sweat poured off Jon's face and stained his ruffled shirt. He was possessed of an enormous rage as the cruel words came out of his mouth, and the tiger stalked, ready to kill.

Neither Tracy nor Jon heard when Dave said quietly, "Roll camera two." It was the second camera that finished the scene, catching on film for all time one of the greatest screen performances ever delivered by an actor.

By the time Jon pushed the pillow over her face, Tracy fully expected him actually to try to smother her.

He did not. As soon as Dave called, "Cut! Print!" Jon loosened his hand on the pillow. Tracy struggled to sit up and both she and Jon, in sheer exhaustion, looked at Dave, who was pumping his fist in the air, seemingly oblivious of the tears that were streaming down his face. "That was great!" he said. "That was great!"

Tracy started to cry. Jon collapsed on the bed as if his legs wouldn't hold him anymore. The technical crew burst into applause. Jon reached out and took her hand. She stared down at the large hand that had engulfed hers and said through her sobs, "I thought perhaps you really might kill me. You were terrifying."

"I even scared myself," he said huskily.

As the crew began to put the scene away, Tracy and Jon sat together on the bed and let the emotions they had built drain slowly from their adrenaline-driven bodies.

After taking off her costume and her makeup, Tracy went up to her bedroom and for two hours fell into a deep, dreamless sleep. When she awakened it was twilight, that lovely time in England when it isn't light but isn't yet dark. Her eyes fell on an envelope bearing her name, which reposed on her night table. She opened it, took out a piece of stationery engraved with the Oliver coat of arms, and read: *"I looked in on you but you were sleeping. I'm going to be at the farm for the rest of the day—see you when I get back. Harry."*

Damn, she thought, annoyed at having missed him.

While she was sleeping an idea had coalesced in her

brain, and she decided to follow up on it and make a telephone call to Gail.

Meg was in the morning room watching television when Tracy came in. She waved to Meg, dialed Gail's number, and turned away to face the dining table.

When Gail picked up the phone, Tracy said, "Have you heard anything from Sanderson?"

"Yes," Gail replied. "But it's not good news. He said that it was impossible to get hold of Mauley's bank records. They're available to the police, of course, but not to a private investigator. He said that if you wanted to charge Mauley, then perhaps the police would demand the records, but his own contact in Scotland Yard doesn't want anything to do with preempting Mauley's records without demonstrable cause."

"Damn. I can't charge Mauley with bribery when I have no evidence, and I can't get evidence unless I charge him."

"Um," Gail said. "Catch 22."

They talked about a few other business matters and then Tracy said, "I do have one more job for Sanderson, Gail."

"Shoot." Gail wrote down what Tracy told her.

"It's probably a waste of time," Tracy said, "but we've already wandered down so many dead ends that one more won't matter."

"Okay. How did the filming go today?"

"We did it in one take, and Dave said it was great."

"That's wonderful," Gail said sincerely.

Tracy laughed. "I don't think I could have gone through it again. It was that intense."

"If it was that intense, then it must be good."

"I think it is. I might even look at the rushes tomorrow."

She hung up and went to join Meg on the sofa. "Is Harry still at the farm?" she asked as she sat down. "It's getting rather late."

Meg turned to her. "No, he came in about half an hour ago. Then he had a call from Tony and went out again."

Tracy felt all the blood drain from her head. "Do you know where he went, Meg?"

Meg shook her head. "What's wrong, Tracy? You look terribly white all of a sudden."

"I don't like these mysterious phone calls," Tracy said.

"This wasn't mysterious," Meg assured her. "I picked up the phone myself. It was Tony."

The fear Tracy had felt this afternoon with Jon was nothing compared to the terror that seized her heart now. Harry was in danger. She felt it as surely as she had felt anything in her life. She looked at Meg and opened her lips to tell her.

The eyes that met hers were the same sky-blue as Tony's, and they regarded Tracy with trusting innocence.

How can I possibly tell her that Harry might not be safe with his own brother?

She fought for control of her voice, so that it would not be shrill with fear, as she said, "What program are you watching, Meggie? Is it any good?"

26

The pub was crowded when Harry opened the oak door and stepped in. Most local businesses had just let out, and there were a number of men, and one or two women, who had stopped by for a pint before they went home. Harry looked around, didn't see Tony, and went to the bar.

"Good evenin', my lord," the gray-haired man behind the counter said respectfully. "How can I serve you today?"

"Actually, Tom, I'm looking for my brother. Do you know if he's here?"

"He's yonder, in the back booth, my lord."

Harry smiled, murmured his thanks, and made his way to the booth, acknowledging greetings along the way.

Tony was hunched over an almost-empty glass of Heineken. He looked up as Harry slid into the opposite side of the stained wooden booth, and said gruffly, "Thank you for coming."

"You're welcome," Harry returned, resting his hands on the scarred tabletop. "What's this all about?"

Tony took a deep breath, and said in a rush, "I know I'm a selfish bastard, Harry. Mum always gave me everything I wanted, and that's what I expect to get. I wanted to manage Mauley's golf complex, and I was angry with you for thwarting me. I've been beastly to you, I know that. But I hope you'll believe that I never never would do anything to harm you."

These words were spoken as if Tony had memorized them and wanted to get them out as fast as he possibly could.

Harry lifted an eyebrow. "Good heavens. What has brought all this on?"

Tony stared at his glass. "I had a meeting with Mauley this afternoon, and I told him that it was all over, that you weren't going to sell him the land." He looked up and met Harry's eyes. "He went totally bonkers, swearing and calling you all sorts of names. When I said that, after all, it was your land and you had the right to keep it if you wanted to, he blew up at me. Said that I'd led him on, that he'd invested a lot of money in this deal, had taken a lot of risks. I suggested that he look for another piece of property, but he insisted that he wanted this property. When I said, 'Well, you're not going to get it,' I thought he was going to punch me. It was then, as I looked at his ugly rooster red face, that the truth struck me. *My God*, I thought. *Harry was right. This bastard has been trying to kill him.*

"It's the only answer that makes any sense," Harry said. "No one else stands to gain by my death."

"Except me," Tony said.

"Except you," Harry agreed mildly.

Tony gripped his hands tightly around his glass. "You must believe me, Harry. I had nothing to do with Mauley's actions. My only culpability lies in my refusal to see the kind of man he was. I wanted what he was offering me too much."

"Can I get you something, my lord?" It was the publican, who was now standing beside their booth.

"Some lemonade," Harry said.

"Good God." Tony's voice was appalled.

"I can't drink alcohol until my head is back to normal."

"Oh. Right. Well, you can fetch me another Heineken, Tom."

"Very good, sir."

They sat in mutual silence until the drinks came. Once they were alone again, Harry said, "Do we have a chance of nailing him? I realize that at the moment we have nothing to take to the police, but can you think of anything we might do to unmask him?"

Tony said decisively, "We need to find his accomplice. If we can find him, perhaps we can get him to testify against Mauley."

Harry said nothing.

A note of impatience sounded in Tony's voice. "You do realize, don't you, that Mauley had to have an accomplice? The setting of the fire, the cutting of your brake lines, those things had to be done by someone whose presence on the property wouldn't be questioned. As it wasn't me, it had to be someone else."

Still Harry was silent.

Tony said, "Ned was right there on the scene when

the stable burned, and he has unquestioned access to the garage. He's knowledgeable enough about machinery to know how to cut your brake lines."

There was a sharp line between Harry's brows. "Ned would never do anything to endanger the horses."

"He got all the horses out," Tony said. "He was conveniently on the scene in time to make sure he did that."

The line between Harry's brows deepened. "It wasn't Ned."

"All right," Tony said reasonably. "If it wasn't Ned, then who was it?"

Harry moved his shoulders. "I don't know. One of the stable lads, perhaps."

"One of the stable lads didn't shoot at you, Harry. You said the shot would have hit you if you hadn't stumbled and fallen. Whoever it was knows how to shoot."

Harry didn't reply, but his expression was somber.

"Ned has a rifle, doesn't he? I believe I remember the two of you going out shooting together."

"Owning a rifle doesn't mean he's a killer."

"Well, someone is."

Silence fell as they both contemplated that statement. Then Tony said, "Until we resolve this matter, you're in danger. I did tell Mauley that if anything should happen to you, I would honor your wishes and keep the land in the family. But I should continue to tread carefully if I were you."

Harry's wide-set brown eyes regarded his brother gravely. "That was well-done of you, Tony."

Tony shrugged. "I can't help thinking that I'm partly to blame for this mess. If I hadn't been such an eager little disciple, Mauley might not ever have thought of trying to do away with you."

Harry slapped his hand on the table. "We can't let him get away with this."

Tony said slowly, "Actually, I do have an idea."

"What is it?"

"The bullets that were shot at you," Tony said. "Did you recover them?"

They looked at each other. "No."

"You said he shot twice?"

"Yes."

"Then the bullets must be there. I suggest we go and look for them. If they match up to Ned's gun, then we have found our accomplice."

Harry looked troubled. "I suppose that's a good idea."

"It's a brilliant idea, culled from years of reading detective stories," Tony shot back. "You would never have thought of it on your own. All you read is *Horse and Hound* and farming journals."

Harry smiled reluctantly. "True enough."

Tony leaned toward his brother. "Look, Harry, I know you don't want it to be Ned. But if it is, then don't you want to know? You don't want to keep a man who tried to kill you in your employ."

"No." Harry ran his fingers through his hair. "I don't."

Tony pushed his beer toward the middle of the table. "Then let's not waste any more time. Let's go down to the lake and look for the bloody bullets."

Both brothers stood up and left the pub together.

*   *   *

Tracy was playing gin rummy with Meg when Harry walked into the morning room later that evening. The rush of relief she felt at the sight of him almost overwhelmed her. She had spent the last few hours in such a state of fear that she had to keep reminding herself to breathe.

"Harry," she said in a trembling voice.

Tony came into the room, and Harry crossed to the table where the two young women were playing cards.

"I hope you're not gambling," he said lightly. He looked down into Tracy's upturned face and continued in the same tone. "I thought I could trust you not to corrupt my sister."

He was giving her a chance to collect herself, she realized. After a moment she managed to say, "Hah. She's killing me. I haven't won a game yet."

Meg hooted. "That's because your thoughts have been a million miles away."

Tony slid gracefully into the chair next to his sister. "What have you been playing?"

"Gin rummy," Meg returned. "But Tracy's been so distracted that it's hardly been a challenge."

"I'll play you a few rounds," Tony said. "Then we'll see what mettle you're really made of."

Meg looked delighted to be receiving this attention from her brother. "Great!" Her eyes went to Tracy. "That is, if you don't mind, Tracy."

"I don't mind at all," Tracy replied, grateful to be released from the torturous charade she had been engaged in for most of the evening.

"Let me get you a glass of wine," Harry said.

"That sounds wonderful." She thought quickly. "There's some white burgundy in the refrigerator. I think I'd like that better than sherry."

His eyes glinted in acknowledgement. "Let's go down to the kitchen, then."

They went down the stairs in silence, Harry going first. As soon as he stepped into the kitchen, he turned on the light and turned to Tracy with his arms held out.

She went to him, leaned against him, and felt the warmth and strength of his arms as they closed around her. She reached her own arms around his waist and held him tight. "I was so frightened," she said. "When Meg told me that you were meeting Tony . . . "

"Did you suspect Tony of being involved in the plot against me?" His voice was muffled as his lips were pressed against her hair.

She didn't answer.

He answered his own question. "Of course you did." He held her a little tighter. "He had both opportunity and motive. I'm ashamed to admit that I thought of him myself once or twice."

"I had his finances investigated to see if he might be dangerously in debt," she said in a small voice. "He wasn't."

"You had his finances *investigated*?" His arms loosened and he held her away so that he could see her face. "How on earth did you do that?"

"I hired a private investigator."

"Tom Edsel?"

"No. Someone in London."

He looked amazed. "Good God."

"You don't think it was Tony, then?"

"No. As a matter of fact, we've spent the last two hours trying to find the bullets that were shot at me down by the lake. Tony had the idea of trying to match them to the correct gun."

"How clever of him! Did you find them?"

"We found one."

She looked puzzled. "But, Harry . . . what gun are you going to try to match it to?"

His mouth looked grim. "Ned's rifle."

"Oh," she said softly.

"Tony is convinced that Mauley had to have an accomplice on the scene, and he thinks that accomplice might be Ned."

"I think Tony is right about the accomplice. And it would be easier if you eliminated Ned as a suspect right away."

He gave her a crooked smile. "Thank you, darling."

"How are you going to get the rifle tested? Do you want me to contact my private investigator and ask him to arrange it?"

"That's an excellent idea," he approved. "I was going to ask the local police to do it, but I'd rather not raise any speculation until we've got some proof. Do you think this investigator could get it done in a hurry?"

"I'll call him right away. Gail has his pager number."

"Come into my office," Harry said.

She followed him into the office and went to the telephone on the corner of his desk. "I'll have to call Gail for the pager number first."

"Okay."

She dialed Gail's cell phone and after Gail had given her Mark Sanderson's pager number, she said, "I'm going to need you to run up to London tomorrow, Gail. I have something that needs to be delivered to Mr. Sanderson ASAP."

After Gail agreed, Tracy told her to be at Silverbridge by seven-thirty the following morning. Harry nodded his agreement to this time, and when she hung up, he said, "That's good. Ned is in the stable by six-thirty. That will give me enough time to let myself into his apartment and get his rifle."

Tracy nodded back and dialed Sanderson's pager number.

"I'll get you some of that white burgundy while we're waiting for him to get back to you," Harry said.

"Great."

She was on her second glass when the phone rang. Tracy picked it up. "Mr. Sanderson. Thank you so much for getting back to me."

It was a short conversation. Sanderson knew a lab that could do the job, but it would be costly to ask them to rush. Tracy assured him that price was no object, and they made arrangements for Gail to deliver the rifle the following day.

When Tracy had hung up, Harry said, "Let me know how much it costs. I don't want you paying for this."

She was about to protest, but one look at his face told her not to. "All right," she said.

"When does Sanderson think we'll have the results?"

"By tomorrow afternoon, if we're lucky."

He nodded somberly.

"Harry . . . if it isn't Tony and it isn't Ned, then who can it be?"

"One of the stable lads, perhaps."

Tracy felt that that was doubtful, but she didn't want to say so.

"Or it could be a complete outsider," he went on. "What with all these film people about the place, the staff would think that any stranger was with the film, and the film people would think that any stranger was part of the staff. Someone could easily pose as a gardener, for example."

That sounded more likely, and Tracy agreed. "That's true. But if it is a stranger, finding the bullet isn't going to help. You have to have a gun to match it to."

He didn't answer, but picked up her wine glass and took it back into the kitchen. Tracy followed.

"You don't think you ought to go to the police?" she asked.

He put the glass on the drain board. "The only thing the police can do is assign a bodyguard to me, and I don't want that. If Mauley were less important, they might agree to check his bank account if I asked them. But he's too powerful a man. They won't risk his wrath, even for me."

"I wish you would accept a bodyguard," Tracy said. "I'm so frightened that something will happen to you, Harry. I feel . . . I feel like we're playing out some already-scripted drama whose end is inevitable. You're in deadly danger. I know you are."

"It's not as bad as that, darling," he said soothingly as he took her gently into his arms. "Believe me, I have no intention of dying."

"Charles didn't intend to die either."

"I'm not Charles. The bullet missed me, remember?"

"Yes. Perhaps you do have a bodyguard after all," she said. "Perhaps Charles is looking out for you."

"I don't know. That sounds pretty weird."

She rested her cheek against his shoulder. "This whole situation is weird. You and I are weird. Good God, I've only known you for a few weeks, and yet I feel that if you should die, then I would want to die with you."

He didn't answer.

She lifted her face from his shoulder and looked up at him. "The first time I saw you, I stopped breathing. Isn't that weird?"

The brown eyes meeting hers were grave. "Yes."

"How did you feel about me?"

"The same."

"So," she said. "That's weird, too."

The faintest smile tugged at the corners of his mouth. "I don't think it's weird," he said. "I think it's wonderful."

She placed her hands on his upper arms. "Harry. I lost Scotty. I couldn't bear it if I lost you."

He kissed her forehead. "Don't worry, darling. Tony told Mauley that if anything happened to me, he would keep the land in the family the way I wanted. If Mauley realizes that he won't get the land if I die, then he has no reason to kill me. I think this whole business is finished."

What he said made sense, but it still did not reassure her. No matter how logical he might be, she still could not rid herself of the sense that time was running out. Following this thought, she said, "We go back to London soon."

A thick lock of tawny hair fell over his forehead, and he stared at her, frowning deeply. "You're leaving Silverbridge?"

"We've almost finished filming, Harry."

"Do you have more shooting to do in London?"

"Some of the other cast members do. I don't."

His brow cleared. "In that case, you're staying here."

"As your guest?"

"As my intended wife," he shot back.

Slowly she began to smile. "I think I could manage that."

His fingers tightened on her shoulders. "I don't know where Charles and the past fits into all of this. As I said before, it all seems pretty weird. But I do know that you and I belong together."

She tilted her face invitingly upward. "Yes."

There was no urgency about this kiss. It was long and gentle and tender, a seal to a covenant made between the two of them. When he finally raised his head, he said anxiously, "I say, do we have to have a big do? Could we possibly just be married quietly without any fuss?"

She thought for a moment. "I don't see why not. I already gave my family one big wedding; they don't need another."

He grinned. "Did I ever tell you that you were perfect?"

"I don't believe you have."

"Well, you are."

"I'm not, but I'm glad you think so."

He frowned. "I just hate the idea of Mauley getting away with burning my stable."

She shook her head in mock disbelief. "His worst crime is not trying to kill you but burning your stable?"

"I'm okay. My stable is not. And if I can't prove that the E.H. officer was bribed, I'm not going to be able to rebuild it."

"Sweetheart," Tracy said softly, "I make twenty million dollars a movie. I'll rebuild the stable as a wedding present."

His mouth dropped open. *"Twenty million dollars?"*

"Yes. And I have a very clever financial manager who has made me more money than I can possibly spend in one lifetime. Rebuilding your stable will be simple."

He stared at her. "I don't know if I like the idea of using your money . . . "

She said reasonably, "One day Silverbridge will belong to my son. You must agree that I have a vested interest in seeing that it is well maintained."

His brown eyes sparkled. "You sound as if you have thought about this."

"Girls always do," she returned demurely.

He didn't reply, just continued to look at her with those sparkling eyes.

She glanced at the kitchen clock. "Do you think it's too early to go to bed?"

His reply was immediate. "No."

"What about Tony and Meg? What will they think if we toddle off to bed together?"

"We'll tell them that we're going to get married. That will legitimize us."

He took her hand and began to walk her toward the kitchen door.

"I foresee only one problem in our marrying, Harry," she said as they went out into the hallway.

He turned his head. "What's that?"

"Ebony."

"Oh." He grinned. "Don't tell me you're afraid of a little cat."

"She doesn't like me."

"She'll learn to love you."

They began to climb the stairs. "Does she like treats?" Tracy asked. "Perhaps I could bribe her with food."

He laughed. "She'll come around, Tracy. Once she realizes she's stuck with you, she'll come around."

They reached the top of the stairs and went into the morning room to break the news to Tony and Meg.

27

Letting Harry go the following morning was perhaps the hardest thing Tracy had ever done. Even with his assurance that Tony had scotched Mauley's plans, she was afraid.

The ghosts are trying to tell me something, she thought as she cuddled up in the warm spot that Harry had left in her bed. *If only I could figure out what it was, then I could keep him safe.*

But the fact was, she had garnered no clue from Charles and Isabel that might help Harry. *You have to show me more,* she begged Charles silently. *There's something I'm missing, and I know it's important.*

She had to get up. Harry had gone to steal Ned's gun, and she had to deliver it to Gail before she reported for makeup. Reluctantly, she swung her legs out of bed and headed for the bathroom.

* * *

Gail left for London with Ned's rifle, and Tracy started work. Meg had an appointment with her therapist, and Harry drove her into Warkfield. They took the Land Rover, which was the only vehicle other than the tractors that Harry had access to at the moment.

"I'm so happy about you and Tracy," Meg said shyly. "You like her, don't you?"

"I adore her. She . . . understands things."

"Yes, she does."

"Will she be coming to live at Silverbridge?"

"Of course."

Meg said a little anxiously, "I hope I won't be in your way."

He smiled. "Meggie, darling, you could never be in my way. If the happiest day of my life will be my wedding day, then the second happiest will be the day when I know that you are really well."

Meg sat up straighter in her seat. "I'm doing better, Harry. The last time I saw Beth she said that if I kept it up, I was on my way to being cured."

"That's great. You look well. You have some flesh on your bones, and there are roses in your cheeks. With just a little bit more weight, you'll be absolutely beautiful."

"Do you think so, Harry?"

He said firmly, "You'll be the best-looking one of us all—and I include Tony in that description."

She laughed. "He wouldn't like that."

"No, he wouldn't. Perhaps we'd better not tell him I said that."

"Dave thinks that I've been doing a great job working with Nancy," she said. "He told me that if I ever wanted to work on one of his movies, I'd have a job."

Harry lifted an eyebrow. "Did he really?"

"Yes, he did."

"Dave is an important director, Meg. You must have impressed him."

She said earnestly, "I like this job, Harry. I'm good at it. Do you think I could make this my career?"

He replied slowly, "I don't see why not. But you need to finish school first, Meg. I'm sure that Dave didn't intend you to go to work for him right away."

"I'm still too young, he said. But I'll be seventeen this June and, if I go back to school in September, I'll be eighteen when I finish in the spring. That's old enough to get a job, isn't it?"

"Yes." A slight frown dented his brow. "But this kind of job involves traveling and eating out, Meg. There wouldn't be anyone monitoring you. You'd have to take care of yourself."

"I can do that! I know you were thinking of having me go to school in Warkfield next year, but what if I went away? Then I could prove to you that I'm able to take care of myself. I can do it, Harry. I know I can."

"What does Beth have to say about this?"

"She thinks it's a good idea. You can talk to her about it today."

"I'll do that."

Privately, Harry wasn't quite as ready to turn Meg loose as he was leading her to believe. If she wanted to work on films, and apparently she had a talent for it, then she could work on Tracy's films. That way there would be someone to keep an eye on her and make sure that she was eating.

"I'll have to find a school that will take you in September," he said. "If you look as good as you look now, perhaps that won't be as much of a problem as it's been in the past."

"I'll look even better," she promised.

"That would be wonderful." He pulled into a parking spot and turned to face her. "And Meggie, remember that Silverbridge will always be your home." He smiled warmly. "To paraphrase an old saying, you won't be losing a brother, you'll be gaining a sister."

When Meg was finished with her session, Harry had a few items to pick up in town. It was lunchtime when they returned to Silverbridge, and Meg went along to the caterer's truck to join the crew while Harry went into the house. He found Tracy waiting for him in the kitchen. She was in full costume and makeup.

"I heard from Sanderson," she said.

"Come into my office."

She followed him in and took the chair he waved her to. "The results of the test were negative. The bullet didn't match Ned's rifle."

Thank God. Harry didn't realize until that moment how much he had been dreading hearing that Ned was involved in the scheme against him.

Tracy was going on, "While this is good news in regard to Ned, it leaves us in the same situation as before.

We have no clue as to who is responsible for the attacks against you."

He drummed impatient fingers on the desk. "It's Mauley. I think we all know that. What we don't have is proof."

She leaned toward him. "Harry, take the bullet to the police and ask them to test all of Mauley's rifles. Even if he hired someone to do the dirty work, he probably had to supply the gun. England isn't like America, where anyone who wants a gun can get one."

"Thank God."

She rolled her eyes. "Yes, I know we have a reprehensible gun policy, but that's not the point. The point is that it's time to get the police involved. Your life is at risk."

"I don't think it is anymore."

"You can't be sure of that." She gave him a severe look. "What is your problem, anyway? Why are you so reluctant to call in the police?"

"I don't need any more newspaper headlines, Tracy. Once the scandal sheets get hold of the news that I have been targeted for murder, they'll have a field day. I'm just not ready to face all that again."

Tracy understood him perfectly. "Ask the police to keep it quiet."

He lifted an eyebrow. "It's impossible to muzzle everyone who knows about something like this."

Tracy turned around in her chair to regard the portrait of Charles that hung on the wall directly behind her. "Charles is trying to tell us something, Harry. If only I could decipher what it was!"

"Perhaps you will," he said. "Perhaps you will."

* * *

Later that afternoon, a car arrived from London with Ned's rifle. The driver had instructions to deliver it to Harry personally, and he tracked him down at the stables. Unfortunately, Ned had just finished riding one of Harry's younger horses and was standing next to Harry holding the horse's reins when the driver presented him with the rifle.

Ned looked at the gun in his employer's hand, and said in a puzzled voice, "That looks like my gun."

The two of them were standing on the path between the paddock and the stable, and Harry replied soberly, "It is."

There was a pause as Ned's eyes moved from the rifle to Harry's face. "May I ask what you were doing with my gun, Harry?"

"I was having it tested," Harry replied in the same sober voice as before. "I wanted to see if the bullets that were shot at me the other day came from your gun."

Ned's eyes widened. "You were shot at?" River God butted his head against Ned's shoulder.

Harry replied, "Someone fired a gun at me twice, down by the lake. I have also been the victim of an attempted hit-and-run, and the brake lines on my car were slashed, which caused me to have the car accident that sent me to hospital."

"Oh my God," Ned said in a horrified voice. "I didn't know anything about those things."

"Apparently you did not." Harry reached out to lay a hand on Ned's sleeve. "I never really suspected you, Ned. We just thought we should exclude as many guns as we could, so we wouldn't waste time suspecting innocent people."

River God began to dance on the gravel path to demonstrate his impatience at being kept standing. Ned called loudly toward the makeshift stable in the manège, "Someone come and take this horse form me."

A young girl came running toward them and took River God's reins, murmuring to him soothingly. When she was out of earshot, Ned turned back to Harry and said hoarsely, "I think I know who is behind these attacks."

Harry's eyes narrowed. "You do?"

"Yes, I think it's Robin Mauley."

There was a pause, then Harry said, "What makes you think that?"

Ned's eyes held a look of desperate courage. "Because he bribed me to burn down your stable."

Harry's jaw dropped. "*What!*"

Ned ran his fingers through his curly hair, and said wretchedly, "God, Harry, what can I say to you? He told me that it would be just a temporary inconvenience for you, that you would have the insurance money to rebuild. I had no idea you were going to run into a problem with the E.H. I never would have done it if I had known such a thing."

There was a shocked look on Harry's face. "But why the hell did you do it, Ned?"

"He gave me twenty thousand pounds. It was enough for me to start my own stable. You know that's been my long-term dream, Harry. And here it was, being handed to me on a silver platter."

Harry said bitterly, "It never occurred to you that you were getting your stable at the cost of mine?"

"I told you, I thought the insurance money would cover the rebuilding. I knew you were insured, because you were always bitching about the price. It just never occurred to me that the insurance wouldn't be adequate. You're always so careful about things like that."

"It should have been adequate," Harry said in the same bitter voice as before. "I think Mauley bribed the E.H. officer to require that I rebuild with the original materials."

"He probably did," Ned said somberly. "And I'm sure he's behind these attempts on your life. He wouldn't tell me why he wanted me to burn the stable, but it was pretty obvious, I thought. He wanted to force you to sell him the land for the golf course. And when that didn't work, he moved on to other methods." He took a step closer. "Think, Harry. If something should happen to you, Silverbridge would go to Tony. And Tony is thick as thieves with Mauley over this golf course venture."

"I have thought about it, and I agree that Mauley is the obvious suspect. But it's also obvious that he had an accomplice. I can't see Mauley himself disabling the brakes on my car, or running me down, or shooting at me in the woods." He blew out a long breath. "Now it appears that there were two accomplices—you to burn the stable and someone else to try to kill me."

Ned rubbed his hand across his eyes. "God, Harry, I don't know what to say to you. I'm so ashamed of myself. I was sorry I had done it the minute the fire caught. I actually tried to put it out, but I couldn't waste much time because I knew I had to get the horses to safety. I don't know what got into me to do such a thing to you, who have always been kindness itself to me. I am terribly terribly sorry, and you can have the twenty thousand pounds Mauley paid me to put toward the rebuilding of the stable."

"I think I will take you up on that offer," Harry said grimly.

"Please do. And if you want me to leave your employ, I shall perfectly understand."

"We'll talk about that another time, Ned. Right now I'm late for a meeting with Tom Neeley."

Ned nodded sadly. "I'll make sure that the horses in the paddocks get their evening hay."

Harry nodded and, without saying anything else, went back toward the house, where he had an appointment to meet with his farm manager.

28

Tracy finished shooting at three-thirty that afternoon, removed her makeup and costume in her dressing room, and returned to the house, where they were still shooting in the downstairs drawing room. She went to the upstairs drawing room, hoping against hope that she would see Charles.

He wasn't there, but Caroline and her brother were.

Caroline, wearing a blue silk afternoon dress and matching slippers, was seated on one of the sofas, and her brother was standing against the wall next to the fireplace, one hand grasping the end of the mantelpiece, the other hand holding a glass of wine. Caroline was crying into a lace-edged handkerchief.

"Try to get hold of yourself, Caro," her brother said impatiently. "I can't help you unless you can tell me what's wrong."

"It's Charles," she wept. She looked up from the handkerchief with watery blue eyes. "He's leaving me."

The man looked thunderstruck. "Leaving you? What the devil do you mean, leaving you?"

Caroline blew her nose and struggled for composure. "He's going to follow Isabel to Boston. He's going to s-stay there, Jeremy! He's going to leave me and the boys and go to live with her in America. I shall be humiliated in front of the whole world." Her blue eyes flashed with sudden anger. "And what am I to tell my sons? That their father has deserted their mother for their *governess*?"

This last word was followed by an audible sob, and tears started to fall again.

Jeremy came over to the sofa and sat down next to her, placing his wineglass on the table in front of them. "Explain this to me from the beginning," he demanded. "Has Charles been having an affair with Isabel?"

Caroline reached for the glass and took a swallow. "Yes. I first suspected it a few months ago, and the more I watched them, the more certain I became."

"Did you ever catch them in a compromising position?"

"No, it was nothing like that." She frowned, trying to find the correct words. "It was . . . it was something in the air between them, Jeremy."

He lifted a derisive eyebrow. "Something in the air?"

"If you had seen it, you would have recognized it, too," she retorted.

"But you had no proof? You never found them in a compromising position?"

"No."

"Damn it, Caroline. Then why didn't you just hold your tongue and wait for Charles to grow out of this infatuation? They were being discreet. All you needed was patience."

She clenched her hand tightly around her soggy handkerchief and stuck her chin defiantly in the air. "I am not one to stand by and watch my husband make a fool of himself over another woman."

"Hundreds of other wives have done so, with the consequence that their husbands did not leave them."

"You're making this sound as if it's my fault," she said indignantly. "Charles is the one who is cheating, not me."

He let out his breath with an impatient sound. "So you faced him with it?"

She sniffed and nodded.

"And did he deny it?"

Her eyes were downcast, focusing on her hands in her lap. "At first he did. Then, when I told him that Isabel had to leave, he got very cold." Her eyes lifted to her brother's face. "You know how he can be, Jeremy." Angry color stained her cheeks. "And then he just walked away and left me standing there!"

He reached for his glass and finished his wine. After he had returned the glass to the table, he turned to her, and said judiciously, "You didn't handle this well, Caro. You should have held your tongue and the affair would have fizzled. You pushed him into doing something he probably never intended to do."

She started to cry again. "When he told me that he was sending Isabel to his cousin in Boston, I was so happy. I thought that things would go back to being what they had been before she came. But then . . . yesterday morning . . . he told me that he was leaving me and going to live with her in America. I couldn't believe it, Jeremy! A man like Charles does not leave his position and his responsibilities to run away with a little nonentity of a governess. I thought he was joking. But he wasn't. He was serious."

He looked a little dubious. "Are you sure he was serious? That he wasn't just trying to punish you for making him send her away?"

She sat up straight and replied indignantly, "He said that she was his 'other self.' He *apologized* to me, Jeremy. He said he was sorry that I was going to be hurt, but that this was something he had to do."

"He must have lost his mind," Jeremy said grimly. "He could easily have set her up in a house of her own and visited her whenever he wanted. There was no necessity to go to these lengths."

Caroline's blond curls trembled with her emotion. "Well he has, and he's serious. He's talked to a solicitor and made legal arrangements to hold the estate in trust for William. And he told me he had provided amply for my own needs." With an anguished movement of her hands, she twisted her handkerchief back and forth. "Can you even begin to imagine the gossip this is going to cause? The Earl of Silverbridge, the great war hero, running off with his mistress like a lovesick boy. I shall be humiliated in front of the entire world. I think I'd rather die."

"The war must have done something to his reason," Jeremy said. His thick, dark eyebrows almost formed a bridge across his nose. "I can't believe that the Silverbridge I knew before the war would be capable of doing such a harebrained thing."

"It will be the scandal of the decade." Caroline began to weep again. "It will be even worse than the Duke of Devonshire making his wife live in the same household as his mistress. Everyone will look at me and think, *Poor Caroline. Such a pity she could not hold on to her husband.*"

Jeremy got to his feet and paced back to the fireplace, where he turned and faced his sister. "It is an insult not only to you, but to me and to our entire family. It is also a deep injustice to his sons. He must not be permitted to carry out this fantastic scheme."

"I don't think I can bear it if he does, Jeremy. Everyone will talk about me, and pretend to be sorry for me, and . . . and . . . I just can't bear it." She tried to dry her eyes with her handkerchief, but it was too soaked to be of much use. "Do you have a handkerchief I can borrow?" she asked.

He came back to the sofa and handed her a clean white cotton square. "Don't worry about this anymore. I'll take care of Silverbridge for you, Caroline. He won't find it so easy to escape his responsibilities as he thinks."

She blew her nose into his handkerchief. "W . . . what will you do?"

His jawline looked very hard. "I'll stop him."

"He won't listen to you. He is so cold about this, Jeremy." Her voice rose slightly. "I have been a faithful wife to him. I took care of his house and children the whole time he was away at war. I was happy to have him home. I don't deserve this!"

"No, you don't." He looked down at her from his position on the other side of the coffee table. "You were right to send for me," he repeated. "If your husband doesn't know how to protect his wife and children, you can rest assured that your brother does."

He walked steadily out of the room, passing quite close to where Tracy stood. She watched him go by, registering the ruthless expression in his eyes, and when she returned her eyes to the sofa, Caroline was gone.

Tracy stood for a long time in the empty room, going over in her mind the scene she had just witnessed. Then she walked to the door that connected the drawing room to the bedroom passage, went through and into her own room.

The late-day sun was slanting in through the windows making all of the tabletops shine. *The cleaning girl who comes in from the village once a week must have come this morning,* she thought, as her eyes rested on the fresh flowers and polished wood of a Regency table. Slowly she walked to the sunlit window and looked out upon the front lawn.

A flow of costumed men and women was spilling out of the house and onto the front drive. Tracy watched them absently as they made their way toward the campers, her mind still caught up with the encounter she had witnessed between Caroline and her brother.

It had to be Jeremy who shot Charles, she thought. *He did it to save his sister from a terrible scandal.*

But how did that situation apply to Harry? Harry didn't have a wife, let alone a brother-in-law.

I have to think about this logically, she told herself, trying to ignore the panicky feeling that was growing in her chest and stomach. *I can figure this out. I have to figure this out.*

She went over to the small French writing desk that was in the corner of her room and opened the single drawer, looking for paper. Inside were a white pad and a pen, neatly lined up next to each other. Tracy took out both and sat down at the desk, the writing materials in front of her.

I'll match the people from Charles's time to the corresponding people from today, she thought. *Perhaps then I'll figure this out.*

The first two lines were easy. *Charles = Harry,* she wrote. Then, *Isabel = Tracy.*

Could Tony still be involved? But Tony was Harry's brother, not his brother-in-law, and it seemed as if Tony had cleared himself of suspicion.

Caroline and her brother must equate with Robin Mauley and his golf course, she thought. Mauley wasn't going to get what he wanted and so he contracted someone to do away with Harry. She picked up the pen again and wrote: *Caroline = Mauley; Jeremy = ?*

It was the question mark that was the problem. Who was the assassin hired by Mauley? And what did he have to do with Jeremy?

She sat for perhaps ten minutes, staring at the paper and trying different names in place of the question mark. *It has to be there,* she thought desperately. *I am seeing these ghosts for a reason, I know I am. There has to be a connection somewhere . . .*

Jeremy = Gwen, she wrote. As she looked at this equation, a thought popped into her mind. *What if we've been on the wrong track this whole time? What if this isn't connected to the golf course at all? What if it's something entirely else?*

After five more minutes of intensive thinking, Tracy got to her feet and went in search of her cell phone so she could get in touch with Mark Sanderson.

It was half an hour before Mark Sanderson called Tracy back. He agreed to do the research she requested and promised to call her as soon as he had anything.

After she had hung up, Tracy glanced at her watch. It was five-thirty. *Perhaps Harry's in the morning room,* she thought, and went to look. But the morning room was deserted, and Harry had not yet taken the newspaper from its usual spot on the sofa table.

Tracy thought briefly about reading the paper herself, but there was a sense of urgency inside her that made the idea of sitting quietly impossible. She wanted to do something.

She went down to the kitchen to see if Mrs. Wilson might know where Harry was.

"He's in his office, Miss Collins," the woman said as she dropped peeled potatoes into the large pot that was cooking on the stove. "He's with Mr. Neeley, his farm manager."

"Then I won't bother him," Tracy said with a smile. She retraced her steps upstairs, but instead of continuing up to the second floor, she opened the door and went outside.

The afternoon light was a mellow gold, and there were only a few fleecy clouds floating in the sky. Tracy felt warm in her sweater and pulled it off over her head and tied it around her waist. Without making a conscious decision, she began to walk toward the back gar-

den and the path that led both to the stables and the
woods. It wasn't until she took the cutoff to the woods
that she recognized where she was going: to the lake.

The scene between Caroline and Jeremy she had witnessed earlier had unnerved her. It seemed as if time
was telescoping, and the fatal moment when Charles
was shot was almost at hand.

I can't prevent Charles from being shot, she thought,
as she walked along the bridle path underneath the
spring-green trees. *It happened in the past. It's done.*

But something was drawing her toward the lake.

The lake was where it happened before, she thought.

She had a feeling that the lake was where it was going
to happen again.

$\mathcal{I}$t was six o'clock when his farm manager finally left
Harry's office. He put away the account books they had
been looking at, then ambled next door to the kitchen to
see what Mrs. Wilson was making for dinner. He found
her folding up her apron and preparing to leave for
home.

"I've a pot roast on the stove for you, my lord," she
said briskly. "It'll be ready whenever you want to eat."

"Thank you, Mrs. Wilson," he replied, as he appre-
ciatively sniffed the aromas coming from the stove.

He left the kitchen before she did and went upstairs
to the morning room, planning to read the evening
paper. He had just fixed himself a whiskey and water
and opened the paper when Jon came into the room.

"Silverbridge. I'm glad I found you." His voice
sounded slightly breathless.

Harry looked up in surprise. Jon was not in the habit of seeking out his company.

Jon went on, "I finished filming earlier and went for a walk in your woods to wind down. I came across an injured deer near the lake path—the poor thing has a broken leg and is suffering quite pitiably—and I was wondering if I could borrow a gun to put her out of her misery." There was a sheen of sweat on Jon's face that, along with the breathlessness, betrayed that he had been hurrying.

Harry folded his paper and stood up. "I'll come along with you. We might have to look for her a bit. It's amazing what animals can do even when they're badly injured."

"That's good of you," Jon replied. He added gruffly, as if embarrassed, "I can't bear to think of an animal in pain."

"Nor can I," Harry said. "I'll just get a gun from my office and meet you outside."

He walked past Jon, who was still standing in the doorway, and went back downstairs to his office, where he unlocked the gun cabinet, removed a rifle, and loaded it. He sent the disappointed spaniels back to their sofa and went up the stairs and outside, where he found Jon awaiting him.

"It seems strange to see you without your dogs," the actor commented, looking at the empty places at Harry's heels where the spaniels usually walked.

"They'd frighten the deer," Harry returned. He rested his gun across his shoulder, said to Jon, "Let's go," and began to walk with long strides in the direction of the woods. Jon walked at his side.

29

I'm probably crazy, Tracy thought, as her steps brought her ever nearer to the lake. *I should have stayed at home and read the paper. Now I'll be late for dinner, and no one will know where I am, and Harry will worry.*

But she didn't turn around. The sense of urgency she had felt at the house was only deepening the closer she got to the lake.

A young deer stepped onto the path about twenty feet in front of her and for a brief, startled moment the two of them looked into each other's eyes. Then the deer leaped into the woods, followed two seconds later by another, larger deer, probably the mother.

Tracy's lips curved. She had never got over feeling honored whenever she caught a glimpse of one of God's most lovely and graceful creatures. Not even growing up in Connecticut, where gardeners spent at least half their time trying, unsuccessfully, to deer-proof their flowers and greenery, had changed that feeling in her.

When finally she reached the lake, the peaceful scene in front of her belied the pulse that had started to beat urgently in her brain. The water was quiet as a mirror under the early-evening sun. The swan family floated serenely, elegant and lovely in the golden light.

Some lines from Yeats came to her mind: "now they drift on the still water / Mysterious, beautiful . . ."

"*The Wild Swans at Coole*," she thought. Symbols of unchanging beauty in a perilous world.

Were the swans on the lake in Charles's day? she wondered. *Were they watching, in their aloof beauty, when he was killed? Did the gunshot frighten them? Did they perhaps gather up their babies and hustle them into the safety of the overhanging willows at the edge of the water?*

A downed tree trunk lay along the border of the woods, and Tracy went over to it and sat, her eyes still on the floating swans. Two brown ducks waded into the lake across from her and began to poke their heads into the water, looking for dinner. Birds called to one another from the greenery of the woods, and out of the corner of her eyes, Tracy saw a bunny hop into the safety of the trees.

It was such a peaceful picture. There was nothing whatsoever in the scene before Tracy to account for the pounding of her heart. She stayed where she was for ten minutes, unmoving, scarcely breathing, filled with an unbearable feeling of helplessness, waiting for something terrible to happen.

The swans continued to drift on the still water. The

two ducks were joined by five or six others. Almost directly across from Tracy, two does came down to the lake for a drink.

Then she heard the sound of horses' hooves, and in a moment, Charles, mounted on the big gray horse Tracy had seen him riding before, came out of the woods some fifty yards to her right.

Tracy stood up. *No,* she thought wildly. *No! This can't be happening. I can't allow this to happen.*

Charles had turned his horse to follow the lake path and was moving in her direction. He had given the gray its head, and the horse was walking along easily, his face turned toward the water so he could watch the ducks.

The picture they made was as perfect and as beautiful as a painting. The sun reflected off the man's golden hair and the horse's dappled coat, and the lake and trees made an ideal background to frame them.

Tracy's pulse was pounding so hard in her head that it drowned out the sound of the birds, and she whirled and searched the woods with straining eyes. She saw the sun flash off what looked like a piece of metal, and she opened her mouth and screamed. The name she cried out, with all the power that terror could impart to her young and healthy lungs, was *"Harry!"*

There was no gunshot, and, when she spun back to look at Charles, he was gone.

Harry and Jon did not follow the bridle path to the lake, as Tracy had. Instead they went through the woods, following the deer tracks that Harry knew so well.

The talked very little. Harry went first, carrying the rifle, and Jon came after, evincing little trouble negotiating the several steep grades they had to descend. As they approached the lake, Harry turned to say, "Show me where you found the deer and, if she isn't there, we'll search the immediate area first."

"Right," Jon returned. "Let's go down to the lake path first, so I can get my bearings."

Harry nodded and once again took the lead. They were perhaps twenty feet from the edge of the woods when a bloodcurdling scream ripped through the quiet air.

Harry's head jerked around in the direction of the scream. A fraction of a second later he felt a powerful blow land on his shoulder, and he crashed to the ground. Intense pain shot down his arm, his fingers loosened their grip, and the rifle slipped out. Then Jon was on him, arm lifted to strike again.

Harry raised instinctive arms to defend himself, scarcely noticing the screaming pain in his shoulder as his adrenaline surged. He grabbed Jon's arm as it descended toward his face and forced it back. For a long while the two men struggled, Jon trying to smash the sharp-edged stone he was holding into Harry's skull, and Harry trying to push it back. Both of them were gasping for breath and perspiring heavily as they fought each other for the prize of Harry's life.

On the surface it would appear that Jon held the advantage. He was heavier and burlier than Harry, and he was uninjured. But Harry had spent his life riding thousand-pound horses, and his upper-body strength was much greater than his slim build suggested. Ever so slowly, that strength began to tell, as Jon's arm was pushed farther and farther away from Harry's head.

"Damn you, Silverbridge," Jon said through clenched teeth, as he struggled to reverse the backward movement of his arm. Harry grunted and fought to maintain the advantage he had so far won.

Then a voice said strongly, "Get away from him, Jon, or I'll shoot you."

Both men froze.

"I'll shoot you," Tracy repeated. "Get away from him."

Harry felt a quiver of indecision in Jon and took advantage of it by levering Jon's arm farther back, then jumping to his feet. In a moment he had snatched the rifle from an extremely pale Tracy and trained it on Jon. He said, "You can drop that stone now, Melbourne. It's all over."

Jon's face looked ashen. He let the lethal stone drop to the ground and said nothing.

"Was that you who screamed?" Harry said to Tracy, his eyes still on Jon.

"Yes," she replied shakily.

"Well, you kept this bugger from landing that stone on my head instead of my shoulder. Good job, darling."

Tracy's body began to shake, too. "Oh God, Harry. I was so frightened. When I heard the noise of you fighting . . ."

"You very sensibly came along and nabbed the gun," he said calmly, his eyes still on Jon. "Later you will

have to tell me how you came to be here, but right now
we have another matter to deal with."

Jon's hazel eyes had begun to glitter in the pallor of
his face. He said intensely, "You're a bastard, Silverbridge. I'm not sorry I tried to kill you. I'm only sorry
that I failed."

"What the hell have I ever done to you?" Harry demanded in genuine bewilderment. "Is this about
Tracy?"

"No," Tracy said steadily from her place at his side.
"I rather think it is about Dana Matthews, Harry."

"Dana Matthews?" Harry scowled. "How the hell
does Dana Matthews come into this?"

"Do you want to tell us, Jon?" Tracy said.

Jon looked at her grimly and did not reply.

"You were her brother, weren't you?" Tracy said.

Harry's shoulder was aflame, but he kept the rifle
trained on Jon and waited for him to answer.

For a long moment, it seemed as if he wasn't going to
reply. Then he said in a staccato-sounding voice, "I was
her stepbrother. My father married her mother when
Dana was eleven and I was fifteen."

"Christ," Harry exclaimed. He glanced at Tracy.
"You mean this had nothing to do with Mauley after
all?"

"The attacks on your life didn't," she replied. "They
were separate from the burning of the stable, but we
didn't realize that. If we had, we might have tracked Jon
down sooner."

"You killed Dana," Jon said with barely controlled
passion. "She called you for help that night, and you
didn't answer. You let her die because it was the easiest

way to get her out of your life. You deserve to die too, you bastard. She needed you, and you turned your back on her."

"I wasn't home when she called," Harry replied.

"Right. That's what you told the police. I'll bet they didn't even check your alibi, *Lord* Silverbridge."

"It's true," Harry said steadily. "As soon as I got in, and got the message off the answering machine, I raced around to her place. Unfortunately, I was too late."

"Unfortunately," Jon sneered. "You dumped her. That's the reason she took those pills. You dumped her and she was heartbroken and that's why she killed herself."

"I couldn't help her, Melbourne," Harry said, still speaking in the same steady voice as before. "I tried. Believe me, I tried. But she couldn't break the cycle. She wanted the drugs more than she wanted anything else. More than she wanted me. More than she wanted her life. It was the drugs that killed her. Not me."

"I'm sure that's what you tell yourself, but that's not the truth," Jon said. The anger in his face was frightening.

Harry began to shrug, then inhaled sharply as the pain ratcheted through his shoulder. "You tried to kill me. You tampered with the brakes on my car, you tried to run me down in the hospital parking lot, you shot at me in the woods, and you just tried to bash my head in with a rock. You're the one who's going to be facing murder charges, Melbourne, not me."

Jon took a menacing step toward him, and Harry lifted the gun, which had been sagging, to point directly at his heart. "I'll blow you away, Melbourne. And, according to you, no one will even question me about it."

Jon stopped.

Harry said, "All right. We are going to return to the house via the bridle path. You go first, Melbourne, and Tracy and I will follow. If you make even one suspicious movement, I'll shoot. Now, we'll go on down to the lake path and turn right so we can pick up the bridle path."

Jon stood still

Harry gestured with the gun. "Move."

Slowly, Jon turned and began to make his way down to the lake.

They were about halfway home when Harry's shoulder gave out. "Do you think you can handle the gun?" he asked Tracy in a low voice.

She had been asking him to give up the gun for the last fifteen minutes, and replied patiently, "Yes. I told you I learned to shoot when I was making *Sweet William.* I am perfectly capable of holding and shooting that gun."

Reluctantly, he handed it over to her. Then he cradled his right arm with his left hand and supported it against his chest. He exhaled with relief as the strain on his shoulder lessened.

Jon said sardonically, "Done some thinking, my lord?"

The two men's eyes held for a brief moment before Tracy demanded, "What do you mean? Done some thinking about what?"

"Nothing," Harry replied. "He's just trying to make a distraction. Let's go on."

They had reached the place where the bridle path made a loop around a stand of grand old trees when Jon made his move. A flock of blackbirds flew overhead, *cawing* loudly, and he turned and bolted toward the cover of the trees.

Tracy lifted the gun to her shoulder, but she was too slow, and by the time she was in position to shoot, Jon was out of sight.

"Oh no!" she cried. "Come on, Harry. We have to catch him!"

She began to run toward the woods.

"No," Harry said strongly. "Let him go."

"What?" At the edge of the woods, she spun around to stare at him incredulously. "Are you crazy? The man tried to kill you. We can't just let him go!"

"Yes, we can," Harry returned.

"Well, you might, but I can't," and, still clutching the gun, she turned her back on him and started once more after Jon. It was with intense relief that she heard Harry coming after her.

Then his hand came down on her shoulder, spinning her around, and before she had quite realized what was happening, Harry had wrested the gun from her.

Tracy's stomach began to churn, and her breathing got quicker and heavier. "What are you doing? Are you crazy? He's getting away!"

"I want him to get away," Harry said.

"Why?" She threw the word at him as if it was a spear.

He rested the rifle barrel on the ground. "Try to calm

down and listen to me. I've been thinking the whole
time we were walking. If I accuse Melbourne, and it
comes out that it was about Dana—which it will have
to—that whole mess will be stirred up again. I can just
see the headlines now: *Brother Tries To Kill Aristocratic
Boyfriend.*" His voice was deeply bitter. "And it will be
even worse than the last time, because it involved Melbourne, who is Britain's most respected actor, and because it involves you."

She shook her head in disagreement. "That's no reason to let him go, Harry! Suppose he tries to kill you
again? You're never going to be safe as long as that man
is free!"

"I don't think he'll try anything again. *You* know
about him, and if anything happens to me, he must
know he will be arrested."

"This is crazy," she cried. "It's something Charles
might have done in the nineteenth century, chosen to
cover up a scandal rather than prosecute a murderer. But
this is the twenty-first century! We don't do those things
anymore. Give me that gun!"

He shook his head. "It's too late, he's gone by now.
But I don't think he's going to go far. We can still have
him arrested if that's what we want."

"What I want is for you to be safe, and for that to happen, Jon Melbourne needs to be behind bars."

He stepped closer to her. "Tracy, think. You're a
movie star. You, of all people, must know how vicious
the press can be." He put his left hand on her shoulder
and looked into her eyes. "I don't want any more of it.
It looks as if Meg will be able to go back to school for
the next term, and she doesn't need a lurid trial for at-

tempted murder hanging over her. After all, all we can hope to accomplish is to wreck Melbourne's career. Even if we can prove a case against him, he will only serve a few years." Gently, he pushed a tendril of her hair off her forehead. "Luckily, he didn't succeed in killing me, did he?"

He could see her struggling with his line of reasoning. "He *tried* to kill you," she repeated. "He shouldn't be allowed to get away with it."

He went back to cradling his right arm with his left hand. "If we lived in a perfect world, I would agree with you. But we don't. We live in a very imperfect world, where there is as much gray as there is black-and-white. This is one of those gray areas. We have to ask ourselves: Will the good accomplished by letting Melbourne go outweigh the good that will be accomplished if we have him arrested? I think it will."

She scowled, still not convinced.

"If this all comes out, our wedding will be hell. There will be reporters and photographers all over us, no matter where we go or how hard we try to hide."

Tracy slowly let out her breath. "You gave me that gun on purpose didn't you? You knew Jon would try to escape if I was holding the gun."

He said, "You had the look of a tigress defending her young. You would never have agreed to let him go."

She narrowed her eyes. "That's what he meant when he said you'd done some thinking. He knew you were giving him an opportunity to get away."

He didn't answer.

"Damn," she cried.

"Darling, I will be perfectly safe, and so will you. I

shall leave a letter with my solicitor that will name Melbourne as a suspect should anything happen to me. And I'll make sure he knows that."

Tracy could feel the adrenaline rush that had powered her desire to catch Jon draining away. Her temper flared. She didn't want to be reasonable about this. She wanted Jon behind bars.

A little breeze ruffled Harry's hair, and he said, "The press are like pit bulls. Once they get their teeth into a juicy story like this, they won't let go. Just think about that."

"Once they find out that I'm marrying the Earl of Silverbridge, they'll swarm all over us anyway," she said sulkily.

"They probably will," he agreed. "But that's a two-day story, not an ongoing scandal. We can live with that."

There was a long moment of silence as Tracy stared into his calm brown eyes. Then she sighed. "I want to see that letter before you send it to your solicitor. And I'll sign it, too, as a witness."

"An excellent idea," he said.

She looked him up and down, assessing his condition. He had let the gun drop to the ground and was still supporting his bad shoulder by holding his arm against his chest. Tracy looked at the injured shoulder and said, "Thank God you didn't get hit on the head again."

He put his good arm around her and kissed her hair. "I would have, if you hadn't screamed my name. What on earth made you do that?"

Briefly, she rested her cheek against his shoulder.

"I'll tell you later. Right now, we need to get your shoulder x-rayed."

"I don't think it's broken," he said reassuringly. "I broke my shoulder once, and it felt worse than this. There's probably just soft tissue damage."

"We'll let a doctor be the judge of that," she said firmly. "Come on, give me the damn gun and let's go back to the house."

Harry was right about the soft tissue damage. The doctor in the hospital gave him a sling and painkillers and told him there was to be absolutely no riding until he had healed.

This last instruction put Harry in a foul mood. "I've already missed too much time," he complained to Tracy the following morning. She had let him sleep in her bed, but sleep was the only thing she let him do. This put him into an even fouler mood.

"It won't kill the horses to have a little time off," she said.

He moved his head in a negative gesture. "Horses lose muscle so fast it isn't funny. What takes a year to put on can disappear in a month."

She replied inconsequently, "Did I ever tell you that I bought Dylan for you?"

He had been contemplating one of the bedposts gloomily, but his head jerked around. "I don't believe you ever did."

"But you have to give me lessons on Pendleton in return."

A faint frown creased his forehead, and he didn't reply.

She said, "I've been meaning to ask you, do I get a coronet or anything like that when I become a countess?"

His frown lifted. "As a matter of fact, you get the Oliver sapphire-and-diamond tiara," he said. "It's been in the family for over three hundred years, and I actually managed to hang on to it. You can wear it when you get presented at court. And when the next coronation finally happens, you'll have a front seat at Westminster Abbey."

"Wow," Tracy said reverentially. "Wait until my mother hears that. I'll finally be doing something that she approves of."

The fingers of his good hand closed around hers. "How can she not approve of *you*?"

Tracy returned the pressure of his hand. "She thinks the people I associate with in films are all addicts, alcoholics, and adulterers."

There was a beat of silence, then he said wryly, "I'm not sure the royal family is much better."

She laughed, and asked, "Will our children have titles?"

"Our eldest son will be called Lord Riverton—that is one of my lesser titles and it is traditionally given to the heir. Our other sons will only be 'Honorables,' but our daughters will be called 'Lady.'"

"Mom will definitely like that," she said with satisfaction. "I can just hear her now at the garden club. 'My grandchildren, Lord Riverton and Lady Sarah, will be coming on a visit shortly.'"

He sighed. "Well, I'm glad I can contribute something to this marriage. So far it has seemed that all the giving is coming from you."

She moved closer to him and rested her head against his good shoulder. "Don't be idiotic. What's mine is yours and what's yours is mine. That's what marriage is all about."

"Mmm." He brought her hand to his mouth and kissed the palm. "My shoulder is feeling much better this morning."

"Is it?" She sounded skeptical.

"A good night's sleep has done wonders."

"Let me see it." She leaned across him, pushed his old-fashioned pajama top out of the way and regarded the deep purple bruising that marred his shoulder.

"Ouch," she said. "It sure looks worse than it did last night."

"Bruising always gets darker. It doesn't mean anything."

She lowered her head and gently kissed the wounded area. "Poor baby. Between your head and your shoulder, you really have taken a beating."

"True. I could certainly use a little comfort right now."

She leaned down and kissed his mouth, her hair spilling around them like a silken tent. "If you lie still and don't move your shoulder," she murmured.

"I promise," he replied fervently.

"All right," she said, and, after removing her pajama bottoms, swung her leg over him and bent forward to kiss him again.

30

Later that same morning, Dave told Tracy that Jon had been called away on urgent family business.

"Thank God we've finished filming his scenes here at Silverbridge," the director said. "He has some more shots in London but, since that's where he's gone, we should be able to get hold of him to finish up."

"I'm sure you can," Tracy replied smoothly. "Dave, I want to let you know that I'm going to be staying here at Silverbridge when you go up to London. I've finished filming, but if you need me to reshoot anything, just let me know."

He smiled at her affectionately. "You'll make a beautiful countess, Tracy."

Her eyes widened in surprise. "How did you know we were planning to marry?" They were standing near the catering truck, which was dispensing elevenses. A number of other people were standing around, drinking tea and eating biscuits, but no one tried to join them.

Dave laughed at her question. "Are you kidding? One would have to be blind, deaf, and dumb not to sense the chemistry between you two."

Tracy didn't know if she should be pleased or embarrassed by this reply. She said, sounding a little flustered, "It doesn't have to mean marriage. We could just be having an affair."

He shook his head. "It's serious with Silverbridge. One can see that immediately."

"It's serious with me, too," she replied.

The elevenses group began to break up, and Dave raised a hand in greeting as two of the electricians passed in front of him. He turned again to Tracy, "I hope this doesn't mean you're going to abandon your career?"

She had given this question some serious thought and so was able to reply firmly, "No, I quite like making movies. I won't do so many, because I want a family, but I won't give it up altogether."

"Good." His face was grave. "You proved yourself on this film, you know. You have real talent as well as beauty."

Tracy felt immensely pleased. "Thank you, Dave. That means something, coming from you."

He nodded. "Right, then. I'll call you if I need you." He leaned over and kissed her cheek. "Good luck, Tracy."

"Thank you, Dave."

At lunchtime, both Meg and Tony wanted to know what had happened to Harry's shoulder, and he gathered the two of them, along with Tracy, into the privacy of his office and told them about what had happened with Jon.

"*Melbourne?*" Tony said incredulously from the comfort of an old leather chair. "Why the hell would *Melbourne* want to kill you, Harry?"

Harry, who was sitting in his desk chair, replied, "Apparently he was Dana Matthews's stepbrother, and he blamed me for her death. He was after revenge."

"I can't believe it," Meg said from her chair next to Harry's desk. "He was always so nice to me!"

"Yes, well, you weren't the one he wanted revenge on," Harry said wryly.

Tony got up, walked to the window, and turned to face his brother. "Are you sure you've done the right thing in letting him go? Won't he be a danger to you in the future?"

Harry explained about the letters that he and Tracy were going to lodge with their solicitors. "So if something should happen to me," he ended lightly, "make certain you see Trumbull. He's got the information against Melbourne."

Tony nodded abruptly, looking as if he was going to say something, changed his mind, and turned away to look out the window.

"Well, I think he should pay!" Meg said indignantly. "This isn't a trivial thing, Harry. He tried to kill you!"

Harry glanced at Tracy and said with gentle humor, "Tracy felt the same way. Whoever said that women are less bloodthirsty than men?"

She smiled at him, and his dark eyes turned very bright.

Tony turned away from the window. "So the stable fire and the attempts on your life were two separate things after all."

Harry nodded.

"Perhaps the fire marshal was wrong," Meg said. "Perhaps the stable fire really was an accident."

Tracy saw how Harry's eyes held Tony's, warning him to keep quiet. Harry replied, "I think you're right, Meggie. Someone must have sneaked kerosene in to keep warm, and that's what caused the fire."

Tracy thought it would be a good idea to remove Meg and let the men talk. She looked at her watch, and said, "You're going to miss your appointment with Beth if we don't hurry, Meg."

Meg looked undecided, then said to Harry, "For how long will I have to keep on with Beth? I'm doing super. I really don't need her anymore."

"One of the reasons you're doing super is because you're seeing Beth," Harry returned. "I want you to stay with her until you leave for school."

Meg hooked her hair, which had actually developed a shine, behind her ears. "I don't mind seeing her, but she's expensive, Harry, and I truly don't think I need her anymore."

Harry shook his head. "Don't worry about the expense. All you need to concentrate on is getting well. That's your job, Meggie. That's what I need you to do."

Meg still looked undecided, but said, "Okay."

Tracy changed the subject. "I saw the neatest jacket in Aldridge's. After your sessions, let's go look at it. I think it would look great on you."

"Really?" Meg's worried expression returned. "Was it very expensive?"

"If you like the jacket, buy it," Harry said. "You're looking so pretty these days that you should have more than just jeans and sweaters to wear."

Meg smiled shyly. "Am I really looking pretty?"

Tony said from his position at the window, "Harry and I are preparing to beat the boys off with cricket bats."

Meg laughed.

Tracy, who had every intention of buying Meg the jacket herself, stood up. "Come on, Meggie. Time to go."

After the women had left, Tony sat in Tracy's vacated chair, and said bluntly, "Was Martin the one who set the stable fire?"

Harry closed his eyes, then opened them, and said, "Yes. He told me that Mauley paid him a lot of money to do it. Ned was vulnerable to a bribe because he wanted to start his own stable."

"You fired him, of course."

"Well . . . no."

Tony's perfect eyebrows drew together, and he said emphatically, "Harry, the man burned down your stable."

"I know." Harry changed the position of his injured shoulder. "But he is deeply sorry. He told me he tried to put the fire out, but he couldn't."

Tony snorted. "Don't tell me you believe that bullshit?"

"Actually, I do."

Tony stared at him, and said tartly, "It's one thing to have a soft heart, but quite another to have a soft brain."

Harry picked up a sterling silver paper knife with his good hand and tried to explain. "Tony, I need Ned. I'll never get another stable manager whom I trust to ride my horses the way I trust him. And I need him more than ever, now that I can't ride myself."

There was silence. Then Tony said carefully, "You think you can trust him? After what he did?"

Harry put the paper knife down. "I can trust him with my horses. I'll never feel the same way about him myself, but I know I can trust him with my horses. And that is what is most important to me."

"You and your damned horses," Tony said, his tone a mixture of exasperation and resignation.

"Ned got them out. He would never hurt the horses."

Tony sighed, "And what do you plan to do about Mauley?"

Harry's reply was instant. "There's no way I can involve Mauley without involving Ned."

Tony did not look surprised by this reply. "So Mauley goes scot-free, along with everybody else?"

Harry's smile was wry. "I suppose so."

Tony slowly shook his head.

Harry continued, "I'm going to go ahead and appeal Howles's decision about the stable to the Secretary for the Environment. With luck, reason will prevail, and I'll be allowed to rebuild with modern materials."

"And if the secretary doesn't overturn the E.H. decision?"

For the first time in the conversation, Harry looked

uneasy. "Tracy said she would rebuild the stable for me as a wedding present."

Tony smiled. "Good for her."

"I suppose," Harry replied, the troubled expression still on his face.

Tony pointed his forefinger at his brother and said sternly, "Don't you dare feel guilty about using Tracy's money to improve Silverbridge. She has a vested interest in the place now. Her son will own it one day."

Harry smiled faintly. "That's what she said."

"No one will think you married her for her money. It's clear as water that you're bonkers over her."

"I didn't realize I was so transparent," Harry said ruefully.

"You both are." Tony leaned back in his chair. "I gather you don't want Meg to know about Ned?"

"No." Harry was positive. "She won't be able to hide her feelings, and I prefer to keep my environment as pleasant as possible."

Tony nodded, put his hands on his chair arms, got to his feet, and said gloomily, "Well, I'm afraid I'm going to have to go back to London and show my face at Witherspoon, Harris and Smith. It looks as if my career as a hotel, golf-course manager is not to be."

Harry's expression was unreadable. "Ambrose Percy is going to build a new hotel somewhere in England. Why don't you talk to him about managing it?"

Tony said derisively, "Do you know how many people will want that job? And I don't have any experience. The reason Mauley was giving me the position was because I'm your brother, and he hoped I could convince you to sell. I don't have any strings to pull with Percy."

Harry said mildly, "You could tell him that your brother and his wife will throw a huge opening party there if you're in charge. We'll guarantee that some of the royals will attend. Even better, Tracy will get some Hollywood stars."

Tony sat down again and stared at Harry. "Will you really do that?"

Harry said, "If you want the job, we'll do it."

"That sort of job would suit me perfectly. And I'd be good at it."

"I know you would be."

Tony's eyes gleamed. "If you and Tracy threw a party like that, it would get an enormous amount of publicity."

"I know," Harry said resignedly.

Tony stood up again. "You're a trump, Harry! I think I *will* talk to Percy."

Harry got to his feet as well. "I'm off to the stables to see Ned. Then I told Tom Neeley that I would ride around the farm with him."

"The country squire," Tony said affectionately.

"It's the life I like," Harry said, and the two brothers left his office together in quiet amity.

$\mathcal{F}$ive days later, Tracy and Harry met in Harry's office with Mark Sanderson, the investigator Tracy had hired. Harry sat behind his desk, his arm still in a sling, the dogs at his feet. Tracy sat in a chair on the right side of the desk, and Sanderson sat on the opposite side, facing them both. He was giving his report on Dana

Matthews's stepbrother, and when he finished he fell silent, waiting for questions.

Tracy let Harry speak first. "I find it damn peculiar that Dana and Melbourne kept their relationship a secret," he said. "What was the reason for that?"

Sanderson smoothed his neat black mustache. "The neighbors told me that when Dana left home, she severed all ties between herself and her family. I assume that she wanted to keep it that way permanently."

"Did something happen to make Dana run away from home when she was only fifteen?" Tracy asked. "It seems such a drastic step."

Sanderson looked at the printed report that lay on the desk in front of Tracy. "In there you'll see that I talked to a woman, Marianne Keys, who had been a school friend of hers. According to Mrs. Keys, Dana's mother had had a succession of men friends before she married William Melbourne. Dana confided that she had been sexually abused by two of them."

Harry made a muffled noise, and Tracy looked at him. His wide-set brown eyes held a mixture of anger and pity.

Sanderson continued, "Mrs. Keys also told me that Dana and Jon were sexually involved."

Harry swore under his breath.

"Mrs. Keys thinks that Dana ran away to get clear of Jon," Sanderson finished.

"Dear God," Tracy said.

"It's not a pretty story," Sanderson agreed.

Tracy looked at Harry. "He took his own guilt out on you. He needed to blame someone else for what she had become, for the way she died, and he chose you."

He nodded, his face looking strained.

Sanderson turned to Tracy. "I also did some investigation into that other matter, Miss Collins."

Harry's head turned in her direction. "What other matter?"

Tracy ignored him and said to the detective, "Did you find anything?"

He nodded. "It's all in the report. I was able to verify that an Isabel Winters sailed from Southampton in June 1820. She landed in Boston, and a few years later she married a Massachusetts state representative named Francis Coke. I was able to trace their offspring."

Harry looked from Sanderson to Tracy then back again to Sanderson. "Did you discover anything that's of particular interest?"

"Indeed I did." Once more his right forefingers smoothed his mustache. "Did you know, Miss Collins, that Isabel Winters is a direct ancestress of yours?"

Harry turned to look at her; Tracy did not look back. "I rather suspected it," she said softly.

"Indeed. The relationship is through your mother. It seems that one of Isabel's great-grandchildren married a Connecticut man at the turn of the century, and your mother is one of their descendants."

"My God," Harry said.

She looked at him and gave a tremulous smile.

Shortly afterward, Mark Sanderson departed, with Tracy assuring him that he would have her check in a few days. After the door had closed behind him, Harry reached across the desk with his good hand and covered hers. "Are you all right?"

She said shakily, "I just feel so sad, Harry. Poor Isabel. How awful it must have been for her, to be all alone in a strange country, and then to learn that Charles was dead."

Harry's hand tightened on hers, and his eyes moved from her face to the portrait of his ancestor. "Do you have any idea how amazing it was for a man of his time to make such a decision? Men in Regency England just did not turn their backs upon an earldom to run away with the governess. Certainly not men of Charles's wealth and power."

Tracy blinked back tears. "He loved her very much."

"He must have." Harry was still looking at the portrait of Charles. "And the poor bastard was shot before he could go to her."

Tracy drew a deep, steadying breath. "He wanted you to have what he did not. That's what this whole re-creation of the past has been about, Harry. You and I are to live out the life together that Charles and Isabel could not."

He continued to look at the portrait. "Don't ever tell anyone else about this, or they'll lock you up in a madhouse."

She said anxiously, "But you believe me, don't you?"

His eyes turned to her once more. "God help me, I do." He patted her hand and withdrew his own. "You are one of the sanest people I know, and if you say you saw ghosts, then you must have seen them."

"You saw them too," she replied.

He sighed. "Yes. I did."

"Harry . . ." For the first time she brought up a subject that had been on her mind for quite some time. "Do you believe in reincarnation?"

He immediately looked wary. "Please don't tell me that you think we are Charles and Isabel come back to life."

She said somberly, "Perhaps we are."

"No." He shook his head in emphatic denial. "I'll accept the ghosts, because we saw them, but not this bizarre theory." He gave her a stern look. "You and I are you and I. We are *not* Charles and Isabel. We look like them because we carry the same genes. But that is all."

Tracy was not so certain, but she could see that this was not a subject on which Harry had an open mind and decided not to push it. She said lightly, "You're probably right. I've been reading too many Shirley MacLaine books."

There was a deep line between his brows. "Who is Shirley MacLaine?"

She smiled. "A movie actress who has written books about her past lives. She remembers being an Egyptian princess, or something like that."

His frown lifted. "You see? You don't want to become like that, Tracy. It's unhealthy."

She got up and went around to the back of his chair. "Okay, we'll forget about it." She smoothed his thick straight hair away from his forehead. "I love you, not Charles."

"I'm very glad to hear that."

Marshal, thinking that if someone was getting petted it should be he, reached up with his paw and claimed Tracy's attention. She obliged by sitting on her heels and stroking his head. She said, "I only hope Ebony is as easily won over as these guys."

"It might take a little time," Harry said cautiously as he swiveled his chair so that he was facing her.

"Yeah. And it might be never," Tracy retorted as she smoothed Marshal's silky ears.

"Once she realizes that if she wants me, she has to accept you too, she'll come around."

Millie, thinking it was unfair for Marshal to have all the attention, butted Harry's leg with her head. Obligingly, he began to pet her. "Do you know something I realized recently?" he said slowly.

"What?"

"Both of the women I have been serious about, Hilary and Dana, were tall and slim and had red hair."

"You were looking for me," she said matter-of-factly.

He nodded thoughtfully. "I fully planned to marry Hilary, and then, when we got close to the date, I just couldn't. It didn't feel right."

Tracy smiled at him mistily and stopped petting Marshal. He nudged her to continue.

"Let's be married right here at Silverbridge," she said, rubbing under the spaniel's chin. "My family can come over, and we'll do it very quietly."

"I'd like that."

"So would I."

There was a knock on the door, and Meg poked her head in. "Guess what? Mrs. Wilson and I have just baked some cookies. Would you like to taste them?"

Both Harry and Tracy made noises of assent and, trailed by the dogs, went with Meg into the kitchen.

Epilogue

One Year Later

"And the Oscar for the Best Performance by an Actress goes to . . ." Harry and Tracy watched the television breathlessly as last year's winning actor opened the envelope and pulled out a card. He looked up with a big smile. "Maria Yearwood."

"Damn!" Harry said.

"Oh well. Everyone said she would win," Tracy returned. But she couldn't quite hide her disappointment.

He glared at her. "She wasn't any better than you. She wasn't *as good* as you. She just had a showier role."

She sighed. "She carried her picture, Harry. Jon carried mine."

They both returned their eyes to the screen as Maria Yearwood, dressed in a plunging red Versace gown, slithered up on the stage to claim her award.

"I'm glad you aren't there," Harry said, as the screen showed a brief glimpse of the losing actresses. "The bloody cameras would be all over your face, hoping to detect disappointment."

"I'm not there because I couldn't fit into one of the

auditorium chairs." As if to demonstrate the truth of her words, Tracy shifted her bulk on the sofa.

He was sitting beside her and turned immediately, scanning her face, which was slightly rounder than it was nine months ago. "Everything all right?"

"Except for the fact that I'm bloody uncomfortable, everything is fine."

"Only another two weeks to go," he said soothingly.

"Yeah, if I deliver on time." She gave him an indignant look. "Today on the phone my mother informed me that she was late with all her children, and I shouldn't be concerned if I go beyond my due date." She stared down at her stomach. "That was not what I needed to hear."

"Don't worry about it," he advised. "Your sister delivered on time, didn't she?"

Tracy's face brightened. "Yes."

"Then don't fret, darling." He turned back to the television. "Hang on. They're about to do the Best Actor award."

Tracy immediately turned her attention to the screen, where the radiant winner of last year's Best Actress award was about to announce the winner. As she opened the envelope, the camera scanned the audience, focusing on the five men who were the nominees. When the camera settled on Jon, Harry gave a disgusted snort.

"If that bounder gets this award, and you didn't . . ."

Tracy regarded him with amusement. "*Bounder?* You sound like Lord Peter Wimsey."

He gave her an affronted stare. "There is nothing wrong with Lord Peter Wimsey. He has birth, breeding, and brains. I consider it an honor to be compared to him."

"*Jonathan Melbourne,*" the actress shouted.

"Shit," said Harry

"Shush."

The two of them sat in silence and watched as a tuxedo-clad Jon walked up to the podium and accepted the Oscar statuette. The clapping subsided when he stepped to the microphone to make his acceptance speech.

"I have so many people to thank for this," he said, his magnificent voice a trifle huskier than usual. He went through a list that included the producer and director and photographer of *Jealousy,* as well as his English agent and his American agent. Then he said, "Last but not least, I would like to offer special thanks to Tracy Collins, whose presence illuminated the film and whose name gave it public recognition."

Applause rang out as Jon left the stage, his Oscar clutched firmly in his fist.

"That was nice of him," Tracy said.

Harry snorted. "It was the least the bastard could do."

She returned a little grimly, "Considering that he should be in jail instead of accepting an Academy Award, I agree with you."

The commercial came on, and Harry helped Tracy up so she could go to the bathroom. When she returned, the academy was ready to hand out its award for Best Director.

"Dave should get it, but I don't know if they'll give it to an Englishman," she said, as she settled back next to Harry, feeling rather like a ship coming into port.

Ebony had followed her back into the morning room, and now she jumped on the sofa and managed to insinuate herself between Harry and Tracy. She squawked to be petted, and Tracy obligingly scratched her favorite spot in front of her tail.

"I do hope she isn't going to be jealous of the baby," Tracy said, regarding the little black cat anxiously.

"She got used to you, she'll get used to him," Harry replied with serenity.

There was a pause as they watched the emcee introduce the winner of last year's award, whose job it was to hand out this year's. As he walked across the stage, Tracy said, "Do you know, I'm still mad at that doctor for telling us the baby's sex? I wanted to be surprised."

"I know you did, darling," Harry replied sympathetically. "We'll make sure the next one is a surprise."

"Did I tell you that I talked to Meg on the phone today? She is so excited about working on Dave's next picture." She stopped petting Ebony and focused her whole attention on the screen. "It would be neat if he got the Oscar for Best Director."

"Um," Harry said, and they both leaned a little forward as the envelope was opened. Last year's winner gave a smile of what looked like genuine delight and said simply, "David Michaels."

"*Yes!*" Tracy pumped her fist in the air.

"Good going," Harry said.

They both watched with smiles on their faces as Dave came up to the stage to accept the Oscar. He, too, mentioned Tracy in his list of people to be thanked, and Harry said, "Hint to the Academy that they chose the wrong actress for their award."

"When I win that award I want to be there," Tracy said firmly. "It's okay that they gave it to Maria. She did a good job, and she deserved it."

Ebony, realizing that Tracy's ministrations had ended, jumped on Harry's lap and remained there comfortably during the remainder of the show. *Jealousy* had received a Best Picture nomination, but it lost to a World War II epic in the voting.

Finally, Harry turned the television off. It was very late, as they had stayed up to watch via satellite.

"Come along, darling," he said to Tracy, holding out his hands so he could help her to her feet. "You and little Lord Riverton need your beauty rests."

His hand rested lightly between Tracy's shoulders as they moved in the direction of their bedroom. "Do you realize that we haven't yet talked about a real name for this baby?" she said. "I certainly don't plan to call him Lord Riverton."

He looked down at her, his eyebrows lifted in surprise. "I didn't think there was any doubt about the name."

She said softly, "Charles?"

"Of course."

She rested her cheek briefly against his shoulder, then they continued on their way to the bedroom.

Dear Reader,

I hope that you enjoyed *Silverbridge*, my first venture into a full-length contemporary novel. I am not entirely new to the genre, however. Many years ago I wrote seven shorter books for NAL's Rapture series, and when the thought occurred to me that I might try a contemporary novel, I remembered those Raptures and how much I had enjoyed doing them.

I decided that I wanted to write a really romantic contemporary novel. Nothing is more romantic than the idea of a love so strong that it cuts across time, and so the idea of *Silverbridge* was born. And, after all these years of writing about the English aristocracy during the Regency, it seemed only natural that the past lovers in the book should be from the Regency period.

The novel I am working on at present has no foothold in the past, however. It is about a New York Yankee baseball player (if you've visited my website you know I am a Yankee fan), and the adoptive mother of his son. *High Meadow* is a true love story; it's about the love of parents for children, children for parents, grandparents for grandchildren, and, most of all, the love of Daniel for Kate.

It has been a nice change of pace to write about the present, and I hope you enjoy reading *High Meadow* as much as I'm enjoying writing it.

Joan Wolf

PLEASE TURN THE PAGE FOR A PREVIEW OF *HIGH MEADOW*, COMING IN 2003 FROM WARNER BOOKS.

"Finish your milk," Kate said just as the doorbell rang. Ben started to get up, but she held up a hand. "I'll get it."

The little boy subsided into his chair. "Can I have another cookie?"

The kitchen was redolent with the smell of the quick-bake oatmeal raisin cookies she had just made, and she helped herself to one as she answered, "One more, if you finish your milk." She looked at the German shepherd lying on a mat in the corner of the sunny room, and said, "Cyrus, stay with Ben."

Before she left the kitchen, she glanced from habit out the window, which gave her a view of the stable. The wooden barn looked peaceful in the September sunlight, with a few horses' heads hanging out the opened top of the Dutch doors on their stalls. As she walked toward the front door of the old Connecticut farmhouse, the doorbell rang again. "I'm coming, I'm coming," she muttered, put her hand on the knob and opened the door halfway.

The extremely thin, blue-jeans-clad man outside on the porch looked vaguely familiar. She looked beyond him, but all she saw was an orange cat curled up on a wicker chair; the man was alone.

"Kate?" he said, and she recognized his voice.

Shit, she thought. Her fingers clenched on the doorknob. *My God, he looks twenty years older.*

"You look great," he said.

"What are you doing here, Marty?"

He shrugged blade-sharp shoulders. "I'm home, and I thought I'd come and see if Colleen was around."

"You haven't been home in eight years," Kate said. "We were all rather hoping you were dead."

Something flared in his pale blue eyes. "Not yet. Is Colleen here?"

Kate's thoughts flew to Ben and her back stiffened. "Didn't you know? Colleen's dead."

His head jerked. "What?"

He had looked terrible before; now he looked even worse. Kate said, "You really must have cared about her, Marty. In all these years you never once asked your parents about how she was doing?"

She started to push the door closed. He wedged his foot against it. "How long has she been dead?"

Kate thought she heard the scrape of a chair against linoleum in the kitchen and replied rapidly, "Seven years. She died in a car crash. So you can go away, Marty. And don't come back. I don't think my mother would be happy to see you."

She pushed the door again. She was a small, slender woman, but she had a lot of upper-body strength. Marty's foot held firm.

A clear treble voice said from behind her, "Who's that man, Mommy?"

Damn. Damn. Damn.

"Nobody," Kate said firmly. "Go back to the kitchen, Ben." Then, to the man in front of her, "Goodbye, Marty."

Cyrus materialized at her side.

Marty looked warily at the dog but held his ground. "Why are you so anxious to get rid of me?"

Kate's voice took on a sarcastic note. "That's easy enough to answer. I don't like you. You took my sister away from us, then you abandoned her. Get lost, Marty. We don't want you here."

They stood at impasse, the door half-open between them, Kate acutely conscious of Ben still in the hall behind her.

Cyrus growled softly deep in his throat and moved closer to Marty. "You'd better go," Kate said warningly. "I can restrain him for only so long."

"I didn't abandon Colleen. She was the one who left me."

Kate's voice was contemptuous. "I guess she finally found out what a worm you are. Too bad she didn't listen to me and Mom before she ran off with you."

Ben said uneasily, "Should I call 911, Mommy?"

Kate gave her son a reassuring smile. "No, honey. That won't be necessary. The man is leaving."

Marty looked at Ben. "This is your son?" he asked.

After a fractional hesitation, she said, "Yes."

"Are you sure?" He kept staring at Ben. "He has black hair like yours, but he's of an age to be Colleen's child."

Fear and fury flamed equally hot in her heart. From behind her a small, strained voice said, "Colleen died. Mommy is my mother now."

She turned to Ben. His large, luminous brown eyes were very dark, and Kate felt a second surge of fury that he had to be subjected to this. She said crisply, "Ben, go back to the kitchen. I'll keep Cyrus with me."

Ben hesitated, his eyes going from the man in the doorway to Kate, then back again to the man. Suddenly, breathlessly, he asked, "Are you my father?"

The words hit Kate like a punch in the stomach.

"No, Ben," she managed to answer steadily. "Marty is not your father. Now do as I say and go to the kitchen."

Mercifully Marty remained silent as Ben did as he was told. Cyrus remained beside Kate, his eyes focused unwaveringly on Marty, who finally spoke. "So he *is* Colleen's child."

His voice sounded triumphant.

"He *was* Colleen's child," Kate said. "I adopted him after Colleen died. And don't get any ideas, Marty. He is *not* your son. Colleen was quite clear about that."

A muscle flickered in his wasted cheek. "Did she give you a name?"

"No. And I'm not interested in finding out. Ben doesn't need a father. He has Mom and me, and he doesn't need anyone else. So go away or I'll sic Cyrus on you."

Marty was carefully not looking into the dog's eyes. "How old is he?"

"None of your business."

"I can get it from the Records Office here in town, Kate. Stop being so obstructive."

If Marty went to the Records Office, someone in the

town clerk's office would be sure to find out what he was doing and rumor would spread that he was Ben's father. Kate struggled to contain her rage that this scumbag had the power to disrupt her relationship with her son. "He will turn seven next month," she said coldly.

"Thank you." He removed his foot from the door. "You haven't asked me why I came home after all this time."

She began to push the door closed. "I haven't asked because I'm not interested."

"I have AIDS," he informed her.

"How nice," she said, and slammed the door in his face.

She took a moment to pat Cyrus reassuringly and collect herself before she walked back to the kitchen to join Ben. He was sitting at the old oak table, his empty glass of milk in front of him, and his arresting dark eyes were troubled. He waited for her to speak first.

She sat at the table across from him. "That man was once a friend of your mother's. He isn't very nice, Ben, and I don't like him."

"Did my mother like him?"

Cyrus went back to his mat in the corner. The window above him was open, and the crisp white cotton curtains rippled in the breeze.

"She was fooled by him, but then she found out about how bad he was and she didn't like him anymore."

"Oh," Ben said.

Kate took a deep, steadying breath. "Ben, why did

you ask him if he was your father? Haven't I told you that your father is dead?"

He made no reply, just regarded her out of those large, long-lashed eyes.

"Didn't you believe me, Ben?"

"Yes."

"Then why—" She broke off. She already knew the answer to her question. He was hoping. No matter what she had said, he was hoping that one day his father would come.

Damn.

She spoke in the most normal voice she could muster. "Soccer practice starts today. Nana will be home soon to take you. Why don't you go and change your clothes?"

"Okay."

He was so quiet and cooperative that he worried her. *Damn Marty Lockwood,* she thought with helpless rage as she watched her son leave the kitchen. *Damn him.*

The first thing Marty did after he left High Meadow Farm was to go to the Glendale Public Library. He sat at a computer, connected to the Internet, and typed in the keyword *Daniel Montero.* When he left the library an hour later, it was to return to his parents' house to carefully compose a letter, which he mailed directly from the post office.

Three weeks later he received a response. "May I speak to Martin Lockwood?" a man's voice asked when Marty picked up the phone on the third ring.

"I'm Martin Lockwood." Marty's heart skipped a

beat. The man had spoken fluently, but his voice had a distinct Spanish accent.

"I'm calling for Daniel Montero. He would like to meet with you."

Marty's heart began to hammer. "That can be arranged."

"Mr. Montero lives in Greenwich. Would it be possible for you to come to his house?"

"Y-yes," Marty stammered. "Of course."

"Shall we say tomorrow at noontime?"

"Give me the address," Marty said, "and I'll be there."

He was still going over his speech the following day as he walked up the flagstone path to the clapboard-and-stone single-floor house that belonged to the New York Yankees ace pitcher. The house was not lavish for Greenwich, but the gardens framing it were magnificent. A small fountain played in the shrubbery-enclosed area that was surrounded by the drive.

I can't let myself be intimidated, he told himself as he pressed the bell button. *I'm the one with the upper hand here*.

The door was opened by a slender, dark-haired man who looked to be in his fifties. Marty introduced himself.

"Yes. Come in." It was the same voice on the telephone the previous day. Marty stepped into a high-ceilinged foyer with polished bare wood flooring and yellow walls and looked around. "Come with me, please," the man said briefly, and Marty followed him down a wide hall that led toward one of the wings. The man pushed open a door, said to the occupant inside,

"Daniel, Martin Lockwood is here," and gestured for Marty to enter.

Marty strode forward and found himself in a comfortable and well-furnished office. It was a medium-size room, with French doors giving a view of the gardens and free-form pool outside. The large rolltop desk was golden oak, as was the computer station and the floor-to-ceiling bookcases. The man who was sitting behind the desk swiveled around in a large coffee-colored leather chair, and Marty found himself looking at one of the most famous faces in all of American sports.

Daniel Montero said, "Stay, Alberto," and the man who had escorted Marty went to take a seat in a leather armchair. No one asked Marty to sit down; both men just looked at him.

Boldly, Marty stared back at the man he had come to see. The Yankee star's bronzed, clean-cut face was familiar from the newspapers, but the large brown eyes were even more remarkable in actuality than they appeared in photos.

"So," Daniel Montero said. "You wish to blackmail me."

Still nobody asked Marty to sit down, so he crossed his arms over his chest and replied with the words he had rehearsed. "As I wrote, I am in possession of information that you have a son who is being raised in ignorance of who his father is. If I inform the child's adoptive mother of your identity, she will most certainly demand a huge sum of money from you. What I am asking for my silence doesn't begin to compare with what you will have to pay in child support over the next eleven years."

Daniel Montero's face was calm and unreadable. "Why do you think that this child is mine?"

"Because I know that eight years ago you had an affair with a girl named Colleen Foley." A trace of bitterness crept into Marty's voice. "I know this because she ditched me so that she could be with you." There was no flicker of recognition on Daniel's face at the mention of Colleen's name, and Marty continued defiantly. "Ten months after she started to sleep with you, Colleen had a baby. I saw him the other day. He looks just like you."

"Can this be true, Daniel?" the man named Alberto asked.

The Yankee pitcher's face remained inscrutable. "I remember Colleen. It was the spring training after I graduated from college. We were together until I left Florida to go to one of the Yankee farm teams. She told me she was going home." There was no trace of an accent in his voice.

"She did go home," Marty said triumphantly. "She went home and she had a baby. Then she was killed in a car crash. Her sister adopted the boy and is bringing him up. She doesn't know who the father is."

For the first time, a flicker of expression crossed Daniel's face. "This is difficult to believe."

Marty said eagerly, "If you like, I'm sure I can get some pictures of him. Once you see him, you'll know he's yours. Colleen had blond hair and blue eyes. This boy has straight black hair, like yours, and his eyes are like yours as well." Marty brought out his *coup de grace*.

"Once I give Kate your name, she can get the court to order DNA testing to prove paternity. Believe me, once that's done, you won't be able to get off the hook."

Daniel said slowly, "And you are telling me this because you think I will pay you to keep my identity a secret, so I will not have to pay child support to my son's adoptive mother?"

Marty smiled. "That's right."

"How fortunate for this child that he does not have you for a father," Daniel Montero said. "I, on the other hand, am perfectly willing to support him—and his mother—if it can be proved that he is in fact my son."

It took Marty a moment to digest the implications of this statement. The smile left his face and he stared at Daniel in outraged disbelief. "You *want* to pay for this child? But you don't even know him!"

"If he is my son, then I am responsible for taking care of him." He leaned forward slightly. "Where may I find him?"

Marty's brain churned frantically as he tried to salvage something from the wreck of his perfect plan. A glitter in Daniel's eyes alerted him to a possible alternate course. "It will cost you to find out."

The glitter became even more pronounced. "You would blackmail me for this information?"

"Yes," Marty said, sure he was onto something now.

Daniel fitted his fingers together, and said, slowly and deliberately, "In that case, let me tell you what I will do, Martin Lockwood. I will give your name to the police and tell them to arrest you for attempted blackmail. Then I will hire a private detective, who will search out the whereabouts of my son. You said that

Colleen's sister is raising him, and that her name is Kate. I do not think it will be very long before he is located."

I told him too much, Marty thought despairingly.

"Kate will refuse to see you," he said.

A straight black eyebrow lifted, "You told me she would sue me for child support."

"She's more likely to get a restraining order to keep you away from him," Marty said. "If you want, I can arrange for you to meet the boy away from her."

"A restraining order will avail her nothing if he is indeed my son. Nor am I going to sneak behind her back." Daniel stood up and the full force of his physical presence struck Marty like a blow. "Now, are you going to tell me where I can find this Kate and my son?"

Checkmate, Marty thought bitterly, and gave Daniel Montero Kate's address.

It was the seventh inning and the Yankees were up by two runs, but Daniel Montero was in trouble. He had loaded the bases by giving up two walks and an infield hit, and Boston's biggest slugger was coming to the plate. There was furious activity in the Yankee bull pen, and when Daniel glanced over at the dugout, he saw the pitching coach on the telephone.

Shit, he thought. *Mel's going to take me out.*

Then the manager himself was walking to the mound. Daniel cursed long and fluently to himself in Spanish as he stood with an impassive face and watched Joe approach.

"I think you've lost a bit of concentration," Joe said,

holding out his hand for the ball. "Let's let Mike finish this up."

It killed Daniel to give up the ball. When he got into a mess, he wanted to be the one who got out of it. "I'm sorry, Joe," he said stiffly as he surrendered the ball. Joe patted him on the shoulder as he walked by. The crowd gave him a standing ovation, which he forced himself to acknowledge by tipping his cap.

He sat by himself in the corner of the dugout, and no one came near him. Everyone in America knew that Daniel Montero hated to come out in the middle of an inning.

And against Boston! he fumed to himself as he squinted into the sunlight on the field. *I couldn't even get the damn ball over the plate! What the hell is the matter with me?*

Daniel knew the answer to his own question. He was meeting after the game with the private investigator he had hired to dig up information about Kate Foley, and he couldn't seem to keep his mind from straying to that future conversation.

I have a son. Every time he said those words to himself, sheer joy bubbled in his chest and stomach. After two years of thinking it would never be possible . . . he had a son. It was like a miracle.

On the field the batter hit a line drive down the left field line. The third baseman, who was playing on the line, snagged it, and the inning was over.

Daniel stood up and shook the hand of the pitcher who had relieved him and saved his chance for his twentieth win. Wins had seemed of the utmost importance to him just a few days ago. He was in a contest to win the Cy Young Award for best pitcher in the American League, and the more wins he rang up, the better his chances of getting the trophy over Boston's ace. Daniel had won it twice, and Boston's pitcher had won it twice, and Daniel wanted to be the one who went to three.

But that was a few days ago. Now all he wanted was to go down to the clubhouse, change into street clothes, and go home so he could meet with the private investigator. He was stuck, however, because of the significance of this possible win.

Twenty-two minutes later, the game was over and the scoreboard flashed the news that this was Daniel Montero's twentieth win. The crowd went wild and he had to step out of the dugout and tip his cap. Then his teammates were giving him high fives and slapping his back and looking so genuinely pleased for him, he felt guilty that he could not be more wholehearted in his response.

Finally, the team went down to the clubhouse, and Daniel steeled himself to be polite to the reporters who were already gathered around his locker, which was marked by a brass plate bearing his name. He had been born into a privileged Colombian family, and his mother had instilled into him from early childhood the necessity of courtesy.

"Did it make you mad to have to come out?" the reporter from the *Daily News* said as Daniel approached.

Daniel flashed his famous grin. "Not at all, Felipe. You know how much I appreciate Mike's help in the middle of an inning."

Everyone laughed, and a television reporter asked

the next question. It was a full hour before Daniel was able to extricate himself from the clubhouse and get into his car to drive home.

Alberto met him in the hallway of his house in Greenwich, and said, "He's in your office."

Daniel didn't want his secretary and his father's old friend to see his face when he was talking to the private investigator. Alberto saw too much sometimes, and there were some feelings a man wanted to keep private. "If you don't mind, I'll handle this alone, Alberto," he said.

"Of course."

Daniel walked quietly to his office door, inhaled deeply, and pushed the door open. The man inside got to his feet as he came in. "Congratulations," Joseph Murphy said. "Twenty wins. That's terrific."

Daniel held out his hand. "Thank you."

The two men shook, and Daniel looked into shrewd blue eyes that were on a level with his own. The other man's thick six-foot-two-inch frame carried considerably more weight than he did, however.

"Won't you please sit down," Daniel said.

Murphy resumed his seat in the leather armchair, and Daniel took the chair in front of his desk. He swiveled around to face Murphy, and said, "So, tell me what you have found out."

"There isn't a whole lot to tell," the detective replied. "Katharine Foley lives a quiet, structured life. She has custody of her sister's child."

Daniel's heart leaped with hope. "Custody? I was

under the impression that there was a legal adoption involved."

"There is."

Damn. Daniel's heart settled down. A legal adoption would make matters more difficult for him.

The detective went on. "The sister died in a car crash when Ben—that's the kid—was only six months old. Katharine Foley adopted him but she and her mother have raised him together. As far as I can discover, there's been no sign of a boyfriend since she took on the boy."

That was good news. He did not want his son being raised by a woman who dated around.

"How does she support him?" he asked.

The detective settled his burly frame more comfortably in his chair. "She teaches riding, and she buys and sells horses."

He stared incredulously. "And she makes money at this?" His father bred horses in Colombia, and in Daniel's experience, horses were money-losers.

"She didn't when she first started the business, but she does now. Her mother's a schoolteacher, and she supported them for the first few years until the business turned around. Now the business pays the bills."

"She must be a genius, to make money on horses," Daniel said with wonder.

"Apparently she's a pretty smart businesswoman," Murphy agreed. "You said you wanted a report on her finances, so I got you a copy of her last tax statement." He opened the briefcase on his lap, took out a sheet of paper, and passed it to Daniel.

The number that Daniel saw typed tander *net in-*

come was respectable, certainly enough for a woman and a child to live on. Daniel frowned as he put the tax statement on his desk.

"Horses are a lot of work," he commented. "Where is Ben while this Katharine is working?"

"You asked me to find that out, and I did. When Ben was a baby, Ms. Foley took care of him while her mother was at school. She did the stable work and teaching when her mother was at home. Now that Ben's in school, she has more time for the business, which is one of the reasons it's been making more money."

"What grade is Ben in?"

"He just started second grade."

Second grade. Daniel shut his eyes. *I have missed so much time.*

A little silence fell.

Murphy said, "I have a picture of the boy, if you would like to see it."

If I would like to see it? "Yes," he said, his voice not quite as steady as he would have liked. "I would like to see it."

Once more the detective opened his briefcase. "It's only a newspaper photo. It appeared in the local rag last year. Apparently Ben's first-grade class went pumpkin picking, and the paper carried the story." He handed over a photocopy of the article. "You can see why they chose Ben for the picture. He's a good-looking kid."

Daniel stared down at the photograph and into a pair of huge, long-lashed brown eyes. It was like looking at a picture of himself when he was seven. Ben's dark hair was styled in the cut that Daniel had seen on the sons of his friends, but the face was the same.

"He looks very much like you," the detective said softly.

"Yes." Shaken, Daniel inhaled and blew out slowly through his nose. "I have only just learned of his existence."

Murphy nodded, his blue eyes speculative. "He appears to be a perfectly normal, happy little boy. Ms. Foley has done a good job with him."

Daniel nodded. "If I can prove that he is mine, can I claim the legal rights of a father?"

"You'll have to consult a lawyer, but I'm sure the court would award you visitation rights."

He wanted more than visitation rights. But that would be for the lawyers to work out.